MARKING TIME

BOOK ONE
THE IMMORTAL DESCENDANTS

APRIL WHITE

CORAZON
ENTERTAINMENT

The Immortal Descendants Series
Marking Time
Tempting Fate
Changing Nature
Waging War
Cheating Death

Edited by Angela Houle
Cover design by Penny Reid
Cover images by Shutterstock

ISBN 978-0-9885368-1-4
Library of Congress Control Number: 2012920469
First American edition, October 2012
Second American edition, March 2015

For Connor, my Wolf
And Logan, my Ringo
And for Ed,
My Love.

CLOCKER

My mother had vanished again.

She did it every two years like clockwork, and her absence meant we'd be moving again ... soon. So I did what I always did when I found the stocked fridge and the note – I ran. The knots in my guts and a startled cat were my only company as I sprinted along the top of a wall and down a dark alley. The wall ended at a narrow gap separating a head shop and tattoo parlor, and I spider-crawled between the buildings with knuckles bitten by the rough edges of the bricks. It was a free-run fueled by an early diet of superhero fiction and a fierce need to lose myself in survival mode. I dropped the last six feet, slipped into the tattoo parlor through the broken back door, and then vaulted the stair rail to hit the basement floor. My lungs burned, but my hands were steady when I stopped to loosen my backpack. I took a deep breath, slipped behind a shelving unit, and stepped into the underworld of Venice.

The prohibition era rumrunner tunnel forked into a bigger branch already colored with graffiti that felt more like one-upmanship than art. The smaller fork was jammed with boxes and pallets and other junk that kept the easy access taggers out. Old places had history, and I loved history – especially anything hidden, secret, or underground – which meant the jammed tunnel wasn't a deterrent to me; it was like an engraved invitation.

I heard the hiss of spray paint just as I turned the corner. Two bangers in respirators were throwing up tags, and though their drawing skills were decent, the tags were all gang signs and territory markers. Bangers were sheep with fangs as far as I was concerned.

1

Anyone who needed to belong to something that badly didn't have the confidence to stand alone. And alone was all people could ever count on in life. I turned the corner and slipped through an opening at the far end before the bangers saw me.

The long, narrow passage was like my own private art gallery, with vintage tags that felt more visionary than vandalism. The standout was an old tag from 1972 signed by someone named Doran – a spiral symbol that looked ancient and vaguely Celtic. A spiral I wanted to copy.

I flipped on my Maglite and a rat darted away down the tunnel. I shuddered, imagining disease-filled fleas leaping off the creature as it ran, then focused my light on the mostly brick walls of the narrow space. There was a clean plaster facing next to Doran's spiral.

I set the Maglite on the floor, pointing up like a candle, opened my backpack, and pulled out a World War I gas mask. Besides not wanting to give myself cancer, I wore the mask to hide my face. My black hooded sweatshirt covered long dark-gold hair tied back in a braid and whatever minor curves I'd managed to grow in seventeen years. The gas mask kept me looking like any other tagger – skinny, fast, and vaguely male. Someone would have to be pretty close to see I was a girl, and frankly, no one ever got that close.

I fitted a new tip to my red can and started on the center spiral. The paint laid down easy, and by the time I got to the fourth one the tightness in my chest was letting go. The sun-like circles were a good way to mark my time living so close to the beach in L.A., and they practically painted themselves. But then things got weird: the spirals started to … glow. Like daylight peeking through the cracks in a door. Not possible with standard Krylon paint. At night. In a dark tunnel. Not possible at all. I flipped off my Maglite to see better. Maybe the fumes really were getting to me.

Something moved. The rat? I froze in place and saw a shadow at the far end of the tunnel shift. I had great night vision and I loved the dark, but shadows creeped me out. Darkness was just dark. Shadows could be anything.

Something was there and it was time to go, so my brain instantly clicked into 'flight' mode. I could drop the backpack if I had to run, but it could be a weapon too. I slid the can back inside just as a scuffling noise came from the tunnel entrance. I was trapped. By the bangers, or someone else?

"Dude, there's nothing down here." A surfer voice. Right, someone else.

"I'm telling you, man, he said it would go down tonight. We're supposed to keep the kid from running." The second whisper sounded nervous. These jokers were up to nothing good, and I backed myself against the wall to become one with the bricks.

"There's no one here. Your intel is faulty." Something in Surfer's voice changed. Like someone else just came in. Someone Surfer was afraid of.

"My 'intel' is never faulty. It's this tunnel. Tonight. Tom saw it." A third voice spoke quietly in a British accent. The Englishman's voice was slick and reptilian, and my guts twisted unaccountably.

"Dude, Tom's so scared of you he'll say you're the King of England if he thinks it's what you wanna hear. And now I'm thinkin', fifty bucks ain't gonna cut it."

"Leave now and you'll never stop looking over your shoulder." Slick's quiet menace made me shiver. I believed him, and instinct screamed at me to run.

"I wanna see what's comin'. Hit the light." Nervous Guy's voice shook.

"No light!" Slick yelled too late. The beam hit me square in the chest.

"What the hell is that?!" I was really glad I still had my respirator on. But Slick's next words sent an earthquake down my spine.

"Grab her."

I spun on the balls of my feet and sprang away down the tunnel. When I was out of range of the flashlight I reached out to both walls and did my best Spiderman impression, practically flying up the sides with all four limbs. My spine pressed against the curved brick ceiling of the tunnel, and I closed my eyes with that 'if I can't see them, they can't see me' rationale.

"Where'd she go?" Nervous Guy screeched. "She was just here!"

Slick's voice was cold in the darkness. "Get the light. She's still in this tunnel."

"No way, Dude. I'm telling you, she disappeared." Surfer walked right under me. And like most people, he didn't think to look up. It's why ceilings made such great hiding places.

I froze as Slick's flashlight beam hit Doran's spiral. He touched it gently, and then retrieved my respirator. I couldn't see his face, but I thought I'd never forget the sound of his voice.

"You can't hide from me little Clocker."

I shuddered at the threat in his words. Clocker? He had the wrong girl, and only sheer force of will kept me silent.

Finally, a few curses and a dying battery later, Slick and his henchmen slithered away.

My night vision cleared and I was alone. I spider-walked myself back down the walls and fumbled for my flashlight. I wanted to be long gone. I found my way back to the tattoo parlor through the door in the basement and was just about to sling my backpack over my shoulders when it was ripped out of my hands. I bolted for the stairs and slammed into someone beefy. "Ooof!" The guy went down hard on one knee.

"Grab him!" A deep voice shouted.

Not if I could help it.

"Stop! Police!"

I closed my eyes with a sigh. This was not going to end well.

I may have lived on the edge of legal sometimes, but I wasn't a *bad* person. Yet here I was being driven home by two pissed-off cops. Officer Beef, named in honor of the massive chest that was losing its war with gravity, had hurt his knee when I accidentally ran into him and was particularly annoyed to discover I was female. Apparently, I hit hard.

"So you think you're pretty tough? Down there defacing private property." The Beef's partner was a short, arrogant Napoleon type.

"The tunnels are non-jurisdictional." The look I got from Napoleon through the back seat grate would have been less painful with a dagger attached. The Beef swallowed a chuckle and then looked out the windshield skeptically. "Windward and Pacific you said?"

"We're in the loft above the Venice Beach market."

"We?" Napoleon had a sneer in his voice I didn't like.

"My mother and me."

"Her name?" He had his notebook poised to write.

"Claire Elian."

"Father?"

"Deceased." My tone stayed perfectly even.

"Hmm. Mother's occupation?"

"Artist."

"Figures. Names her kid Saira – 'Sigh-ra' – instead of something normal and pronounceable." I didn't bother to point out he had just pronounced it.

I directed them to the back alley and led them upstairs. I already had my key in my fist, and was startled to find I didn't need it. The door was wide open.

The Beef looked sideways at me. "You leave it like this?"

I shook my head and the Beef was in front of me in a flash, weapon out, signaling to Napoleon. The main room was in chaos, with art supplies, books and papers everywhere. I followed The Beef into my mother's bedroom and sucked in a breath. Total disaster. I grabbed the key hidden at the bottom of Mom's headboard and unlocked the paint cabinet. Passports and cash were still there, but the antique clock necklace my dad gave her a million years ago was not. Napoleon entered from the kitchen. "Clear. No sign of the mother."

"She's working." The lie sat heavily on my tongue. And worse, they knew it.

Napoleon smiled. "There's the phone. Call her." Jerk.

I didn't move. Napoleon nodded at The Beef. "Once she's in I don't see much chance of her getting out, especially when they see this."

"Who? When who sees this?" I didn't like the pity in The Beef's eyes.

5

"Child protective services." Napoleon was dangerously smug. "They're the first call for minors."

"I'm seventeen."

"Still a minor in California."

"I have a British passport."

Napoleon snatched it from my hand. "Immigration is next on my list."

I glared at him, and The Beef must have felt bad because his tone softened. "Are you sure there isn't someone we could contact?"

I looked from The Beef to Napoleon, and bit my tongue, hard. "My mom will be back in a couple of days."

"Then she can bail you out, if she can get through the paperwork before you're assigned."

The Beef looked me right in the eyes. "We need a family member, Saira. There must be someone who can prove a relationship."

I tasted blood. There was someone.

That someone was waiting for me when I stepped off the British Airways flight in London: Millicent Elian. I hadn't seen my grandmother since I was three years old, and yet she still matched my vague memory of a tall, steely woman with iron eyes and a grim mouth. My mother couldn't stand her. Not a big surprise given the way she was sizing me up, probably wondering if I was worth the effort. Granted, I wasn't really dressed to impress in skinny jeans, combat boots, and a hooded sweatshirt. Perfect for the street. Not so impressive to a proper English noblewoman.

"I see you got his height." Millicent's tone was not flattering.

"Hello, Millicent." I knew I should be more polite and call her "Grandmother," considering she just kept me out of foster care, but she hadn't really earned the title.

"And his manners, too, evidently."

"I wouldn't know."

Millicent gave me a once-over like I was about to get wiped off her shoe. "At least you favor Claire."

"I don't suppose you've heard from my mother."

6

Millicent's eyes narrowed. "How long has she been gone?"

"Since Tuesday."

"Four days. She'll call tomorrow, or Monday at the latest."

I glared. "How do you know that?"

She ignored me. "I have a car waiting." Of course she did. Millicent's fancy gray Rolls Royce waited at the curb outside the airport, and her fancy gray driver held the door open for us.

"Home, Jeeves," she said with total authority.

"Jeeves? You're joking."

"I don't joke." Millicent's expression didn't change.

Jeeves caught my eye in the rear-view mirror and very slowly, he winked. It wasn't much, that wink, but it was something.

"I trust you still go to school?" Millicent's gaze was direct.

"Yes." A new one every two years. Not so conducive to making friends, which was fine with me, but it made my mother nuts. She didn't get that friends were a liability to the perpetual new kid. It was easier for me to just blend into the background, and practically a rule of thumb for a seventeen-year-old free-running graffiti artist.

"Then you shall start at St. Brigid's boarding school on Monday."

"Boarding school? I don't think so."

Millicent spoke sharply. "Our family has gone to St. Brigid's since 1554, and it's appalling to me that you've never been educated there."

"Considering you kicked my mother out of the family, it shouldn't be a surprise." I was already on thin ice – might as well see what it took to crack.

To my complete surprise, Millicent practically snorted. "I didn't kick her out of the family. She left us."

"Right." I said it under my breath, but it was full of snark and her eyes narrowed.

"Saira Emily Elian. Like it or not, you are a lady, and you will behave like a lady in my presence. Is that clear?" I looked away. My mom was not strict with me, and I was used to doing pretty much what I wanted. This thing with Millicent wasn't about my manners, it was about control. Over me. She wanted it, and I didn't want to give it up.

I fogged the window next to me with my breath and absently began tracing Doran's spiral design from the Venice tunnel, but when I felt Millicent's gaze burning a hole in the back of my neck, I wiped the window clean.

The Rolls Royce turned down a long driveway guarded by huge trees on all sides. They made me feel like a little girl stepping into a fairy tale – the kind with evil queens and enchanted forests that swallowed wandering kids into their depths. When the trees opened up, a massive building loomed in front of us. The place felt like a fortress with forbidding stone walls, and I could feel Millicent's eyes on me.

"Welcome to Elian Manor."

MANOR OF SECRETS

I looked around the enormous entry hall that was bigger than our whole loft in Venice. Millicent's voice shook me out of my awe. "Take Saira to the east wing."

A small, dark-haired, hobbit-sized woman seemed to materialize from nowhere as Millicent dismissed me. "Dinner is at seven. I assume you brought a dress?" It was a completely rhetorical question since she swept out of the room without waiting for an answer. Which was "no," but I didn't think she was in the mood to hear it just then.

The Hobbit was already at the end of the hall, lugging my bag with her. I had to run to catch up. "East wing, she says. Hrmph. West wing is for family." The Hobbit's voice sounded like it needed oil, and the "hrmph" she made was something between clearing her throat and hawking a loogie. Almost made me want to practice it.

We passed huge rooms filled with art and rugs and furniture that could be in a museum, and here and there I caught sight of uniformed maids polishing gleaming side tables inlaid with bone and ebony, or cleaning fireplaces big enough for a person to stand inside. We finally stopped in front of a large wooden door on the second floor.

The Hobbit produced an old-fashioned iron key that opened the lock. I wasn't excited to be staying in a room with an exterior lock, but to her credit, she left the key on the dresser. She set my bag down at the foot of the bed and studied me. "Ye have the look of your mother. It's why herself won't care for ye overmuch." The Hobbit raised an eyebrow. "Ye'll be needing a skin of iron, ye will.

The People hope ye have it." And with those strange words, she was gone.

A four-poster bed with carved wood posts and a faded silk canopy dominated the room. I flopped back onto it and took a deep breath, the first one since landing in England. I'd been living on pure adrenaline since the night in the tunnels, and I finally felt it start to loosen its hold on my body. Maybe too well, because three hours later I snapped awake and suddenly realized I was going to be late for dinner.

I slammed the bedroom door behind me and flew down the hall, tying my hair into a knot as I ran. It wasn't a dress, but at least I made an effort. I was probably already busted for being late, so jeans and a sweatshirt couldn't make it worse.

At least that's what I thought until I saw Millicent's face.

My grandmother was wearing a long dress that was practically a ball gown with a diamond choker around her neck. On anyone else it would have been a costume, but on Millicent it was armor. I realized then that late would have been much better than jeans, but there was nothing I could do now. Her jaw was already set.

"If you weren't Claire's daughter you would be eating in the kitchen with the staff."

I had just taken a seat at the only other place set at the long table, but I immediately stood back up. "Show me the way and I'll go." My cheeks flushed and I was being snotty to cover it up. Apparently Millicent was onto me though, because she coldly waved me to my seat.

"You won't get off so easily with me, Saira. Please sit down." She took a sip of her wine, and my gaze was trapped by the glittering jewels on her fingers. The woman sparkled everywhere but her eyes.

I sat. Every instinct in me wanted to run away from the gilded stranger across the table, but that's exactly why I wrapped my ankles around the chair legs. My mom always said fight and flight were at war in me, and considering how I ended up here, she wasn't too far wrong.

A mousy maid put steaming bowls of soup in front of us. Millicent studied me as she ate. "Why, exactly, are you here, Saira?"

"You're better than foster care."

Millicent raised an eyebrow with a look that said my thin ice was cracking. "The last time your mother left, were you alone then, too?"

"Every time since I was about thirteen."

"Don't you have friends? People you could stay with?"

"You say that like it's normal for a mom to disappear for a week every couple of years."

"Yours has to." The matter-of-fact way my grandmother spoke about something that was basically child abandonment told me volumes about her.

"Whatever. All I know is that if she had been home like a normal mom, our place wouldn't have been trashed, her clock necklace stolen, and I'd be sleeping in my own bed right now."

Millicent stared at me like I'd just sprouted wings. "Clock necklace?"

"The one my dad gave her before I was born. She never wears it, but it was locked in the paint cabinet with our passports and money *they didn't take.*"

She finally schooled her expression and then spoke in a voice that was trying too hard to be casual. "Show me the design you were drawing on the window in the car. Here, on the tablecloth, with your finger."

Okay, weird. I got up and moved to the other end of the table. She smelled of some fancy old perfume, powdery and really expensive. I used my finger like a pen and started drawing the spirals on the white tablecloth. Before I was even halfway done she stopped my hand. "That's enough." I'd just gotten in a groove and my fingers itched to finish. "Do not draw that design again … ever."

I stared at her. "You don't tell me what I can draw. Nobody does."

"Saira," Millicent's voice finally got some emotion in it, but I didn't like the tone. "Do as I say. It's for your own good." I snorted and her voice turned steely. "I am your elder and you will respect me."

"Respect gets earned." I pulled my hand out of Millicent's grasp and stalked to the door. "I understand why my mother left here." I was angry, but for some reason my eyes welled up with tears, which made me even madder. "You act like you have the right to fling rules at me because we're 'family,' but family cares, and you never did. Don't pretend to now."

I wiped the tears away fiercely and gave myself credit for not slamming the door, no matter how badly I wanted to make brick dust fall. The Hobbit was watching me from a darkened doorway, shaking her head. And with her disappointment, I felt the protective armor I'd spent seventeen years wrapping around myself begin to fracture.

The fancy bed with all the luxurious sheets was hard as a rock. I was fairly sure the mattress wasn't actually from the sixteenth century, but no amount of tossing and turning could make me comfortable enough to sleep. After trying for an hour or two I gave it up as a lost cause and around eleven pm, I got up to explore.

But the doorknob wouldn't budge. I tried again with more force and then flipped a light on to grab the key from the dresser. Not there. I did a full search of the area. No key.

Millicent had officially hit monster status. I glanced around the room looking for something I could use to get myself out of my new prison. There was a botanical print hanging on the wall, backed by a piece of cardboard that could work. I detached the cardboard from the frame, then untwisted the wire. With that I had my tools.

Everything was quiet in the hall. I slid the cardboard under the door, angling the piece so only a small corner was left on my side of the room, then stuck the wire into the old lock and hoped my warden was too lazy to take the key. The wire hit something that moved, so I jiggled it carefully and finally pushed. The key fell to the hall floor with a soft thud, hopefully landing on the cardboard underneath.

Bit by bit I pulled the cardboard in, like reeling in a fish on a line. The glint of metal showed under the door. Another inch and I had it in hand. I tried the key in the lock and the doorknob turned. I was free.

Now what? I knew my stay at Elian Manor had just expired, but I wasn't quite sure of my options. I quickly reassembled the print, threw on my clothes, then stuffed extra clothes, my passport, money, and toothbrush into my backpack. A last-minute addition was a heavy black marker and a can of red spray paint.

With my Maglite in my back pocket, I slipped out of the bedroom and secured the door behind me, leaving the key in the lock. Make them wonder how I got out if nothing else. I navigated my way through the east wing and down to the kitchen where I thought there'd be a servants' entrance. The door was latched from the inside with a heavy wooden bar – very middle-ages of them, but effective. I closed it quietly behind me and stepped out into darkness.

It wasn't the first time I was glad for great night vision as I picked my way along the unfamiliar perimeter of the house. The manor seemed like a fortress, built of solid stone with high windows and few doors. Everything about this place screamed 'prison'.

A cat suddenly yowled in front of me, and I stumbled and went down on all fours. Hard. Something sharp cut my hand and I hissed in pain and waited for a light to flick on inside the house. None did. The cat was long gone, and even though my mother swears I'm part feline, I silently re-confirmed my preference for dogs.

I picked myself up and bolted for the garages, but stopped short when I saw a lit window. Jeeves was inside the garage apartment looking as startled to see me as I was to see him. I nodded respectfully to him, and Jeeves cocked an eyebrow, slowly nodded back, and then waved his hand at me to scoot. I blew him a kiss and saw him smile as I ran for the woods.

When I got too tall for gymnastics, free-running had been the next logical step in my stealth-tagging habit. It's using acrobatics to move around urban environments at high speeds, and for me it made running around a nighttime city like playing on a giant jungle gym. And since a bad landing or a missed vault could break an arm, I didn't have the brain space to worry about a little thing like my lack of a permanent residence, so it was my escape too. I'd just never used it to actually escape before.

The forest along the long driveway was seriously creepy. Ancient trees were like sentries standing guard, while the underbrush probably teemed with hidden – and hopefully sleeping – wildlife. I would have preferred no moon to the almost full one that cast huge pools of darkness around me. My thing about shadows was kicking in hard, and I fought down a rising panic as I headed toward the main road.

As much as I wanted to believe every sound I heard was a normal nighttime noise, and every movement was just my eyeballs playing tricks, I knew in my soul that I wasn't alone in the woods. My most primal instinct screamed out that something, or someone, was tracking me. So the question was, animal or human? Predator or just curious?

A car engine sounded in the distance and I froze. It came from the main road ahead, not the manor behind me. I hoped that meant I might be able to hitch a ride toward London, maybe from an early commuter? I could see the glimmer of headlights through the trees, so I broke into a run ... and whatever was tracking me started running too. I could hear two feet hit the ground behind me instead of four. A biped then. A much scarier prospect than an animal.

I dodged around low branches and over fallen logs that tripped my pursuer, then broke from the trees. I spotted a dark-colored luxury car, maybe an Audi or a BMW, pulled over by the side of the road. It looked like the driver was reading a map and I made an instant decision to call out. "Help! Help me!"

The driver was a middle-aged guy in a suit, with blond hair and refined features. He looked shocked to see some girl sprinting down the road in the middle of the night. I dropped into the passenger seat and looked up to find him smiling at me. "Hello, Clocker. I wondered when we might finally meet."

That reptilian voice liquefied my guts, and a shot of pure adrenaline went coursing through my veins. Slick – from the Venice tunnels – with a menacing smile on his almost handsome face. Slick looked past me to a tall guy who had just run up outside my window. My biped pursuer. Instinctively, I grabbed the keys that were dangling from the steering column and hurled them out the window past Slick. Then I threw open the passenger door and nailed Biped right in the nuts. He went down, swearing loudly, and I took off running.

"Grab her!" Slick yelled.

I heard the rev of a car engine, then saw the shadow of headlights coming up behind me. A silver sports car appeared, and a guy called through the open window, "Get in!" He sped ahead and slammed on his brakes just as I reached his car. Primal survival instinct was back in spades as I flew into the passenger seat. He hit the gas pedal, and we did zero to sixty in about half a second. I looked over at my rescuer who was driving with one eye on the rear-view mirror. In the light from the dashboard he looked young, maybe early twenties, with dark hair and a strong profile. His jaw was tense as he watched to see if they were following us, and I could see muscles working as if he was grinding his teeth. Then my rescuer turned to look at me, and I felt his eyes reach right down into my lungs and suck all the air out.

With that look I knew I'd just jumped straight from the kettle into the fire.

WHITECHAPEL

He sniffed and then looked down at my hand. "You're bleeding."

The scrape on my palm was deep, and a trail of blood had smeared down my fingers. I was about to wipe my hands on my jeans when he caught my wrist. "Don't."

I stared at him. The force of his response was more than a simple scrape warranted. But then he nodded toward the glove compartment. "There's tissue in there."

I grabbed a tissue and clenched it in my fist. He looked at me again for a long moment, then his eyes were caught by something in the rear-view mirror.

"They're following us."

I spun in my seat to see, and sure enough, headlights were zooming up the road behind us. My rescuer stepped on the gas and my head flew back against the seat. "Sorry." He smiled and the light glinted off his teeth, making him look like a wolf. I buckled my seatbelt and held on while Wolf drove the Aston Martin sports car like he was playing an arcade game.

We zoomed past a "London City Limits" sign, and I started looking for my chance to bolt. I knew there'd be a stoplight somewhere; I just had to be smart about the part of town I jumped out in.

I needed to land in a working-class area. Not so poor that crime was an issue, but not so upscale that I couldn't blend in with my current wardrobe.

Wolf spoke quietly, his eyes darting to the rear-view mirror. "Wait for my signal before you try to run."

"What makes you think I'm going to run?" The squeak in my voice gave away the level of my fear.

"I know you better than you think, Saira."

I stared at him, open-mouthed. I suddenly wanted out of that car very badly. My hand clutched the door handle with white knuckles as Wolf steered hard to the left. If I tried to jump now I'd probably be killed. I had no choice but to wait.

"The Upminster station is just around the corner. Go directly to the train. If they don't see you go down, they'll assume you're hiding at street level." Wolf screeched around another turn, completely ignoring traffic signals.

"How do I know it isn't a trap?"

"You don't. And it isn't. The District line will take you into London proper, but you have to run to make the last train."

Wolf suddenly spun into an alley and slammed on the brakes. "Out! Now!"

I didn't wait to be told twice. I jumped out of the car and sprinted down the alley toward the street. I had heard him say something just as I slammed the door. The words "Spiral at Whitechapel" didn't make sense to me, but at this point, nothing did.

I saw the entrance to the Tube station across the street and I dashed for it. Suddenly the screech of brakes filled my head and my knees buckled as a taxi sent me flying over its hood. It happened in slow motion, and I saw the cabbie's face for one brief, horrifying moment right before I sailed over the windshield.

Miraculously, I landed on my feet - wobbly, but still standing. The cabbie reached for his door handle but I was already gone, racing down the stairs to the Tube station. The gates were open, but the place looked deserted. I sprinted down to the lower tracks just as a train rumbled into the platform.

My legs were shaking and my breath came in ragged gasps. I didn't think I was hurt, but I'd probably feel like a bag of bruises in the morning. Finally the warning bell bonged and an electronic

English accent chimed, "Mind the gap." After a last quick glance at the empty stairs, I darted into the nearest compartment.

The London Underground is an eerie place in the middle of the night, and by the time the nearly deserted train reached the Whitechapel station, I was feeling exposed and jumpy. Curious about Wolf's "spiral at Whitechapel" statement, I hopped off the train to see what I could find. I figured things were already so strange in my world, one more thing couldn't tip the balance either way.

Boy was I wrong.

There was a distant screech of tires, a car door slamming, and the sound of running feet. Footsteps exploded into the tunnel behind me and I bolted, ducking into a service alcove to hide. I realized I had switched into a kind of cat and mouse mentality without even knowing it. Somehow, I had become hunted.

The footsteps stopped near the service alcove where I was hiding. Panic rose up in my throat and I firmly told myself to keep it together. Looking around for any distraction from the terror clawing at my skin, I found some scratch marks in the tile wall and focused on their shape. I just barely managed to swallow my gasp. It was a spiral, leading to another, and another. This was a smaller version of Doran's spiral, hidden in an alcove at the Whitechapel station in London.

A "D" was scratched at the bottom of the spiral. Was this what Wolf meant? But how could he know about this design my grandmonster had specifically forbidden me to draw?

My fingers found the grooves and began to tingle as I traced the pattern. Then I heard it. A footstep, light like a cat's. And a soft, menacing voice. "I think we found our little Clocker."

A buzzing started in my head. This couldn't be happening! There's no way Slick could have found me at Whitechapel station. Not unless Wolf told him to look here. The buzzing sound in my head got louder, and still my fingers traced the spirals of Doran's design. There was a dim light coming from the edges, and the sound in my head was so loud I finally realized it wasn't in my head at all. I felt myself starting to freak - about Slick, the light, the noise, but I couldn't stop tracing the design. I had absolutely no choice about it, and I felt like I was about to scream!

And then I *was* screaming. My lungs ached and my throat burned and my brain reeled with a sound my ears couldn't hear. And then I was falling and my body felt like it was a giant rubber band. Stretched and pulled, with a thrumming sound underneath my silent screams. Bile rose up in my throat and I tasted the sourness of puke.

And then suddenly, everything stopped.

It was pitch black and cold, and I felt like I'd just stepped off the teacup ride at Disneyland. Or maybe I really did hit my head when I went over the taxi, and I had a concussion. But then my vision started to clear, and I could make out the flicker of dim lights.

I was still in the service alcove. My spine stiffened and I held my breath, expecting Slick's hand to come snaking around the corner to grab me. But nothing happened. And except for the hammering of my heart and the silent screams still ringing in my ears, the station was completely quiet.

The flickering light had an orange cast and made shadows dance on the tile walls. I had to will my muscles to take a half step out of the alcove so I could peek around the corner. No one was there. But there was no reason I could think of that Slick wouldn't be waiting for me. Not that I understood why he *would* be waiting for me, but I'd come to accept that I was somehow his prey.

The lights were really flickering, and I looked up to see if there was some sort of power surge. Weird. It looked like real flames in the wall-mounted brackets. I didn't think that was legal, but then again, this was London, not earthquake-prone L.A. Coming from the tracks was the sound of heavy boots and the jangle of keys. Mine was pretty much the last train, so someone must be coming to lock up. I stuck close to the wall as I slunk away from the night watchman, back to the steps and across the tracks bridge toward the street exit for Whitechapel Road.

I adjusted the straps on my backpack and pulled my hoodie up to cover my head, hunching down like boys do when they're minding their own business. It's a pose that doesn't work for girls because they look afraid, and that turns them into victims. But most guys just look like sullen jerks when they walk like that, and I was counting on my jeans, boots, and hoodie to make me anonymously male in this nighttime city.

Whitechapel Road was deserted when I left the Tube station. It was a wide street with low buildings running its length on either side. Across the street was a huge Victorian edifice with a sign proclaiming the "Royal London Hospital."

I heard the clatter of footsteps and a man's laughter coming down an alley so I instantly switched direction and turned down a side street. It was darker there, with no streetlamps and no porch lights on any of the houses. A good place to disappear, but not knowing the geography was making me very jumpy.

I veered down Berner Street and stuck to the sides of the narrow road where I could duck into a doorway for cover. I needed a plan. I didn't have enough money to buy a ticket home to L.A., but I could probably make it in London long enough for my mom to get back. Then life could go back to normal – whatever that was.

I had a twenty pound note stuck in my pocket and dollars in my backpack that couldn't be changed until I found an open bank in the morning. I hoped I could work my magic and blend into the city. But so far, I wasn't feeling it.

Coming toward me down the street were a man and a woman dressed like they just stepped off a stage. She was wearing a long black dress with a full skirt and a black hat like something Steampunk girls would thread chains and old pocket watches through and call fashion. She had a long, fur-trimmed coat over the dress with a red rose pinned to the collar, and was holding the arm of a short guy in another long black coat. He had a pockmarked face and a wide-brimmed hat, and he pulled a flask from his pocket. The woman took a drink from the flask, wiped her mouth and gave it back. The whole effect of the two of them was like some weird costume prom.

I ducked into an alleyway while the costume couple passed. She was laughing in a way that told me it wasn't coffee in that flask. They crossed the street and stopped for a moment. The sound of noisy kissing made my stomach lurch. Ugh! Boozy breath and sloppy drunks.

But who was I to judge? So far I'd avoided any form of physical connection. I managed to be so intimidating or stand-offish that no one had ever asked me out. I was fine with it, but other people thought I was a freak. Who turns seventeen without ever having been kissed?

It didn't seem too smart to stay tucked into a covered alley for very long, and I tried to see down the far end to make sure I was actually alone. My night vision, usually awesome, was really being put to the test as it seemed there was almost no light anywhere. I looked up and was comforted to at least see stars in the London sky.

I heard a woman scream then, but quiet, like she was muffled. I couldn't tell where the sound came from, but every nerve in my body jangled electrically.

I didn't even think, I just ran ... *toward* the screams. I'm not the hero-type. I don't think it's my duty to save people, but I can't stand bullies. This flies directly in the face of my need for camouflage, but there are times it just isn't right to blend.

Across the street was an open gate to an empty space. There was a little wooden sign above it that said "Dutfield's Yard" which became one of those useless facts that got lodged in my brain. And then a shadow moved and I gasped. A figure in a black cape was crouched over a woman's body, and I must have surprised him because he stumbled backwards.

"You!" In my shock I wasn't even aware that I'd spoken. The pale face of Wolf stared up at me in alarm. "What are you doing?"

"I was determining her condition." His voice sounded very nervous and formal. He got his feet back under him and stood up, blocking my view of the woman on the ground.

"Which is?"

"Deceased."

I stared at Wolf in complete disbelief. I'd never met the guy before tonight, and he'd already managed to freak me out more than anyone had in my entire life.

"As in... dead? What did you do to her?"

Wolf looked appalled. "Do I know you, sir?"

"It's me." I pulled off my hood, releasing my long braid from the confines of my sweatshirt.

Wolf's eyes widened in surprise. "I'm sorry, miss, but you have me at a disadvantage." A clatter of what sounded like hooves was entering Dutfield's Yard from the other side. "But unless you'd like to find yourself associated with the lady's demise, may I suggest we make ourselves scarce."

Wolf moved toward the gate so fast I could only follow. We left the yard just as a horse-drawn cart came down the path, and I could hear the driver shouting, "Whoa there, girl! Whoa!" For a second I thought the driver meant me and I almost stopped, but a light touch at my elbow kept me moving forward.

"In here." Wolf's voice was low, and his hand at my elbow directed me toward a narrow covered alley. He practically shoved me into the doorway and put a finger to his lips.

The official-sounding footsteps of the bobby tapped down the road. He paused for a moment outside the entrance to our alley and I held my breath. A shout of "Police!" came from the direction of Dutfield's Yard. The bobby hesitated a moment, then finally took off running.

"He saw us come in here. When he realizes the woman's dead, he'll come looking for us." Wolf's voice had the same low tones I knew, but his words seemed more formal – and less sure – than before. "We should go."

"Why should I trust you?" This whole thing felt wrong, like I'd been thrown in the middle of a stage play. That had to be it. This whole thing with the 'dead' woman and the bobby, and the horse and cart, it must be all part of one of those haunted city tours. Why Wolf was involved mystified me, but for some reason he was penciled in as my tour guide for the night.

"You're right. You don't know me and have no reason to trust me." Wolf looked me up and down with a critical eye. "Despite your choice of garments, you are a woman. And given your strange way of speaking, a foreign woman at that." He looked me in the eyes. "That places you in a certain amount of danger. If you choose to travel with me, that danger will be somewhat mitigated."

"Assuming the danger isn't coming from you."

Wolf searched my face with a very frank gaze. "Quite true." Shouts of alarm were coming from Dutfield's Yard and running footsteps pounded by. Wolf turned away from Berner Street and faced down the pitch black alley. "This alley leads toward Commercial Road East and a less criminal district. You're welcome to join me if you're willing to risk life and limb in my company." I couldn't tell if he was being sarcastic as he strode away down the alley with a quick glance over his shoulder at the growing foot traffic on Berner Street.

So, somehow I'd managed to lose the creepy Slick guy and land myself in the middle of a murder mystery thing. I didn't know who Wolf was, or why he was following me, but I did know that no amount of night vision was going to help me in that pitch-black alley, and Wolf seemed to have a road map of London lodged in his brain. So I shoved my skepticism and pride down to somewhere around my ankles and took off down the alley after him.

And even though it made me cringe to think it, whatever this guy's game was, the nighttime city seemed slightly less menacing with him standing next to me.

 WOLF

After Commercial Road we headed west, toward solidly middle class neighborhoods. I had to admit, walking with Wolf gave me a sense of security I definitely didn't have on my own.

I'd never had a tagging partner, so I didn't know what it felt like to have someone watch my back. Not that I trusted him, but I had the sense he was putting some distance between us and Dutfield's Yard. And that was just fine by me.

The next corner put us squarely back on Whitechapel High Street. A pub door opened and a couple of drunks spilled out, laughing and teetering down the steps. Wolf grabbed me and spun me into a darkened doorway, out of sight of the drunks. But not before I saw their costumes. Wool hats, knickers, long socks and linen shirts. Working men's clothing ... from another century.

I stared at Wolf, really looking at him for the first time. He was wearing a white shirt with a small collar, a thin black tie, a black suit with a long coat, and a cape which smelled like some warm spice – maybe cinnamon or nutmeg. A cape? Who wears a cape? His face was pale, and his dark hair was longish with a piece that fell over one eye. The fact that I actually thought about brushing it back irritated me even more than the whole situation I found myself in.

"Is everyone in this city completely nuts?" I whispered as fiercely as I could.

Wolf raised an eyebrow. "That depends on your definition of insanity."

I glared at him. "You're all dressed like you stepped off some Victorian stage. Well guess what? You can let go of the character

24

now. I'm not the damsel in distress who needs to be rescued from drunks."

"That lot wouldn't give you time to explain your manner of dress before they threw the first punch. They don't much care for *different.*"

"*I'm* different? You're wearing a cape, for God's sake!"

"God had almost nothing to do with my wardrobe choice tonight, the theatre did."

"Of course it did. Your little murder mystery get-up must go over really well with the goth set." And then it hit me. "That's right! I got off the train in Whitechapel. It must be some sort of Jack the Ripper thing."

I didn't think it was possible for Wolf's already pale face to get any more bloodless, but it was, and it did. He stared at me. "How did you know it was the Ripper?"

"Oh, come on! You're dressed like some Victorian dude crouching over a 'dead' woman in Whitechapel, how dumb do you think I am?"

Wolf's eyes widened. "The police haven't even tied these killings together yet. How could you possibly guess the Ripper could be involved?"

I scoffed. "He's only the most famous serial killer in history. Who else could it be?"

"In history? I suppose two prior killings would make the news, but to link them to tonight ...?"

"Two? No, five I think. Maybe more." My mom was completely hooked on all things Victorian and I'd absorbed some of her near-encyclopedic knowledge of the era by osmosis.

Wolf took a step forward, staring at me like *I* was the nutjob. "Who are you?" He was uncomfortably close to me in the doorway, and I pushed past him out into the street.

"A better question is who are *you?*" Ever since I'd stepped out of the Whitechapel station I'd felt like I was in some alternate universe where the little things weren't adding up.

Wolf offered his hand to shake. "Archer Devereux at your service."

25

I smirked. "Archer? That's so much more noble than what I've been calling you." One of Archer's eyebrows arched up arrogantly, and I decided his real name was just as appropriate as his nickname. "I'm Saira Elian."

Archer stumbled and had to catch himself against a wall. "Elian?"

My eyes narrowed. "Yeah?"

"But it couldn't … you aren't …"

Now I was getting mad. "I'm not what?"

Archer grabbed my hand and pulled me off the main street into a small brick courtyard. I yanked my arm from his grasp and glared at him. "What is your problem?"

The intensity of his gaze was starting to freak me out. "Miss Elian, when were you born?"

I gaped at him. "When was I …? What are you, a cop? Why do you want to know how old I am?"

His voice was calm and quiet, like he was talking to a skittish animal. "I didn't ask how old you are; I asked what year you were born."

"In the nineties. Why? When were you born?" My voice was beyond snarky and I didn't care. I had lost my patience with this whole night.

"The 1890s?"

"Do I look like I'm over a hundred years old?" No amount of sarcasm seemed to get through to this guy.

Archer took a step backward and looked me up and down. "It certainly fits. The dress, the speech, the manner …"

"What are you talking about?"

"You're a Clocker."

"A what?" I started pacing furiously. "What's a Clocker? Slick called me that too."

"A time traveler. Who is Slick?"

I stared at Archer. "A time traveler?"

"It's the only explanation. And I repeat, who is Slick?" He looked a bit concerned, probably for my sanity.

I answered automatically. "He was in Venice, and then chased me to London. And you drove me to Upminster station and told me to run."

Now Archer looked at me like I was losing it. "I'm sure I don't know what you're talking about, Miss Elian. I've never met you before tonight." His tone got all formal again, and now I was really annoyed.

"If I really did travel back in time, you did too." I turned to face him, our noses inches apart. It made him uncomfortable, but he didn't back down.

"Of course I didn't." he scoffed.

"And neither did I."

He glared at me a moment longer, then grabbed my hand again and pulled me back onto the main street. Boy, was this guy ever pissing me off! I tried to yank my hand away, but his grip tightened and he pulled me toward some kid standing on the street corner. The kid was dressed in the same type of costume as everyone else, but wearing possibly the grubbiest newsboy cap I've ever seen in my life.

"What's the date today?" Archer demanded of the kid.

Bright green eyes narrowed dangerously, and the kid barked back in a thick East End accent. "Wot's it to yer?"

Archer raised an eyebrow as if his patience was on the line. He pulled a coin out of his pocket and handed it to the kid. "The date, please."

The kid bit the coin and slipped it in his pocket almost faster than my eye could follow.

"September 30th, a course."

"The year?"

"Wot're ye daft?" The kid looked nervously at Archer, like he expected him to lunge.

"My friend here just arrived from a long journey and doesn't believe me about the date."

Now the kid turned his narrowed eyes to me. "1888. 'Tis the year after t' Queen's jubilee. Now move along wi' ye. Me mates'll be none too 'appy wi' company."

Archer pulled me away from the kid and I stumbled after him, until I ripped my hand out of his.

"You can't expect me to believe some grubby-capped urchin you just *paid* to tell me something totally ridiculous."

"Oy! I ain't no urchin!" The kid yelled at me as we hurried down the street.

I turned and shouted back. "Well, you obviously found your hat in the sewer. What else would you call yourself?"

It was official, all my self-protective instincts to blend in and hide had just run away screaming, and I parked my hands on my hips defiantly. "People don't travel through time, except the normal way, one day at a time. So, don't try to sell me your story about time travel just to explain the lame costumes you all are wearing."

He was back to that calm, quiet voice again. "It's 1888, Miss Elian."

"It's Saira. And no it's not." I stalked away angrily. Archer must have realized it was pointless to argue because he let me go, even though I heard him walking a few feet behind me. My brain was spinning a mile a minute.

Time travel? Jack the Ripper?

Seriously?

I used the silence to examine my surroundings, looking for any evidence at all that I *hadn't* time traveled to Victorian London. There were no modern buildings or cars anywhere. The only lights on the street were from gas lamps that made shadows dance on the walls.

And then there were the people. The few I'd seen looked like they'd stepped out of a Charles Dickens novel, or maybe a Sherlock Holmes story. A Haunted History tour explained some of them, but everyone? I stopped and faced Archer, with his long black cape and formal clothes.

"Why are you staring?" His low voice snapped me out of my daze.

At him? Around me? Like a drooling idiot? Take your pick; I was doing it all. "There's no way I'm in Victorian England."

Archer sighed and seemed to search around him for something. Then he reached into his pocket, pulled out some coins, and handed one to me. It was very shiny silver with a portrait of Queen Victoria on the front, and the date "1887" on the back.

"It looks brand new."

"It was minted for the Queen's Golden Jubilee which was, as the lad said, last year."

Victoria had been queen for fifty years in 1887. My mom and her history conversations had drummed that into my brain. I reached into my back pocket and pulled out the twenty pound note I'd stuck there. Queen Elizabeth II's face stared back at me. Archer looked at the bill in my hand and his expression suddenly registered shock.

"Good God, is that twenty pounds?"

I nodded. "The rest of my money is still in American dollars."

He stared at me. "You mean you have more? This is more money than most people earn in a month."

Then it was my turn to stare. "You're not kidding, are you?"

He shook his head, staring at the note. "And that's the queen from your time?"

"Elizabeth the Second. She had her Golden Jubilee when I was a kid."

He reached out to touch the paper tentatively. "Fascinating. Is that a lot of money?"

I shrugged. "Not that much. It might buy dinner in a restaurant." He looked horrified. "But I bet the coin you showed me is worth more."

"How is that possible?"

"Because that's a practically brand new coin that doesn't look a hundred and twenty-five years old."

"It's not."

It's not, he says.

Breathing was suddenly hard to do, and I was having trouble focusing. There was a war between reason and, well … insanity raging in my brain, and it was all I could do to rein the madness in. So I *got* mad instead.

"Then explain this, genius. Why do you look exactly the same now as you do in more than a hundred and twenty-five years?" I couldn't believe I'd just said that with a straight face.

Archer paled. "We know each other in your time?"

"Whatever the hell that means – my time. But yeah, I've seen you drive an Aston Martin sports car like you stole it."

"I'm sure I didn't—"

"Shut up! Stick to the facts, Jack. And the facts are, you drove me to London like, two hours ago, dumped me at the curb, and next time I see you you're kneeling over some woman you claim got killed by Jack the Ripper. Tell me how that's possible?"

Archer's eyes went vacant. "It's not possible, is it?"

"That's what I'm saying!"

"But I've never seen you before tonight." His voice was uncertain.

"Yeah, you told me that. In practically the same breath as you told me about time travel. You can't have it both ways. In fact, I'm sick of playing this … whatever game this is. Have a nice life, *Wolf.* Don't call me and I won't call you, okay?"

He looked like he was about to say something else, but I didn't give him the chance. I took off running. At a dead sprint. The speed I go so nothing can catch me.

If Archer followed me at all, it wasn't very far. I wasn't consciously trying to lose him, but I did make a point of darting down small alleys and staying off the main roads. I was free-running with a vengeance and the kind of single-minded determination that usually ended in a sprained wrist or a cracked rib. I didn't do reckless because it drew attention, but since I felt like I was losing it anyway, I might as well see how far I could go.

I scaled a high stone wall, and every hand and foothold was exactly right. The top was wide enough that I could crouch there for a moment to catch my breath, looking for all the world like a stone gargoyle. Except for the heavy breathing.

Behind the wall was a cemetery with straight paths and headstones arranged in grids. The moon passed out from behind a cloud, and a sudden shaft of milky light revealed two men near the opposite wall. One man seemed to be keeping watch on the main gates while the other flung dirt over his shoulder with a shovel. Grave diggers or robbers? I didn't want to find out. Staying low, I crept along the top of the wall to the next alley and dropped down into the shadow of the tenement building it served.

Moving kept my mind off everything that had happened since Millicent locked me in the room at Elian Manor. Like a shark, as long as I kept moving I could breathe. But no amount of running could keep the picture of Archer Devereux out of my mind. First, as the Wolf, with gleaming teeth and a predatory smile, speeding away from Slick and his bipedal goon. And then, as the formal young man in a cape, looking so shocked at the thought that I could already know him. None of it added up, and all of it made my head hurt.

A door suddenly swung open right in front of me, and I had to jump out of the way to miss being hit by a yowling ball of fur. A sweaty drunk growled from inside the slum, "Piss off, cat!" Then he aimed a kick in its general direction and landed flat on his butt. He caught sight of me from his ignoble position on the floor. "Help me up." He spat when he talked and his eyes were barely focused. Human compassion battled with self-preservation for a moment, and I almost took a step forward. Until he spoke again. "Help me up, damn ye, or I'll hunt ye down and cut yer ears from yer bloody 'ead." So much for human compassion. I had to hurdle the cat that was sitting in the middle of the alley grooming himself, and he hissed at me. Damn cat.

And who does that? Who threatens to cut someone's ears off? All I wanted at that moment was a well-lit café, an overpriced coffee, and a bitchy waitress to ignore me. Was that so much to ask?

Apparently it was, because when I rounded the corner I ran smack into a group of young men. From the looks of them they were the same variety as the newsboy urchin, only older and more criminal. One of them had a long flat board and looked like he'd been about to swing at the window of a hat shop.

The first thought that went through my head was 'How much loot could someone possibly get from a hat shop?' The second thought made infinitely more sense than the first because it involved velocity and distance. Mine from them.

"Oy! Mate!" I was already halfway down the block when the first thug yelled. And just rounding the corner when the call to arms came. "Get 'im, lads!"

Crap. I'd been running at nearly full speed since I'd bolted from Archer, and I wasn't sure exactly how much I had left. I needed to get out of sight, fast. I spun down another alley, trying to stay well away from the wide open main streets where I could be spotted. Another turn down an even smaller alley, and the final turn led to a dead end. Perfect.

The wall was brick, but the old kind with wide mortar lines and good footholds. It was just tall enough that I was confident the thugs wouldn't guess I'd scaled it. I dropped down the other side and winced with the hard landing. I was at the end of a wider street that looked like a completely different part of town.

The first alley to my right led to a square that looked like a market, with several roads and passages leading from it. I sprinted toward a covered one called St. James Passage and stayed close to the wall as I navigated the pitch-black. When the tunnel ended I was in a cobblestone square, surrounded on three sides by tall warehouses. There was a plaque mounted in the wall that announced "Mitre Square" with a gaslight above it. The shadows moved ominously on the walls, compelled by the flickering flames, so I stayed in the deepest darkness at the far end of the square. God, I hated shadows.

I crept forward cautiously, listening for any sound beyond my steps. The wall must have stopped the thugs from following me, and the square was nearly silent. And then my foot touched something weirdly soft and hard at the same time. I recoiled backwards, stumbling over a cobblestone and breaking the eerie quiet of the deserted square. Except it wasn't deserted. Something shifted in the shadows and I turned to run, but not before an image was burned into my brain. It was a body I'd kicked. A woman. I wished I'd never seen it, because now I could never forget.

A Long Dark Night

Adrenaline surged through my veins and I bolted for the tunnel, running at full speed toward the yawning darkness. Except now there was something blocking it. A man. In a long coat. Drawing a knife. He stepped toward me, scraping the blade along the brick wall menacingly. Like he was sharpening it.

A clock began to strike the hour. BONG!

Without conscious thought I ran *toward* him, then suddenly bounded up a wall, scaled a fence above his head and picked my way across a tiled roof like a cat. If I had stopped to think about it, I might have been impressed with myself, but the only thought in my head was "RUN!"

BONG!

And then the killer started after me. I could hear him scrambling up the wall with brute force, and I was acutely aware of the sound my boots made on the slate roof tiles. Free-runners avoid tile roofs like the plague because when a tile breaks it sounds like a gunshot. I didn't have a choice. Every roof in this part of town was slate or metal, which was worse. I picked my way carefully across the pitched roof, listening intently for the sound of the killer on my heels. He had reached the tiled roof but didn't slow down.

BONG!

I had a choice to make. Keep picking my way across the tile, or jump and take my chances. I looked over my shoulder just as the killer cleared a pitch behind me. I couldn't see his face, but I could feel his eyes burning through me.

I jumped.

BONG!

There was a balcony about ten feet below me with another one about five feet lower. I barely had time to plan my landing before I reached for the rails of the next one.

I felt the fresh scab on my palm catch on the rail, but I ignored the sharp pain and concentrated on controlling my fall. A wide window ledge, a drainpipe, another balcony, and finally I was on the ground.

I looked up as slate tiles rained down from the roof and the cloaked figure leapt to the balcony rail I'd just left. He stopped there for a moment, and it looked like he touched the rail and rubbed my blood between his fingertips. Gross!

I took off sprinting, and in a couple of minutes I was back at the fruit market square. Some merchants were already setting up their stalls for the coming day, and I thought I probably shouldn't race in with my strange clothes. Above me were two buildings with fairly easy roof access. I scaled the wall and balcony, then found a protected alcove where I could see much of the square below me.

I settled in to wait, watch, and listen.

At first there was nothing, just the sound of my own heart hammering in my chest. Then the slap of running feet joined the beat and a man's voice cried out.

"A body! In Mitre Square!"

Another voice, farther away, called out, "Call the coppers!"

Hoping the killer wouldn't stick around with people emerging, I carefully picked my way down a drainpipe and quietly dropped to the ground. An iron grip caught my arms and dragged me back into the shadows. I opened my mouth to scream and a hand clapped over it.

And then I smelled spice. My legs turned to Jell-O, and I sagged against Archer's chest in relief. He whispered in my ear. "We need to go."

"He chased me up to the rooftops."

Concern immediately flooded his eyes. "Are you hurt?" I shook my head. "We need to leave this place. Once the rabble is aroused, they'll be out for blood. Dressed as you are, we'll both become targets."

"I can take care of myself." Instant defensiveness. Maybe because I'd just come really close to actually needing help, something my self-preservation instincts would barely allow.

Archer's eyebrow raised and he let go of my shoulders. I missed the reassurance of his touch, and then got mad at myself for it. "Perhaps in the time you come from, Miss Elian, but it's clear you're not used to this era's criminal element."

I glared at him. "I do just fine in any city. Why should London be any worse than Los Angeles?"

"Were you feeling 'just fine' when the young thugs were intent on beating you senseless with a plank when you wandered into their territory?"

My eyes narrowed at him. "You saw that?"

"I caught up to the tail end of their chase, just as you lost them over the wall. I had to hide in a doorway so I didn't become their next target. Surviving in this city requires never being caught alone in the dark, lest one become a victim."

"I am not a victim." I spoke through gritted teeth. Why did this guy seem to know every button to push with me?

Archer glared right back at me in a display of temper that would have impressed me if it hadn't pissed me off so much. "Miss Elian, you are a victim of so much more than you can possibly know at this moment. I don't know where to begin to enumerate all the dangers you face just by being here. If you were locked in a cell in the Tower of London you would be safer than you are alone out here on the streets of Whitechapel."

"And you're what? My knight in shining armor? You can't even keep up with me." I was beyond mad, and worse, I knew some part of him was right. There were rules to this city I didn't understand, and I hated being out of my element. So I was determined to show him just how capable I was. I bolted, then put on a burst of speed when he caught up to me, pulling myself over walls Archer had to climb, and practically flying down staircases. The look on his face was grim determination, and I found energy reserves I didn't know I had. Making Archer chase me suddenly became a game, and I tested his abilities with tumbles, leaps, scrambles, and jumps he'd probably never seen a girl do before.

When I had pushed my own endurance to its limit, I finally stopped running. Archer caught up to me a moment later, gasping for breath. "You're not human."

I snorted, holding my sides as I took deep, gulping breaths. "You should be impressed you almost beat me."

"Do all Clockers move like cats?"

"We're going there again? I don't know. In fact, as you so helpfully pointed out, I don't know anything."

He sat down on a stoop to catch his breath. It was an oddly relaxed pose for him and made him look like a regular guy, not a stuffy Victorian gentleman. Then he looked at me carefully. "What was I doing when you saw me in … your time?"

"As much as it chaps me to admit it, you rescued me. But if Slick shows up here now, I'll know for sure you're in on whatever this is with him and his cronies."

"I don't have … cronies."

I scoffed. "Friends, then."

"No."

"Why not?"

Archer held my eyes. "Because among other outlandish things, I believe in time travel, and unfortunately, in my social circles, that confirms for most people that I'm quite mad."

Cool. I was hanging out with a lunatic I'd found lurking over a dead person. I had a choice here. I could roll with this and somehow figure out how to get back to my real life, or I could freak out and end up in a loony bin of truly epic Victorian ugliness, never to be seen again.

I blinked and took a deep breath. I was tired. Too tired to stay angry and righteous and so very sure of everything. So … roll with it. I sat down next to him on the stoop.

"Are you actually crazy or just weird?"

After an astonished moment, Archer laughed.

I spoke under my breath. "Just weird."

He studied me. "Doesn't it shock you?"

"Which part? That you say I time traveled back to 1888, or that you say you're a nutjob? Or maybe it's the fact that I've just spent the night running away from criminals and killers. Take your pick. That you might be a nutjob is about the only one of the three that makes any sense."

Archer smiled at that and settled back to look up at the stars. I was still having trouble reconciling the idea of visible stars in London, so I watched his face instead. His eyes were a dark gray-blue and his hair was almost black in the pale moonlight. Broad cheekbones and a strong jaw saved him from prettiness, but his face was most interesting when he talked.

"What do you know about the Immortals?" He turned to hold my gaze and I didn't look away. I didn't want him to think he could unsettle me.

"Immortal means 'lives forever'; that's what I know."

Archer seemed like he was debating something. Finally he took a deep breath, stood up, and helped me to my feet. We continued walking. "Consider the possibility that things most people take for granted as just part of life are actually embodied in Immortals – five of them to be exact."

"You lost me."

He seemed amused by my exasperation, then composed his face. "All right, consider this. You are a child of Time. Others are children of Nature, War, Fate, and even Death."

I stared at him, barely comprehending his words. "You mean like Time and Death are people?"

"Immortals."

I scoffed. "I know who my mother is, and she's definitely not immortal."

"When I say child of Time, I actually mean Descendent. As I understand it, the Immortals have created Family lines that stretch thousands of years. Within those Families exist the traits of the Immortals themselves. You can travel across time. That ability came from either your mother or your father." Archer was watching me carefully.

I shook my head. "My parents are just regular people."

"From whom did you get the name Elian?"

"It's my mother's maiden name. My dad died before I was born."

He nodded. "Then it's most likely your mother who travels. Elian is one of the old families of Time."

I glared at Archer. "How do you know any of this?"

He sighed. "I don't think I can tell you that."

"Right! You can tell me I'm a time traveler and you claim there's such a thing as Immortals, but you can't tell me how you know any of it?"

"Everything I've said is true." He sounded frustrated. Well, too bad. I was way worse than frustrated.

"I need to get back home." It was a statement with so many possible meanings; I wasn't totally sure which home I meant. I started to walk away, but Archer's voice stopped me.

"Miss Elian?"

I spun angrily. "What."

"I'd like to help you."

That simple sentence rocked me back like a blast of wind. Other people didn't do things for me. I took care of myself. Even my mother hadn't been able to do more than make sure we had a roof and food since I got old enough to realize no one else we knew moved every two years. And then it was easier to just stop knowing people. My eyes filled with tears and it appalled me. I bent to re-tie my boot laces until I could get myself back under control.

"Where did you come through?"

"Come through?" I stalled with the laces until my traitorous emotions were in check.

"As I understand it, Clockers come through portals. I'm not entirely sure how it works, as the families are very close-mouthed about their particular gifts, but apparently there are physical places that Clockers can open in order to move through time."

"Open? How?" Since when was I not completely denying the possibility of time travel?

Archer shrugged. "I don't know. I've never seen it done."

My brain was going a mile a minute about everything that had gone down in the last four days. I felt like the answers were there, I just needed to sift through the madness to find them. I sat on a low wall and Archer dropped down next to me.

"Saira?" His eyes were full of concern.

"I'm fine. I just need to think." And distract myself from the intensity of Archer's gaze. He was looking at me in a way that made my heart pound. Something nobody had ever done to me before. I wasn't sure it was a good thing.

I closed my eyes, aware that Archer was still on his knees, still staring at me, still way too close. I took a deep breath. Break-in at the loft. Elian Manor. Millicent locks me in. Escape and run from Slick and his goon. Archer. Upminster station. The spiral at Whitechapel. The spiral …

My eyes popped open. Archer was still there, still too close, but his expression had shifted from concern to something speculative. I stood up abruptly, almost knocking him off balance. Served him right for doing it to me. "*If* I believe you about the time travel thing, and that's a *very* big 'if,' I might have come through a spiral at Whitechapel station."

"A spiral?"

"I think so." I explained. "I was tracing a design that was etched into the wall, and it started glowing and humming. And then my whole body was being stretched and pulled, like I was a giant rubber band. And there was a sound that vibrated through my skin and into my stomach, which is probably what made me want to puke— er, vomit."

Archer smiled wryly. "They don't make it easy on you, do they?"

We started walking down the avenue in the direction of Whitechapel. "*They* as in the Immortals?"

He nodded. Our stride was almost exactly the same as we walked, and I noticed I was almost his equal in height. I guessed he was probably tall for the times because I'm about 5'10", tall for a modern teenager, but positively gargantuan for one in 1888.

"Have you ever met one – an Immortal, I mean?"

Archer shook his head. "Apparently no one sees them anymore, and there's even question as to whether some of them still exist."

"Just *some* of them? Call me a skeptic, but unless I've seen something with my own eyes, I have a hard time believing in it."

"How do you reconcile the idea of something like God then?"

"I'm not really the church-going type." I looked closely at him. "Are you?"

We turned down a smaller side street, out of the flow of foot traffic that was beginning to pick up as early morning vendors went about their business. "I'm in the AKC program at King's College, getting a special degree in ethics and theology."

"Sounds like you go to church then."

Archer smiled. "My tutor is a bishop in the Church of England, so I suppose that counts."

"And what about someone like Jack the Ripper? Does God love him too?"

Archer stopped and held my gaze. "A man chooses what he becomes, and he must accept responsibility for his choices."

"You didn't answer my question."

"I don't know how to."

We started walking down Brady Street. Across the way was a cemetery with massive gates, and Archer abruptly turned and entered it. I had to run to catch up with him as he moved easily among the old headstones.

I looked around at the very deserted place. "A cemetery? After the night we've had?"

Archer looked around as if seeing the place through my eyes. "It's been closed for thirty years. If no one else is buried here in the next seventy years it'll probably become row houses. I like it because it's quiet."

The place definitely had the feeling of abandonment. There were Stars of David carved onto the headstones, and names like Hannah Hyams and Nathaniel Rothschild written in English and Hebrew. "Is this *the* Rothschild? The wine guy or the bank guy?"

Archer looked at the headstone I was reading in surprise. "The bank chap I believe. You know about him?"

I shrugged. "Lots of useless facts get stored away in my brain. One of the pitfalls of being on my own so much." I stepped carefully around Mr. Rothschild's headstone and squatted down to brush some dirt away from his wife's.

Archer knelt next to me. "It's just you and your mother then?" I nodded. He was quiet for a moment. "I didn't know my mother. She died when I was born."

"I'm really sorry."

He shrugged slightly and carefully avoided my eyes. "I'm told I favor her. Perhaps it's why my father sent me to the university rather than let me help my older brother run his estates."

"Do you miss him? Your dad?"

Archer's expression was unreadable. "There was a time when I was young that I believed he cared for me. When he taught me things that mattered to him. That time is past." He stood and brushed himself off, then held his hand out to help me up. "Come. It's almost dawn. The station will open soon."

I pulled my black marker out of the side pocket of my backpack and reached up to a protected spot under the eaves of the arched gate to the Houle family garden.

"What are you doing?"

"Making my mark." I quickly drew my standard tag, a spiral question mark I'd invented for myself when I knew my mom and I were about to leave a place. It made me feel like my presence would be noted even if my identity was a mystery.

Archer watched me cap my pen and shove it into my backpack, and then his eyes traveled back up to the mark. "Is that like the spiral you came through?"

I shook my head as I shouldered my pack. "It's my own invention, but now I wonder where I got it."

At the hospital we stayed on the opposite side of Whitechapel Road to avoid the people dumping bedpans and dustbins. A very pale light was beginning to brighten the sky. "We're here. Whitechapel station." Archer looked at his pocket watch, a gesture that reminded me it was 1888. "It opens in five minutes."

41

I nodded and looked for someplace to wait. There was a staircase leading to a basement apartment. "Can you wait with me, or do you have to go?"

"I can wait."

We sat on the lower steps, away from any prying eyes at the street level. The flickering gaslight dimmed, then went out, and we whispered so we wouldn't wake any tenants in the nearby flat. Archer looked tired in the dusty light of dawn.

"Archer? How did you know to find me outside Elian Manor?"

"I have no idea, Saira. But maybe if you tell me exactly what happened, I'll remember to do it then."

That sounded about as insane as anything else he'd said all night, so I told him the story of how we met. He let me speak without interruption, even as his expression showed everything from disbelief, to shock, to outrage, and finally anger.

"And what of your family? Is anyone searching for your mother?" Interesting that of all the things he could have asked it was my family Archer wanted to know about – the thing about which I knew the least.

"My grandmonster seemed confident my mom would be back in a couple of days."

Archer smirked. "Grandmonster? I assume you don't hold her in high regard?"

"You assume correctly."

"And your father?"

"I never knew him."

Archer was silent at that. I guessed that in this time, not knowing your father was about the same as admitting your mother had questionable morals. But I wasn't up to explanations.

There was a box of produce stashed behind the stairs, maybe a fruit-seller's wares. Archer dropped a coin into the box and picked out an apple. "It's his loss, then." He brushed the apple off with his sleeve and handed it to me. I accepted it gratefully.

"Thanks." I wasn't sure if I was thanking him for the apple or the fact that he didn't judge me for my parents' choices. I bit into the fruit and Archer smirked.

"I'm sure there's symbolism in offering an innocent an apple."

"That's a pretty big assumption." I tried to sound haughty but probably failed miserably.

"That you're innocent? I don't think I'm assuming anything." He smiled, and my stomach flip-flopped in a way that smiles from strange, good-looking guys didn't generally bring on in my world.

"What makes you think so?" I'm pretty sure I wasn't flirting, but thought I might be dangerously close.

"You lack the artifice of someone practiced in social graces, which, in itself, is a form of seduction." Archer was enjoying the outrage on my face.

"So basically I have no manners. Is that what you're saying?"

He laughed, and I tried hard not to stare at his mouth. "Not at all. If anything, there's more truth to you than most women I've known. Only little girls are as honest and straightforward, thus my assessment of your innocence."

"And now you're saying I'm a child. You know, if you're trying to be charming, you suck at it."

It was Archer's turn to raise an eyebrow. "I ... suck? That hardly seems an appropriate thing to say." I tried to keep a straight face but couldn't, and I burst out laughing. It felt good to laugh, like a lightness in my lungs that hadn't been there since the cops busted me in Venice a lifetime ago.

Then I noticed the way Archer was watching me, and it made me flush with heat. His eyes wouldn't let go of mine and it almost felt like he was trying to memorize my face. Then his gaze moved to my mouth and I covered my embarrassment with a last bite of my apple.

"Saira—"

I interrupted him. I didn't know what he was about to say and didn't want to know. Everything about Archer had put me off balance and I tried to find my footing again, even with the question I'd been dreading.

"What if it doesn't work?"

He knew exactly what I was talking about. "You came here, didn't you?"

"Did I? I'm still wrestling with that one."

Archer thought for a moment, then reached into his pocket and pulled out the silver coin he'd shown me earlier. "Take this with you. It was minted last year in my time. See if it's really worth something in yours."

He put the coin in my palm and then closed my hand around it. His skin was warm and his eyes danced as he smiled at me. "Or keep it as a memory of a strange night with an odd young man who told you unbelievable stories."

"Are you an odd young man?"

Archer shrugged. "People who think they know me would say yes."

"And what about those who really do know you?"

He held my gaze for a long moment with the ghost of a smile on his lips. "I've never met one."

There was something very sad about the way he said it, and I realized he really believed he was alone. I didn't have friends, but at least I had my mother. And even though her version of parenting was moving us from place to place and teaching me art and Victorian history while letting me take care of myself, she still knew me all the way to my soul. I reached out for Archer's hand and he smiled.

"Well, isn't this the perfect picture of young love?" A graveled English voice above us spoke. Archer leapt to his feet while I stared in horror and a deep, primal fear twisted my guts.

A powerful, stocky man with a pockmarked face and a sneering smile stood at the top of the stairs. I knew that face. Even though I'd only caught a glimpse of him in the darkness of Mitre Square and on the rooftop above it, I knew him from Berner Street. From passing him on the road as his lady-friend took a drink from his flask and laughed too loudly at his stupid joke.

It was Jack the Ripper.

I've never seen anyone move as fast as Archer did *up* the stairs as he lunged at the Ripper. I stared at the two men, just as shocked by Archer's speed as his willingness to jump into danger. His yell broke my paralysis. "Go *home*, Saira!"

Fueled by pure adrenaline, I leapt on top of a garbage can, grabbed the lower rails of the street-level guard, and hoisted myself up and away from Archer and the Ripper. They were boxing, and Archer's blows were surprisingly accurate and ferocious. The Ripper was a dirty fighter, and the sound of fists hitting flesh made my stomach hurt. I couldn't watch.

A guy in a uniform was just unlocking the gates to Whitechapel station when I flew through them. "Oy!" was all I heard as I raced down the passageway. My feet sounded like hammers on the rickety metal stairs, and I sprinted across the bridge just as a steam engine train pulled into the station below me.

I raced down the steps on the other side of the tracks, barely conscious of the people swarming toward the train. I scanned the passage for the service alcove. There! About halfway down toward the tracks, on the left side of the corridor. I bumped into a lady in a green dress as I ran for the alcove, but was past her so fast I didn't even look at her.

Voices shouted from the tracks over the steam hiss of the engine, and I slipped into the alcove and started tracing the design with my fingers. Almost immediately the cold porcelain warmed beneath my fingertips and the wall began to hum.

The shouting voices grew louder and more insistent. "Oy! Stop there! Ye can't do that!" My fingers shook as I traced the spirals faster. The tile was practically hot, and a white light seeped around the edges of the design.

A thud of fists and flesh, and a groan of pain followed the sound of running feet, then Archer's voice gasped. "Go, Saira! Go!" The design was almost totally lit. Just one last spiral to trace.

A hand grabbed my backpack and I screamed. It was the Ripper. The blood from Archer's punches made the leer on his face look like horrific clown make-up. "You're not going anywhere!" He jerked me backwards, and my fingers lost contact with the wall as my head cracked against the tile behind me.

"No!" I was desperate to get back to the spirals. Then the pressure slackened on my pack and I knew Archer had pulled him away. The Ripper growled and drew a knife on him, and I whipped my backpack around just as he lunged. The wicked-looking blade struck through my pack and suddenly a fine red mist sprayed the white tiles.

Oh, God! Archer?

No. Red spray paint. Archer and the Ripper seemed mesmerized by the hiss and spray coming from my slashed pack. I leapt forward to finish tracing the design. The humming filled my ears, and my body was beginning to feel the stretch like a giant rubber band was pulling me apart.

The sharp blast of steam and the peal of the train whistle signaled the departure of the iron beast as it pushed forward. Passengers raced to board, and others began to surround the fighting men.

My vision was blurring and my body felt disconnected from the tile under my feet. Archer and the Ripper still grappled with each other, and there was a flash of green at the corner of my vision. My fingers grasped to finish tracing the design.

"Saira!"

I turned in horror at the sound of my name. Just as I slipped through the spiral portal, I managed to scream one word to the woman in green who appeared across the track as the train pulled out of the station.

"Mom!"

GOING BACK

This time I did puke. My head was pounding, and I slid down the wall to sit for a minute. Or maybe an hour. Had last night happened, or did I have a concussion that gave me delusions of dead bodies and crazed killers? And had that really been Claire Elian, looking like a proper Victorian lady in a long green dress, screaming my name from across the tracks? I cranked my head around to look at the platform where she'd stood just moments before.

A train rushed into the station in a blur of silver, then slowed to a stop, disgorging early morning commuters. She wasn't there and an electronic voice announced the train to Upminster station. That, more than anything else, convinced me I was back in twenty-first-century London. Which meant Jack the Ripper wouldn't be waiting to grab me? Maybe.

Or maybe I was just losing my mind.

Because according to Archer, I had time traveled to 1888 through a spiral some old tagger had scratched in the Whitechapel Underground station. And even worse, apparently I was descended from a whole line of time travelers, including my mom.

Mom. I whimpered and struggled to my feet. My head was pounding and I couldn't think, and it was the thing I needed to do most of all. I wiped my mouth and took a deep breath, then poked my head around the corner.

"Welcome back, Clocker." The reptilian voice sank into the pit of my stomach like a dagger, and before I even knew my feet were doing it, I took off running.

Slick's vague expletive followed me as I dodged early morning commuters on the platform. I raced up the metal staircase to the green bridge that crossed the Whitechapel station track, and Slick had made it about halfway up the stairs behind me when I slid down the bannister on the other side, and stepped into the train that was getting ready to leave. I found an empty seat halfway down the car between a woman reading a newspaper and a kid in headphones, rocking out to an old Clash song that echoed the thought in my head. Stay or go?

My eyes were locked on Slick's progress as he descended the steps and scanned the platform, searching for me. The warning bong sounded and I tensed. His gaze finally found me and his eyes locked on mine. He smiled and slid onto the train through the closing door. But he telegraphed his move just enough that I had time to bolt for the door at the other end of the car and dart outside. As the train pulled out of Whitechapel station, Slick's handsome face was a mask of rage at the window. I just barely resisted the snarky urge to blow him a kiss for his trouble.

I had no idea why the guy had been stalking me, but the fact that he had waited at the station all night for me to return from my jaunt through time gave me chills that had nothing to do with the early London morning.

I was back in a time where my disguise counted, so I pulled my hoodie up over my long braid again, shoved my hands in my pockets, slouched into my best tough-guy stance, and strolled out of the Underground station toward Whitechapel Road.

Even in the gray light of dawn, this London was busy. Traffic already clogged intersections as vendors opened shops and kiosks for early morning commuter business. The modern city was really loud and made me kind of miss the silence of 1888.

I was cautious as I left the underground station. My backpack was with the Ripper, with my passport and most of my money. That was going to be a tough one to explain. "Sorry, I seem to have left my passport in 1888." At that moment though, I couldn't find it in me to care too much. A major inconvenience? Yes. A life-threatening one? Not after the night I'd had.

48

The twenty-pound note was still in my back pocket, and I could feel the outline of a coin in the front. Archer's coin. I couldn't look at it yet. Because if that coin was still shiny and brand new looking it meant the night hadn't been a dream. I took a deep breath. Twenty pounds was enough for a cup of coffee and a phone call. I needed them both.

I found an open coffee shop and grabbed an empty booth near the window – I was in danger of slipping into an exhausted coma if I didn't get some caffeine into me soon. The waitress behind the counter was eyeing me suspiciously, but she suddenly relaxed when I pulled off my hood. I must have looked like hell because she brought me a cup of strong black coffee with my menu. "Thank you. You're a lifesaver." I gasped as the coffee scalded my mouth, but I sipped it greedily anyway.

"You're American?" The waitress was probably just a couple years older than me, twenty at most, and one of the most striking people I'd ever seen. She had mahogany-colored skin, almond-shaped eyes, and long black hair pulled back in a bun. Her face was completely bare of make-up, and she moved like a dancer. I'd bet money she was.

I nodded and held out my hand to shake. "I'm Saira."

The skin on her hand was soft, like she hadn't been working in kitchens long. "I'm Alex. Are you on holiday?" I didn't realize I'd made a face until Alex grimaced. "Right. Not a pleasure trip?"

"Not so far."

"Sorry about that." A cook yelled for her. "Can I get you something to eat?"

"Toast would be awesome." I must have sighed when I said it because she shot me a quick look of sympathy and pirouetted away. Unfortunately, that meant I was alone with just my thoughts to keep me company.

Burned into my brain like a still from a movie was the image of my mother, wearing a heavy green dress and a feathered hat totally appropriate to Victorian times, staring at me in shock across the tracks. What was she doing in Victorian England? Did the time travel thing only work between now and 1888? And why had she been gone almost a week?

I needed a plan, but a coherent thought would be a good start. Millicent. The woman my mother despised would know what was going on. She obviously knew about the spiral portal, otherwise why would she forbid me to draw it? And if Archer had been right about the Elians, she was probably a time traveler too.

Alex was back with my toast and more coffee and I thanked her in a way I hoped would invite conversation, but she was already off and running for another customer. I wondered how she'd ever have the energy to dance after a shift in this place.

I looked out the window and suddenly there was Slick, looking like a Russian mobster with his greased-back blond hair and designer suit. He and some boy-next-door type about my age were outside Whitechapel station talking to a maintenance man.

I slouched down in my seat. What *was* it with Slick?

Alex showed up with my check. "Anything else?" Her air of distraction disappeared, and was replaced by something that seemed like fear as she looked out the window.

I fished in my back pocket for the twenty-pound note and handed it to her, wrenching my head around. The only thing I saw was my own nemesis, still lurking on the street corner with the young guy. "There's a guy out there I'd like to avoid running into. Any chance I could use a back door?" Alex's attention shifted to me as she counted out my change.

"Down the hall past the toilets. It goes to the back alley." She scanned the people across the street again, but Slick and the young guy had stepped inside the station.

I quickly grabbed all but a one-pound coin and slid out of the booth. I upped the wattage on my smile in an unfamiliar attempt at friendliness. "Thanks for everything."

Alex smiled, and I had the sense she didn't do that too often. "Good luck."

"Thanks." I headed down the hall to the back door. "I'll need it," I added under my breath. Now to get back to Elian Manor. As much as I hated the thought of facing Millicent again, she had information I needed.

I stepped out of the alley and made a left turn, away from Whitechapel station. My hoodie went back up and I turned on my "guy" walk. About a block later I realized I was on Brady Street when I passed the old Jewish cemetery where Archer and I had talked about an hour before, give or take a century. The cemetery was somehow more deteriorated yet less overgrown than when I saw it in 1888. It wasn't a block of row houses, so I assumed someone had been buried in it in the past one hundred years.

I picked my way over the broken paths to the Houle family garden. Despite falling plaster and smashed roof tiles, the gated entrance was still standing. I peered up under the eaves, expecting to find nothing. It would be easier if I found nothing. It could all be a dream if there was nothing there. Except it was there, my spiral question, faded and chipped, but still marking my presence. Proving my night in another time.

I held my breath and reached into my front pocket. The coin was warm in my fingers and I opened my hand. It was beautiful, shiny, brand new, and dated 1887. Oh. I quickly closed my fist and shoved the coin back in my pocket. Seeing it made me miss Archer. And if that wasn't shocking enough to the girl-who-needs-no-one, I realized that I wanted to see him again.

I had only met the guy last night, first in this time when he'd rescued me from Slick on the road outside Elian Manor, and then, inexplicably, in 1888 when I'd found him crouched over one of Jack the Ripper's victims. Maybe he was a time traveler too? Or maybe he was somehow able to access the portal I'd opened in Whitechapel station? But if he had figured out the time travel thing, why hadn't he been waiting for me at Whitechapel when I came back?

A train rumbled underground and snapped me out of my futile search for answers. I spotted a sign for the Bethnal Green rail station and headed toward it. I needed public transportation and a good map to figure out how to get back to the manor, Millicent, and the answers to my questions.

The station was full of early morning commuters coming into London from the outer boroughs. Bethnal Green put me directly in line toward Brentwood in Essex. One of the few things I knew about Elian Manor was that it was outside a small village near Brentwood.

At the ticket window a bored cashier sold me a one-way ticket to Shenfield for "ten pounds sixty" just as my train was just pulling into the station. I ran past a spray paint artist and dropped a pound coin into his can as I boarded my train. He looked up in surprise and then winked as he saw me sink into my seat onboard. The rock of the train was comforting as it rolled out of the city.

The trip was only an hour and I knew there was no way I'd be able to stay awake that long. I leaned over the empty seat to an older lady across the aisle.

"Excuse me. I'm going to Shenfield and I'm afraid I'll fall asleep and miss my stop."

"Don't worry, dear, I get off at Brentwood. I'll wake you then." She had a crisp English voice that made me think of tea and crumpets and walled gardens.

I smiled at her. "Thank you so much."

"It's no trouble at all. Sleep well." She looked like the grandmother I wished I had instead of Millicent-the-Battle-Ax.

It felt like barely five minutes had passed when the lady gently shook me awake. "Wake up, dear. We're at Brentwood." I cracked my eyelids and mustered a heartfelt "Thank you." The lady smiled as she moved off down the aisle.

I sat and looked out the window as the train rolled on to Shenfield. The scenery was picturesque, with stone cottages and walled kitchen gardens that looked … familiar? Then I realized why. These were the places in my mom's paintings. This was her English countryside.

I really missed her. To the casual observer my mom and I were nothing alike. I dressed sort of like a rocker boy, and fancy for me was a white linen shirt with jeans and boots instead of a hoodie or an anime t-shirt. My only jewelry was the pearl necklace my mother gave me when I turned sixteen. It had been hers when she was young, and was in my suitcase under the bed in Elian Manor. I'd never worn it but I didn't leave it in L.A.

My mom dressed like the artist version of a woman who wears pearls. Slightly tailored and slightly bohemian. She always wore a man's white dress shirt tucked into jeans when she was working, or linen pants when she wasn't. She owned skirts but didn't wear them, and when she went out in the Venice sun, she always wore a big, elegant sun hat. My mom never lost her Englishness; she wore it every day like a second skin, not like the armor my uniform of boots and jeans was.

Claire Elian had been raised a lady and she never lost the habit of it. I, on the other hand, had been raised by a lady to be a vagabond. My upbringing gave me a different set of skills, and my priorities definitely made my mom a little nuts. But I was as much a product of her choices as my own.

The train pulled into the station with a creak of wheels and the hiss of air brakes. I stepped onto the platform before the doors were fully open and was already down to street level when the train pulled away.

I stood in the shelter of the doorway for a moment, scanning the street for signs of someone waiting for me. Suspicion and caution had settled in like old friends. Slick was still hunting me, and I hoped Millicent could tell me why.

A long silver car pulled up to the curb and parked just down the block from where I stood, half-hidden in the train station arch. I couldn't imagine there was more than one Silver Cloud Rolls Royce in town. I was right.

Jeeves, my grandmonster's chauffeur, stepped out of the driver's side and entered a shop nearby. So, now what? Go bold and brassy and bum a ride from him, or stick with the feeble plan of navigating my way back to the manor on foot?

I wasn't exactly sure how to get to the manor from the village, so I decided to put my fate in Jeeves' hands. I left the train station and casually strolled over to the Rolls. She looked like a classy old lady with the guts to tell you what she thought and the elegance to do it nicely.

I tried the door and it opened. I guess a car like the Rolls defies theft. Either that or everyone knew who it belonged to and no one wanted to risk the wrath of Millicent if they messed with her ride.

I had barely closed the car door behind me when Jeeves emerged from the shop. I slipped down out of view before he got in the car.

"You look ridiculous lying down in the seat like that. Please sit up like a respectable passenger of this car." Jeeves didn't even look behind him as he spoke.

I sat up sheepishly and met his eyes in the rear view mirror. "Hi, Jeeves."

"Good morning, young lady. I believe your grandmother is very near setting the groundskeepers to drag the pond for your remains. I trust you had a good night?"

"Not really." I didn't elaborate, and Jeeves' eyebrows went up a notch.

"May I suggest you find Lady Elian immediately then so she can call off her dogs? They're ruining my flower beds." The faintest hint of a smile played at the corners of his mouth.

I settled back into the cushy leather seat. "I'm sorry about your flowers."

"I'm sorry about your night."

The impending confrontation with Millicent was already making my stomach churn. Hopefully I could eat crow convincingly so I could get the information I needed. I would almost rather face off against The Ripper again than grovel to my grandmonster.

The Rolls turned onto the long drive leading up to Elian Manor, and then glided smoothly to a stop. Jeeves got out and held the back door open for me like I was the Queen. It felt weird to be treated so nicely when I was pretty sure I was about to get yelled at, but I'd take kindness wherever I could get it. I slid out of the car with a smile for him. "Thanks for the ride."

He leaned in with a whisper. "Don't let Lady Millicent scare you. She was more worried than angry and she'll be glad you're back."

I doubted it. "We'll see." I took a deep breath, straightened my spine, and headed for the massive front door.

SECRETS OF ELIAN

The ancient oak creaked like a bad horror film when I entered the dim hall. Of course, the Hobbit appeared out of thin air and made me jump, but I probably would have been more surprised if she hadn't. She stood completely motionless. I smiled, and it seemed to break the spell. She beckoned me with one gnarled finger. I knew if I hesitated even a moment she'd be down a passageway and gone like Alice's White Rabbit.

I made my feet follow the stooped little old woman down a hallway to a door I hadn't seen before. "Herself isn't the enemy, no matter what she'd have you believe. But she isn't a friend to us either." Then the Hobbit knocked twice on the door and faded back into the shadows of the hall.

"Come." Millicent's voice sounded stern and edgy through the closed door, and I could feel my temper rise. I reached for the handle, but it was flung back out of my grasp. Millicent stood glowering. Then she saw me and her expression shifted from anger to something more like surprise, or maybe even fear.

She spun on her heels and strode across the room to the massive desk in its center. She picked up the phone and spoke into it. "Tell Thomas she's back." Millicent didn't wait for a response before hanging up the phone with a firm click. She rubbed her temples, and then turned to face me. "You may as well come in and sit down, Saira."

I stood next to a spindly gold chair, but Millicent didn't sit, so neither did I. "I'm sorry if I worried you." I tried not to sound sarcastic.

Millicent looked sharply at me. "I thought you were lost."

"Lost? Why?"

She didn't answer. Instead she seemed to study me from head to toe for a long moment before finally speaking again. "Where were you last night?"

"1888."

It looked like she was about to clutch the desk but managed to control the instinct. "Interesting. How?" She might have been talking about the weather, but there was a tightness to her voice that told me she believed me.

"You tell me."

Her eyes narrowed. "You found a spiral."

Very interesting. Millicent knew what a spiral could do, and intriguingly, she didn't ask where the spiral was. Doran, the graffiti artist, had done the one in a Venice tunnel and maybe even the one scratched into the tile of the Whitechapel Underground station. What if I drew a spiral right here? Would I be able to travel through it back to Elian Manor before Millicent was born so I wouldn't have to be having this conversation?

"I should have left you in Los Angeles."

That's nice. Way to make me feel wanted. "Why didn't you?"

"Because you are your mother's daughter and therefore my blood."

"That didn't seem to bother you before when you threw my mom out."

"I'm sure it's easier for you to believe Claire was pushed out of this family."

"Easier than what?"

Millicent actually sighed, like I was making her tired. "Your father was a completely inappropriate match for Claire. When she didn't get permission to marry him, she ran away from the family instead of facing up to her responsibilities as an Elian."

"Responsibility? She was pregnant! Her responsibility was to me! I would have run away from a family that dictated who I could love, too."

56

"And how, exactly, did that turn out for her? Or you? It seems to me that if your father had been worth any of the drama, you would all still be together. A happy little family."

"You must have really hated him."

"I hated what he did to this family." Millicent's tone said the subject was closed.

"Yeah, well, he's dead, so it's ancient history now." I can close my own subjects. I was seriously ready to walk out. I figured I'd grab my suitcase and maybe go stay in a youth hostel or something until my mom got back ... from 1888.

"Why is my mom hanging out in Victorian England?"

The look on Millicent's face almost made the whole fight worth it. I loved that I could jolt her out of her superiority. She stared at me. "How do you know that?"

"I saw her there, I mean then. She was at the Whitechapel station."

Millicent got up and started for the door. "Come with me, Saira."

We were still on the main floor of the manor, but in a totally unfamiliar section. The hallways were narrower and the doors we passed were plain, solid wood. It seemed like an older part of the house, if such a thing were possible. Millicent confirmed it as she stopped in front of the last door at the end of the hall.

"There was a stone keep built on this property when Adelaide Elian built the manor house. She incorporated the keep into her design so well that no one remembers it was ever here."

"That's why this part is so much colder?"

I surprised her again, but only her eyes showed it. "It is?"

I reached out to touch a stone wall and the chill seemed to seep directly into my bones. I snatched my hand back like I'd been burned. "It's freezing."

Millicent looked thoughtful as she pulled a big iron key ring out of her pocket. She chose a plain, black, oddly-shaped key and unlocked the heavy wooden door in front of us. It opened into a low-ceilinged, dark room. Millicent crossed to a table in the middle and picked up a barbecue lighter lying next to an old-fashioned lantern. She lit the wick inside the lamp, then went around the room lighting other oil lamps hung like sconces on the walls.

"No electricity?"

Millicent shook her head. "The keep was never wired for it. The walls are too thick."

"Creepy."

I thought I saw a tiny smile at the corner of her mouth, but it was gone in an instant. The lamps were all lit and the room had a warm yellow glow that seemed to banish a little of the cold.

Millicent went over to a shelf and pulled down a big, leather-bound book. She brought it over to the table and opened it. "This is the Elian Family History. Begun by Adelaide Elian in the 1500s, it's as complete as we've been able to make it."

The paper crackled with age as she found a page and showed it to me. Two little girls looked solemnly back from an old-looking formal photograph.

Both girls looked somehow familiar, even though I was sure I didn't know them. The older girl was maybe five and looked like she was about to laugh. The younger one was probably three and clearly loved her big sister.

"The one on the left is your mother." Millicent watched me for a reaction, and it was a big one.

"You're lying! That picture's ancient!" I didn't know why she was messing with me like that but I wasn't an idiot. The photo was practically a tin-type.

"And the younger girl is my grandmother."

Millicent's grandmother. There was the bombshell. The one I'd halfway been waiting for since all this weirdness began. I suddenly couldn't get enough air and started circling the room like a wild animal in a cage as Millicent watched me silently. I needed something to fix on, like a dancer does when they're spinning. A painting in an elaborate gold frame caught my eye and I made a beeline for it. It was painted in a Renaissance style and looked a little like the Last Supper, except there were five people at the table, not thirteen. Two women and three men, dressed in robes painted to look almost sheer, even though you couldn't see much of their bodies underneath.

All five people were beautiful. There was no other way to describe them. Even with the long-faced Renaissance style of the painting, they had an ethereal look to them.

The blonde woman sat at one end of the table staring off into the distance with a dreamy look on her face. A ridiculously handsome blond guy stood behind his chair next to her. He held something that looked like a long staff in one hand, and his face had kind of a sneer on it. Even though he was model material, he looked stuck up and superior, and there was something about him that reminded me a little of Slick. I shuddered. Next to him sat a dark-skinned man who was kind of a stunning mountain man. If it was possible to look graceful, strong and capable while sitting in a chair, he did it. His gaze rested on the auburn-haired woman to his right.

I'm not sure how it's possible to see it in a painting, but I felt like the auburn-haired woman had just looked away from the mountain man and was now looking directly at me. Obviously, not me exactly. But the artist had made it seem like she looked straight out of the canvas. I moved closer to study her eyes.

"That's Jera." Millicent's voice startled me. I was so engrossed in the painting, I forgot she was there.

"She's staring at me."

"She does that."

That seemed as unreasonable as anything else Millicent had said so far, so I ignored her and continued to examine the painting. Sitting on the far side of the scene, a full space beyond Jera, was a black-haired man who was the most striking person there. Everything about him seemed dark, and even his sheer robe was two shades darker than everyone else's. He wasn't glaring arrogantly like the blond guy, but the intensity in his gaze was unsettling.

I couldn't tell if the dark man was looking at Jera or the mountain man or both of them. I just knew I wouldn't want to be on the receiving end of that stare.

There didn't seem to be any particular race or ethnicity to any of the people in the painting – just shades of skin, hair and eyes. The strangest thing about the painting though was not the cast of characters in it. It was the space between Jera and the dark man. It was what wasn't there. The artist had a perfect sense of proportion and scale. Every person was fully occupying their own space in the scene, and their body positions were completely balanced by the person next to them. It made the gap feel like a hole, a mistake, or maybe like something was missing.

I looked closer but couldn't find any marks to show that someone had been painted out. That was even more unsettling. It was like the artist wanted the viewer to feel the wrongness of the scene.

Jera was still staring at me from the painting, and her eyes felt alive. I gasped and stepped back, and with the extra foot of distance her eyes became painted again.

"It's beautiful, isn't it?" Millicent sounded awed. I turned to her, surprised at how angry I suddenly was.

"It's wrong."

She took a step back from me. "What do you mean by that? What's wrong with it?"

I scoffed at her. "If you can't see it on your own, nothing I say will make you see it." I turned away from the remarkable painting and went back to the leather-bound book on the table. Millicent was studying the painting so I had the book to myself. I turned pages beyond the two little girls. The photos were old, and the clothes and hairstyles were probably from around Victorian times. The photos were family shots mostly, of the girls and their parents doing things around the manor house.

I turned another page and barely contained another gasp. A young woman stared out of a sepia photograph – a young woman wearing pearls, my pearls, who would eventually become my mother. Millicent wasn't lying about that. Could she be telling the truth about everything else? The final picture of my mom showed her at about twenty-one or -two. She was laughing at whoever took the photo, and she looked totally happy.

I stared at Millicent, realization suddenly dawning. "So you're not really my grandmother." It wasn't a question and she didn't answer it.

"I never had any children."

I had to fight a feeling of sympathy that single statement roused in me. Like her weird bitterness about my mother leaving the family, this was personal, and probably way more information than I'd ever get from Millicent in any other circumstance.

"So why did you help me?"

Millicent sighed. "I am your first cousin once removed and, as your mother will have nothing to do with us, the current matriarch of our Family. Regardless of my personal feelings about what she's done, it is my duty to care for every member of it."

This woman sounded like she was saddled with the weight of the world and it was all my mother's fault. I suddenly felt sorry for Millicent. She must have sensed it because her eyes narrowed dangerously.

"Even the illegitimate ones."

That did it. Sympathy gone. Millicent was absently stroking the back of a velvet and gold chair, waiting for my reaction. "Well, the job doesn't seem to be without its perks." Scorn crept into my voice and I didn't bother to hide it.

The lines on Millicent's face were etched in stone and her voice was suddenly flat. "Or costs." She suddenly turned back to the painting and spoke as if she were reciting a lesson. "Like time itself, the rules for Jera's family are strict and cannot be changed lest we invite catastrophe." Millicent turned back and spoke to me in the softest voice I'd ever heard from her. "What I might want has no place in Jera's rules for us."

"Jera's rules? You lost me."

Millicent indicated the painting. "Has anyone ever spoken to you of the Immortals?"

Not since last night, I thought with some satisfaction. But I decided to play dumb. I shook my head. Millicent pointed to the vague-looking blonde on the left of the painting. "Aislin. The Immortal, Fate." Her hand moved right to the handsome warrior guy with the sneer. "Duncan. The Immortal, War." She kept moving across the painting. "Goran. Nature."

I interrupted her. "Isn't Nature usually depicted as a woman in mythology?"

"Mortals have always tried to tame nature and make it soft and gentle, so they've created female representations. But Nature is unforgiving, harsh, strong, and totally careless in its destruction. It is also unexpected and striking and can take your breath away with its gifts. And as you can see, Goran, as the Immortal, Nature, is unquestionably male."

No doubt about it. He was about as manly as they came.

"Jera is the Immortal, Time. Thus we are of her Family."

"So, we're time travelers?"

"The Elians are the Descendants of Time. The ability to travel in time flows through our family lines as a direct inheritance from Jera herself."

"Can everyone in our family do it?"

Millicent seemed to pause slightly before answering. "No."

And I got nothing else on that one. She pointed at the black-haired man on the end of the painting, effectively changing the subject. "This is Aeron. He is the Immortal, Death."

"Death that can't die? Sort of an oxymoron."

Without a trace of humor, Millicent remarked, "Aeron isn't fond of the term. I'd advise you not to use it in his presence."

I stared at her. "In his presence? You mean there's a chance I could meet Death?"

"A certainty, I'd say. One of the few in life." The corners of Millicent's mouth rose very slightly. Her attempt at a smile apparently.

"Okay, Millicent – do you mind if I call you Millicent?"

"I suppose it's more appropriate than 'Grandmother.'"

Not to mention the other things I'd been calling her in my head. "So, the people in this painting are Immortals, and supposedly Jera, the Immortal of Time, is our ancestor ..." I looked to Millicent for a reaction. She nodded but didn't interrupt. "Which is nice and all, to know who you're descended from, but I'm sorry, I don't understand how all this Immortal Descendant thing works at all."

Millicent recited again. "Each Immortal created his or her own lineage and endowed the Descendants with their own gifts. We, of Jera's line, have the gift of time travel."

"I understand the concept of the legacy, but time travel? How is that even possible?"

"Think of time as a circle. Actually, it's more like a spiral that expands upwards. Elians aren't bound by the edges of the circles. We can slip from one ring to the next through spiral portals like the one you traveled through."

"Still not getting it."

Millicent scowled and took a breath. "Let me put it into real terms then. Your mother, Claire, was born in 1850, and my grandmother in 1853. That's their native time. Claire ran away in 1871, but instead of merely running away through space, she also ran through time. She traveled through a portal to the next ring, if you will, approximately 125 years ahead, to what has become your native time.'"

That actually made sense, but it felt like just barely scratching the surface of everything I wanted to know. "You keep saying 'native time.' What does that have to do with anything?"

"Many things. But in Claire's case, there's one thing in particular that makes traveling back to 1888 vital. In one of Time's remarkable traits, our family doesn't physically age unless we are in our native time."

I stared at Millicent, then said something really mean that I instantly regretted. "You must not travel much then, do you?"

The expression on her face slammed shut and Millicent strode toward the door. "Your remarkable cruelty is a trait you inherited from your father." Her tone was as cold as ice.

"I'm sorry, Millicent. I shouldn't have said that."

She spun to face me. "As you say, I don't travel. My family duties keep me as chained to this time as if I were wearing real shackles. And unlike some members of this family, I take my responsibilities very seriously."

She waited for me to leave the room in front of her, so I had no choice but to go. I really wanted another crack at the Elian family history, but doubted she was in the mood to loan it to me now. Millicent closed the door behind me with a loud 'click' and locked it firmly. "And when you have washed and dressed for dinner, we'll discuss your punishment for disobeying me." With that she strode away, forcing me to run after her like a puppy rather than lose my way in the bowels of the manor.

The main hall was bright with daylight. I'd forgotten what time it was in the windowless keep. Once we made it back to where we started, Millicent disappeared into another room, closing the door firmly behind her. I waited for a moment in the hall, half-expecting the Hobbit to appear out of thin air and lock me up in my room again.

That didn't happen. I was forced to find my own way back to my bedroom, and more importantly, my suitcase that was hopefully still stashed under the bed. I took my time getting back to the east wing. I made a point of memorizing landmarks as I went – a painting here, a carved wooden bench there.

The art in this place was actually pretty remarkable. A lot of landscapes and some fairly impressive portraits. Most of it was in older styles that didn't really appeal to my own aesthetic, but I still appreciated the collection.

Some of the landscapes looked familiar, and I looked more closely at one in particular. It was a small stone cottage perched on the edge of a forest. A big cat, like a mountain lion maybe, stared across the painting at the cottage door as if waiting for someone to emerge. Instead of being menacing, the animal looked lonely, and it infused the painting with a sense of longing. There was a small metal tag attached to the frame that said 'Epping Place.' I'd never seen the place, but the style of painting was unmistakable. In the bottom right corner was my mother's perfect signature. And the date. 1871. The year she ran away.

I looked around me to figure out where I was. I knew if I continued on to the left I'd be in the east wing, but this section of hall seemed to be a crossroads. Turn left, go east. Turn right, go west. The painting was on the right side of the intersecting halls, so I decided to go right.

Just beyond the painting was a door, and on a whim, I tried the doorknob. It opened. Inside was a bedroom, but unlike my own very impersonal room, this one was clearly meant for a young girl.

I'd be lying if I said I didn't immediately hope it was my mom's childhood room, but I also knew the chances of that were slim. The room was clean, like every other room I'd seen in the manor so far, but looked like it hadn't been used in a long time. The furniture was all antique, and the bedspread on the pretty iron bed was a faded patchwork quilt made with pieces of what looked like very fancy fabric.

There were still some personal things on the shelves along with old fairy tale books inscribed to "Emily." I flipped the lid open on an inlaid wood box and found a collection of colorful pebbles and stones. A jewelry box had hairpins decorated with little fake jewels that would have been pretty tucked into long hair or braids. Everything in the room was really girly, and I wondered who Emily was.

I considered what Millicent had said. In our family we don't age when we are out of our native time. So life was going on as normal for me right now, but the night I spent back in 1888 had stopped the clock for about twelve hours.

So the converse must be true too. My mom could only age when she went back to her time. I wondered if the aging happened all at once, or only for the amount of time a person spent there. During the week she was gone, did she age one week, or did she age two years? Based on how tired she always looked when she got back, I guessed it was the whole two years.

It explained a lot. It would be pretty weird to people around us if my mom never aged, and I'd probably notice too. Maybe it was voluntary, or maybe keeping in touch with your native time was mandatory for Clockers. I couldn't suppress a shudder at the name, 'Clocker.' The way Slick had said the word still made my skin crawl, and reminded me I'd completely forgotten to ask Millicent why he was hunting me. Note to self: grill Millicent *before* the punishments were handed down, because it was inevitable I'd say something I'd regret after.

Absently, I tried the door on a cabinet. It was locked. I looked around the room, then went to the bed out of habit and felt around the bottom of the headboard where my mom always hid her keys.

One was there, tucked into the frame of the bed. I tried the key in the cabinet lock and it opened. Inside was empty except for an artist's portfolio, which I carefully removed. I leafed through the charcoal and pencil drawings with hands like a museum curator, holding everything by the edges as I spread them out flat on the bed.

It was like looking into a secret life of madness. The drawings were beautiful in a dark and disturbing way, depicting snapshots of life in an institution. There were images of hospital beds filled with shackled sleepers, a young woman in a straightjacket staring right at the artist, a group of men playing dice while another man behind them sat alone in a chair staring off into space. The most haunting one was of the outside of a massive stone building with a long row of barred windows. Behind the glass of each one stood a person in a hospital gown staring out. One of the men had the palm of his hand pressed to the glass as if in greeting.

The drawings were unmistakably the work of my mother, and one was even signed "C.E." on the back.

When had Claire Elian been to a mental institution?

With questions pinging around in my brain, I carefully gathered up the drawings and placed them back inside the portfolio, then locked them inside the cabinet. I'd had no problem snooping through Emily's things, but somehow taking the drawings would require answering questions about my mom I wasn't really prepared to dig into. They'd obviously been hidden for a reason, and could stay that way as far as I was concerned. I replaced the key in its hiding spot and left the room.

Finding those drawings had unsettled me, and I firmly told my brain to mind its own business on this one. Mental denial in place, I gave myself to the business of finding my way back to the east wing room I'd been assigned. If a daughter of the family slept in the west wing, it seemed likely the east wing was reserved for visitors. Ever since I arrived at Elian Manor I've felt more like a visitor than family, even with all of Millicent's talk about clan and responsibility.

The door to my room was unlocked and the key was back on my dresser. Inside, the room was exactly as I had left it. I pulled my suitcase from under the bed. Everything seemed to be there, but I could tell it had been gone through. Not a huge surprise, but still annoying.

I grabbed a clean t-shirt and sweats and went to turn on the bath. The tub was enormous and long enough for me to lay all the way back without bending my knees too far. And surprisingly, considering how old the house was, the hot water didn't run out before it was comfortably full. I'd been in brand new hotels with my mom that couldn't fill a tub even halfway. Unbraiding my hair and scrubbing it clean in that tub was the single most relaxing thing I'd done since landing in England. I felt like I was scrubbing off centuries of grime, and I probably was.

Our Venice loft didn't have a bathtub. Showers were fine for every day, but baths were pure luxury. I wondered if this house had running water in the bathrooms when my mom lived here. I was pretty sure they would have had to heat the water someplace else for baths, which meant a lot of running around for servants just so some rich person could get clean. I definitely took stuff for granted about my 'native time,' and hot running water, flushing toilets, and electricity were among them.

I figured I'd probably fall asleep in the bath if I wasn't careful, so I braided my wet hair and climbed under the covers. Even the rock hard mattress couldn't keep me awake. Within seconds of slipping between soft linen sheets I was out cold.

St. Brigid's

A very light tap at my door woke me hours later. "Yeah," I managed to croak. The door cracked open and the Hobbit stood there, peering in.

"I have a dress for ye." After a night spent listening to Whitechapel English from 1888, the Hobbit's gravel mouth was easier to understand.

I scowled. "My ... Millicent sent you?"

The wizened old woman slipped into the room and laid a simple emerald green sheath dress on the bed. She shook her head. "'Twas I went through your things. Ye have no finery, and Mistress expects it. And ye don't need to add fuel to that fire, as I see it."

I sat up in bed and rubbed my bleary eyes. So, the Hobbit was on my side? "Thank you, Miss—" I realized I didn't know her name.

"I am Sanda. Not a Miss for a long time."

I smiled at the wry tone in her voice. Sanda had a sense of humor buried under that Hobbit exterior, and I decided I liked her. "Thanks for the dress, Sanda." She nodded curtly and slipped out of the room. I realized her entrance was probably my cue to get dressed for dinner. I climbed out of the covers and held the dress up that Sanda had brought me. It was a rich, green silk and looked like it might be something from the 1920s. Kind of flapper style with a dropped waist. I figured there must be closets full of clothes to choose from in this house, and the '20s was probably an appropriate choice for someone my age.

It also couldn't have been my mom's – too new, or even Millicent's – too old. That was good. I was already in so much trouble with Millicent that raiding her closets would have started the dinner conversation off badly. And to get the information I wanted, I had to avoid as much trouble as I could.

The dress actually fit pretty well, but I felt like a total fraud in it. I didn't wear girl clothes because frankly, I didn't usually feel like a girl. Archer didn't know how close he'd hit to home when he said I was basically without feminine wiles. I stuck with jeans and t-shirts because dresses made me feel too vulnerable. Not the best way to go to a meeting with Millicent, but I didn't see I had much choice. I was, however, totally screwed in the shoe department. I had combat boots, Keds I had painted myself in art class, and flip flops. I chose the flip flops and hoped I could stay behind the table so Millicent didn't take offense.

I brushed my hair out and tied it back in a knot. No jewelry, no make-up. The eyeliner and Chapstick I usually had with me were both in my stuck-in-the-nineteenth-century backpack. Which made me tense to even think about. It was probably just as well to look as young and innocent as possible around Millicent. Maybe it would help keep her off guard.

The flip flops were loud on the bare wood floors of the manor, so I took them off and went barefoot. Cold, but not unpleasant. My feet were pretty tough anyway from summers on the beach. But when I got downstairs the stone floor was freezing. Stealth vs. warmth – a tough call. I chose stealth and made my way down the hall carrying my shoes.

Just outside the dining room I stopped to slip them back on. The door was open just a crack, and I could hear Millicent speaking to someone in the room. Her voice was quiet, but distinct. "See that she's kept away from the other Descendants. For once, I'm grateful that Jane Simpson has allowed Ungifteds into our school." The disgust in Millicent's voice sounded like pure intolerance to me.

"If I may be so bold, ma'am. Why send her there if you don't want her trained?" That sounded like Jeeves, but the voice was so low it was hard to be sure.

"That will be Claire's problem when she returns. I just want her out of this house until then."

"Of course, ma'am."

I've always thought eavesdropping was sneaky and I was about to push the door open when it was pulled from behind. Jeeves was as startled as I was. I gave him a reflexive smile and a nod before I went into the lion's den. I think I caught a glimpse of his return smile, but given Millicent's scowl, I didn't think I should call attention to it.

"Hello, Millicent."

The scowl deepened. "Saira. I'm glad to see you can look presentable when you choose to."

I was determined to be as nice as possible to get information. "Thank you. That's a pretty necklace."

And in fact, it was. Opals and moonstones glittered on tiers of gold chains. The whole effect looked like a cascade of milky ice. "It was my grandmother's."

My compliment seemed to mollify her for the moment, and I was able to slide into my seat without comment on my inappropriate choice of footwear. The woman had truly stunning jewelry, and I can only imagine what she would have thought about the plain bronze choker embedded with a tasseled clock that my mother sometimes wore.

"You slept well, I presume?"

"Yes, thank you."

The scowl was back, and I had the thought she was looking for something to criticize, so I headed her off at the pass. "Can you tell me about the other families? We can time travel; what can they do?"

Millicent gave a big sigh. It was killing her to tell me anything. "The descendants of Aislin – Fate – are mostly Gypsies, palm readers and fortune-tellers. Nothing to take seriously. Duncan's brood are hooligans and trouble-makers with no real skill beyond causing chaos. The only Immortal with Descendants of any skill is Goran. They can shapeshift into animal form."

"Like werewolves?"

Millicent looked pained. "Don't be ridiculous. Of course not. The ones with ability take the form of a specific animal, to be

70

determined by heredity. They're not limited to the bigger creatures like were-animals are, though I admit, the men of the Shifter clans like to show off in carnivore form often enough."

I stared at her. "So there's such a thing as werewolves?"

Another scowl. I switched gears.

"What about Death? What can his Descendants do?"

Millicent checked the delicate gold watch at her wrist and rang the tiny silver bell near her plate. "There's someplace I'd like to take you this evening, but we'll be late if we don't get our food quickly." Mistress Mouse came scurrying out of the kitchen, carrying a tray laden with two bowls and some steaming French bread. Dinner was a lamb stew that smelled amazing. Still trying not to offend, I waited until Millicent had tasted her stew before I picked up my spoon. It was as delicious as it smelled, but before I'd gotten a second bite into my mouth, Millicent pushed her bowl away. "The carrots are overcooked. Take it away."

The ever-scurrying Mistress Mouse whisked the offending stew away from Millicent's plate. "Sorry, miss," she murmured as she stole my lamb stew out from under my spoon.

"Hey! I wasn't done with that."

"Of course you are, Saira. It's inedible." Millicent seemed impatient and on edge, so I let the Mouse take my bowl, even though I was starving for the stew. As much as I tried to keep my mood polite and friendly, my stomach was growling and it made me grumpy. I snagged a piece of bread and tore it into pieces, not caring what Millicent thought of my manners anymore.

"Does my mom *have* to go back to her native time, or could she just stay in my time and never age?"

This startled Millicent out of her annoyance for a moment. "We don't stay out of our native times," she said severely.

"Don't or can't? There's a difference."

"I'm well aware of the difference, young lady. It just isn't done."

I shrugged. "My mom's doing it."

"And she goes back every few years to reset."

"Do you 'reset' to the age you should be, or does your clock just start again?"

Millicent suddenly pushed back from the table. "We're late and dinner's taking too long. We're going."

"But I'm starving."

Millicent looked at the roll I'd shredded with disdain. "If you ate your food rather than played with it, you wouldn't be." She strode to the dining room door and beckoned imperiously. "Come. There will be time for dinner later."

I felt like my tongue was almost bitten in half with all the things I didn't say to Millicent Elian.

Lucky for me there was a wool blanket in the back seat of the Rolls, because as pretty as the green silk dress was for dinner, it was nearly October and already freezing outside. Jeeves had handed Millicent her own fur coat when we left the house, but he'd had nothing for me except a look I can only describe as pity.

I had a bad feeling about that look.

Millicent refused to discuss where we were going, except to say that it would give me much more insight into my mother and our family.

The fading light was completely gone by the time we pulled into the long driveway that ended at a massive, gothic edifice. I thought Elian Manor was big, but this place was like a castle out of a horror film. It was probably really striking in the daytime, but at night the shadows made the turrets look like tusks … or fangs.

Jeeves parked the Rolls in front of the heavy iron gates and then helped Millicent from the car. When she finally saw my feet, she gasped.

"Saira! Really! Do you own no proper shoes?"

"I thought the combat boots would clash."

Millicent actually huffed. I almost laughed out loud until Jeeves squeezed my hand and shook his head very slightly. When he let go, there was something clutched in my palm, something he had slipped to me. I quickly put it into the pocket of my dress. It felt like a key, one of the old-fashioned metal kind that fit the door locks of the manor, only smaller. But a key to what? I looked over at Jeeves, but he didn't meet my eyes again as we walked up to the massive iron gates. Written above them, in scrolling iron letters, were the words, "St. Brigid's School."

I promptly forgot the key and stopped in my tracks. "I told you I'm not going to your boarding school."

"And I told you you're here to learn about your mother." Millicent actually grabbed my arm and pulled me forward. I yanked out of her grasp, but realized resistance was probably futile. There weren't so many places I could run in flip flops, and I silently cursed Millicent and my footwear once again.

Millicent pushed the heavy iron gate open with a gothic CREEEEAK! She looked furious. The iron gate banged shut behind me, and I was propelled forward by Jeeves' presence at my elbow. The front door to the mansion was studded with iron and looked like a medieval torture device. It opened suddenly, and a beam of warm light emerged.

A small, white-haired woman in slacks and a blouse stepped out to greet us, and I was so surprised, I almost stumbled up the steps. It was my alarm-clock lady from the train, and she smiled at me warmly.

"How delightful to see you again, my dear."

Millicent looked from me to the woman. "And how do you know my granddaughter, Jane?"

"Miss Simpson, thank you." Anyone who corrected Millicent got points in my book. "I met her on the train from London this morning." Miss Simpson's voice was clipped and courteous, but definitely no-nonsense. But she gave me a slight smile, and I gave her a bigger one back.

"Please come in, Lady Elian. Miss Elian."

"Saira." I found myself wanting to make a good impression on Miss Simpson.

She gestured for us to enter the enormous entry hall and then closed the door behind Jeeves. "You have a beautiful name. Does it have a meaning?"

Millicent surprised me when she spoke up. "It means 'traveler.'"

I stared at her. "It does?"

"At least your mother got that right."

"Well, it's lovely, and I'm sure it suits you very well." Miss Simpson's voice was warm and genuine, and the more she annoyed Millicent, the more I liked her. "Let me take your wrap, dear. It's warm in the library by the fire." Miss Simpson held out her hand for my blanket and indicated the next room where the world's biggest fireplace crackled with yellow, red, and orange flames. She was being very gracious to call the old blanket a wrap, and I thought that must be what 'impeccable manners' were.

"Thank you," I said, really meaning it as I handed her the rough wool and made a beeline for the flickering fire. I sat on a footstool practically in the fireplace, huddled against the thin fabric of my dress.

Everywhere in the room, floor to ceiling and stacked on every surface, were books. This was my kind of room. Within seconds the cold was forgotten and I was on my feet, scanning titles on the shelves.

Millicent and Miss Simpson entered the room after me. I didn't know where Jeeves had gone, but it was my guess that he was back out at the car. My attention was caught by a book about the underground art scene in 1960s London, and I didn't turn around when the two women sat down.

Millicent spoke first and I pretended not to pay attention. "Saira wishes to learn more about our family, and especially about her mother. I've told her you can help her with that information."

"I can teach her what I know, of course, and I believe Miss Rogers knew your grandmother, Emily, and may have some additional details."

"As Saira is my ward until her mother returns, I'd like to enroll her here for regular classwork."

I spun around suddenly. "Hey! I didn't agree to that!"

"And I didn't agree to having a teenager foisted on me, running away from the manor and disobeying my direct orders every chance she gets." Millicent's voice was tight and angry.

I glared at her with all the venom I could muster. "I came back, didn't I?"

"Because you had no alternative." Her tone was equally fierce.

74

Miss Simpson's voice was smooth and calming. "Ladies, please. I'm certain that every bit of anger is justified between you. For this reason, I believe Lady Elian's plan is not a bad one. Saira, you are welcome to stay here until your mother returns. You will have access to my library, my knowledge, and the not-inconsiderable knowledge of my staff. And you and Lady Elian will no longer be able to 'push each other's buttons' I believe is the term?"

Miss Simpson smiled and spoke directly to me. "I think you'll find St. Brigid's a very interesting place, especially to someone of your family history." I saw Millicent tense behind Miss Simpson and that basically clinched it for me. Anyone who annoyed Millicent was one of the good guys.

I nodded. "I'll need my stuff from the manor."

Millicent sounded superior. "It's here. Jeeves has had it sent up to your room."

I spun to her angrily. I was furious, but instead of yelling, I went very cold and quiet. "Don't for a minute think you control me, Millicent! Because you don't!"

Miss Simpson seemed to realize that anything Millicent said back to me was going to set me off, so she directed me back to the main hall where a girl stood waiting. "Olivia will see you to your room, Saira. Thank you for choosing to spend your time here with us."

I looked back at Millicent one last time. Her eyes narrowed and never left mine as she spoke to Miss Simpson. "She is to be taught only theory. If I hear she's learned anything practical, I'll withdraw my Family's financial support from the school."

Nice. Dump me at a school, and then tell them not to teach me. I broke Millicent's stare, and without looking back, I turned and followed Olivia from the hall.

Olivia was one of the tiniest people I'd ever seen. By her face and figure I guessed she was around fourteen, but she was like a miniature version of a teenager. She had corkscrew curls, and huge eyes, and her voice was surprisingly normal for someone so small.

"Lady Elian is your grandmother?" Olivia asked as she led me up massive stone steps.

"You know her?"

"She's a patroness of this school. And my aunt works for her."

"Who's your aunt?"

"Lady Elian's housekeeper. Sanda."

"Wow. Being tiny must run in your family."

Olivia stopped in her tracks and turned to stare at me, hands on her hips and eyes flashing dangerously. She was two steps above me so she looked me in the eye. A good trick for a little person to do.

"Are you making fun of me?"

"I am so sorry, Olivia. I've always been so tall I'm just really aware of height."

The stern look on Olivia's face remained as she narrowed her eyes. "Before you ask, or even if you don't, I'm not a midget, I'm not a dwarf, I'm not a brownie or a fairy, and I'm fifteen years old, not five."

I stared at Olivia, open-mouthed, then I couldn't help it, I busted up laughing. She glared at me. "Oh my God, you have the perfect comeback to every idiotic question anyone could come up with. That's awesome!"

The corners of Olivia's mouth twitched and the fierce look in her eyes relaxed. "I've had a lot of practice."

"I bet you have. And I'm sorry if I was offensive. Tact is not my strong suit."

Olivia's expression shifted in an instant and her eyes actually twinkled. She hadn't said she wasn't a Pixie, so I didn't rule it out. "Get under your grandmother's skin, did you?" Now I could hear the echo of her aunt's Welsh accent.

I grimaced. "She's not my grandmother, and I got dumped here, didn't I?" Olivia laughed, and I realized I liked her. She might be prickly and quick to take offense, but she was equally quick to let it go.

We climbed another set of stairs to the third floor and turned down a hall lined with portraits of stern-faced people. Olivia stopped outside a door.

"Miss Simpson put you in with Raven. Her last roommate just went home in tears."

"That's encouraging."

Olivia leaned in and dropped her voice. "Consider asking for a new roommate *before* she picks a fight." She knocked on the door, and a clear voice called from inside. "Come in."

The door opened and the girl inside regarded me with a bored expression. She was pretty, with long, straight blonde hair pulled back in a ponytail, but there was something about her I instantly disliked. In fact, my reaction to her was so strong I had trouble entering the room.

She stood up and extended her hand with a smile. "Hi, I'm Raven. Miss Simpson told me you'd be coming." I shook her hand and tried to paint a smile over my discomfort, but it made my voice come out too bright. "I'm Saira. Sorry to be a last minute drop-in."

"No, don't worry about it. I happen to have the only free bed in school at the moment."

"Really? This place seems so big."

"It's massive. And it's kind of like a compass. But they've shut down the east and north wings, and the whole third floor, so we're left with girls in the south wing and boys in the west. And the main floor for classes, of course."

I realized I was staring at her as she spoke. Raven raised an eyebrow and looked pointedly at Olivia. Her tone cooled. "Thank you, Olivia. That will be all."

That kind of tone shift reminded me of how Millicent spoke to Sanda – like servants were less than people. I was sure it was only a matter of time before Raven turned that superiority against me. I guessed that despite the gleaming blonde hair, Raven was appropriately named.

"Thanks, Olivia. I really appreciate your help."

"See you around." Olivia shot Raven a look before she left. Raven got up to close the door.

"Olivia's here on scholarship and apparently her aunt is a housekeeper or something. Can you imagine?" Raven shrugged. "She's nice enough, I guess. But she's sort of like a talking doll, don't you think?"

This was not a road I wanted to go down with Raven since she was obviously not shy about spilling anyone's personal information. I noticed my suitcase standing next to a bed on one side of the room. Raven saw my glance.

"Your driver delivered it himself." She indicated the window. "My family has a Rolls Phantom, so I recognized the sound of yours right away." Somehow I had the feeling my reception from her would have been different if I'd arrived in a Honda. I went to look out the window and realized it had a view out toward the woods just past the front drive.

Something white flashed behind a tree, and then someone stepped out into the dim moonlight. Archer! I gasped.

"Are you okay?" Raven was coming up behind me, so I quickly turned and covered my reaction with a yawn. "Sorry, it's been a really long day." I hoped Archer had gotten the hint and was blending back into the trees.

"Oh, well lights out is in ten minutes anyway. We're allowed to stay up reading if we want, but we can't be out of bed."

I pulled my suitcase up on the bed and unzipped it to get out sweats, a t-shirt and my toothbrush. I looked around to find Raven watching me closely. "Where's the bathroom?"

"Down the corridor on the right. We share it with about ten other girls." Raven wrinkled her nose delicately to show her distaste. "Do you want me to show you?"

"No, I can find it." I reached into my suitcase to pull out my hoodie and felt something hard wrapped in it. Hoping I was being casual enough to avoid Raven's notice, I kept the hoodie folded and added it to the bundle of clothes in my arms. Then I closed the suitcase and zipped it up securely. If Raven was the kind of girl to go through my stuff there was nothing I could do to keep her out. I had the feeling she was already revising her opinion of my worth as she checked out my ratty, non-designer sweats.

I left the room and closed the door behind me with an audible click. Another girl left a room in front of me and headed down the hall. I followed her and she turned to enter the bathroom. I found an empty stall and closed the door behind me to change my clothes. I'm

78

not a prude about dressing in front of people, but I also don't usually strip down around strangers. My sweats were warm and familiar, and as pretty as the dress was, I'd been cold all night.

I unwrapped my hoodie and found a small flat box inside. It was locked, but with sudden inspiration I dug into the pocket of the silk dress and found the key Jeeves had given me. It fit the lock perfectly.

Inside the box was a folded up map of England, with a city map of London on the other side. Weird. I glanced at it briefly and saw nothing but a couple red dots marking it. I didn't want to study it too carefully right now because the sound of paper crinkling while I was in a bathroom stall was not a message I wanted to send about my personal habits. I replaced the map in the box, and put the key back into the pocket of the silk dress.

"I heard your brother's ex ran off with your cousin. That's gotta hurt." The voice outside the stall was snarky and mean, and I held my breath, expecting the slap her tone deserved. Instead, there was the sound of running water, then a soft voice.

"Watch for the water, Kelly."

"Why? Are you going to splash me with it? Freak."

I quickly wrapped the box up in the dress and shoved them both into the front pocket of my hoodie, then opened the stall door. There were two girls at the sinks. The blonde, who was pretty in a watery way, looked at me in the mirror while the fake-bake ginger-haired girl was brushing her teeth angrily. The faucet at Ginger's sink suddenly exploded off and water sprayed everywhere, soaking through the front of her nightgown. Ginger glared at the blonde.

"You'll pay for that!" She stalked out of the bathroom.

The blonde reached over and calmly shut the offending faucet off, then smiled at me in the mirror.

"I saw you come in." The blonde's voice was soft and almost musical, like she was seconds away from breaking into song.

"I'm Saira."

"Oh! That's your name? I only saw the S A I and couldn't figure it out."

That was just odd enough that I took a stab in the dark. "Did you make the faucet explode?"

"Kelly thinks I did. And she's gone to get her friends to threaten me. They won't touch me though. They all think I'm crazy."

"Oh. Are you?"

The blonde smiled. "No more than anyone else who can see things before they happen."

"You're a … Seer?" I tried the word out to see what kind of reaction I would get.

Her eyes widened, and then the blonde laughed. "I told Adam it was you. He didn't believe me." She started brushing her teeth, watching me in the mirror with twinkling eyes. I brushed my own teeth and wondered what the hell she was talking about.

"Yes, I'm a Seer. I'm Ava."

I rinsed out my mouth. "Hi, Ava. Who, exactly, were you expecting? And who's Adam?"

"Adam's my twin – he's over in the west wing with the other boys. And you're the girl we've been waiting for." Just then Raven came in. She took in the scene at a glance and her eyes narrowed at Ava. "Kelly said you're causing problems, and now you're freaking Saira out with crazy talk. You know how Miss Simpson feels about that, especially around someone who wouldn't understand."

Ava looked directly at Raven and smiled prettily. "She understands more than you ever will, Raven." Ava left the room with another bright smile for me. Raven shook her head, pityingly.

"Her family is one of the original donors to the school, so Miss Simpson has to let her in. She's a freak."

I headed for the bathroom door too. "See you back at the room." I didn't wait for an answer. Raven's attitude was seriously snotty, and I didn't want to stick around long enough to snap at her. Besides, I needed whatever time alone I could steal to look over the map Jeeves had hidden for me.

My suitcase was just where I'd left it, still zipped closed. I went back to the window and looked out toward the woods where I'd seen Archer. No one was there. My imagination seemed to be active enough for me to start doubting what I'd seen, but if I couldn't trust myself, I was well and truly screwed.

The bedroom door handle turned, and I shoved the emerald silk dress with both box and key back into my suitcase. Then I pulled out my combat boots and a pair of clean socks and set them by the bed. Someone had slipped a book into my suitcase, *Caves and Caverns of England*. Weird, but cool. It was my kind of book. I set the book on my nightstand before heaving the suitcase to the floor and pushing it under my bed.

Raven eyed my boots as she came in, but said nothing and went straight to her desk. She pulled out her cell phone and started texting. Within minutes an adult voice called down the hall, "Lights out! Goodnight, ladies!"

It was a long time before the sounds of texting in the dark finally stilled.

NIGHT OUT

I jolted awake from a dream. I'd been free-running in the woods with Archer and was afraid I had laughed out loud in my sleep. The room was pitch black and silent, and I lay still for a long moment listening for Raven's breathing. It seemed steady, and I hoped she was a deep sleeper.

The creaks of my bed and the floor were unfamiliar to me so I moved like molasses as I got out of bed. I found my boots by touch, and after another minute of creeping in slow motion, finally made it to the door.

Raven's breathing hadn't changed at all, but the true test would be the door. It was a lever-type handle and I had the momentary fear that we'd be locked in. Clearly, my recent experience at Millicent's house had given me a complex.

The door opened, and I felt instantly better as I stepped out into the hall. The corridor was quiet as I crept down it to the stairs.

I carried my boots, and my feet were frozen by the time I made my way downstairs. I tried the front doors first. Locked. The windows in the library were next, but they were tall, skinny, and made of leaded glass that didn't open. No good.

At the end of the hall was an archway leading into a huge dining hall filled with long tables. The room had a totally gothic feel to it, complete with gargoyle wall sconces and huge tapestries. The shadows in here were impressive too, with big swaths of darkness reaching out from the corners like tentacles. I hoped the kitchen was close because I was starting to get the creeps.

Fortunately, the next door led to an enormous kitchen, and, just as I'd hoped, there was a door leading outside just past the big fireplace.

I grabbed an apple from a bowl on one of the tables and I shoved it in my hoodie pocket. The door wasn't barred from the inside and I couldn't see a key in the lock. Not a good sign. I tried the door handle and it, too, was locked. I swept my hand on the lintel above the door in case there was a key hidden there, but no luck. I guessed there must be a housekeeper somewhere with a big ring of keys. Maybe that was smart with all the girls in the house, but my impression of prison just came back.

Okay, Plan B. Fire escapes.

The back stairs were creakier because they were wood, but as long as I stayed off the middle of each step, I was good. There was a small balcony on the third floor with a fire escape. The door was locked, but the window next to it wasn't. I opened the catch and prayed the window wasn't painted shut like in so many apartments my mom and I had lived in. The mark of a cheap landlord was painted-shut windows instead of proper security. Effective, but miserable on hot summer nights.

A blast of cold air hit me in the face. I slipped out quickly and closed the window down to just a crack so the draft wouldn't bring someone out of their room to investigate.

The fire escape was an old kind, probably put on during one of the World Wars, which meant I needed to be more monkey than human to climb it. I huddled on the balcony trying not to shiver as I laced up my boots, then grabbed the ladder and descended as far as I could go. It was stuck of course, probably rusted in place, so the last drop was about fifteen feet. I dangled from the bottom rung, which made my drop closer to nine feet. Except it wasn't.

I let go and got ready to tuck and roll for impact. Strong arms caught me and I barely stifled a scream, half-expecting to see Slick grinning evilly at me. But it was Archer.

"What the hell?" I demanded in a whisper. Archer put his finger to his lips. The sound of an exterior door closing had our full attention.

"Come," he whispered. He set me down gently and ran for the woods. I had to sprint at full speed to catch up with him. Archer led me deep into the trees, dodging branches and jumping rocks like he'd been free-running his whole life. I didn't think Victorian gentlemen were into that sort of thing. But I had to admit, it felt really good to run. I was free of all the stone walls that had been trapping me since I got to England.

He finally stopped in a little clearing completely surrounded by tall trees – a tiny meadow that glowed silver in the nearly-full moonlight. I had to bend double to catch my breath, but Archer hadn't even broken a sweat. I stared at him. "Why are you here?"

"For you."

That startled me and I deflected. "How can you be here? Did you go through the spiral too?"

He winced a little. "It's complicated, Saira."

My guts did a little half-twist at the way he said my name. When did I become such a *girl*? "Tell me anyway."

And then *he* deflected. "So you've had no word of your mother?"

His words felt like a punch, and I shook my head. "What happened after I left Whitechapel station?" The conversation was starting to sound surreal, and I knew I was just going to have to roll with it.

"A crowd had gathered around our fight, and pandemonium broke out."

I stared at Archer. "Did I just disappear in front of a bunch of people's eyes?"

He smirked slightly. "The few people who actually did see you wink out seemed to disappear fairly quickly themselves, rubbing their eyes and looking dazed. No, the melee was caused by the Ripper himself. When you vanished, he suddenly went charging past me to the platform where he knocked several people down onto the tracks."

I stared at Archer in horror. I've always shuddered at the idea of falling in the way of a train. It's why I've never tagged a rail station. "Was anyone hurt?"

He shook his head. "We got them out before the next train came through. But that time cost me the Ripper."

"And my mom?"

"She was gone."

I whispered, almost to myself. "And she hasn't come back."

Archer took a step closer to me, and his eyes bored into mine with the intensity of his gaze. "Then go find her." He was inches away from my face, and I couldn't move or look away.

My voice cracked with the desperation I felt. "But I don't know anything! I don't even know if I can go back."

Archer wouldn't let me look away. "I can help you, but you have to trust me."

"I don't understand any of this. I don't know what I can do, or why you're even here. I don't even know you, but you keep showing up in my life. Why?"

Archer's eyes were locked on mine. "Before that night I had my studies to keep me occupied. Then I met you." He sounded agonized. I was afraid to even twitch in case I broke the spell that held us there. "Falling for a Clocker from the future shattered my careful peace and left me vulnerable to things I'd never imagined."

I took a step backward from the anger and pain in his voice, and Archer finally broke his gaze and turned away from me. My insides were twisted up in a rat's nest of emotion. Shock, excitement, terror – they all pretty much felt the same. My automatic response was fight or flight.

Which was probably a good thing. A sudden crash in the underbrush put us both on high alert. Archer grabbed me and pulled me behind him protectively, and I practically jumped out of my skin when a big stag leapt through our clearing. I sagged against him in relief as the stag took one look at us and jumped away, but Archer was still coiled. A dog barked behind us, and a man's voice called out in the distance. "He's got 'em!"

"Run!" Archer whispered fervently to me. I looked into his eyes. There was terror in them, and I was instantly back to being prey. "I'll draw them away. Get to the school!" He pushed me away from him and suddenly growled in the direction of the dog's bark. It was a sound I'd never heard a person make, and it raised goose bumps on my arms. I took off running.

I moved by pure instinct. Over a rock, up a fieldstone wall, across a log. The woods around me faded into the background as obstacles came into pin-sharp focus. I heard voices behind me, and a commotion coming from the direction of the little glen, just as I broke out of the woods on a different side of St. Brigid's than the one I'd left.

There was no fire escape, but I spotted a second floor balcony with a decent-sized tree close enough to be a viable option. I scrambled up the trunk, thankful for long-sleeves and boots. The tree was pretty easy to climb once I was up in the branches, and it was just a matter of getting as high and far over as I could without breaking any of them.

In the distance I heard a car peeling out at full speed, and I felt sick in the pit of my stomach. Whatever was going on in the woods, Archer was out there with no back-up. I debated jumping down and going back out there after him, but realized how stupid that was. Somehow Archer had gotten here, so he clearly had skills I wasn't aware of.

I sat still for a moment and allowed my brain to process what Archer had said to me in the meadow. The idea that the Ripper had gotten away from Archer was horrifying enough. That he had almost killed people in the train station to do it was unthinkable. Where was my mother during all this? And why had she been in Whitechapel station in 1888 in the first place?

The cold finally ate through the body heat I'd managed to generate running. I had probably run away from Archer and the intense feelings he laid on me as much as from the hunters and dogs. I shivered again. Okay, time to move.

The coast seemed clear enough, and I found a fairly sturdy branch reaching out toward the second floor balcony. It was easier to walk it than to crawl, and in less than a minute I was across. I stayed low on the balcony for a second, partly to catch my breath, but also to look for anyone who might have seen me. Nothing moved outside the mansion, so I stood up to try the door.

And looked right into a huge pair of eyes.

Fortunately, the eyes were just as startled to see me as I was to see them. "Crap!" I whispered to myself as I dropped back down below the level of the windows. Which was a stupid thing to do and didn't change the fact that some guy was standing on the other side of the glass. I took a deep breath and stood back up again. The guy was still there, but the shock on his face had been replaced with a smirk.

I actually wanted to punch him just for his expression. This from someone who does everything she can to avoid a fight and the attention it brings. What was wrong with me?

To cover up my reaction, I put on the same cocky attitude the guy had. I raised an eyebrow and tried the door. Locked of course. So I pointed at the handle. "Open it." I mustered as much arrogance as I could. He considered me for a moment through the window and then held up a key.

"With this?" He mouthed, through the glass. Jerk.

"No, with your superpowers, idiot!" I leaned against the railing with my arms crossed in front of me.

The guy laughed at me. "What will you give me?" I couldn't hear his voice, but the words were clear enough.

I stuck my middle finger in the air in a very unladylike gesture – one I'm sure Millicent would have disapproved of with every fiber of her being.

The guy laughed again and made a show of pocketing the key. I narrowed my eyes at him and tried to look threatening, until the crunch of gravel under tires echoed from the front of the house. I whipped around to see what was coming, but caught only the shadow of headlights.

The balcony door clicked open and hands grabbed me from behind. "Come on." The guy's voice was low and he spoke directly into my ear. He propelled me inside and quickly locked the door behind me.

We were at the end of a hall in an unfamiliar wing of the school. I turned to face him and barely had time to register what he looked like before he spoke. "The Crow's new roommate?" I nodded. 'The Crow.' A perfect name for Raven.

"Let's go. Before they do a room check." He took off at a run down the hall, and I jogged behind him to catch up. My guide was tall, probably 6'3", with sandy blond hair that fell to almost shoulder length. He was wearing sweats and a Pink Floyd t-shirt that looked like it was from the '80s. It was the kind of shirt I would have slept in, and probably, so did he.

Floyd, named in honor of his shirt, led me down an odd little back corridor to a set of service stairs. He stopped suddenly and then pulled off his t-shirt, using it to protect his hand from the heat as he unscrewed the light bulb in a wall sconce. The staircase was plunged into darkness, and Floyd continued up the staircase. I hugged the outer edge of the wooden steps, aware of every creak and groan Floyd's feet made. If he was so worried about being seen, he might have been a little more careful about being heard.

He paused at the top of the stairs to pull his t-shirt back on and grinned as I looked away – I was vaguely uncomfortable at the sight of toned abs and rippled shoulders. The guy reminded me of a surfer from Venice Beach, about as out of place at a boarding school in England as someone could get. The smirk on his face was totally consistent with surfer arrogance.

"Come on, Clocker. Before they find out you're not in bed."

I stopped in my tracks and stared at Floyd through narrowed eyes, hoping my shock didn't show. "What did you call me?"

"Sshh!" He put a finger to my mouth and almost seemed to cover my body with his. A door opened down the hall and someone looked out of their room. I thought my pounding heart would give us away, but the head disappeared back inside the room and the door closed softly.

I let out a breath, but Floyd held his hand over my mouth. I hate that! The door opened again quickly, as if the room occupant hoped to catch someone sneaking by. But after another moment, it closed again with a firm click, and the pressure against my lips relaxed. I glared at Floyd fiercely. He shrugged. "Radar's the worst one. Unless she's drinking, she can hear a mouse fart." His whispered voice was inches from my ear. I pushed him away from me harder than I meant to. He nearly lost his balance and caught himself against the wall in surprise.

"Tell me how to get back then, so you don't have to get in trouble too." My whisper was laced with as much venom as I could muster. Floyd grinned at me again and shook his head.

"I won't get in trouble. But thanks for caring."

Floyd was an annoying, yet effective tour guide. He led the way down a different corridor, up some creaky stairs to the fourth floor, across an outer hallway, then back down. I recognized a portrait of a glaring old guy and realized we were just outside my room. Floyd grabbed my hand before I could touch the door handle.

"Boots!" I looked down at my feet, mystified. "The Crow will know you've been out."

"Right." Our voices were quiet whispers and I dropped down to untie the laces and pull off my combat boots. Floyd dropped down next to me and his eyes caught mine.

"Check the Crow's phone. You'll need something on her to keep her in line."

My eyebrows arched up in surprise. "Thanks." I meant it. Until he smirked.

"No worries. I like it when hot girls owe me."

Ew.

I stood up quickly and held my boots behind my back as I opened the bedroom door and slipped inside. Floyd was already gone by the time I'd closed the door. I quietly set my boots down on the floor next to my bed, and let my eyes adjust to the darkness of the room. I could hear Raven's regular breathing and hoped it meant she was still asleep.

I slipped across the room to the window. A truck was parked outside, and the floodlights were on at the front of the school. I could see a dog and an empty gun rack inside the truck. Great. I could only hope Archer had gotten away from whoever had been hunting in the woods tonight.

I still needed to get information on Raven. For all his attitude, Floyd was right. Raven needed a leash. Her phone was next to her on the nightstand, and I was able to reach it without making a sound. Texting history was first, to somebody named "chaotic1." Apparently about me.

"new roomie. bitchy." Nice. Thanks.

"Family?"

"don't know."

"find out."

Okay, whoever chaotic1 was I didn't like. And as enlightening as the conversation was, it wasn't ammo. I scrolled around Raven's phone some more but didn't find anything that made sense until I got to her pictures. The first one was of an open suitcase. My open suitcase! She had opened my bag and photographed the contents.

She'd found the locked box in my hoodie, took pictures of my spray paint cans, and even the *Caves and Caverns* book that somehow made it into my bag. Unbelievable!

My first instinct was to delete the pictures, but then I realized the threat of exposing her blatant snooping might be enough to keep her in line. I quickly e-mailed the photos to myself and put the phone down before making my way back to my own bed. The truck engine echoed outside and Raven startled awake at the noise.

"What was that?" She immediately took in my seated and dressed state. "Where were you?"

"Asleep. The noise woke me up." I tried to make my voice crackly and sleepy. I didn't have to try hard.

"Why are you dressed?" She asked, suspiciously.

"Fell asleep with my clothes on. What time is it?" Raven reached for her phone to flip it open and read the clock. "3:30." She set the phone down again, apparently not wondering why it was warm.

I swung my legs under the covers and settled them over myself. I rolled away from Raven to face the wall, pretending to drift off to sleep. I could hear her moving around in her bed restlessly, and held my breath when I heard her reach for her phone again and start texting. Finally, she shut it off and settled back down to sleep. It was a long time before I could do the same.

LOCK DOWN

Raven poked me the next morning. I felt like I'd been kicked in the head and I wasn't in a great mood. "What's your problem?" I sounded practically Welsh with all the gravel in my voice.

"Breakfast ends in ten minutes. You're welcome." Raven flounced out of the room in a huff. I cracked my eyelids open just as she left and caught a glimpse of a denim mini skirt, striped tights, and some kind of sweater. Painfully stylish and probably really expensive. I was perversely glad to see her style was totally different than mine, because the more I knew about my roommate, the less I liked her.

I got up and dragged my suitcase out from under the bed. The box was still wrapped up where I'd left it, but the Crow was so nosy, it was only a matter of time before she found the key. I dug it out of the pocket of the green silk dress and strung it on a cord I kept wrapped around my drawing pencils. I put it on like a necklace, and the key dropped low enough into my shirt to be invisible.

As much as I wanted to open the box and check out the map again, I was starving. I pulled on my uniform of jeans, combat boots, my Amp'dGear t-shirt and a clean hoodie, then I quickly braided my hair down my back and headed down to breakfast.

I just barely made it to the dining hall before they took the food off the buffet. I grabbed toast, eggs, and sausage and sat at a long table to eat.

"Didn't your mother ever tell you to chew your food or you'd get a stomach ache?" I looked up to see Olivia smirking at me. She was holding a piece of sausage and parked herself on the bench across from me.

91

"Sorry, I didn't eat yesterday."

"I figured it had to be something because the food here's not that great. How was your first night with Raven?"

"She went through my bags and only tolerates me because she thinks Millicent's money is mine. But she's already starting to turn on me, so I'm sure it's just a matter of time until one of us is in tears." I grinned and Olivia laughed.

"I told you she was a piece of work. You could probably talk to Simpson about getting moved, but I don't know if they'd open another room just for you."

"What is it with this place? It's huge, but it seems deserted." I looked around the nearly empty dining hall where I saw a couple of younger kids, maybe ten or eleven years old, and a group of fifteen-year-old boys horsing around on their way out. "The way Millicent talks about this place, you'd think it was the most exclusive school in England."

"It probably is. It's why the two wings are closed off. Not enough bodies to fill it."

"It can't be that exclusive. I'm here, aren't I?"

Olivia laughed. "You and me, both. Actually, when Miss Simpson got here about ten years ago, she made it possible for a whole new group of kids to come. But families have been pulling their kids out right and left, especially in the last three months. At the rate they're dropping, I'd be amazed if the school can stay open next year. With the kids goes the money, which means my scholarship dries up too. I'm sure Raven informed you of that the instant I was out of the room last night."

I rolled my eyes and Olivia laughed.

"Yeah, I wouldn't have been here before Miss Simpson came."

"Would Raven?" I asked.

Olivia shrugged again. "She's part of this whole exclusive Family thing here that no one talks about. Her crowd has stupid names for each other, private study groups, and one-on-one apprenticeships with teachers. But those are the kids that are getting pulled, so the rest of us usually just ignore them."

Olivia checked her watch. "Come on. We have assembly in the solarium." She popped the last of her sausage in her mouth and started for the door. I quickly cleared my plate and followed her out.

The solarium was a stunning room. I was shocked I hadn't seen it from the outside during my adventures last night because it was unmistakable. The whole room was floor-to-ceiling glass that looked out onto a big rolling lawn. I couldn't take my eyes from the view and didn't even notice that the room was filled with benches until Olivia pushed me down on one.

We sat in the back, and I guessed the room contained about fifty kids. That hardly seemed enough to fill more than three classes, so I couldn't imagine how St. Brigid's could be a proper school.

Miss Simpson stood at the front of the solarium with four other adults. Teachers or staff I supposed. An ancient, half-asleep looking woman sat directly to Miss Simpson's right. Next to her was a youngish, pretty woman who was trying to look confident, but seemed less at ease than I was. Seated on the other side of Miss Simpson was a perfectly-dressed, immaculately groomed woman about my mother's age with an imperious expression on her face. About two weeks ago I would have done everything possible to stay out of her way. Now, after dealing with Millicent for a couple of days, the woman's attitude just made me tired.

And at the end of the group, seated just enough away from the others to really set him apart, sat a man who looked exactly like Millicent's portrait of Goran, the Immortal mountain man.

It was so jolting to see him lounging insolently in the seat that I almost got up and backed out of the room. I had the very distinct impression that this was not a man to turn your back on. Ever. I was dimly aware that Miss Simpson was greeting the students and wishing them a good morning. My eyes were locked on Goran's twin, and I only realized I was staring when his gaze wandered over the assembled group and found mine. I had to keep myself from physically ducking behind the person in front of me. I tried to look casual so he didn't notice my stare.

Unfortunately, the place my casual look landed was on Floyd, smirking at me from the next row. I gave Miss Simpson my attention just so I could ignore him.

"Last night our groundskeepers spotted a … predator in the woods outside the school." Miss Simpson had my undivided attention now. "And a window on the third floor of the south wing was found open." She looked around the room meaningfully, and I'm pretty sure her eyes found mine in the crowd.

"I don't know if someone tried to leave the building, or let someone in, or just felt the need for fresh air. The point is, with a predator in the vicinity, we can have no breaches of security in this school. All windows and doors will be locked at sundown, and for additional safety, the staff will take shifts to patrol the halls of the dormitory wings. I'm sorry to say that until our woods are clear again, St. Brigid's will be in lock-down."

A quiet, collective gasp went up around the room but nobody spoke up. Apparently the idea of lockdown wasn't as appalling to these guys as it was to me.

"All right, you're dismissed to your classes." Miss Simpson turned away from the students to speak with the old lady on her right. The students were all up and moving toward the exits.

I overheard students around me talking about the possible break-in. "I heard the groundskeepers actually came inside the school and almost caught someone on the second floor of the west wing, but one of them tripped down a dark staircase."

"Those staircases are always lit."

"The sconce was burned out and the stairs were dark. That's what I heard."

The group moved away and I turned to look for Floyd. Could he have been the one they chased through the hallways? Was that why he unscrewed the light bulb on that staircase? Floyd appeared in front of me with an arrogant, lazy grin on his face. "Hey, Clocker. Let's get you to class."

"Sure, Floyd. Lead the way." I managed to unsettle him just a little bit. A very small victory, but a meaningful one.

"Floyd?" His eyebrow arched up.

"Clocker?" I tried for the same tone.

"We don't get many Elians here anymore. It was worth a shot. Why 'Floyd?'"

"Your t-shirt last night. Thanks again, by the way. Was that you the groundskeepers chased through the school?"

Floyd looked around quickly to make sure no one was in earshot, and then he grinned. "Just one, but the guy made a total racket when he fell down the stairs."

"Impressive use of said t-shirt."

"You figured that out?"

"I didn't think you were stripping for my benefit."

He laughed. "How little you know me." Floyd's eyes narrowed and he suddenly got serious. "Did you leave the window open?" I nodded and Floyd's eyes narrowed. "To meet a Sucker in the woods?"

I scowled at him. "I don't know what you're talking about."

"The 'predator' Simpson's talking about. It has to be a blood-sucker, otherwise why start patrolling at sundown and worry about a third floor window?" He stared at the compete bafflement on my face. "Did they lock you away in a cellar all your life? There was a Vampire out last night."

My eyeballs almost departed their sockets. The casual way he talked about 'Vampire' was deeply disturbing to my fragile sense of reality. I decided I needed to just accept that everything I thought I knew about the world was probably wrong, and to start paying attention if I wanted to keep my head from exploding.

I took a deep breath and changed the subject as we departed the solarium. "Where are we going?"

"To class. You're probably with us in Rogers' study. She's pretty cool when she's conscious. At least she knows a lot about the Families."

I stared at Floyd. "The Families?"

He stopped suddenly in the hall, forcing some girls to go around us. "You *are* a Clocker, aren't you?"

I folded my arms across my chest, forcing myself to keep breathing. "Maybe."

Just then the Goran look-a-like stepped out of a room along the hall. "Adam Arman, you're late for class. Not the best first impression for Miss Elian to be making. Move it!" He had a deep, bear-like voice and sounded like someone I didn't want to mess with. Apparently, neither did Floyd. Wait, Adam?

"You're Ava's twin? You guys are Seers?"

Adam looked around quickly. "Took you long enough. C'mon. There's Ungees around, and Mr. Shaw's still watching us." I looked back to spot the huge man standing in his doorway glaring at us through narrowed eyes.

"What the hell are Ungees?" I whispered as we walked.

"Our grandparents called them 'Ungifteds.' Adam grinned as he entered a classroom at the end of the hall. "Which makes us gifted, obviously."

Miss Rogers was already there, seated in a big wing chair by a fireplace. "Thank you for escorting our new student to class, Adam." Miss Rogers' voice was surprisingly strong for someone who looked like she would blow over in a stiff wind.

I stopped inside the door and took in the room. Instead of a proper classroom like I expected, it was set up more like a study. Comfortable-looking chairs were grouped around the fireplace facing Miss Rogers, enough for four students. Raven was there next to a pretty brunette girl with her head in a book, and Ava, Adam's twin was seated off to one side.

"Saira Elian, welcome to the sixth form at St. Brigid's."

That sounded so important and substantial. As far as I was concerned, this little stopover was for just a couple of days until my mom got back. And I had to keep telling myself that or I'd go totally nuts.

"Thanks." I nodded to Miss Rogers and vaguely included the rest of the class in a smile.

"Adam, please pull a chair over for Saira so we can begin."

Adam made a gallant show of offering me a chair. I wouldn't have taken it, except I saw Raven scowl at Adam's gesture and I knew it would bug her. So I sat down next to Ava while he pulled another big chair over and plunked down next to us.

Ava leaned in. "Hi, Saira. I'm glad you're finally here." She looked at the brunette who was putting away her book. "Saira's the one I told you about, Stella."

I thought I could like Ava, but the way she said things was a tad unsettling. Especially when Stella's expression shifted to something speculative as she said a polite hello.

The class seemed to be in the middle of a discussion about the American and French revolutions, but from the British perspective, so I sort of tuned out until Miss Rogers addressed her question directly to me.

"Saira, I believe your mother traveled back to the time of the French Revolution when she was young. What did she tell you of her experiences in Paris?" My jaw, seriously, hit the floor. I thought I might actually have a bruise from the impact. Raven sniggered. I've always hated that sound. It's the sound of arrogance and attitude and it never fails to make me mad.

Miss Rogers seemed to understand her mistake, and to her credit, she tried to backpedal. "I'm sorry; I might have her confused with her sister, Emily. My grandmother taught them both, you see."

"I wouldn't know. You should ask Millicent."

Miss Rogers looked at me a little sadly. I must have sounded bitter, and she nodded. "Yes, I think I will."

I pretty much tuned out the rest of the history lesson as my brain spun on the idea that my mom could have time traveled to the 1780s. I wasn't even aware of the passage of time until chairs were suddenly scraping back and people were standing to leave. Adam leaned over and my eyes suddenly focused again.

"We're going to the library to study. You want to come?"

Ava waited behind him and I stood up quickly. "I'll meet you there. Thanks."

Adam looked at me oddly for a moment, and then quickly repositioned my chair behind me. My knees suddenly buckled and I went down – fortunately right into the chair. If he hadn't moved it, I would have hit the floor. My vision doubled for a moment, then righted itself, and I struggled to my feet again. Maybe the knocks I'd taken to the head had actually done some damage, or, more likely, my capacity for overwhelm had just hit its limit.

"Are you okay?" Ava hovered nervously.

"Yeah, fine." I clutched the back of the chair for support, and then looked at Adam. "Thanks. Again."

I caught a glimpse of a concerned look, but his expression shifted almost immediately to the familiar smirk. "I have that effect on girls."

"Oh, you mean the nausea? Yeah, I can understand."

Ava laughed and pulled her brother out of the room. "See you later, Saira."

I waited until the room was empty except for Miss Rogers shuffling through papers on her desk in the corner. "Miss Rogers? Do you have a minute?"

I still felt a little shaky, and my voice must have echoed it because Miss Rogers looked concerned. "Yes, Saira. Of course."

"I'm sorry about earlier. The fact is, I didn't even know the people in my family were time travelers until this week, and as for my mom, I can't ask her about the French Revolution because she's not here. And the last place anyone saw her was in Whitechapel, in 1888." I paused to breathe and watch her reaction.

Miss Rogers sank into her seat, but her expression didn't change and she regarded me thoughtfully. "Who saw your mother in 1888?"

"Me."

"I see." Miss Rogers shuffled some more papers. "I'd like to do private lessons with you in the afternoons to bring your education current with your abilities. I believe I can arrange things with Miss Simpson to clear your schedule if you agree."

Relief coursed through me. "I'd appreciate that."

"Good. Now I'd advise that you stick with Adam and Ava Arman as much as possible. They'll be able to keep you out of trouble as you learn your way around this school."

"I'm not a troublemaker, Miss Rogers."

Miss Rogers looked at me sharply. "No, but others are. I'll see you back here at three."

I found the Seer twins sitting with Stella in the library at the front of the school. Raven was in a corner, texting on her cell phone. My own cell phone didn't work in the U.K. and I didn't miss it. Besides my mom, I didn't really have anyone to text or talk to anyway.

I dropped into a seat beside Ava. She gave me a bright smile. "The Crow's nosing around your stuff again. You need a better hiding spot for the box."

"Do you guys do that often?"

"What? See things? Yeah, but we don't usually say anything. Mostly because it freaks people out." Ava gestured around the library. "But as you can see, no Ungees in sight."

I shuddered. "I think I hate that word."

Miss Simpson entered the library and came straight over to our table. "Miss Elian, may I speak with you?"

I looked up in surprise, and then nodded. "Sure."

"Privately, please." She smiled at the others, and I got up to follow her.

Miss Simpson led the way to a small room just off the library. It was also full of books, but they looked older and more interesting than anything in the other room. She closed the door behind me. "Miss Rogers just asked me for permission to give you private tutoring." I nodded mutely. "Unfortunately, as valuable as I believe that would be, I can't allow it."

I stared at her. "Why not?"

"Your guardian gave specific instructions about your education."

I scoffed. "Theoretical, not practical."

Miss Simpson nodded. "Indeed."

"Technically, I'm her great-aunt. That should give me some rights, shouldn't it?"

Miss Simpson smiled wryly. "Unfortunately, you are underage, and she is the 'technical' head of the Elian family."

"Cool. So I'm at a school where I can't learn anything."

"I will try to make as much information available to you as I can without disobeying your guardian's wishes."

I looked Miss Simpson in the eye. "I'm willing to learn anything you're willing to teach me."

"I wish I had more students like you, Saira." She opened the door and ushered me out of the room. Adam and Ava were still waiting for me at the table.

"I need air. Anyone want to come for a walk with me?"

Ava looked at Adam. "Told you they cancelled her tutoring."

"Okay, seriously? Knock it off."

Ava asked Adam, "Will they let us out since it's daytime?"

"We're not prisoners; they're just worried about a Sucker on the loose."

I hated that name even more than 'Ungee.' And the totally casual way it rolled off Adam's tongue was the proof he wasn't just making it up to see my reaction. He was talking about something real – something I needed way more information about. And information seemed to be the thing most lacking at this school.

I headed for the door and the twins got up to follow me. Raven called out from her corner, "Where do you think you guys are going?"

Ava shot back, "To look through your stuff. Why should you have all the fun?"

Raven's eyes narrowed. "Freaks."

"So much for my grace period." I turned to Adam. "And you were right about getting something on her. She has been going through my stuff."

Ava snorted. "Don't let her get to you. Mongers have always been bullies."

"Mongers?"

"Wow, you seriously don't know anything."

"You're right. I don't. So educate me." My tone of voice didn't even faze Ava. She was just so cheerful it was hard to be annoyed with her. "Well, Mongers are, you know, like war-mongers."

It clicked. "The Descendants of War." I stopped in my tracks, just outside the front door. It was so strange to put reality together with the stories I'd been hearing about Immortals for the past two days. It made the lines I'd drawn around my life for seventeen years seem imaginary. I jumped down several steps at a time and headed for the woods.

"I don't think we should go into the forest." Ava sounded concerned.

I shrugged. "Stay here if you want." I didn't look back to see who would follow; I just took off running.

THE PROPHECY

Free running in the woods was a little more challenging than in the city because there were more potential obstacles on the ground with every step. I picked up speed, scaling boulders and leaping felled trees at a full run.

Adam had followed me, and was clearly out of his league. After a few minutes, I took pity on the guy and stopped at a fallen log to wait and mull over what I'd picked up so far. This place was a special school for the kids of the Immortals' Families – and regular kids too, but they didn't seem to count. Obviously there was a lot for me to learn here. I was trying really hard to stay loyal to my mom, but the realization that she had kept so many secrets was eating away at me.

And then, of course, there were the Vampires. I couldn't even think that thought with a straight face.

Adam finally showed up, sucking air like a guy who just scaled Everest. How come Archer could keep up with me and a super-athlete like Adam was out of his league?

"What's your problem?" He could barely get the words out, and it made me grin.

"I'm not the one gasping like a guppy out of water."

"And I didn't realize I was chasing a jack rabbit. It explains how you climbed that damn tree last night." He collapsed on the log next to me, holding a stitch in his side.

I laughed, which annoyed Adam. A bonus. He threw me a disgusted glance, got up and started hobbling back the way he came, still holding his sides. "I'm sorry." I was still giggling, but I tried to make my voice sound properly contrite. He ignored me and kept walking.

I realized I actually did want to pick his brain, so I caught up to him. "I take it you've never done any free-running?" I tried to keep my voice totally neutral.

"There's a name for what you just did?"

I nodded. "The French name is parkour, and I think it came from military obstacle courses or something. It's all about going over and under things in the most efficient way possible."

"Over or under? What about around?" His annoyance seemed to have faded. We walked along at a normal pace, and his breathing had slowed down to a heavy pant. "Show me." He nodded at a tree about ten feet away. It had a big trunk, and the lower branches were above my reach. "Climb that."

"Gotta see it to believe it, huh, Seer?" He looked like he was working up a smart-ass comment, but I was already gone. I leapt onto a fallen log about eight feet from the tree. From that I jumped for the lower branches of a nearby pine, caught one and pulled myself over in a move straight from the playground monkey bars. The bark bit into my palms a little but didn't leave splinters.

I scampered up the trunk of the pine until I was even with an upper arterial branch of my target tree. I looked down just to make sure Adam was watching, then shifted my body around and leapt. The upper branch of the big tree was a solid one, and I landed on my feet, grabbing a cross branch for support. I stood there and looked out at the view for a second to get my bearings.

We weren't actually that far away from school, though from my perch, St. Brigid's was mostly just rooftops and chimneys. Finally, I swung down the trunk to the lower branches and dropped to the ground. It would have been nice to stick my landing, but at least I didn't fall on my butt.

I brushed off my hands and strolled toward Adam. His jaw was hanging somewhere around his knee region, and his stare was actually a little unsettling. I stopped. "What?"

"Teach me how to do that."

I took a deep breath. "Teach me about the Immortals— about what I can do." It was hard to admit that I was clueless about this part of myself. Adam seemed to get it. He held out his hand to shake. "Deal."

His hand was warm and strong as I shook it. "Deal."

On our way back to school I gave him the basic theory of free-running and explained how the obstacles in the path became a way to use gymnastic skills. Instead of going around things, the game was to go in a straight line up, over, and under.

True parkour is all about efficiency – getting from A to B without detour. Free-running tends to be a little showier, with spins and flips in mid-air that look cool but don't get the job done any faster. "I'm not so much about the tricks when I run," I told Adam. "For me it's more about never being stopped. Like anything that could get in my way is just something to be climbed or jumped and it's my job to figure out how – at full speed."

Adam smirked. "Yeah, it's that 'at full speed' thing that I keep tripping over."

"You need to train your brain to look for the hardest way to go, not the easiest. And then make your body do it."

"Why do I think that's easier said than done?"

I looked around quickly and spotted an apple tree growing behind a high stone wall. "Get me an apple."

He followed my gaze to the apple tree and stared at me in shock. "No way. The tree's too high."

"The wall isn't. Don't focus on the tree. Look for handholds and footholds in the rocks instead."

Adam squinted at the wall and started walking toward it. He shifted direction slightly, heading for a rough patch that looked older than the wall directly under the tree. I nodded with approval as he reached for a handhold I would have grabbed. His feet went to the right spots, and only once did he reach for a rock that would have trapped him. I was about to say something when he shook his head slightly and backed off it, reaching for a better stone above it. With one final grab he pulled himself to the top of the wall. He didn't look at me as he balanced his way across to the apple tree, but the grin on his face gave away his excitement. Adam plucked two apples from the upper branches and turned to toss one down to me. But I wasn't there anymore. I had scrambled up the wall behind him.

"What the hell? How'd you do that?"

I took an apple out of his hand and grinned. "Same way you did, only faster." I sat happily on the wall and dangled my legs over the edge as I bit into the apple. "Good one. Thanks."

Adam sat beside me. "That was cool."

I nodded. "You realized you were about to put a hand wrong and changed your grip. Most newbies don't get that."

"Believe it or not, I actually Saw it going wrong."

"As in, Saw the future?"

"I guess. Those are the visions I usually ignore because they get in the way."

"But if you could train yourself to See the right way at speed, you could get really good at this."

Adam contemplated me for a moment. "Interesting. I think I wouldn't mind being good at something."

"Yeah, right. You're probably one of those guys who does everything well the first time they try it."

Adam scoffed. "Did you happen to see how long it took me to get up here?"

I shrugged. "Never done it before. You'll get faster." We sat in silence for a moment before I finally spoke again. I kept my eyes on the view. "Tell me about Clockers."

Adam grinned slowly. "I thought you didn't like the name."

I shrugged. "I've been called worse."

"I'll bet."

I glared at him. "Are you going to tell me or not?"

He held up his hands in mock surrender and laughed. "Relax. Family history's just a big subject, that's all. It's weird that you didn't learn any of it from your parents like everyone else does."

I looked sharply at Adam to see if he was digging at me. He seemed sincere enough, and I figured I could always push him off the wall if he made fun of me. "My mom has moved us from city to city every couple of years since I was born. I only just found out she was born in 1850. She left her native time to have me. And my dad's dead. I never knew him."

Adam was staring at me oddly, and it kind of wigged me out.

"What? I'm a freak because my parents split before I was born?"

"Was your dad from the 1800s too?"

"I don't know. I don't know anything about him."

"Just think, Saira. Was your mum already pregnant with you when she left her native time?"

"Why? Does that make her a slut?" I could feel invisible claws coming out, and I was debating whether to draw blood or bolt.

"Was she? This could be important."

"It's none of your business. I'm sorry I even told you anything."

I climbed halfway down the wall and leapt to the ground. My legs felt shaky, and I just wanted to run very far away from St. Brigid's and everyone there.

Adam dropped down next to me with a heavy thud. He grunted in pain and I stared at him. "That was ten feet, you idiot! You could take out an ankle or knee from that height." I was shocked that he'd done it, and more shocked that he was standing so close to me. Our faces were literally inches apart.

"Have you ever heard the Prophecy of the Child?"

I glared at him. "No. Why would I have?"

"Because it's the oldest unfulfilled prophecy of my Family – one Fate herself made about a thousand years ago."

"Of course it is." I couldn't have kept the snark out of my voice if I'd tried. "Well, I'm listening." My ignorance on the whole subject was like a mosquito bite that itched worse the more it got scratched.

Adam quoted like it was engraved on the wall in front of him.

"Fated for one, born to another,
The child must seek to claim the Mother.
The Stream will split and branches will fight
Death will divide, and lovers unite.
The child of opposites will be the one
To heal the Dream that War's undone."

106

I stared at him for a long moment. His words had given me chills all the way down to my toes. Something in that prophecy went "clunk" in my brain, and that, of course, sent resistance shooting straight up my spine. No way did I have anything to do with that prophecy.

"Am I supposed to know what that means?" My voice came out more defensively than I meant it to, but it was too late to take it back. Adam didn't move or look away. I was totally unnerved that I could smell the clean, soap-and-sweat scent of his skin. Avoiding popular, arrogant guys like Adam was pure self-defense, and I was standing far too close to this one for my comfort.

He shrugged in a way that brought his casual arrogant pose right back. I crossed my arms across my chest. I was mad that I'd let him get to me, and even more mad when his smirk came back. "Just wondering if it could be you."

I glared at him through narrowed eyes. "If what could be me?"

"The *child of opposites.* The one who reunites the families."

"Why would you think that?"

"*Fated for one, born to another?* People have been speculating about that for as long as I can remember. The most common theory is that the 'one' and 'another' are either places or times. So either it's someone born in the wrong place or the wrong time. That part, at least, could be you."

I shook my head and started walking back toward the school. Adam caught up to me with easy strides. He didn't say anything as we walked, and his silence was way too loud in my head. I finally stopped and faced him.

"Okay, as fascinating as this word puzzle may be, what does it matter? What bearing could a thousand-year-old prophecy possibly have on today?"

Adam's eyes searched my face. "People say we're at war. The *child of opposites* is the one who will save us."

A bell jolted me out of my shock. Adam grabbed my hand and dragged me after him. "Come on! That's an assembly bell. They'll do a head count." We sprinted back toward St. Brigid's, which was looming up in front of us like Vlad's castle. The bell was still ringing, and Adam suddenly veered to the left, toward the big glass solarium. He didn't drop my hand until we got right up to the glass walls, then he pried his fingers around the edges of a pane near the stone wall. It took two hands, but with a little tug the glass slid open.

"This would have saved me a little trouble last night." I climbed through the open window and got out of the way so Adam could come in behind me.

"Yeah, but then you wouldn't have met me."

I arched an eyebrow at Adam and he grinned. He slid the windowpane closed behind us and dropped his voice. "Feel free not to mention that entrance to anyone else."

"Sure, if you forget to tell people about your theory on the prophecy."

Adam suddenly looked serious. "I need to tell Ava."

"You're joking about this, aren't you?"

"It's not funny."

"But it's not real. It can't be."

A deep voice boomed through the solarium. "The snog-fest is over! To the library, both of you!"

I spun around to find Mr. Shaw glaring at us.

"What's going on?" Adam's voice was calm and sounded very grown up to my ears.

"What's going on is that you two were obviously out on the grounds while there's a known threat in the woods." There was a load of sarcasm in Mr. Shaw's voice that made me flinch.

Adam's voice maintained its neutral tone and he looked Mr. Shaw in the eyes. "We were only told there was a predator in the woods, which, as we all know, is code for a Sucker. And since that's clearly not a threat during daylight, I didn't think there'd be a problem."

Mr. Shaw's voice thundered. "You don't think. You assume you know better than all of us because of your little talent. Sight does not equal skill, Mr. Arman, something I expect you, of all people, to remember. Now get yourselves to the library!" He stormed off without another glance at us, yelling at some kid down the hall who wasn't running fast enough. I quickly looked at Adam. His jaw was clenched.

"Come on. If I have to hear another word from him I'm going to throw a punch." Adam led the way through the nearly empty hallways back to the library. It seemed impossible that such a huge room could be full, but the place felt crowded with kids and staff milling around.

Ava saw us and raised her hand to get our attention. We wove our way around the edges of the room until we reached her. "What's going on?" Adam's voice was pitched low, but Ava was looking at me.

"I rescued your suitcase. It's locked up in a third floor linen closet." She slipped me a key and winked at my startled look.

"Thanks," I whispered back, but Ava's attention had already shifted. She stared at the front of the room where Miss Simpson stood with Mr. Shaw on one side of her, and a man I'd never seen before on the other.

"What's *he* doing here?" she whispered furiously to Adam. His mouth tightened into a grim line, and he settled himself so he was slightly behind me.

"Who is he?" I whispered to Ava, but Miss Simpson raised her hands for quiet.

"Students, I need your attention please. Most of you know Mr. Landers from several months ago. He's here to give you an update on the search for his son, Tom, and to deliver some news that is important to all of us. Mr. Landers?"

Miss Simpson stepped away from the man the twins weren't happy to see. He was thin and wore an expensive-looking suit. His hair was perfectly combed, and everything about him looked professional. When he spoke it was with a posh accent that dripped money. "As most of you know, my son, Tom Landers, disappeared from St. Brigid's three months ago. The police, of course, found nothing." There was disdain in his voice, or maybe it was just the money talking. "But my people have found a lead to a gang operating out of London."

There were murmurs among the students. Landers held up his hand and the room quieted again. "I know that most of you who had any information about Tom's last few months here came forward when he disappeared ..." Landers paused and seemed to be scanning the room. Adam's feet slipped under my chair as he slunk even lower behind me. Landers continued, the edge in his voice getting sharper. "If any of you didn't come forward with information then, there's no excuse for withholding it now. If he's still alive, Tom's life is most certainly in danger."

This was like Venice Beach gang stuff, not British boarding school drama. Olivia had mentioned that people had been pulling their kids out for the past three months. Was this why?

Miss Simpson stepped forward and spoke to the crowd of students. "If you have any information that might help Mr. Landers, please come to my office. The general dusk-to-dawn lockdown is still in effect, and I expect all students to please respect our rules of conduct, especially during these stressful times. Please go back to your regular classes. You are dismissed." Miss Simpson left the room with Landers and Mr. Shaw. The minute they were gone, I spun around to face Adam.

"Let's hear it."

He shook his head, looking grim. "Too many ears." He caught Ava's eye. "The Seer Tower in ten." He got up and strode from the room without a backward glance. Ava watched him go for a few minutes, then looked around at the students left in the room. Raven sat in a corner with Ginger, and they were deep in conversation with a dark-haired guy who looked like Dracula. Ava scowled and stood up to leave the nearly empty library. She spoke directly to Raven.

"Miss Simpson won't believe you, so don't even bother."

Ginger and the Count looked startled, but Raven just looked venomous. "I'm surprised your uncle can't use his gifts to find his precious boy. I guess you lot aren't so very useful after all."

Ava's mild expression never left her face, but her eyes went cold as she stared Raven down. Suddenly she laughed. "Sorry about your skirt, Raven."

Raven tipped her chair back from the table to look at her skirt and knocked into Mr. Shaw's hand that happened to be holding a mug of tea. The tea rained down on Raven's lap, drenching her skirt in dark liquid.

Ava grabbed my hand and bolted from the library, laughing at the sounds of rage and indignation from both Raven and Mr. Shaw.

"Did you make that happen or just see it?"

Ava smiled. "I'm not telekinetic." She looked at her watch. "I have to go."

"I'm coming with you."

Ava sounded dreamy. "Oh, right. You are."

I seriously didn't know what was her Sight and what was just plain wackiness. Either way, the girl had no filters and she had a wicked sense of humor. My favorite kind.

We climbed the main staircase to the second floor, and then turned down an unfamiliar hall. Then we went up more stairs, down another hall, and by the time we got to a small study, I was thoroughly lost.

She closed the door behind us and walked over to the bookshelf. It was lined with old textbooks that looked like they hadn't been read in twenty years. "This used to be the headmaster's private study back in the days when the school was full. Miss Simpson prefers to be closer to the students downstairs."

Ava felt along the inside of an upper shelf. Click. A latch opened and the bookshelf swung forward on a hinge. Ava grinned. "I love secret passageways, don't you?"

I loved them like I loved books, running, and chocolate. "This leads to the tower Adam was talking about?"

"Our grandfather was headmaster here before we were born. He used to tell us stories of what this school was like when it was full of just Descendants."

"Something closer to a looney-bin than a school, I'd guess."

She shrugged as we climbed the dark staircase behind the bookshelf door. "To an Ungee, probably. But we have to be so secret about our gifts; it must have been nice to be open about them at school back then."

111

It was something I hadn't considered. I was close-mouthed about pretty much everything in my life, so another secret more or less didn't make a huge difference. But to someone like Ava, who was such an open book, keeping her gift a secret was probably like living a daily lie.

We reached the top of the stairs. The space opened up into a circular room – one of the fang-like towers I'd seen from the outside of the building. The room seemed to glitter, and I realized that nearly every surface held some sort of mercury glass. Old gilt-framed mirrors hung on every wall, and even the candlesticks in the corners were reflective silver.

Adam was pacing like a caged lion, and he glared at Ava. "Why did you bring her?"

"Look, *Seer*, my family has totally shut me out of the information chain, and I'm sick of it. We have a deal – you teach me, I teach you, remember?"

Ava turned to her brother. "What is she teaching you?"

He mumbled under his breath. "Nothing." He turned the glare on me. "How do we know we can trust you?"

"Are you kidding? You're Seers. Just ... look!"

My eyes caught my own reflection in all the mirrors around the room, and suddenly I understood. Seers need to See. Maybe reflections gave them extra access to that Sight.

"It doesn't work like that." He sounded annoyed, but Ava nodded.

"She's right, though. I don't See betrayal around her."

That fascinated me. I turned to Ava. "Like, as a general state of being, or a specific action?"

Ava shrugged. "Major things leave a color trace. Betrayal leaves a dark purple mark, like a bruise. You don't have any bruises on your aura. Just ... movement." Ava's expression was quizzical. "Weird. A shifty aura."

I stared at her. "Do you talk like that to everyone?"

She shrugged and grinned. "They all think I'm a nutter, so they don't listen to half of what I say anyway."

"Fine. You can stay." Adam's tone was grudging, and I could tell it irked him to give in.

"Gee, thanks, big guy." The sarcasm was back in my tone. I was tired and hungry and cranky, and I had a million questions. "So, what's the deal with your cousin?"

Adam sighed and sat down in the middle of the floor. The room had no chairs, so I sat cross-legged in front of him. I shivered. "Why is it so cold in here?"

"You can feel that?" Ava looked surprised.

"The room has wards on it." Adam had mellowed out a little.

I got up to touch a wall. "Freezing."

"Weird that you can feel it. It's totally normal to me." Ava said, thoughtfully.

"What are wards?" I didn't want to sit down again. The cold seemed to suck all the heat out of my body.

"They're kind of like spells put on rooms to protect whoever's inside."

"Protect them from what?"

Adam shrugged. "No one really knows. The wards were put on a long time ago, and I don't even think anyone knows how to do them anymore."

"Just add it to the list of things I know nothing about, I guess."

That got a partial smile from Adam. "Sorry. I really don't know anything else about them. I've always just taken the wards for granted. Our house has a warded room, and I think this place has a couple."

"Elian Manor has one, freezing, like this place. And Millicent can't feel the chill either. But tell me about Tom."

"Are you going to sit?" Adam leaned back to look up at me. I shook my head.

"Too cold." I went over to the window and looked out. The view of the school grounds and the woods beyond was incredible.

"Tom's dad is our mum's brother. And he can't stand us for a lot of reasons, but mostly because of succession." I faced Adam with a raised eyebrow and he explained. "Seers are matrilineal, so Ava's next in line for Head of our Family after our mother."

113

I nodded. Matrilineal succession is the only thing that makes sense as far as I'm concerned, since you always know who the mother is, and the father could be anyone.

"What about you? You guys are twins?"

Adam shook his head with a grin. "Born lucky."

Ava grimaced. "Being Head sucks. Too many branches on our Family tree, with every gypsy and mall psychic claiming to be a blood relative."

Ava and Adam shared a twin look of pain before Adam continued. "Anyway, our uncle believes he should be the Head because he's the older brother and he actually really wants the job."

Ava interrupted. "He's also been spending too much time with Mongers and Shifters if he thinks men have any right to Seer succession."

Adam nodded. "He's constantly barging in on meetings and trying to stir it up with some of the other branches. Tom can't stand his dad and was always really happy to come back to school after holidays."

Adam stretched and got to his feet, then helped Ava up. "Anyway, Tom was my roommate and best friend—"

"Besides me."

"Obviously." Adam smiled at his sister in a way that made me wish he was my brother.

Ava took over. "If I was the jealous type, the boys would have turned me green. They were even more like twins than we are sometimes."

"Okay, what happened?"

Ava turned to me. "About a month before he disappeared, Tom went to London for some benefit thing with his parents. Something was different about him when he got back."

"He turned into a wanker." Only the anger in Adam's voice kept me from laughing. What a great word.

"Tom was always the sincere guy. The one the girls would turn to for solace when Adam broke their hearts."

Adam looked indignant. "I don't break girls' hearts."

"Oh come on, Adam. You walk into any pub and can instantly see who's lonely or easy or thinks you're cute. You have inside information you don't hesitate to use whenever it suits you. You don't play fair and you know it." Ava was teasing Adam, but I had the feeling she was telling the absolute truth.

Adam glanced at me quickly and changed the subject. "Anyway, Tom came back from London arrogant and aggressive. Like he should be the one the girls went to first, and I should be the one picking up his pieces. And he started texting all the time. Especially after lights-out."

I shrugged. "Raven does that."

Adam scowled. "Raven's a Rothchild. She figures rules were meant for other people without her pedigree."

I thought about making a female dog joke, but decided it was too easy, and therefore not worth it. "Did you ask Tom about the texting?"

Adam scoffed. "He said it was someone he met in London."

Ava interrupted. "You never even got a name, did you?"

"I saw it when I finally threw his phone across the room. 'Chaotic1.'"

"The Crow knows him. She texted 'chaotic1' about me."

Adam stared. "Why the hell would Tom be talking to someone a Monger knows?"

Ava laid a hand on his arm. "It might have something to do with some Family thing. We'll talk to Mum and Dad in Paris next month."

I stared at them. "You're going to Paris?"

Ava shrugged. "It's Mum's birthday and she wants truffles for dinner."

I was stunned. "You guys must come from serious money."

"So do you. All the Families have money." Ava shrugged.

"I don't have anything but the suitcase I came with."

"You're an Elian, right?"

"It's my last name, but that's about all the connection I have with Millicent and that family."

Ava looked at me strangely. "I don't think there are any other full-blooded Clocker families besides you guys anymore."

"Nothing like being a dinosaur in your own time, huh?" Adam was entirely too smug.

"Is that a time travel joke, or something I should take personally?" Actually, I took back the brother wish. He made me glad I was an only child. I turned to Ava. "You said your Family tree is full of branches. Why wouldn't mine be the same way?"

"Apparently gifted Clockers are rare. Sight can be strong or weak, but it's still there. You lot either travel or you don't. There's no half way. Since it's hard to find other full Clockers, most of the Clocker families intermarried with Ungees. It's why Miss Rogers is only a Quarter-Time."

"She is? Can she travel?"

Ava shook her head. "I think her mother could, and I heard it was a huge disappointment to the Families when she didn't marry another Clocker."

"You guys really take your bloodlines seriously. It's like you're breeding racehorses."

Ava's expression suddenly got solemn. "The Families are protective of their gifts. We're lucky ours is so large. We have a lot of people to choose from when it's time for us to marry. But Clocker and Shifter families are much more limited."

"It's all stupid if you ask me. They can't tell you who to love." Adam's voice surprised me with its anger. I looked at Ava for an answer, but her gaze was on her brother and it was full of sympathy.

Then Ava turned to me. "You've got it the worst though. The Elian family has always been the main line, so it's pretty rare for them to marry Ungees."

"As if Millicent has any say over who I can marry, or even if I do." I thought I saw approval in Adam's eyes, but more disturbing was the glimpse of pity in Ava's. Seriously though, the bloodlines stuff was crap, and I definitely wasn't buying into it.

"What about the other Families. How do they work?"

Adam answered. "Shifters are similar to Clockers in that only certain Shifters can change, mostly just the full-bloods. But half-bloods can still have the enhancements of animals – extra sight, sensitive hearing, strength or speed. Some of the best pro athletes have some Shifter in them."

"Come on though, there must be other Clocker students besides me."

The twins shook their heads. "Clockers are rare." Ava looked at me sorrowfully. "They're somewhat prone to getting lost."

"You mean 'in time' don't you?" Ava nodded.

I spoke under my breath. "Sounds familiar."

"What?" Ava asked.

"It explains a lot about my life in the past week, including the lock and key I seem to be under right now."

"I'm surprised you're allowed to be here." Ava turned to Adam. "You don't think the lockdown is because of Saira, do you?"

"No, I really think there was a Sucker in the woods last night." He looked directly at me.

"I have no idea what you're talking about."

He looked skeptical. "Really? You didn't meet anyone tall, dark, and dangerous out there?"

I glared at him, ignoring the tangled knot in my stomach. "You're an asshole."

Ava tried to play peacemaker. "We don't know for sure it was a Sucker."

"By 'Sucker' I assume you mean Vampire?"

"A Descendant of Death." Ava spoke matter-of-factly.

I stared at her. Where to begin? "Assuming such a thing as Vampires exist, don't you have to be born to be a Descendent?"

They both looked at me like I just crawled out from under a rock. "Of course Vampires exist. Who else could be descended from Death? It's oxymoronic for death to be born, so he *created* his offspring instead." Weirdly, Ava's explanation made sense. Death can't be born, it just is. And according to every legend I've ever heard about Vampires, they have to die in order to exist.

Adam scoffed. "Suckers are not Descendants. They're abominations."

"Apparently you're not a fan?"

117

Ava explained. "Aeron's line has been cut off since almost the beginning. He did something to get himself kicked out of the Families, and no one's really heard from him since."

"So how do you know Vampires aren't just some legend made up to scare little kids into minding their parents?"

Adam's voice was full of scorn. "Because you and I exist, and we're Descendants of Fate and Time."

"Come on. We have class with Mr. Shaw in a few minutes and he yells if you're late." Ava was a master at subject changing.

I looked at Adam. "Are you coming?"

"I got kicked out of Shaw's class last year. He knows who you are. You'll be fine."

I grimaced. "And I'm sure being seen with you this morning will work in my favor."

Adam grinned. "Exactly."

SHIFTER CLASS

As Ava and I raced down the tower stairs and out through the bookcase door, she gave me a little more background on their cousin, Tom.

"Adam and Tom had a big fight the night Adam threw the phone. He ended up storming out of their room."

"What was he so mad about?"

"My brother has always had a lot of friends in all different social groups. Tom used to sort of come along for the ride, but ever since that trip to London he had been turning his nose up at our Ungee friends, saying they were second class and not worth his time."

"Great. A new kind of prejudice. Because race and class isn't enough?" I've always hated bigots.

"Exactly. That night Adam had wanted Tom to come into the village with him to meet a couple of local girls at the pub. Tom got all puffed up and said he was done being Adam's wing man, especially for Ungee trash. That's when Adam threw Tom's phone and stormed out."

We raced down the main staircase to the first floor and ran past an open classroom just as Olivia stepped out. Ava grinned and waved. "Hey, Liv!"

Olivia smiled and waved at us both as we passed her. "Hi, guys. How's the Crow treating you, Saira?"

I laughed and said over my shoulder, "Exactly as you'd expect."

"Oh good. Wouldn't want to disappoint."

Olivia was still laughing as Ava and I rounded a corner and almost ran straight into Mr. Shaw. He looked at his watch and growled, "Late."

Ava smiled sweetly at him. "Thanks for holding the door for us, Mr. Shaw. Saira was lost on the second floor and I had to track her down." We slipped around the giant man into his classroom, and I mumbled under my breath.

"Thanks for throwing me under the bus."

The smile never left her face as she murmured, "Watch this."

The room was set up like a science lab, and Raven was already seated at a long table next to Ginger and the Count. Ava strolled past their table.

"Heard they found 'chaotic1' in Tom Landers' phone."

Raven stared at Ava, the color draining from her face. She stood up, grabbed her bag, and bolted for the door. Mr. Shaw slammed it shut before Raven could leave.

"Sit down, Miss Walters." His voice boomed across the room.

"I have to go." Raven pulled her arrogance on like a cloak, but her imperious tone had no effect on Mr. Shaw.

He turned the key in the lock and pocketed it. "Take your seat."

Raven tried another tactic. She sounded desperate and even crossed her legs for effect. "But I really have to go, Mr. Shaw."

Mr. Shaw's mouth tightened and he glared at her. "There's a coffee tin at the back of which you can avail yourself if it's truly an emergency. Otherwise, *sit down!*" Raven looked blown away that someone had dared to thwart her. She sat down without another word.

Mr. Shaw took his place at the front of the room and scowled at all of us equally.

"We begin a new project today. It's called survival." He unrolled a chart that looked like a botanical print of weeds. Someone groaned. Mr. Shaw practically growled. "You think the study of botany is a waste of your time? You are dead wrong. Or you will be if you don't learn what I'm going to teach you." The guy was seriously abrasive, and he had me at the word "survival."

I looked around at the other students. Ava seemed interested, Raven's whole table had their heads together whispering something that I'm sure had nothing to do with botany, and the others just seemed bored. I turned my attention back to the front of the room and found myself staring directly into Mr. Shaw's amber-colored eyes.

"Some of you may someday find yourselves in situations where you'll need to scavenge to eat." Raven scoffed loudly, but Mr. Shaw ignored her. He was still looking at me. "Even more importantly, you may find yourselves sick or wounded in places where modern medicine isn't available."

Raven muttered under her breath. "We're not going to bloody Borneo."

Mr. Shaw finally turned his attention to Raven. "I've no doubt that someone of your limited skills would not take the risks I'm talking about." His gaze traveled over the other students before finally resting back on me. "But others of you will, and do already."

Raven's eyes narrowed at me, and she went back to whispering with her friends.

"The dandelion plant, for example, is completely edible. The leaves are excellent in salads, rich in vitamins A, B, C, D, potassium and iron. The flowers make a decent wine, and the roots are a coffee substitute." I was completely fascinated. Dandelions had always just seemed like pretty weeds to me. "But in addition to its edible properties, this humble plant is one of nature's great medicines. A decoction of the whole plant is an excellent cure for stomachaches and constipation." There were sniggers at this and Mr. Shaw smirked. "If you've ever lived on a high protein diet, you'll recognize the value in this."

Ava leaned over and whispered to me. "He usually turns into a Bear. He would know."

I stared at her. A Bear? Obviously the man looked like Goran, the Immortal Nature, but seriously? He was actually a Shifter? Mr. Shaw continued. "And this might interest some of you. Did you know the sap of the dandelion can cure warts, pimples and bee stings?"

A boy behind us laughed. "Good to know."

Mr. Shaw smiled for the first time since I'd seen him. It warmed his face up like a fire had just been lit. "I thought you might like that." He pointed to another plant. "This is commonly known as shepherd's purse. The leaves can be eaten as a vegetable, the seeds can be cultivated as a spice, and a poultice of the plant can stop bleeding."

He indicated another one. "And this is chickweed. Chickens love it, the leaves are a great source of vitamins, but its primary benefit is as a poultice or ointment for skin irritations and ulcers."

Mr. Shaw pointed at several other plants on the chart. "You can eat miner's lettuce, sea holly – the boiled root tastes like chestnuts – and young bracken. The tightly coiled heads can be eaten raw, and the rootstock can be made into glue." He rolled down another chart and pointed to a bigger fern. "But avoid mature bracken, which destroys vitamin B in the body." His expression was serious. "Avoid any plant with milky sap except dandelion. Avoid fruits that are divided into five segments. Avoid red plants – hemlock has reddish-purple splotches on its stem, and though the red stem of rhubarb can be eaten if cooked, its leaves are poisonous. And avoid anything that tastes or smells of bitter almonds or peaches, or anything that stings or numbs the skin or tongue."

Mr. Shaw unlocked the classroom door and opened it. "Miss Walters, now's your chance. We'll be in the field beyond the kitchen gardens. I expect you to join us there."

It took some effort for Raven to keep from glaring at him as she swept from the room, her cell phone already in hand. She'd be texting 'chaotic1' before she was even down the hall.

Mr. Shaw held the door open for the rest of us. A short girl with a huge mass of kinky curls spoke. "Do we need to bring anything?"

"Only your eyes, noses, brains, and common sense."

We filed out of the classroom and followed the enormous man down the hallway. With all my urban survival tactics, I'd never even considered what would happen if I had to find my own food or medicine. And the nineteenth century didn't exactly have convenience stores. Despite what I'd said to Archer, I knew I was going back.

I caught up to Ava as we were walking out. "Does he really change shape?" Mr. Shaw was far enough ahead of us I figured he couldn't hear. I should have known better.

Mr. Shaw stopped and turned and looked directly at me. "Walk with me, Miss Elian." Ava shot me a sympathetic smile and walked ahead. He waited until the other students had gone before he spoke. "I understand there's been a moratorium placed on what you are permitted to learn." I looked sharply at him. "It may interest you to know that I intend to disregard it."

I nodded, barely resisting the impulse to give him a high-five, and Mr. Shaw continued. "Lesson number one: your fellow Descendants are ever fewer in number here at St. Brigid's, and therefore, the tone of what we teach has changed. Unless you are in a small study group of Descendants only, you will not discuss Family business with other students. And you will certainly never speak of it in the halls."

"I'm sorry. I didn't think—"

He cut me off. "No, you did not. But it's clear that you are lacking some fundamental information that would mitigate that problem. I have office hours after dinner this evening. Have Mr. Arman bring you at six."

"But I thought he wasn't your student."

His eyes narrowed at me a moment. "Mr. Arman is well acquainted with the location of my office, and until you're better equipped, it is inappropriate for you to be wandering the halls alone."

He strode away, leaving me gaping after him. I quickly followed the class out of the building and past the walls of the kitchen garden. One of the cooks was planting something, and I suddenly flashed to an image of my mother doing the same thing in the little garden we had in Oregon. It was right before we moved to Venice, and I remembered thinking it was weird she was planting food we'd never get a chance to eat. It was like she was leaving a secret stash for someone else to uncover. I wondered if that was a Clocker thing to do, to leave stashes. It would make sense, especially if you knew you might return some time. We never went back to that little cottage, but I'd bet the asparagus she planted still grew there.

I caught up with Ava in the big field. She was sniffing a wildflower and listening to Mr. Shaw talk. "Your assignment is to identify and harvest as many wild plants as you can find."

"But we don't have the chart out here," someone whined.

"Nor will you when you're lost in the woods one day with nothing to eat." He glared at all of us. "If you studied the drawings in the classroom, you should be able to find at least three edible plants."

The October air was cold, but the sun had broken through the clouds and felt good on my back as I wandered around the field. I found a dandelion right away, and saw that other students had found them too. One boy had broken a stem and was surreptitiously dotting sap on his chin.

The middle of the field was getting trampled so I headed toward the outer edge for my search. The drawings in class had been well done, so I spotted chickweed, a low matting creeper plant, easily. I pulled up a handful and tasted a small leaf, hoping I'd actually identified it properly. It tasted ... green. I broke off a piece of dandelion leaf and tasted that too. Again, green, but fairly bitter too. Wouldn't be my first choice for food, but good to know I could feed myself with it if I had to.

I saw some ferns at the edge of the forest tucked in the shade of a big tree. I thought Mr. Shaw's description of bracken was pretty cool. Try to eat the old fern and it sucks all the vitamin B out of your body, but the young curls are okay. Slightly dangerous, but also useful. My kind of plant.

Up close it was pretty clear the bracken was all too mature to eat, but I pulled one up anyway. The roots were thick and sprawling, and I shook off the extra dirt. I tried to mash a piece of root with my fingers but realized I'd probably need a rock to be able to make glue.

Goosebumps crept up the back of my neck and I spun to find Mr. Shaw approaching. He looked a little startled. "You heard me?" I shook my head. "How did you know I was behind you?"

"I felt you." Another person, more or less, thinking I'm crazy wasn't going to make me lose sleep. But the look I got from Mr. Shaw wasn't "she's a whack job," it was more like "hmmm."

"What else can you do?"

Now it was my turn to stare. "Uh, well, I have a freakshow ability to fall through spirals into other times. Is that what you mean?"

"Must be a little disconcerting, that."

"A little. The puking's fun though." Mr. Shaw laughed. I'd made the man laugh. Score one for the Clocker.

"Show me what you've found."

I unclenched my hand. "The bracken's too old to eat, but I was wondering about making glue from the roots. Do you have to pound it or boil it?"

"If you crush it with a rock, you can generally get enough viscous fluid for glue. And this?"

"Dandelion, of course. And chickweed. The chickweed tastes better, but I figure you'd have to eat a whole lot more of it than dandelion, and I'm not sure what would be worse."

"You tasted the plants?"

I shrugged. "What's the good of finding them if you don't know if you'd ever eat them?"

He looked at me speculatively. Then he bent down and pulled up a weed. "Marsh mallow."

"As in, the sweet, white fluffy stuff?"

"There's a substance in the stem that has a gelatin-like quality that they used to add to marshmallows. Now they just use gelatin." He handed it to me.

"So this is edible?" The plant was about three feet tall with pale yellow roots and tapered, round, short-stemmed leaves. I sniffed a leaf.

"It won't hurt you. But marsh mallow is most useful as a medicine."

"Poultice or infusion?"

He smiled. "You've been paying attention."

"It's interesting."

"Good." Mr. Shaw took the plant back and began stripping off the leaves. "The most effective way to prepare it is as an infusion of the flowers, stem, and leaves." He knelt down and grabbed a rock. "Crush them first to release as much of the oils and juices as you can, then pour boiling water over them and let them steep until the water is cool."

"What if you don't have fire to boil water?"

He nodded. "Smart girl. If you don't have boiling water, use half the amount of cold water and stand it in the sun."

I grinned. "This is England. You don't have sun."

He laughed. "Then suck the leaves and stems for all the juices and spit out the pulp."

I grimaced. "Nasty."

"Indeed." He used the rock to scrape at the roots of the marsh mallow. "You can also make a decoction of the roots by scraping and mashing them, then boiling them down."

I nodded. "Okay, what's it good for?"

"Because of the high mucilage content – the gelatin stuff – it's good for treating inflammation and ulceration of the stomach. As a poultice it can clean and soothe wounds, and you can drink it to treat colds, coughs, and respiratory infections."

His amber eyes looked challenging. "Bring a healing poultice with you this evening when you come to my office hours." Mr. Shaw brushed off his hands and walked away without a backward glance.

A test? I smiled to myself and pulled up several marsh mallow plants, then caught up to Ava as the class headed back inside. "Where's Adam?"

"He has a private class with Miss Simpson. Why?"

"Mr. Shaw wants your brother to 'escort' me to his office hours at six. Could you let him know?"

Ava shrugged. "Sure. I'll have him meet you in the library."

"Thanks."

We walked past the kitchen garden, and Ava called out to the woman pulling herbs. "Hi, Mrs. Taylor!" Mrs. Taylor looked up to see Ava smiling and waving at her. She dropped a fistful of rosemary into her basket. "Any chance you're making roast chicken tonight?"

126

Mrs. Taylor sniffed. "Might be."

Ava grinned. "I love her roast chicken."

I had a sudden inspiration. "Introduce me."

We walked over to the door of the walled garden. "Mrs. Taylor, this is Saira Elian. She's new to St. Brigid's."

Mrs. Taylor looked me over. "Eat all you can at mealtimes as there'll be no food in your rooms."

I nodded politely. "Yes, ma'am."

Mrs. Taylor squinted at me. "Elian, you said?"

Ava answered. "She's American."

Mrs. Taylor sniffed again and said nothing, turning back to her herbs. "Um, Mrs. Taylor?" She looked up wordlessly. "I was wondering if I could use a corner of your kitchen this afternoon to make a poultice for Mr. Shaw."

Mrs. Taylor looked at me oddly. "Did he not give you the key to the laboratory for that?"

"No, ma'am."

She sighed. "Sets you to a task with no means to accomplish it. Sounds like Shaw." Mrs. Taylor gave me an appraising look. "If you keep to yourself and clean up whatever mess you make, I'll set you up in the staff kitchen."

"Thank you, Mrs. Taylor. I really appreciate it."

She sniffed again and filled her basket with the herbs she had just picked. "Five minutes," she said, and brushed her hands off on her apron.

Ava looked at the weeds in my hands. "I guess I know what you're doing for the rest of the afternoon."

"I don't really have a schedule, do I? I mean, no one has told me anything."

"I'm sure Miss Simpson is working it out with the other teachers. We don't usually get Family kids who just drop in mid-term." Ava checked her watch. "Well, I'm off to class."

"Which one?"

"Miss Simpson is a Seer, so she works with me and Adam on our skills."

"Are there any other Seer kids here?"

Ava shook her head. "Our other cousins are too little, and Tom left …" Ava's eyes went slightly unfocused, and then she shuddered. "Oh!"

"What?" The way Ava was looking at me gave me chills.

"I have to talk to Adam." Ava started to turn away, but I grabbed her arm.

"What did you just see?"

Ava's eyes cleared, but her expression didn't inspire confidence. "I just saw you … and Tom."

"Your cousin?"

"You were running."

I stared at her. "Like out for a jog?"

She shook her head. "Away."

"From …?"

Ava looked confused and scared, like a deer in headlights. "From shadows."

That might just have been the most terrifying thing she could have said to me. I opened my mouth to respond, but Ava was already racing down the hall. "I'll find you later, Saira," she called over her shoulder.

I hoped Mrs. Taylor was ready for me, because I was craving the comfort of a busy kitchen right about now.

I found her at a big sink full of steaming water plucking a chicken. I had never seen anyone actually prep a real chicken before and I had to admit, I was pretty fascinated. "You dunk it first in hot water to loosen the feathers. I hold them by the feet so I don't burn my hands." Mrs. Taylor spoke in a very matter-of-fact tone as she nodded toward an unplucked bird on the sideboard. "Try to pull the feathers out of that one." I tugged on a tail feather, but it wouldn't budge. I pulled harder, but it was like trying to pull out a fingernail. Mrs. Taylor held up the bird she was working on. "Now this one." I reached for a wing feather and it came out with just a gentle tug. Mrs. Taylor looked at me with approval. "You think you can finish this one for me while I clear a workspace for your poultice?"

"Sure." She handed me the half-plucked chicken.

"If the feathers stick, dunk it again."

I started pulling feathers out and leaving them in the sink. Somehow I doubted this was what Millicent had in mind when she sent me to St. Brigid's. In her world, that's what servants were for. But plucking a chicken seemed like a good skill for a Clocker to have. I needed survival skills, not just blending ability. Things like building shelter and starting fires, dealing with wounds or injuries, and feeding myself.

Mrs. Taylor came back and nodded approvingly. "Not squeamish, are you." It wasn't a question. I shrugged.

"I've never actually done this before."

"It's the killing that's the hard part. Dressing it's just a matter of scalding, plucking, and gutting. Are you any good with a knife?" I took a deep breath. I wasn't sure I was prepared to gut the naked chicken in my hands, but I knew I should learn how.

"Will you show me?"

Mrs. Taylor smiled, the first I'd seen from her. "Good lass. Okay, use the bone-handled knife over there. It's just been sharpened."

Mrs. Taylor showed me how to use the knife to cut the head and feet off, open both cavities, then reach in and pull out the guts. I ran it under water again until it was clean.

Mrs. Taylor gave me a handful of rosemary to stuff it with. She showed me how to salt and pepper it and cover it in olive oil. Then she plucked a lemon out of a pot of boiling water, stabbed it a couple of times, and shoved it into the cavity with the rosemary. "To steam it from the inside," she said. She popped the whole thing into the oven, and we washed our hands.

"You're a quick study. Better than most of 'em." The compliment made me feel good. I got the impression Mrs. Taylor didn't think too highly of many people.

She set me up with a sink, a really old-looking marble mortar and pestle, and a cast iron pot. I got to work grinding the marsh mallow plants with the mortar and pestle, then I dumped them in the pot, covered the mess with water, and set the whole thing deep into the fireplace. I wanted to keep whatever respect I'd managed to earn from Mrs. Taylor, so I was extra thorough as I cleaned my workspace. She was busy preparing the other chickens for dinner, but I thought I caught an approving glance from her as I worked.

I had to wait for the water to boil anyway, so I wandered back over to Mrs. Taylor. "How can I help you?" The chickens were all plucked and prepared, but there was only one other cook in the kitchen, and she was making pies at the far end.

Mrs. Taylor eyed me. "Don't you have classes?"

"Not yet. Today's my first day."

"Hmmmph." It was a great noise and probably meant about a dozen things. I tried to hide a smile. "There's potatoes in the root cellar that need peeling. Grab a basket and pick out forty or fifty medium-sized ones." I was almost sorry I asked, but the idea of a root cellar instantly appealed to the underground junkie in me.

I picked up the big wicker basket Mrs. Taylor indicated and hesitated. "Annie," Mrs. Taylor called to the other cook, "show Saira the cellar, would you?"

I smiled at Annie. "You can just tell me where to go."

She wiped her hands on her apron and shook her head. "You'll never find it on your own." Annie's voice had the same Welsh gravel as Sanda's did.

"Do you know Sanda, in my … in Millicent Elian's house?"

Annie raised an eyebrow, and she looked at me for maybe the first time. "Olivia's Sanda?" I nodded. "I've known Sanda's people since Olivia's mum and me were bairns together in Gosefordsich. They're all born there, but come here and to Elian Manor to serve when they're grown." The Welsh accent sounded soothing as it rolled off Annie's tongue. "And how do ye know Sanda?"

"She works for my mother's family."

Annie stopped in her tracks and looked at me through narrowed eyes. "You're an Elian then?" I nodded, suddenly nervous that being an Elian would be considered a bad thing to this tiny woman. "And an American?" The raised eyebrow was back.

I winced. "Yeah."

Annie laughed. "It's not as bad as all that. Being an American Elian gives ye a fighting chance." We stepped outside the kitchen door, and Annie lifted a heavy iron ring from the ground. A wooden door came up with it and a black hole yawned open below. Annie propped an iron bar under the door like the stick that holds the hood of a car up, and then reached down to pluck a flashlight from just inside the hole. She turned it on and handed the light to me.

"The potato bins are at the back. Mind the steps, and don't leave the torch behind. And if ye wouldn't mind, shut the trap when ye finish?" I said I would, and Annie gave me a quick smile before slipping back inside the warm kitchen. The sun had gone behind the clouds and it was starting to get cold. I was glad to be wearing my hoodie and boots as I started down the creaky wooden steps into the root cellar.

The flashlight was one of the big old kind that shone wide but not bright. It illuminated a huge space under the kitchen, and I fell instantly in love with the mood of it. It was dark and gloomy, but the flashlight wasn't powerful enough to make shadows, so I was right in my element.

Brick columns supported the arched ceiling, and wooden shelves lined the wall closest to me. The other walls were cloaked in total darkness, but I assumed they probably also held food storage shelves and bins. The floor was made of flagstones, and the temperature was at least twenty degrees colder in the cellar than outside.

I explored methodically, circling the walls to find my way to the back where the potatoes were kept. Every kind of food imaginable was stored down there, probably enough to feed a hundred people for at least a week. I loved the idea of having provisions. My mother and I never really had more than a week's worth of food at a time, and because we moved so often, things got abandoned every couple of years. But this place was like having a supermarket under the school. Incredibly cool.

I found the potato bins and counted out forty-five medium-sized ones into the wicker basket. The big flashlight was too hard to hold with potatoes in my hands so I set it on its end like my little Maglite candles. The ceiling above me was beautifully domed, but oddly cut off by the potato bin wall. Almost as if the room continued beyond, and the wall was built to divide it.

131

My curiosity was starting to ping, and I left the basket on the floor to explore the room more thoroughly. The wall was built of brick, just like the rest of the room, and a food storage rack covered most of it.

My nose was literally inches away from the wall when I spotted a small metal latch behind the storage rack that seemed too flimsy to carry the weight of the heavy unit. I reached behind the shelves and unfastened the latch. It came free easily.

Something glinted on the floor and I knelt down to study it. Buried in the flagstone was a thin metal track that ran under the shelf unit and all the way across. I shone the light up and saw a groove set into the bricks about eight feet up, the same height as the top of the shelves.

I tugged on the shelves and they creaked slightly but were clearly designed to slide sideways. The mechanism seemed old but it was still functional, and I slid the shelves about three feet to the right. The wall behind was a wooden panel with another small latch, which I unfastened with quick fingers.

I slipped through the opening and then shone my flashlight around the hidden space. It felt like another storage room, but instead of food it was full of odds and ends of furniture, art, and books. My light passed over armchairs, old desks, two bookcases full of dusty books, a sofa, and rolls of what looked like tapestries or rugs. Two eyes glinted at me from the wall, and I fought back a gasp when I saw it was just a taxidermy owl, with wings spread out as if it were taking off in flight. The place was cold and dark, but it wasn't creepy in that way old places sometimes were. It felt like the kind of place I wanted to explore for lost objects and treasure.

I started with the bookcases, but quickly realized they were just old textbooks. The really important books were probably all upstairs in the library and in Miss Simpson's office. There was a gap between the cases, just wide enough for a person to pass through. So I did.

Behind the bookcases was more furniture and rugs, but they were arranged like a bedroom and study. A desk dominated one wall, a sofa the other, and a huge four-poster bed hung with heavy drapes filled the back of the room. A rug covered the flagstones, and there were more bookcases lining the walls. These actually looked arranged on purpose, with books and small objects filling the shelves. It was quite beautifully furnished, despite the darkness and chill.

I crossed the old Persian carpet to check out the books on the shelves. They weren't textbooks, they were older than that and included novels, history books, scientific references, and volumes about world politics. I was curious to see if the bed still had sheets on it, so I pulled the heavy drape back – a move I regretted the moment my brain processed what my eyes saw.

There was a body on the bed.

RESTING PLACE

I wanted to run screaming from the room.

"Keep it together, Elian," I whispered to myself fiercely. I took a deep breath. No smell. So if it was dead, it had been that way for a long time. The light from the flashlight barely shook as I slid it slowly up the body. It was dressed – always a bonus – and was wearing black pants and a black cloak.

Cloak? I quickly shifted the light to the man's face.

Archer. What the hell?

I shook him. Hard. "Archer!" I whispered as loud as I dared. Nothing. I shook him again, panic rising in my throat. His head flopped alarmingly with my shaking, so I stopped and put my ear to his chest. I could hear a heartbeat, but I couldn't tell if it was his or my own thundering in my ears. I tried to find a pulse at his neck. Nothing, and his skin was cool to the touch.

Was he dead? Or undead?

"Archer!"

The panicky stutter of my heart was in my throat as I studied his face in the dim glow of my flashlight. His skin was perfect, but pale and waxy like a mannequin. He looked exactly as I remembered, but like the Madame Toussaud's version of himself.

Adam had asked me if I'd gone to meet the 'Sucker' in the woods. Could Archer be the one everyone was so freaked out about? Was this the daytime resting place of a Vampire?

I poked his cheek. His skin bounced back into place like live skin does, although I didn't have a lot of experience poking dead people for the comparison. I lifted his arm and dropped it to the bed.

The muscles were limp, as if he was unconscious, but not stiff like a corpse would be. I wracked my brain thinking of other tests I could do to determine Archer's status, but knowing absolutely nothing about Vampires put me at a distinct disadvantage. I looked around the bed. There was an old fashioned gas lantern on the bedside table, with a Zippo lighter and a magazine next to it. I picked up the magazine, the British version of Fortune. A page was marked and I flipped it open.

It was an article about the Rothchild Family, 'not to be confused with the French Rothschilds, the great wine and banking families,' according to the writer. These Rothchilds were English and had made their fortune buying and selling money. The current head of the family was Markham Rothchild, a brilliant and ruthless businessman who, because he'd only had daughters, was grooming his son-in-law, Laurence Walters, to follow him in the business. I flipped to the front for the publication date. It was this month's issue.

I took a deep breath. I'd seen Archer last night in the woods, very much alive. He was hiding out in a secret cellar room reading a current issue magazine, and despite looking like a corpse, he didn't smell or feel like one.

And the more I pieced together about my own Family, the more it seemed that random people can't time-travel through spirals. So the idea of Archer traveling here from 1888 seemed pretty unlikely.

I looked at him and decided to consider the impossible. *Archer was a Vampire.* Ho boy, was he ever going to have some explaining to do when he woke up.

It was a little weird to study him so closely when he was unconscious, but I figured he deserved it for being an even bigger freakshow than me. His hair was a little longer than most men wore it, which probably made it easier for him to fit into all the different decades of the past two centuries.

As I was considering this, the conversation from the woods came rushing back to me. This guy who I barely knew – a *Vampire* – had somehow managed to fall in love with me even though we only spent one night walking around Victorian London together. Well, running too, but mostly just walking and talking.

Had he been a Vampire when we met? When did he become one? What had he been doing since then? If I was totally honest with myself, the logistics of him being a Vampire weren't as intimidating to me as his intensity had been. The things Archer had said to me in the woods weren't something I could just dismiss as a guy trying to put the moves on. He was too serious for that, and the way he looked at me was like he was burning the words into my skin.

But now, looking down at his dead-to-the-world body lying so peacefully in a secret room under the school, I felt protective of him. Scary creature or not, he was totally helpless in this state. A piece of dark hair had fallen over one eye, and I brushed it to the side before I could stop myself.

I glanced around the secret room again. Had Archer set this place up as a daytime resting place, or did he just find someone else's hiding spot and use it as his own? I had so many questions, but if I didn't get back upstairs with the potatoes, someone was going to come looking for me.

I looked at Archer's face, so peaceful and perfect, and I had a crazy impulse. I leaned over and gave him the smallest kiss on the cheek. My heartbeat jumped in my chest and I pulled back before he could move or grab me or something, but he stayed perfectly still. I told myself my jumpy heart was from nerves, but I've never been very good at lying to myself.

"See you later, Sucker," I whispered, and as I turned the flashlight back toward the room, I thought I caught the hint of a smile at the corner of his mouth. Chills prickled my skin.

When I got back to the kitchen Mrs. Taylor threw me a sideways glance. "Get lost down there?"

"Sorry. I've never seen a root cellar before. Is all that food from your garden?"

"Of course it is. Why buy what you can grow?"

"My mom feels the same way. She really missed having a garden when we lived in the city."

Mrs. Taylor made a grumbling noise, and I bit my lip to keep from laughing. "Cities. No point in them if you ask me. Just set the potatoes on that table and tend to your poultice. It's bubbling away something fierce in there."

I had totally forgotten about the cast iron pot in the fire. I used the long tongs to carefully lift the heavy pot off the rack in the fireplace and set it down on the stone hearth. Almost all the water had bubbled away, and the mixture inside was like a soupy paste. Mrs. Taylor looked over my shoulder.

"There's a wee pot with a lid in the spice rack that used to hold ginger. My grandmother put ginger in her compresses for muscle aches. I'll bet your Mr. Shaw won't have known that."

I thanked her and scooped the marsh mallow poultice into the little pot. The ginger smell cut through the green plant smell and made it kind of spicy, so I mixed the poultice around the pot to absorb the leftover ginger powder.

I cleaned all the dishes I'd used and scrubbed out the cast iron pot with a rough sponge. When my workspace was clean, I checked the big kitchen clock over the door. It was five o'clock. "Thank you for everything, Mrs. Taylor."

"You've been a big help, Saira. You're welcome in my kitchens anytime."

Annie's eyes caught mine and she winked. I grinned at her and left the one place at St. Brigid's it was easy to feel welcome in.

The room I shared with the Crow was empty, thankfully, and I set the little poultice pot on my bedside table and dropped onto the bed. I felt like a wind-up toy that had just wound down, and everything from my feet to my brain hurt.

I looked around the little room and realized I didn't want to stay there at all. If I was going to be trapped in this school until my mom came back, I needed to find my own space. Someplace private and secure. I thought about the secret cellar room but dismissed that as too cold. Not to mention there was a Vampire living in it. Even if he might be okay with the idea of me moving in, I wasn't sure I was.

Besides, I'd run the risk of leading other people right to him if even one person saw me going in and out of the cellar.

No, my best bet was one of the empty wings. I groaned at my achy legs as I got up off the bed. It was time to go exploring, and of course the ornate doors leading to the east and north wings were locked. But, when doors failed, there were always windows, and the one near the fire escape was unlocked.

From there it was an easy climb to the roof. Running the length of the north wing was like scampering across a playground for me, and at the end of it, just where I'd hoped it would be, was another fire escape ladder leading down. I tried a second floor window and slipped inside the dark hall. It was gloomy in there, but enough light still shone from the window that I could see. The doorknobs were all locked – no surprise there – but the keyholes were the old-fashioned kind, and it looked like the keys were on the insides of the doors.

That discovery made me smile. Now, to just find the perfect piece of art. Halfway down the hall hung a print behind glass, which meant it had a backing I could use. I quickly pulled the print off the wall and dismantled both wire and backing for my key drop trick – this time to get *into* a locked room instead of out of one.

I chose the room closest to the fire escape. It didn't take long to work the key out of the lock and slide it under the door. I re-assembled the print and hung it back on the wall. A missing piece of artwork would turn a routine patrol into a search, and I didn't need anyone poking around my empty wing.

The lock was a little stiff, but the key finally turned and opened the bedroom door. The room was small but neat, and was furnished with a single mattress, a desk, and a dresser. There were heavy drapes on the window, but no bedding or rugs. I wrenched the window open to air out the room, then sat on the bed and sank into a decent mattress. Ava said she had hidden my suitcase in a linen closet, and I hoped I could find bedding and towels there. My room. I grinned to myself, satisfied with my discovery. I quietly locked my bedroom door, pocketed the key, then went in search of the bathroom and a way out.

The bathroom was halfway down the hall and still functional, even if the first water out of the pipes was rusty. Finding a way in and out that didn't involve scaling walls and running across rooftops was actually surprisingly easy. The key to my bedroom also worked on the main door to the hall. It made sense that students should be able to get in and out with just one key.

I had left my poultice on the nightstand of my old room and walked in to find Raven sniffing it with a disgusted look on her face. "Eeeww. That smells rank."

I took the pot out of her hands and clapped the lid on it. "Then don't open it."

She scowled at me. "Where have you been?"

"Class."

"With whom?"

"Why did you go through my stuff last night?"

She recoiled. "I don't know what you're talking about."

"I have the picture of my open suitcase from your phone. And I can only assume that someone who rifles through their roommate's things can't be trusted. So I'm leaving this room." I leaned in closer for emphasis. "If you tell anyone I'm gone, I'll make sure Miss Simpson gets a copy of that photo."

I made my voice as quietly threatening as I could, and I stared Raven right in the eye. She reacted just like the bully she was. She backed down. Without fail, if you stand up to a bully, they tuck tail and run.

"And if you or any of your little posse harass Olivia or Ava again, the photo goes on the school server and everyone finds out what a sneak you are."

"Where will you sleep?"

I smirked. "In the west wing."

Oh, she hated that. I could tell that a million thoughts were scrambling around her evil little brain at once. The west wing was for boys. Adam sleeps there. I must be a total slut. Probably the worst part for her was that she couldn't even tell anyone.

139

I put my finger to my lips with a smile as I left the room. "Not a word, Crow," I whispered as I left. Her eyes were angry little slits, and I laughed as I shut the door. I felt instantly free.

I took the stairs at a jog, passing a group of younger girls on their way up. "What time is it?" I called to them.

"Five forty-five," one called back in a high voice.

"Thanks!" I've never been able to wear a watch because I magnetize them. About three months on my skin and watches stop working. My mom says I inherited it from her, and the only watch she can wear is the one on her necklace. I had fifteen minutes to find Adam in the library and make it to the Bear's office.

Both the twins were waiting for me there. Adam was leaning against a table with his arms crossed in front of him, clearly annoyed. "What's your problem?"

"I don't remember signing up to be the school tour guide."

"Shut up, Adam. It's not Saira's fault Mr. Shaw wanted you to take her." Ava smiled, and I turned to her.

"I need to get my suitcase after this. Where, exactly, is it?"

"Third floor, south wing. The linen closet by the bathroom."

"Thanks for rescuing it. The Crow's pretty much on the warpath with me now."

Ava looked concerned. "Do you want to bunk with me and Melody? I could make a bed on the floor."

I shook my head. "Don't worry about it, I'll be fine." I looked at Adam. "The Bear won't deal well if I'm late again. Can we go?"

"The Bear? Has he heard that?"

"Not a chance." I grinned at him, and he finally lightened up.

"Let's go." He was out the door with me right on his heels.

 ## THE BEAR

Adam led me down a main floor hall, past closed doors, to the west wing. "The classrooms are in the main hall and south wing. Teachers have their studies all over the school, but Mr. Shaw likes being in the west wing. Probably so he can listen in on us upstairs."

"Are you guys really that loud?"

"Nah, besides the occasional football game down the hall." By football he meant soccer, of course. "But I'm sure he'd be up there in a second if he heard female voices."

"So, no girls in the boys' wing and no boys' in the girls' wing."

Adam shot me a lecherous look. "There are all kinds of cozy little nooks in this place. I'd be happy to take you on a tour."

"And I'm sure you've found them all." I played up the disgust, but his comment made me nervous. I didn't want my new room to be discovered by anyone, much less some horny teenagers hunting for a hang-out.

We stopped outside a heavy wooden door. "Here you are. Offices of Doctor Shaw, PhD and MD, right on time."

The door swung open suddenly, and Mr. Shaw stood glaring down at us. Actually, he wasn't that much taller than Adam, but he looked so imposing it made perfect sense he could change into a Bear. The man was practically one already.

"That'll be all, Arman." His voice boomed, but Adam didn't even flinch.

"What time should I be back for her?"

141

Mr. Shaw looked at me, then back at Adam. I spoke quickly. "I can find my way back." I didn't know what the story was with Adam and Mr. Shaw, but the air was thick with it.

"I will walk Miss Elian back to the library. You are excused for the evening."

Adam grinned. "Later!" He bolted down the hall and I was alone with Mr. Shaw. I had the thought that I should be nervous, but I wasn't. Mr. Shaw's office looked like the kind of room I imagined Sherlock Holmes living in. There were plant specimens and deer antlers sitting on shelves full of books. The furniture was old and comfortable with a massive desk that looked like a Rolls Royce after a fender-bender. Scarred and battered, but still gorgeous and well made.

I set my poultice on the desk and turned toward the bookcases. A fantastic brass microscope was set up on a shelf next to an open wood case with various eyepiece fittings. It was definitely an antique, but it looked brand new.

"A Ross binocular microscope, circa 1870."

"It's beautiful."

"I come from a very long line of scientists and medical doctors." The distance in the Bear's eyes suddenly cleared and his gaze became pin sharp. "Sit down, Miss Elian."

I obeyed. His voice didn't allow for anything else. He picked up my jar of poultice, opened the lid and smelled it. One eyebrow raised, and he pinched some between his fingers and rubbed it thoughtfully. Then he finally nodded. Mr. Shaw put down the jar and unbuttoned his shirt. I had a moment of pure flight instinct. The man was taking his shirt off in a private office with a female student. But then my reason took over, and I realized I wasn't afraid of Mr. Shaw. Maybe it was stupidity because the guy was enormous and could easily take me down physically, but on a purely gut level, I knew I had nothing to fear from him.

And in fact, Mr. Shaw himself suddenly seemed to realize that what he was doing must seem very odd. His eyes widened, and I could swear I saw a hint of redness creeping up his neck. But then he turned his back to me, peeled open a big, white, square bandage, and bared a very nasty gash on his shoulder.

"I need your help." His voice was gruff, and I guessed it was probably very hard for him to say those words to anyone, much less a seventeen-year-old girl. "It's getting infected, and I don't do well with antibiotics."

I came around the desk to his side and picked up my poultice. "Should I rub it into the wound or just pack it on?"

Mr. Shaw looked at me with that eyebrow again. "I don't think I could take rubbing it in." There was a half smirk on his face, and I responded with the same.

"Right. Should I reuse this bandage when I'm done?"

"No, I have a fresh one."

I went to work on the gash, trying to be gentle as I packed it with the poultice, but I had to push the green mess in pretty hard to keep it from falling off. I could tell it hurt him, but Mr. Shaw just clenched his teeth and let me work.

"A bit of olive oil or animal grease mixed in will help keep a poultice in place." His voice sounded tight.

"Yeah, sorry about that." I wiped my hands on my jeans and peeled the backing off the new bandage. When I was done, the Bear flexed his shoulder experimentally, then nodded and pulled his shirt back on. "Thank you. We'll see tomorrow whether you're any good at this or not." The words were harsh, but his tone was almost playful. "And I'd appreciate if you'd keep this business to yourself." He indicated his shoulder, and I smirked.

"A little tough to explain bite marks to your fellow teachers?"

Mr. Shaw stared at me through narrowed eyes. "What makes you think it's a bite?"

I shrugged. "Jagged edges and infection. Mouths are the dirtiest things on the planet."

"Human mouths."

"Animals too, if they've just eaten."

The Bear's voice sharpened. "Perhaps I was mistaken to trust you."

"No, just mistaken if you think I'm stupid." I could not believe I was getting snarky with a guy who turned into a Bear. I thought I was going to have to run, but the rage that crossed Mr. Shaw's face lasted only a second before he erupted into booming laughter.

"Impetuous maybe, but not stupid. Yes, it was an animal bite. One of the groundskeepers' damn hunting dogs."

"So you were out last night?"

Uh oh. Too far. Mr. Shaw's eyes narrowed again and he studied me carefully. "What would you know about last night?"

"Nothing. I just thought I heard a dog, that's all."

"Indeed." Mr. Shaw stood suddenly and crossed the room. He took the old microscope down from the shelf and set it on the desk between us. "What, exactly, do you know of the Immortals' Families?"

The abrupt change in subject startled me. I took a deep breath. "I know the Elians can travel through time. I know the Armans are Seers, and the Rothchilds are descended from War." Mr. Shaw nodded, so I continued. "I've heard you're a shape-shifter, and judging from the wound on your shoulder, the rumors that you're a Bear are probably true. And apparently Vampires exist because Death made them."

Mr. Shaw scowled again. "That's hardly comprehensive knowledge."

"You're right. I only know what I've found out in the past three days. And believe me, that's not a lot."

He sat back in his chair and studied me.

"Can I ask you something?" I thought of a million questions I wanted to ask, but one had been nagging at me all afternoon.

"Yes."

"Are there other time traveler kids besides me?"

He drummed his fingers together as he considered his answer. "It's possible. But not likely."

"Why?"

"Occupational hazard, I suppose."

"Oh come on, that many people have disappeared in time?" No way did I believe I was descended from a Family of idiots.

He smiled at my indignation. "There have never really been too many of you to begin with. I'm actually surprised to meet you. When Millicent didn't marry, I assumed the Elian line would die out with her." Mr. Shaw closed his eyes for a moment and took a breath. Then he touched the microscope on his desk. "There used to be another branch of your family who held the Clocker Family council seat for a time in the 1800s."

"Millicent didn't say anything about them."

"She wouldn't. She's descended from a younger sister. Her elder, childless cousin held the seat."

"So? What happened to her?"

"She was murdered in 1871. Along with the entire council."

My eyes widened. "What? Why? Who did it?"

A fierce glint came into the Bear's eyes. "*Why* remains a mystery. *Who,* unfortunately, does not. My great-great-grandfather's brother was the murderer."

The Bear was watching me closely; his eyes seemed to challenge my reaction. So I gave him none. "Is murder a hereditary trait, or can I consider myself safe?"

He cracked a wry smile. "You're safe. For the moment."

I shrugged. "I guess that's all I can hope for in the circumstances." I sat back in my chair. "So, what happened?"

Mr. Shaw touched the microscope on his desk absently as he spoke. "William Elliot Shaw was the oldest son of the oldest son. His father was Speaker of the Council and the most powerful Shifter of all the Clan families. Will was being groomed to take over his father's council seat and leadership of the Shifter Clans."

The way the Bear's eyes glanced at me could be considered casual, but I knew a predator when I saw one. He was judging me, looking for weakness, surprise, horror, whatever would give him the advantage. Half my brain was listening to his story; the other half was busy trying to stay one step ahead of him.

The Bear's voice was hypnotic as he continued. "Will had everything: brains, looks, money, charm, and power. His younger brother saw him as a hero and his family adored him. Even the Ungifteds considered Will Shaw a leader among men."

Mr. Shaw's fingers stroked the microscope with something close to adoration. "He was an acclaimed scientist who did amazing work in genetics at a time when it was a brand new field of study. This microscope was his. He acquired it the year before he split."

"He 'split'? As in 'left'?"

Mr. Shaw shook his head. "Not the American slang. We use the term 'split' to describe a very rare condition among Shifters. In fact it's only been documented one other time among the Clans, but the case of Will Shaw is the most famous."

"He's famous?"

"Robert Louis Stevenson learned of his case from a doctor at the Bethlem Royal Hospital where Will was committed after the murders. You may have heard it called 'Bedlam.' He was diagnosed with what we now call multiple personality disorder, but apparently he lost complete control over his animal form and was in a constant state of partial Shift – sometimes coherent as a human, but usually more bestial in behavior and appearance. Stevenson based his story of Dr. Jekyll and Mr. Hyde on Will Shaw."

It took a moment for me to process this. I'd read *Jekyll and Hyde* in sophomore English, and the idea that the character could have been a real person was as horrifying as it was sad. I almost felt sorry for Will Shaw.

Then the Bear pulled me back to reality. "Shaw went to a council meeting presided over by his father, Jonathan Shaw, your ancestor, Melinda Elian, the Arman twins' great-great-great grandmother, Lisette Arman, and the seat-holder for War, Spencer Rothchild."

Mr. Shaw's voice was emotionless, like he was reading a newspaper account, rather than telling painful Family history. "There is no record of what happened in the meeting; we only know that it ended in a bloodbath. The local constable described the scene as 'carnage, with bone, blood, and tissue the only identification of humanity in the room at all.'"

The Bear's eyes glinted in the lamplight as he watched for my reaction. "They arrested Will Shaw, still covered in the council's blood and raving about an execution. Had it been left up to the

146

Shifter Clans they would have torn him limb from limb. But he was in Ungifted custody, and the Families didn't need any more attention than they'd already gotten. When he was committed to Bedlam, they left him there, a raving lunatic and a disgrace to our Clan."

Mr. Shaw smiled wryly and sat back in his chair. "The other Families look at the council murders as an unfortunate, but isolated event that happened a very long time ago."

I studied Mr. Shaw. He seemed relaxed in his chair, posed as if he had just told a ghost story to a child. But underneath the nonchalance was something else. The predator watching to see if the creature in front of him was a threat, an equal, or food. I spoke carefully. "But it was a Shifter who killed the council."

"And a son who killed his father." The Bear's voice matched mine in its careful tone.

"The Clans haven't forgotten, have they?"

"The Shaw family was stripped of its lineage. We no longer have the right to lead, or even speak at either Clan Council or the Descendants' Council. Goran's Descendants don't forget … or forgive." His tone of voice was still carefully neutral, but the muscles of his jaw clenched tightly. The accident of birth that made him a Shaw cost the Bear a lot more than being a Shifter did. And somehow this giant man had trusted me with that knowledge.

I decided I liked him.

"Does that microscope still work?"

He smiled. "You want to try it?" I nodded, and he set it up on his desk so I could see. Then he took a box of slides from the bookshelf, selected one, and motioned for me to look.

I put my eye to the eyepiece. There were two strands of hair on the slide. One I recognized as human, and the other one looked coarser, like it was maybe from an animal.

I looked at Mr. Shaw. "Human hair. Female Caucasian, in her forties or fifties. And an animal, possibly dog, but something with a fairly fine coat that gets groomed often."

He raised his eyebrows at me. "You sure about that?"

I set my jaw. "About the human hair, definitely."

"How did you get gender, race, and age?"

147

"From the color. It's blonde, but uniform like it's been dyed. A Caucasian woman is the most likely person to do her hair that shade of blonde."

"And her age?" He couldn't hide the disbelief in his voice.

"The dye job starts at the root and looks expensive. Most young women get highlights if they're going to color their hair. Older women who are just starting to go gray will begin at the roots." I shrugged. "It's a logical guess."

"It's an educated one." The Bear's voice actually sounded friendly for a second. But only a second. "But you're wrong about the dog."

"Okay. Not a dog. But an animal of some kind. It's too coarse to be that color and human."

"It's mine."

I looked at his head then back at his face. "No, it's not. Your hair is way finer than that."

He smiled in that predatory way that gave me the creeps. "But I'm a Shifter."

I stared at him, then crossed my arms in front of me. "So?"

The Bear seemed amused at me. He plucked a sandy brown hair from his head and laid it on a fresh glass slide. "Look again at the two strands of hair." I obliged. The non-human hair was clearly much thicker and coarser than the blonde hair, and I highly doubted it came from Mr. Shaw's head.

He replaced the slide with the fresh one, and I looked again. It was the same coarse, dog-like hair from the other slide. I shook my head as I looked at him. "Your hair looks totally normal. There's no way this is the same hair."

He bent his head toward me. "Touch it."

I reached a tentative hand forward, which he grabbed and put on his head. "See?"

His hair felt completely normal to me, and I pulled my hand back. "You're full of crap. It's exactly like mine." I don't know what possessed me to speak that way to a teacher, but I was getting annoyed.

Mr. Shaw sat back with an amused smirk on his face. "You think so? Prove it."

"Fine." I pulled one of my own long hairs, then reached my hand out for the Bear's head.

"I need another one, and I'm pulling it this time."

I could tell he was trying not to laugh and it annoyed me even more. He inclined his head toward me and I intentionally grabbed a couple of extra hairs.

"Got enough?"

"No, stay there. I might need another handful." The expression of amusement on Mr. Shaw's face was contagious. I positioned my hair and one of his side by side, directly under the lens. The old microscope was very cool to use; the knobs felt good in my hands and the optics were really precise. I fiddled with the knobs, playing with focus and light. But what I saw didn't make sense.

Except for the color, my hair and Mr. Shaw's were exactly the same.

And Mr. Shaw was a Shifter.

I stood suddenly, sweeping the hair off the slide and knocking into his desk as I did. His hand shot out to steady the microscope, but I was already at the door.

"Sorry. I just ... I have to go." I slipped out of his office door before Mr. Shaw could reach me.

"Saira—?"

I didn't look behind me. I just left.

LINEAGE

Everyone must have still been at dinner because I saw no one in the halls. And the whirlpool in my stomach wasn't from hunger, so I wouldn't be joining them.

I was hiding, and I was fine with it.

Somehow my feet took me up to the third floor and I realized I wanted my stuff. I found the linen closet Ava hid my suitcase in, threw some clean towels, a set of sheets, and a duvet on top, and wheeled the whole thing toward my north wing.

My luck with deserted corridors held, and I was able to maneuver everything down to my new digs without being seen. I started breathing again once the north wing door was locked behind me, but nothing calmed my hammering heart. Why the hell did a Clocker girl have the same hair as a Shifter, when Shifter hair was so obviously different than the normal human kind? There had to be a rational explanation. Like maybe all the Families had wacky hair, and it was the thing that made us genetically different from regular humans?

I spent the next fifteen minutes silencing my brain. I made my bed, unpacked my suitcase, and put stuff away. I realized it was the first time I'd unpacked since I'd landed in England. I had no intention of staying at St. Brigid's longer than it took my mom to get back, but I finally felt like I had a little space to call my own.

I set the *Caves and Caverns* book on my nightstand and tucked my spray paint cans into the bottom drawer of the dresser. The red can had been lost with my backpack in the nineteenth century along with my passport and extra money. And my mom. And Archer.

Archer! I looked out the window at the last few slivers of light in the sky. He'd be waking soon. I pictured him in his hidden cellar room, lighting his oil lamp, maybe reading until the school got quiet enough to venture out. I needed to talk to him. And yet talking to anyone was pretty much the last thing I wanted to do at that moment.

I lay back on the bed and closed my eyes, trying to block thoughts out of my head. And failing miserably. Genetic heritage, traveling in time - those were just the beginning of the list of things I needed to learn about myself. At least the Bear was willing to teach me. And despite the fact he was huge, gruff, slightly predatory, and had a tendency toward strictness, I liked the guy. I hoped I hadn't ruined things by bolting from his office, because he was my best shot at learning anything in this place.

My stomach growled and I hoped there was still some of Mrs. Taylor's roast chicken left. I found a back-stair route down to the dining room, which was nearly empty. The food had already been cleared away, and Annie was just pulling the last of the dinner rolls.

"Wait!" I snatched the bread from the basket Annie carried. She was about to smack my hand away but then saw it was me. I did my best to look sheepish. "I'm sorry – I didn't get to eat."

Annie clucked and shook her head. "I've a bit saved in the kitchen. Ye can have some if ye keep it quiet." I beamed at her and picked up some empty food trays to help her carry. "You're the best!"

She winked at me. "And don't ye forget it!"

I tried to help Annie clear the rest of the dining room but she shooed me away, so I took my covered plate of chicken and potatoes and slipped out to the walled kitchen garden. I closed the heavy wooden door behind me and found a bench near a wall to sit on and eat my picnic dinner.

After inhaling the excellent food I got up to explore the space a little. I bent to smell some mint and uncovered a forgotten tomato lurking in the leaves. I poked around some more, finding rosemary, thyme and even some new winter savory. Every discovery reminded me of my mom. Gardening was her thing, and she had always dragged me out to do it with her.

We would pull weeds or plant tomatoes while she asked me about school or what I was reading. She insisted that I could tell her *anything*. Ironic, considering how much she hadn't told me about her family, her history, her abilities, *my* ability – nothing that was really important to my understanding of who I am. And if I couldn't count on that from my own mother …

"Saira." A smooth voice from somewhere behind me murmured my name. Archer.

I turned to face him. "It's a little early for you to be out, isn't it?"

He stared at me, frozen still. The placid look on his face couldn't hide the look in his eyes. Nervousness? Fear? I wasn't sure. "You know." It wasn't a question.

"Yeah. I know. When were you going to tell me?"

"I didn't have a plan."

He was seriously nervous about my reaction to his Vampireness. I decided to lighten things up. I looked around at the still pale sky. "You're smashing stereotypes by being out in daylight."

He smiled very slightly. "The sun set ten minutes ago."

"Isn't that just a technicality?"

He shrugged. "It's life or radiation burns to me, so I think I'll take the technicality."

I arched my eyebrow. "Well, life-ish."

He grinned. "Another technicality."

He squatted down near my feet and crushed a leaf between his fingers to smell. "Mmm, tarragon. Our cook used to brown butter with it to brush onto roasted fish."

I stared at him. "That was what? About a million years ago?"

He smiled faintly. "There are things I'll never stop missing until the day I end."

Interesting choice of words. But I was already dwelling in morbidity and didn't want to go there. "Like what? What do you miss?"

"My father was a hunter. All the nobility were, but he was especially well-known for his excellent hunting dogs." Archer's voice finally found a relaxed and easy-going cadence. "They were magnificent. Nobles from all around England tried to buy his dogs, but he always refused."

"What's so special about hunting dogs? They had guns back then, right? Why use dogs to kill the animals?"

"Oh, the dogs didn't kill them. They drove them. The hunters were really just along for the ride. Horsemanship was important and it was always an honor to be chosen for the kill, but the dogs did all the work."

"English honor at its finest," I scoffed.

"Hunters are honorable."

"Why? Did they need the meat to survive?"

"Oh, they never ate the animal they hunted. The meat was too often poisoned by adrenaline, which tastes foul."

I narrowed my eyes. "And I guess you would know."

To his credit, he winced. "I would know."

"So, explain the honor in your hunts?"

"Well, stags – actually all deer – are unable to sweat, so to keep from overheating as they ran, the stags would invariably end up in a lake or pond. That's where the dogs cornered them." I scoffed, but Archer continued. "Every once in a while a stag would give the hunters a particularly good run, and my father would reward it by letting the animal live."

"Sure – beaten, exhausted, and easy prey for the next predator that came along."

Archer sighed. "The point is the beast earned its freedom."

"So how is it you miss that? It seems like something you could do nightly now. Even the honorable part of letting your prey go every once in a while."

Archer looked at me for a long moment. I'd stepped way over the line with that comment, I was sure, but I didn't back down. I wanted to see who he had become in the last hundred and twenty-five years.

"I miss that feeling of being mentored by my father. He was very strict with his instructions and I hated it at the time, but I knew he was training me to be the kind of man he could admire. Someone with honor and a sense of fair play, even inside something as seemingly barbaric as killing an animal for sport." Archer picked up a pebble from the path and threw it against the far wall. "It was an interesting lesson to learn."

"But you said you didn't think your dad cared about you."

He turned toward me and looked me in the eyes. "Which isn't to say I didn't want him to." Archer stood and brushed himself off. He held out his hand to help me up, and I took it to stand. He didn't let go and we walked along the path in silence.

"Are you learning what you came here to find out?"

I nodded. "In bits and pieces."

His eyes locked on mine. "There are things I can teach you too. As soon as you're ready, meet me here and we'll go." His eyes never left mine. The last of the sunlight dipped from the sky, and I knew someone would come looking for me soon.

"When did you build the room in the cellar?"

Archer's eyes widened. "How do you know about that?"

"I found it today. I saw you sleeping." Archer's expression was suddenly cold and very distant. Whatever line I'd danced on before was nothing in comparison to the one I'd just crossed. I backpedaled. "No one saw me go in, and it obviously hasn't been found by anyone else."

His features were still like stone. "People get careless. If you come again, I'll leave this place. Alone."

I could feel my skin prickle defensively. "Do what you want. I won't go anywhere near your room again."

I turned to leave, and Archer's voice came quietly out of the darkness. "I've been coming to St. Brigid's for a hundred years. I used to watch the Elian children at school, always hoping I'd see some sign of you in them."

I spun around to face him, ask questions, accuse him of something, but he was gone.

DISCOVERIES

I woke up in my little room with the sun just coming up over the horizon. *The Caves and Caverns of England* book was still on my chest and I was stiff from not moving all night. I'd fallen asleep reading about the London Bridge Catacombs.

I tried not to make old-person noises as I creaked my way out of bed, but I finally felt the last few days of craziness embedded in my muscles. Not to mention the army that had taken up residence in my mouth and stomped their muddy boots all over my teeth. Blech.

I hoped it was early enough that I could do a little exploring in the library before anyone else got up. It was also cold, so I threw on jeans, boots, and a big white fisherman's sweater my mom had made when she was young. I'd always assumed the sweater was for my dad, but she'd never talked about it, and I found it in the bottom of a trunk when we moved to Venice.

I'd showered quickly the night before, hoping people wouldn't wonder about the sound of running water in an empty hall. But no one investigated, and I was beginning to relax a little about my private room. I only hoped the Crow would keep her mouth shut.

I checked out my reflection in the bathroom mirror. Teeth brushed, face scrubbed, hair in a single braid down my back. That was about it for my morning ritual. There was no one I felt like impressing, and I couldn't be bothered to put on make-up. I still had a little tan left from Venice, so I didn't look like a corpse in the white sweater. Funny how these things take on a whole new meaning in a world with Vampires.

It was barely six a.m., and I made it to the library without meeting anyone. I brought my little Maglite with me, stuck in my back pocket, and I was in search of anything that could help me understand my Family and all the other Immortal Descendants. After a fairly dusty search in the stacks, I found an interesting historical genealogy-type book about Shifters and settled down at a table by the window to flip through it.

I had to search a little to find the Shaw family line, but I finally found Mr. Shaw at the bottom of a small branch. I traced up from him and found his ancestor, Brian Shaw, younger brother of William Shaw. But there was a line next to Will's name and a single line down under it. Since he was the oldest son, he was expected to marry and have a kid, but I guess going on a mass-murder rampage put an end to that idea.

I looked at the bottom of the Shifter tree to find Mr. Shaw. He wasn't listed as married, though it looked like his sister had three kids. The oldest was a boy named Connor Edwards, who should be fourteen years old according to his birth year. His brother Logan would probably come to school here next year, and they had a little sister named Sophia. It looked like there was an older half-sister named Alexandra Rowen who had probably graduated last year or the year before. I wondered if Mr. Shaw was close to his nieces and nephews or if he missed not having a family of his own.

Miss Simpson bustled into the library. She flipped the main switch and the overhead lights came on, bathing the books in bright light. "Oh! Miss Elian! I didn't realize you were up already."

"I wasn't sure what time my first class started, and I wanted to look around the library some more."

"Oh, I'm so sorry, Saira. I meant to give you a schedule yesterday, but I got caught up in all the business with Tom Landers' father. Please forgive me for leaving you to your own devices."

"No worries. I managed to fill up my day." With a free run outside, break-ins at the solarium, the Seer Tower, a new bedroom, discovery of a Vampire's lair, and a visit with said Vampire in the kitchen gardens. All in all, a busy day.

Miss Simpson regarded me a moment. "The minute I do complete your curriculum, Lady Elian will need to review it and make her notes. Perhaps we'll just leave your schedule a little ... loose at the moment?"

I loved this woman. "That works for me."

She nodded. "Good. Now, come in. Can I make you a cup of tea?" Miss Simpson had such a proper Englishness to her it made me smile.

"Yes, please." I entered the annex and my eyes instantly traveled over the spines of books on the shelf closest to me. Miss Simpson filled an electric kettle and then added loose tea leaves to a delicate porcelain teapot. She set out two gorgeous china cups and poured the boiling water into the teapot to steep. All her business of making tea gave me a chance to get a look at some of the titles on the shelves.

"Do you have any Clocker Family genealogies I could look at?"

Miss Simpson thought for a moment. "I believe the Family book is kept by Millicent and would be the most comprehensive."

I grimaced. "Yeah, she's not so generous with information."

"Of course."

"Can I ask you something, Miss Simpson?"

"I'll answer what I can."

"Why are the Families at war?"

Miss Simpson busied herself pouring the tea. "That's an enormous question with an even bigger answer, I'm sure you realize."

"Actually, I didn't realize. I thought it might be simple."

She smiled wryly. "The enormity comes from the fact that each Family will give a different version of the truth. All will be true, but like any painting, until all the colors are applied to the canvas, you'll never be able to see the whole picture."

I nodded. "Got it."

"So, I'll try to answer as a teacher might answer a student and hope I can keep politics out of it." Miss Simpson took a sip of her tea and sat back in her chair. "You are familiar with the original Immortals?"

"I've seen a painting at Elian Manor."

"Ah yes, the Jera painting. It's beautiful, is it not?"

I considered my answer for a moment. Miss Simpson noticed the hesitation. "The Immortals are beautiful, but the painting isn't."

She looked intrigued. "Indeed? Why not?"

"Because the composition is wrong. There's a gap where something is missing and it throws off the balance."

Miss Simpson considered me for a long moment. "I believe I must pay Millicent a visit soon and entice her to show me that painting again. It's been years since I've seen it."

"She's totally clueless. She doesn't notice there's anything wrong in it."

"And yet you do. Fascinating." Miss Simpson continued. "The stories of the Immortals are very old and have almost passed completely into legend by now. But a few of those stories continue to shape our relationships in unfortunate ways. There is a story that tells of Nature's love for Time. The legend says that Goran pursued Jera and was determined that she should feel the same passion for him that he did for her. He courted her, charmed and delighted her, and finally he seduced her until the last of her resistance melted away."

"Aislin, the Immortal Fate, tried to stop the relationship before it could start. Jera and Goran each had their own powers and responsibilities, and Aislin felt that a coupling of Time and Nature could potentially bring chaos to their carefully ordered world. Of course the Warrior, Duncan, was heavily in favor of chaos, so he did all he could to encourage the relationship."

"And Death? Where did he land on the whole issue?"

"Aeron was in love with Jera. He couldn't bear the idea of anyone having her if it wasn't himself."

"How did Jera feel about Aeron?"

Miss Simpson gave a delicate shrug of her shoulders. "How does Time feel about Death? Time resists Death with every fiber of its being. Yet in the end, Death inevitably wins."

"So Aeron got Jera?"

"In a manner of speaking. They are immortal, so Death could never fully claim Time. But he could take what was most precious to her. The very thing Fate feared would cause chaos and undermine the Immortals' powers." Miss Simpson paused to drink her tea and her eyes had a far-away look in them. "Jera was pregnant with Goran's child, and because its parents were immortal, it, too, would have been. War suddenly realized the potential danger to his own influence if a child of Nature and Time were allowed to come into its power, and Death couldn't bear the idea of this child's existence."

"So it would have been a sixth Immortal?"

"If the child had lived, yes."

"What happened?"

Miss Simpson sighed. "This is where legend fails us. My Family histories record that Fate told Time to hide the child so Death and War could never find it. I believe that the Clans tell of a great battle between Nature and Death, with only War's treachery finally allowing Death to win and take the life of the child."

"And my Family? What does Jera's history say?"

"Only that she wept for her child, denounced all the other Immortals, and remains in mourning to this day." Miss Simpson finished her tea and set down her cup. "And to this day, there is a wedge of mistrust that runs between the Families. Very strict laws were made to keep Descendants from intermarrying, and after Jera's child was lost, the Immortals never again loved each other. They created their Family lines with Ungifteds so there would be no threat of a new Immortal, and it is forbidden for their Descendants to breed with those of other Immortals."

I stared at Miss Simpson with a feeling of dread. "So a Clocker, for example, could never marry a Shifter?"

Miss Simpson looked directly at me. "Or a Seer, or, God forbid, a Monger. The marriage would never be allowed, and any children from such a union would be killed."

I was horrified. "By whom?"

Miss Simpson sighed. "The Descendants of War have taken the policing duties on themselves. It is said they once kept a secret genealogy to keep track of all the Families. But since that kind of book would be tantamount to a blacklist, it was never sanctioned by the other Families."

"Have they ever done it? Have the Mongers ever killed a mixed kid?"

Miss Simpson's gaze never left mine. "To my knowledge, there's never been one." If she knew, she wasn't saying. And I didn't want to think about the fact that I apparently had Shifter hair.

I took a deep breath. "Wow. The whole thing stinks."

Miss Simpson smiled sadly. "Indeed it does."

I finished my tea and carefully set the fragile china cup and saucer on the desk. "I'm looking for other people in my Family. Cousins or anyone else who can travel in time. Do you know if there's anyone besides Millicent, my mom, and me?"

Miss Simpson got up and rummaged around in her bookcase for a moment. She finally pulled down a book and flipped through it until she found a page of photographs. It looked like a school yearbook from the '60s or '70s.

"My first year at St. Brigid's I taught a young man named Doran Vane." She pointed to a picture of a guy who looked a little like a hippie, or maybe like the California surfer version of Jesus. "I believe he was distantly related to the Elians, and he seemed to have many of your Family's skills."

"Doran."

"You know of him?"

I smiled. "I've seen his work."

Miss Simpson's attention was caught by students talking in the main library outside her office. "I'm sorry, Miss Elian, but I need to cut our meeting short. I understand you've become friendly with Ava and Adam Arman? Would you mind shadowing them to their classes for another day?"

"No problem." I got up to leave. She had given me a boatload of stuff to process, and I wanted much more time with her. Morning tea with Miss Simpson had been very enlightening.

I was on my second helping of sausage and potatoes when Adam walked into the dining room with a couple other decent-looking guys. All the girls' heads turned to follow him as the group made their way through the food line to their table.

Adam had an easy way about him that spoke of total confidence. Some of the guys he was with were clearly trying to be studly, but next to him, they just looked like posers.

I stood up to clear my plate, and suddenly Adam was standing in front of me. "What's up, Clocker?" His grin was infectious, but I wasn't going to give him the satisfaction of smiling.

"Hey Floyd."

His cocky grin faded just a tiny bit and I bit back my own grin.

"Got any classes yet?"

"Depends."

He raised a quizzical eyebrow, and I could see female eyes all around the room riveted on our conversation. "On what?"

"On whether any of yours are interesting."

He laughed and his fan club visibly sagged. Poor girls. Didn't they know how dumb it was to fall for the handsome ones? Guys like Adam had it way too easy. They got lazy when it came to girls because they never had to work for them. And with Adam it was probably worse, since he could sense who was a sure thing before she ever batted her eyelashes.

"We've got study hall in the library first up."

I raised an eyebrow with an evil little smile. "Then we're going running."

"Give me a minute to ditch my mates and you're on."

I chuckled as I cleared my plate. Annie caught my eye from the buffet and I grinned at her. She nodded toward Adam with raised eyebrows. I rolled my eyes and shook my head. She nodded once, and went back to filling the sausage platter. A whole conversation had just happened without a word. That must be what it was like to have friends. Crazy.

Adam met me in the hall outside the dining room. "So, back outside?"

I shook my head. "When does the first class start?"

He checked his watch. "Twenty minutes."

"Come on." I took off running.

I made a point of taking hallways at full sprint, staircases on the silent sides of treads, leaping over the bottoms of banisters, and sliding down rails where I could. Adam did a fair job of keeping up with me, and though we startled a couple of students in the halls, the grins on our faces probably kept us from getting yelled at. When we finally made it back to the solarium, half the room had been cleared of benches, and some students in fencing gear were warming up. I raised an eyebrow and Adam laughed.

"Gym class for Mongers."

Of course. Why wouldn't they work out with weapons? I couldn't see anyone's face under their helmets, so I pretended they couldn't see us.

Adam was out of breath but he had done pretty well. I gave him a minute, then pointed to the far side of the solarium where the benches were still set up.

"Pick the straightest line to the podium."

He scanned the room for a moment then shrugged. "It's through benches."

"Or over them." I took off, up and onto the tops of the benches, balancing on the back of one for barely a second before leaping to the next. The benches were solid enough to hold my weight, but it was a lot like skipping across stones in a stream. I was laughing by the time I made it to the other side, and I called to him. "Now you!"

His mouth was set in a line of determination when he first started across the backs of the benches He stumbled, teetered, and I thought he was going to wipe out. But after a ballet-style pirouette, he regained his balance. Suddenly a smile lit up his face, and the last half of the benches were like tap dancing for him. Fun, energetic and noisy.

Adam was grinning when he jumped down off the last bench. He grabbed me for a huge hug in his giddiness. "That was awesome!"

His tall, rangy body wrapped around me like a blanket, and it felt good to be in his arms. Good but weird. And the instant I stiffened, it got awkward, and he let go like I had burned him.

"Sorry. I didn't mean to hug you."

"Who knew you had some ballet dancer in you?"

He laughed. "I was hot for one once. Does that count?"

162

"I don't even want to know how you got your moves then." I winced and he laughed harder.

I glanced across the solarium where the fencers had stopped to watch us. One group was off to one side, and from the annoyed pose of one girl, I guessed it was Raven under the mask. I could feel the hatred rolling off her in waves, and it was making me tense. I wondered if Adam's display of affection was getting noted in some little black book somewhere under "Mixed Bloodlines Alert!"

A bell rang in the hallway and Adam looked at his watch. "First classes start."

"Okay, where can we go that's off the main floor? I want to show you some climbing techniques."

He shrugged his shoulders. "Want to explore?"

"Only if we can look for secret passages."

"You'd like to find someplace hidden with me, wouldn't you?"

I hit him in the shoulder, hard. "Don't wreck a good thing."

"Oh, ye of little faith." He tried leering at me but was laughing too hard to pull it off. We left the solarium and the fencers behind, and instantly the oppressive tenseness was gone. Adam was contrite but still laughing. "Okay, okay, I'll lay off. It's a habit I have no control over."

"Bad pick-up lines and cheesy comments are a habit worth breaking."

"Yes, ma'am."

I resisted punching him. Barely. "Show me another old headmaster office."

He went a little unfocused in that way I was beginning to learn was his Sight going clear. Then he was back, with all trace of laughter gone from his face. He looked at me a little quizzically.

"What?" The sound of my voice seemed to bring him back to himself. He grabbed my hand and led me down the hall at a run.

"Come on. You're going to want to see this." Adam seemed to realize he was holding my hand when we were about halfway up a back staircase. He dropped it and then covered the moment by pointing out a built-in cupboard hidden in the paneling.

"Cupboards like those are empty now, but back when the school was full, the housekeepers used them for supplies. Now they mostly just hold notes about secret meetings and rendezvous between students."

"So where's your stash?"

He grinned. "I dare you to find it."

"I never take dares. Only bets."

"Okay, then a bet. I'll leave a note for you somewhere in the school."

"Not fair. It has to be a stash cupboard someplace public."

"Okay, fine. You have a week to find my note."

"Or what?"

"Or ... you owe me a kiss."

I raised my eyebrows. "Seriously? That's the best you can come up with?"

"We can go bigger if you want, but I figure I just need an opening move and you'll be begging for more."

I looked sideways at him. "Aren't you breaking about a million Family rules even pretending to flirt with me?"

Adam suddenly scowled. "You're talking about the mixed bloodlines bollocks? There's no way some filthy Mongrel is going to tell me who I can or can't date. They tried it once ..."

He suddenly shut up, as if he'd said too much.

I didn't let it go. "Who tried?"

He hesitated, but anger and injustice won. "Shaw and the Rothbitch. They sent Alex away." Alex? "The shite thing was she agreed to go. Couldn't take the heat, I guess. It wasn't worth my effort if she didn't care enough to stand up to them." Adam was heading down a dark path, and I figured I should deflect with humor.

"So, you think one kiss from you will rock my world, huh?

Adam shrugged. "Why pretend otherwise when I know how it ends up?"

I looked sharply at him. "What are you saying? Have you seen something you're not telling me?" He smirked and I glared at him, hands on my hips. "Okay, fine. Here's the bet. If I find your note within a week, you tell me every vision or insight you've had about me, and any you have in the future. You hold nothing back, no matter what it is. Deal?"

Adam's eyes narrowed. "That's not always a great idea, Saira."

"I don't care. I want to hear it all. Do we have a bet?"

"Then I want a kiss and a grope."

"Not a chance. A kiss is all you'll get, and not even that if I find your stash. But you have to be honorable about it. Hide it today and don't touch it again until a week is up."

He held out his hand to shake. "Deal." His grip was warm and firm and he didn't let go of my hand right away. "Now, do you want to see this, or don't you?"

"Lead the way." We went up another flight of stairs, down a long hall, and then into a corridor that seemed to lead to another tower. I looked out the window to see if I could get my bearings. "North tower?"

"Very good. Now let's see if they've locked us out." He tried the handle of the large door but it wouldn't budge. Adam looked confused. "But I saw us in there."

I stepped in front of him and swept my hand across the door lintel. Nope. There was an old wall clock hanging about four feet away. It was the wind-up kind, and judging by the dust, had been stopped a long time. I opened the pendulum door and pulled out an old iron key.

"Maybe this?"

Adam fitted the key into the lock and after jiggling it a couple of times, got it to turn. "Impressive. How did you know it would be there?"

"Common sense. Lazy people and confident people hide their keys close to the lock." The door creaked open when he pushed it. The room was dim with only a couple of narrow shafts of light beaming through heavy velvet curtains. There was so much dust in the place that little clouds seemed to raise at our feet with every step.

A massive desk dominated the center of the room, round, just like the tower itself. In fact, most of the shapes around the room were circles. A chandelier, a chair, an end table, even the carpet was round. The iron curtain rods conformed to the circular shape of the room, and even the hems of the curtains were rounded. Clocks hung from every wall and all had stopped at different times. The room was silent now, but I imagined that when all the clocks were wound it would sound like a heartbeat.

"What is this place?" I was fascinated.

"I have no idea."

I looked at him. "But your vision told you to find it?"

"More or less." He walked to an expanse of closed drapes.

"There's no window behind that one," I said. It was completely dark between the velvet panels.

"Exactly." Adam grabbed hold of one of the drapes and flung it open. Hanging on the brick wall behind was a large painting in an elaborate gold frame. It was a landscape of an old bridge crossing what looked like the Thames in London. The painting was nice, but it was more than just a painting.

Swirled through the paint in intricate brushstrokes that covered the whole canvas was a time traveler's spiral.

"Oh my God." I thought I'd whispered, but Adam was by my side in an instant.

"What is it?" Adam reached out a finger to trace the spiral. "Wow!"

I knocked his hand away. "Don't touch it!"

"Why?"

"Because it's a portal."

 DORAN

"A what?"

"A doorway."

Adam stared at me for a long moment, and then understanding dawned in his eyes. "Like *your* kind of doorway?"

I nodded, and backed away from the painting as if it had teeth.

"This must have been the Clocker Tower." Adam looked around him in wonder. "I don't think there's been a Clocker headmaster in a hundred years."

"Would you mind if we closed the drapes again? That thing is giving me the creeps."

"Sure, but why? It's just a painting."

I shook my head. "It's a vortex of puke."

He looked at me in frank assessment. "Seriously?"

"The first time I went through I wanted to vomit. The second time I did. Not pretty."

He shrugged his shoulders with a grin. "I can do that in a night at the pub. What's the big deal?"

"The big deal is, I'm guessing you usually know where you are when you wake up." I narrowed my eyes at him. "On second thought, maybe you don't."

Adam laughed and closed the drapes over the painting. I immediately felt less anxious and I took a deep breath. "You saw that painting in your vision?"

Adam nodded. "I saw us looking at it together."

"How did you know the room was here?"

167

"I saw the round walls, and this is the only tower I've never explored. I could never get in."

"So, the other tower rooms belonged to the other Family headmasters?" I wandered slowly around the room, looking at objects that had been left behind. A couple of books, a magnifying glass, an old fountain pen with several different nibs – I picked that up and felt its weight.

"What is it?"

"It's for pen and ink drawings." I pulled a piece of blank paper out of the desk drawer and shook the pen before I tried it. The ink was old and the tip was crusted with it, but I got it cleared and quickly did a rough sketch of the bridge from the painting that was now behind the curtain.

Adam looked over my shoulder and then stared at me. "You're really good."

I shrugged. "Thanks. It's a really good pen." I put the fountain pen back into its case and was about to close it into the desk drawer when Adam stopped me.

"You should keep it." I looked in his eyes for any sign that he was laughing at me, but he was serious – and about six inches away from my face. I took a step back.

"Yeah, I guess I will." I shoved the pen case into my back pocket and headed for the door. "We should probably go."

"Hang on; you wanted to climb, right? Let's see where this tower goes." Adam was looking up at the flat ceiling about twelve feet above us. "The tower roofs are pitched, and the ceiling in here is flat. Which means it's probably the floor of something else."

I examined the room with a critical eye. "Over there. The wardrobe."

Adam stopped in front of a large, gothic-looking carved wood cabinet. I joined him there. "It's too deep."

Adam put his hand inside. "No it's not. It's just a wardrobe."

I moved him over to the side of the wardrobe. "It's way deeper than your arm. Look."

Understanding dawned in his eyes, and I grinned. We spoke simultaneously. "A secret entrance." Adam stepped into the wardrobe. "It's too dark. I can't see."

I switched on my Maglite and shone it inside. Adam nodded approvingly. "Impressive. What else do you carry around in your pockets?"

"Wouldn't you like to know?" I focused on the outside edges of the back, feeling along the seams in the wood until finally I found the catch I was looking for.

"Here." I flipped the invisible catch, and the back of the wardrobe swung open.

"Cool." There was awe in his voice. It made him sound like a kid. Way better than the arrogant jerk he sounded like when he was trying to be smooth.

I shone my flashlight in and immediately saw circular stone steps. "Going up?" I grinned at him and stepped into the darkness. The staircase wound about halfway around the tower, and the steps were steep. The door at the top opened with a push.

The tower room was filled with sunlight, and the view from the windows was spectacular. The room felt warm and welcoming in a way the Seer Tower had not.

"This room's not warded." I touched the stone walls and they felt warmed by sunlight. My skin soaked up the sun like it had been starved for light and heat, and I breathed a sigh of deep contentment.

"You look happy." I opened my eyes to see Adam watching me.

"I'm warm. Everything in England is cold."

"Our tower has the same view." Adam sounded a little defensive, and I smiled.

"Yeah, but it's cold. I guess if they warded a room used for Clocking, they might not be able to get back in." It made sense. Warded rooms were supposed to be like safe-houses. Someplace a person could go to keep others out. It kind of fascinated and disturbed me that Clockers would be vulnerable at the points of entry.

169

Adam looked down out the window and saw a class heading outside. He quickly checked his watch. "Oh crap! I've got economics with the Rothbitch."

"You seriously call someone that?"

"Yeah, Ms. Rothchild. You saw her in the solarium your first day. She looks like she eats small children with caviar for breakfast." Ah yes, the snooty one I hated on sight. Adam pulled open the door and bolted down the stone steps. I followed quickly on his heels, making sure to close the top door behind me so light wouldn't shine down and give away the entrance.

He was already at the main door to the tower when I closed the wardrobe door behind me. "Hang on, I'm coming with you." I pocketed my Maglite and followed him out. He quickly locked the door and re-hid the key in the clock.

"Thanks for finding this place." I really meant it. I actually felt like I might belong somewhere; like friends might even be a possibility. Adam turned up the wattage on his grin. "As I said, I love it when hot girls owe me." He bolted down the hall before my slap could connect, but I was laughing.

Adam raced to his economics class, and I figured I should head back to the library and find some answers. Several younger students were filing out of the big room when I arrived, and for a moment, I was totally alone. I found the school computers in a corner, and lucky for me someone was lazy about logging off.

Okay, 'Jack the Ripper.' First, the killings. It was very odd to read about the two murders I'd witnessed first-hand, and very disheartening to realize the next one would be in three weeks. Well, a hundred and twenty-odd years ago and three weeks. He basically disappeared from the media after the death of Mary Kelly on November 9th, 1888. There were other murders they tried to pin on the Ripper after that, but most investigators look at the "canonical five" women as the primary Ripper killings.

Most importantly, none of the other victims were unidentified. And none of them were wearing a green dress. So my mom's name wasn't among the victims. That, at least, was a good thing. There were pages and pages of investigative documents on the Ripper, but the sound of students coming in made me log off the computer, and I slipped back out to the main stacks.

Miss Rogers sat at a table, looking calmly right at me. "There you are, Miss Elian. I've been hoping to run into you."

I dropped into the chair across from her. "I could have come to your class to see you."

"Sadly, you could not. That would be a preordained meeting. This way is much better." Miss Rogers waited until a group of kids passed our table. They were younger boys and one of them, a boy with tousled blond hair and an easy grin winked at me. "Off with you, Connor Edwards, before I tell your uncle you're flirting with older women."

The kid grinned at Miss Rogers. "He'll say I've got good taste, Miss Rogers. You look nice today."

She laughed and made a shooing gesture. "Rascal!"

Connor and his friends left the library shoving each other playfully. Miss Rogers sighed. "That one is too smart for his own good, and when his brother gets here, the pair of them will be insufferable." Miss Rogers turned her attention to me. "Now, for you, Miss Elian, I have five minutes before my next class, and as you may have heard by now, I do know something of your abilities. Ask what you will."

"Are spirals the only way to time travel?"

"If there are other ways, I haven't heard of them."

Her answers were just as no-nonsense and rapid fire as my questions. "Can I make my own spiral to travel?"

"Some can, but it's rare. I haven't heard of a modern Clocker strong enough to do so."

Interesting. Thank you, Doran, for making my spirals. "Will I go to the same time and place each time?"

She had to think about that one for a moment. "Not necessarily. I believe each time ring … you are aware of those?" I nodded. "Good. Each one defaults at approximately one hundred and twenty-five years. But I understand there have been skilled Clockers with more control – perhaps even enough to have determined the place and time to which they traveled."

"How do I get that skill?"

"I don't know if it can be taught. I've never known one who could do it." Miss Roger's voice sounded tired, and I had the feeling my Q&A session was ending.

"Is there a cost to time traveling?" I suddenly had the thought I could be taking years off my life every time I went through a spiral. Miss Rogers seemed to know exactly what I meant though, and I think she was impressed with the question.

"As I understand it, and please realize I'm merely a Quarter-Time with no traveling skill whatsoever, the only cost to Clocking is the risk of getting lost."

"But as long as there's a spiral on the other end, there's no way to get lost, right?"

She smiled at me, eyes sparkling. "My dear, I can get lost between my bed and the toilet these days. I find presumptions to be a source of false confidence. But then again, confidence may be exactly what you need." She took a deep, raspy breath, and I wondered how old she really was. "Your guardian, Lady Elian, never learned the finer points of Clocking because there was no one left to teach her, and she didn't have the courage to try it on her own and risk failure. Sometimes our failures are the only way to truly learn."

A class of older students began filing into the library, and Miss Rogers pushed back her chair. I raced around the table and helped her to her feet.

"Thank you, my dear. You asked about the costs of Clocking? I can't speak to that so much as the costs of being one of our Family." I was holding her arm as I walked her to the door of the library. "Time moves more slowly for us than for others – a blessing when we're young, but less interesting when our bones are brittle and our eyesight fails."

I tried not to stare at her parchment skin and snow-white hair. "Can I ask how old you are?"

Her eyes sparkled again, and I could hear the laughter in her voice. "You can ask, and I won't tell. Suffice it to say, I remember when the Titanic sank." She took her arm out of my hand and walked gracefully, if a little slowly, down the hall.

Some kids ran past Miss Rogers on their way to class and I wanted to yell at them to watch out for her, but she didn't seem to mind them a bit.

I spun back into the library and found an encyclopedia from 1990. Old, but still useful for my purpose. I flipped through the T's to 'Titanic,' did some quick mental math, and then picked my jaw up off the floor. The Titanic sank in 1912. Miss Rogers was over a hundred years old.

Wow.

"Hey, new girl!"

I looked for the speaker. It was the blond kid, Connor. He grinned at me and gave me a thumbs-up. I waved back at the kid, and then did what I always did when I needed to think. I ran.

I leapt over a railing and took a set of stairs three at a time, then climbed more stairs, raced down halls, turned corners, and climbed again. It was only when I finally stopped right outside the heavy wooden door did I realize where my feet had taken me. The Clocker Tower. I unlocked the door, slipped inside, and turned the lock behind me.

I was already starting to think of it as a space just for me, and I grabbed a couple pieces of yellowed paper from the desk and a board to write on. Then I opened the secret stairway door in the back of the wardrobe and bounded up the stairs to my gloriously sunny tower.

I picked the brightest spot in the room and sat on the floor with my drawing pens and paper. It was warm there and I stretched out like a cat, closed my eyes, and let my mind go blank.

And then slowly, almost like a reflection clearing on a rippled pond, the image of Archer came into my brain. Not Archer the Vampire I'd just seen the night before, but Archer the Victorian University Student. He was smiling in the picture in my head, and I started trying to sketch that smile. I realized pretty quickly that I couldn't draw his mouth without first drawing his eyes since that's where his smile started. And before I was even aware I'd done it, a rough sketch of Archer's face stared back at me from the paper.

I looked at the sketch with critical eyes. The nose wasn't quite right, and I didn't think his eyebrows were so arched. I wanted to see him in person. It was an irrational thing, maybe just so I could get the details of the drawing exactly right. I tucked the pens back into my pocket and stood up.

And came face to face with a man.

"I thought I'd find you here."

Every hair on my body stood straight up. "Who are you?" My voice squeaked, and it was barely above a whisper. His face looked oddly familiar. Not like I'd necessarily seen him before, but maybe I knew his parents or something.

"Nice work on the portrait. It looks like him." His eyes lit up merrily. He was probably in his mid-twenties with longish, shaggy, brown hair and the look of an adventurer or outdoorsman. Like the kind of guy who climbed pyramids to watch the sun rise or went skydiving for the view.

I stared at him. "You know Archer?"

He shrugged as if he knew everyone, then held out his hand to shake. "I'm Doran."

I think my mouth fell open. I'm not sure, but I had the distinct feeling I looked like a fish. Okay. Breathe. "Thanks for the spirals."

He grinned. "Glad you found them."

I looked behind him at the staircase leading to the Clocker room. He caught my look and anticipated my question. "I came in through the painting."

"Why?"

He shrugged. "It was time to introduce myself."

"Finally." I spoke almost to myself, and then blurted out, "Can I travel between portals in the same time?"

He laughed at me. I didn't care.

"Yes, absolutely. But it helps to have a really strong image of something on the other side."

"A landmark like the bridge in the painting?"

He nodded. "It's easiest if you already have a visual of the place, though I have traveled to places I've never seen before."

"How?"

"A strong emotional connection can link you there."

"Like to a person?"

"Sometimes."

My eyes narrowed as I looked at Doran. "You're not exactly big on details, are you?"

He shrugged. "I've never had to teach anyone before. It's hard to teach what you just know."

"Great. That's helpful."

"The Family has a timepiece. About the size of a pocket watch. I've heard of some of them using that to focus their travels."

"What do you mean, focus?"

"Well, like this. You've gone to 1888. A fairly simple one-ring jump into the past. Your native time draws you back to it like a magnet each time, so going between these two times is always easiest. If you wanted to do a two-ring jump, or jump to a specific year, you'd have to focus your travel. Some of us do it on our own, but the less skilled would use the Family timepiece like a conduit to that time."

"I supposed Millicent has that clock now?" As head of the Elian family it made sense.

"I don't think the clock has been seen since Melinda's time. I believe she may have mounted it in a necklace, and they thought she might have died with it on."

Melinda. I'd heard that name before. Melinda Elian. Oh! I gasped. "You mean the council massacre."

He nodded. "I heard it got bloody. But that's what happens when you bring Weres in to do your dirty work."

Weres? As in Werewolves? He had to be kidding. Doran made a move for the stairs, then turned back. "Got anything else for me?"

"About a million things. Miss Simpson said she taught you in the '70s. How come you aren't that old?"

He shrugged like it was no big deal. "I jump around a lot in time. Oh, by the way, you won't be able to go anywhere you already are."

"What do you mean?"

"It's a paradox to be in the same time as yourself. So if you try to travel within your own lifetime, the spiral will skip you back to a time before you were born."

I had followed Doran down to the main tower room, and he stepped up to the painting. He started tracing the spirals with a lazy grin. "You're pretty sharp. You'll figure it out."

I couldn't believe he was leaving. "Wait, Doran! Do you know where my mom is?" He was fading before my eyes. He threw me a salute, and I heard him say "native time" before he winked out.

Why couldn't the guy have just sat down with me over a cup of coffee and given me the full rundown about being a Clocker? Why did everything have to be so cryptic and mysterious?

I wondered if I could follow him. The first time had been an accident. What would happen if I did it on purpose now? Miss Rogers seemed to think trial and error was the way to learn. Maybe this was an easy trial? Go through the spiral, turn around, come back.

I started tracing the spirals with my finger and almost immediately the humming began. I hesitated for just a second as my stomach jolted with the memory of traveling. I was completely nuts, wasn't I? Traveling through a spiral painting? Best case scenario I just hopped one spiral and went back to 1888. Worst case scenario ...?

I tried to stop tracing the patterned paint, but short of cutting my hand off, I couldn't do it. I finished the fourth spiral and was starting on the fifth when the thrumming and stretching feeling began. I wanted to scream! And then I was screaming! And spiraling.

London Bridge - 1888

And suddenly I did stop. Screaming, falling, spiraling – it all stopped. And everything around me was silent.

Where was I? My vision was blurry and I staggered when I stood up. I needed to see the spiral for my return trip, but first I needed to puke.

I'm not a good hurler. My eyes tear and my nose runs and I make the kind of retching sounds that send other people running for the bathroom. When I finally wiped my face, my vision had cleared enough so I could see around me for the first time. I was outside by a river. Not in the tower at St. Brigid's.

I turned around and stared. I had Clocked to the London Bridge. I searched the pillars closest to me for my spiral, but it wasn't there. A panicky need to get back to my tower was building, and I pushed it down so I could think. The sky was filled with dark, ominous clouds that threatened rain, and there were people in another century's clothes hurrying along the quay.

"Oy, mate!"

I barely heard the voice until it repeated. "Mate! Are ye daft?"

I spun to realize I was about five feet away from a group of young men gathered around something that looked like a bag of silverware. They were dressed in working clothes, and every one of them looked at me with a scowl. And from the loot-splitting looks of the gathering, I'd stepped right into a hornet's nest of epic proportion. A slightly younger kid than the rest, maybe about fifteen, stepped forward and looked at me with interest. "Ye'd best get back to yer ship, mate." I realized my dad's white fishing sweater and all the hurling must have made me look like a drunken sailor.

He was giving me an out that lasted exactly one second before the biggest guy in the group stood up. "'E'll not be goin' nowhere."

Oh crap. Here we go. I had no choice. I ran. I leapt up the wall of the quay in a move that left about half my pursuers behind, then took the stairs three at a time and was over the rails before a couple of them had even cleared the wall. That left two still on my tail. The bigger one dropped back when I scaled a brick wall and ran through someone's little garden, down an alley, and out to a different street.

That just left the kid who had suggested I get back to my ship. He looked familiar somehow, but I didn't have time to dwell on that because he was keeping pace easily, just a few steps behind me. And he wasn't breathing hard enough to keep him from speaking.

"Keep runnin'. I need to chase ye another coupla blocks before they'll drop away."

I glanced back at him. He was dressed in possibly the rattiest clothes I'd ever seen, but his newsboy cap was almost new. And then I recognized him. The kid Archer had used to convince me I was in 1888 on my first visit. The one I'd called an urchin. My comments must have landed with him because at least he'd upgraded his headwear. The kid had a mischievous grin on his face that probably meant he'd done something worthy of a slap, and he was laughing at me, the little bastard. I put on a burst of speed and left him behind as I leapt up another wall. The kid scrambled up behind me, but I'd managed to put a few more feet of distance between us. I suddenly halted at the top, wavering from my forward momentum. In the yard below me were two wolfhounds with hungry eyes trained directly on me and a single line of drool running from each vicious mouth.

The kid leapt to the wall next to me and looked down at the snarling hounds. He glanced at my face, probably expecting fear, which wasn't there. Just determination to find my way across the yard. He laughed and whistled for the dogs.

"Maggie! Tolly! Come!"

He dropped down into the yard and ruffled the fur on both sets of ears. The wolfhounds looked at him adoringly. He squinted up at me, crouched on the wall above him.

"Are ye coming down yet? The 'ounds in the next yard are vicious, and there's a cat that'll rip yer eyes out just as soon as spit at ye. The lasses 'ere are yer best bet. They don't like most gents, but maybe they won't eat ye, will ye girls?" He ruffled their fur again and they practically purred against his legs.

I jumped and landed in front of the kid. His eyes suddenly widened in surprise. "Oy, but ye ain't no gent, are ye?"

I looked the kid in the eyes and narrowed my gaze. "So? What of it?"

He regarded me for a long moment. "I let ye beat me, and the lads saw it. If any of 'em saw yer a lass, I'll never 'ear the end of it."

"Then don't bring me back there."

He stared at me like I'd gone mad. "Why would I do such a daft thing? Ye outran me and ye got away. I was thinkin' ye'd buy me a bit o' lunch for my trouble though."

"I don't have any money."

He stared at me. "Then what good are ye?" He had me there.

"Actually, I could use your help."

"Why? Ye've got nothin' to pay me with."

"I need to get back to the bridge."

His voice was cautious again. "I can't take ye back there yet. The lads are still divvyin' up. Where are ye from? Ye talk funny."

"America."

The kid nodded. "Explains the kit."

I must have looked confused because he gestured to my clothes. "Ye know, yer get-up."

Jeans, boots and a big sweater. I'd been having no luck blending when I traveled, and questions about *when* I was would be too weird, especially if he recognized me. I absently scratched a dog's ear, and then had a sudden inspiration.

"I came to see the Jubilee."

The boy looked startled. "The golden one?"

I nodded. "Of Queen Victoria."

He scoffed dismissively. "Don't they teach yer nothin' in America? That was last year." Perfect. I was back in 1888. He gave the dogs a last pat on their heads, then headed toward the door at the far side of the yard. "Are ye comin'?"

I nodded and scratched the dogs before following him from the yard. We were on a commercial street filled with shops and pubs. I had a sudden thought. Call it a whim. "If I can't go back to the bridge yet, could you take me to King's College?"

The kid looked me up and down, as if he was trying to decide how much trouble I was worth. The expression on his face was comical, and I was suddenly inspired. I spotted a wall with notices posted and grabbed a handwritten one from the board – something about saving Wilton's Music Hall from the Methodists. I had to laugh at that, and the kid peered over my shoulder.

"What's funny?"

"Nothing." I flipped the page over to the blank side and pulled out my pen case. The kid's eyes got wide.

"What are ye doing with that?"

"It's a drawing pen."

"It's for writin' and lasses don't write."

I glared. "Can you write?"

He scowled. "No."

"Then don't act like girls are stupid." I wrote the word U R C H I N out on the top of the paper.

The kid stared at me like I'd grown a second head. "What's that say?"

I smiled. "It's a name. Now be still a minute and let me draw you." He stood frozen, staring at me with huge eyes.

I sketched out his face, gave his mouth the little lilt of the troublemaker I was sure he was, and added the shock of blond hair that kept falling over one eye.

I handed him the paper and his mouth dropped open. "Who is it?"

Had the kid never seen a mirror? "It's you."

He tried to hand it back, pulling away from me. "Huh uh, not me. I don't look like that."

"Yes you do." I pointed at the hat I'd drawn on his head. "See, this is your hat." He ripped the cap off his head and stared at it, then the sketch, and back again.

"And that's your hair that keeps falling over your eyes." The kid was just swiping the hair off his forehead. He stopped, mid-swipe, and touched his hair gingerly.

"It's you."

He held the sketch very close to his face and seemed to study every detail of it. When he finally looked back into my eyes, there was something like awe there. He held the sketch out to me.

"You can keep it if you like."

As quick as a flash, the suspicion was back in his eyes. "What do ye want for it?"

"I told you. I need a guide to King's College. But it has to be someone really trustworthy." The kid actually got defensive at that, just like I'd hoped he would. He was a proud kid and I kind of liked him for it. "No one knows the city like me. And no one's more trusty—"

"Trustworthy."

"Right. That. I'll do it for the pen then."

I actually did have something of value on me. "Done."

He stared me up and down for a long minute. "Can ye 'ide yer 'air?"

I tucked the end of my braid into the back of my sweater. He studied it critically, then grabbed the hat off his head and plopped it on mine. "That's better. Folks won't mess if they think yer a lad."

It was everything I could do not to snatch the hat off my head and check it for lice. I suppressed a shudder and smiled at him. "Thanks."

He dismissed me with a wave. "It's me own skin I'm protectin', not yer's. I've a reputation to keep. Bein' seen with a lass in trousers, 'specially one I let outrun me, would ruin me forever."

I shot him a disbelieving look, which he returned with a scowl. Then he sighed, like I was just trouble waiting to happen. "C'mon then. Let's go." The kid loped, he didn't walk. He moved like the wolfhounds. Kind of gangly, but with every motion under control.

181

"What're ye called?" The boy's accent was so thick it took me a second to get it. He reminded me of movies I'd seen of the drummer for the Beatles, Ringo Starr. I mentally dubbed him 'Ringo,' for the accent and the attitude.

"My name's Saira."

"Like siren? Them ladies of the sea that'll call a man to 'is death?"

It was my turn to be astonished. How did a street kid in London learn about Greek mythology? "I've been told my name means 'traveler.'"

"Well that's true enough, isn't it?"

I snorted. "I guess it is."

Ringo grinned self-importantly. "I'm called 'Keys.' An' I'm the best there is."

"Keys?"

"There ain't a locked door in the city I can't open."

The obvious pride in his voice almost made me smile, but I kept my face carefully neutral. I thought 'Ringo' suited him better.

"So you're a lock-pick?"

Ringo looked at me scornfully. "Nah. Picks cost. I use these." He held up his fingers and wiggled them.

I narrowed my eyes at him. "C'mon, you can't pick locks with your fingers."

"Door locks? Nah. But windows ..." He waggled his eyebrows at me meaningfully. I laughed.

"Not so thick fer a lass."

I lunged to smack him on the arm, but he danced out of the way and took off running. We were on a main street, but he immediately turned down a smaller side one with less traffic. And he free ran.

It felt like flying. The kid was better than me as he dodged and wove and leapt his way down the street. I almost caught him at the corner, but he surprised me and went over a rock wall that was higher than my head. The stones were old and fit together well so the holds weren't obvious, but I'd seen where Ringo put his first foot and his route gave me mine.

I paused at the top of the wall to look before I leapt. And I was happy I did. The view was phenomenal. There was a huge area behind the wall that looked like a park, and dominating the center was a massive four-story red-brick building. Ringo stepped out from behind a tree and gestured for me fiercely.

"Get down!" He whispered his shout, but the intent was clear enough. I jumped. Ringo dragged me behind his tree in an instant. "Are ye daft? Ye'll be seen."

"What is this place?"

From Ringo's expression it was clear he thought I was an idiot. "Ye said King's College didn't ye? Over there's Guy's Hospital."

"Hospital? I don't want the hospital. I want the college."

"This is the college."

"But it's a hospital."

"Ye didn't say *which* college ye wanted. Just that ye wanted to get to King's College."

I sighed. I didn't know the system, and the only thing I had going for me was that I was American, and therefore, expected to be ignorant. Some things never changed.

"I need to find a theology student."

Ringo thought for a moment. "Them that study religions – yeah, there's a chapel around the side. As good a place as any to ask, eh?"

I nodded. "Let's go."

We kept to the trees around the outside of the park. Ringo was clearly used to blending into the background and his skills were impressive.

One of the second floor windows of the huge building opened, and I could see someone in a black coat. Ringo and I both froze instinctively, and I silently cursed my bright white sweater. The man in the window had dark hair and seemed to be talking to someone inside the room.

"I don't like that window being open," Ringo whispered practically in my ear.

"Would we get in trouble for being here?"

He nodded curtly. "Unless yer a student or ye have business with one."

A cold gust of wind suddenly blew through the trees and I shivered. The dark-haired man turned to pull the window closed. For just a moment, the face seemed to look right at me and I gasped. Archer!

"Wot's it?" Ringo's accent sliced through my surprise.

"I think that was my friend, but I'm not sure. I couldn't really see him."

Ringo looked at me for a long moment, then his eyes scanned the building in front of us, and finally he nodded. "Let's go!" He bolted across the grass to the closest corner of the massive red brick structure, and the instant he grabbed hold of a brick above his head, I knew he meant to climb the wall. Worse, the kid meant for me to climb it too. Crap! Brick sucked to climb. The handholds were tiny, and unless there were clinker bricks – the kind that stuck out funny – a person was better off being barefoot than wearing anything that prevented wedging toes into mortar lines. But there was absolutely no point in Ringo climbing up to get a look at Archer unless he meant for me to follow.

So I did. Running across a wide open lawn felt like being in the middle of a field with a gun-sight on me. I made it to the wall of the building without anyone raising an obvious alarm, but by that time Ringo was already up to a window ledge on the second story. The kid was really good, and the more I watched him the more I thought he could actually teach me something. I started to reach for the bricks above my head, but Ringo made a noise that sounded like "Chhhht!" I looked up. He held up a finger, as if to tell me to wait there, and then he disappeared.

Huh? People didn't just disappear from window ledges twenty feet off the ground. I stepped back, away from the wall, and scanned the place he had just been. Somehow, in the space of less than a minute, Ringo had managed to unlatch the window and drop inside. He was just closing it behind him when I caught his eye. He grinned mischievously at me, winked, and slipped deeper into the room.

I hugged the corner of the building again, and waited … which unfortunately gave me time to think about what I was doing, and was definitely too little, too late. Seriously. Leaping into that spiral just because I wanted to test a skill and maybe see some guy? Some future Vampire guy? And now here I was, waiting for a nineteenth-century street urchin I'd named "Ringo" outside King's College, with absolutely no idea what was going to happen next.

"Chhht!" Ringo's noise came from close by. I slid to the edge of the building and peered around the corner. There he was, standing in a doorway with a grin on his face like he'd just unlocked the gates of heaven. I finally got it. They called him "Keys" because he was a break-and-enter guy. No wonder he didn't want his mates to see me. He must run with a tough crowd. I gave him an arched eyebrow of respect. "Nicely done."

He practically bowed as he let me in. "M'lady."

I suppressed a laugh. "Now, how do we find him?"

"Right this way." Ringo took the lead down a narrow hallway, turning two corners, and up a back staircase. We were totally silent as we moved through the building. There were private studies or offices behind some open doors, but otherwise the place looked completely institutional.

Finally, Ringo stopped and quietly slipped over to a closed door. I held my breath as it opened and the voices of two men could be heard inside.

"It's for his own good. He'll never be whole or even functional again; you realize that, don't you?"

"But it isn't right." That was Archer. I felt something unfurl in my chest at the sound of his voice. He continued. "We're scholars, not physicians. We don't decide that sort of thing."

Ringo pulled the door closed, and I was just about to protest when he slipped into the room next to it like a ghost. I followed him inside and he closed the door to the hall. Ringo whispered into my ear. "We can see them from the window ledge."

I nodded. Even though I had recognized Archer's voice instantly, I wanted to see who he was talking to.

Ringo unlatched the window and carefully pushed the window open just far enough for the glass to catch the reflection inside the next room.

The room was dim and at first I couldn't see anyone. Then Archer stepped forward into the light, and a butterfly the size of a pterodactyl hit my stomach when I looked at his face. The guy was good looking in an everything-fits-together way. He was tall for the times, but not that much taller than me, with a way of moving that made him seem comfortable anywhere. But was he handsome? Not really movie-star knockout handsome, but when I remembered how his smile lit up his face, and how his eyes seemed like the deepest lakes when he looked at me, the pterodactyl fluttered.

He wasn't smiling now.

I searched the shadows for the man he'd been talking to. He was there, but I could barely see him sitting placidly behind a desk deep in the room. He had salt and pepper hair and looked like he was in his fifties. The way he held himself, he reminded me of a silverback gorilla I once saw in a zoo. Totally confident of his own power, and I hated him on sight. When he spoke again, the pterodactyl fled, and my guts twisted instead.

"Despite all you now know about the Families, you're still defending them?"

The Families? As in, my Families? I didn't stop to wonder when I'd claimed them. Probably somewhere around the time Silverback seemed to threaten them.

"This has nothing to do with them. This is about a human being."

"He's an animal. And the split just confirms it."

"Shaw is a man, no matter what he's done."

Mr. Shaw's ancestor who killed the council? He was still alive?

Silverback stood up to go. "When no one came to testify for him at the hearing on the 30th, the decision was made. We'll have the doctor's orders by the end of the month. I'll see to it you're off the floor when it's done. It's the best I'll do."

Archer's jaw clenched. "Thank you, sir."

"I trust we won't be having this conversation again?"

"No, sir."

"Excellent. And now, Devereux, there are young minds to mold and shape into men of character. Would you care to teach my

Theological Ethics seminar today? Perhaps you could put your arguments to use?"

It looked like Archer was biting back a sarcastic comment. His voice was even when he spoke. "I'm sorry, sir. I have some work to do on the Whitechapel report."

Silverback smiled indulgently at Archer. "Of course, your notebooks. Still under lock and key, I presume?"

"Of course, sir. The key remains with me at all times."

"Because in the wrong hands, the information you possess could be quite deadly for many people."

"I'm very aware of the need for secrecy about the Immortals, sir."

Silverback regarded Archer a long moment, and then finally nodded. "Yes, I do believe you are."

Silverback glided from the room and I could see he was not tall but he moved like a powerful man. I shuddered with relief as he left.

Archer dropped into a chair with a suddenness that made me jump. And good thing I did, because his gaze was lifting to the window just as I retreated from view.

Ringo was idly flipping through a book on the desk when I turned to face him. "Yer man?" I nodded. "Right. Ye finished with me then?" He had the book in his hand and looked half way out the door already.

"You're taking that?" I nodded at the book. "Encyclopedia of Cottage, Farm, and Villa Architecture?"

Ringo shrugged with a grin. "The more I know a place, the easier it is to get in." Oh excellent. It was like practically handing him blueprints of houses to rob. He stopped at the door and turned to me. "Thanks fer the drawin'."

Despite his sticky fingers and questionable morality, I liked this kid. I grinned at him and handed him the fountain pen from my back pocket. "Thanks for the guiding."

The pen disappeared into his jacket and he tipped his cap to me before slipping out of the room. I missed Ringo the second he was gone. Weird. Probably just nerves at the idea of seeing Archer again face to face. But that was why I'd come here.

THE BISHOP

I peered out the door and saw no one in the hall. The place was eerily silent as I slid from one room to the other so quietly Archer didn't hear me come in. I let the door close with a "click" to warn him of my presence. It didn't help. The poor guy practically hit the ceiling in his shock. At least it shattered my own anxiety as I burst out laughing.

"Miss ... Elian?" His voice was so tentative it knocked the giggles right out of me.

"Hi, Archer."

"You're here?"

"Apparently."

"But, why?" There was confusion in his voice, and something else. Maybe ... wariness? Suddenly this wasn't going well, and I felt myself getting defensive.

"Is it a problem?"

Archer considered me for a long moment. A really long moment. I started to lose my nerve. Finally he seemed to come to a conclusion and looked me straight in the eyes. "If I'm completely honest with myself, I'm very glad to see you. And that makes me afraid for you as well." He sighed and went to the window, looking out at the view as he spoke. "It is a dangerous time for Descendants of Immortals. You are being hunted and catalogued for a purpose I do not fully understand."

"By the old Silverback guy that was just here?"

Archer looked confused for a moment. "Silverback? Do you mean Bishop Wilder?"

"Short, powerful, silver hair, moves like he's on rails?"

Archer permitted himself a tiny smile. "That's Bishop Wilder, my mentor. Why do you name him Silverback?"

I shrugged. "He looks like a silverback gorilla."

Archer struggled to keep a straight face. "Indeed."

"So why is Silverback hunting Immortal Descendants?"

"Hunting is perhaps a strong word. The bishop has been compiling a list of the living members of each Family. A genealogy of sorts."

"Why?"

"That's what I haven't figured out yet." There was an edge to Archer's voice I didn't understand.

"And you're working with him?"

Archer spun to face me. "Yes."

"So you're hunting us, too?"

Archer looked directly into my eyes. "I'm learning how to protect us."

I stared at him. "Us?"

The silence between us stretched longer than I could hold my breath. Finally Archer spoke again. "My mother had Seer blood."

Fascinating. And with implications I couldn't even begin to fathom yet. "What can you 'See'?"

Archer shook his head and sighed. "I have a sense of people – whether they're fundamentally good or bad." He looked like he expected me to laugh, but I matched his serious tone.

"Does it show up as colors?"

That shocked him. He nodded. "How did you know?"

"I know someone else who can See a thing like 'betrayal' by the color around a person."

He seemed suddenly excited. "Betrayal. Did your friend say what color that is?"

"Purple."

"Purple." He seemed to be committing it to memory.

"You said 'good' and 'bad.' What else can you See?"

"Lies." The way he said the word gave it an inevitable feeling. Like he expected everyone would lie to him, and maybe everyone had.

"What color is a lie?"

"Green. Poisonous."

"I guess that makes sense."

"It's the thing I dislike most to see, and yet there is green around almost everyone I've ever met."

Since I was about to step in it with both feet, I decided to pull on the hip-waders and stride right in. "What about me? How's my green?"

Archer considered me very thoughtfully. He finally spoke. "It's different."

That surprised me. I figured people assumed I was a liar because of my anti-social tendencies. "How?"

"I don't see the pure green of lies around you. It's more a blue-green color, like the ocean."

"Which means …?"

"Blue means something is closed, usually emotions or faith. So I can only assume that the blue green around you is a sign of something withheld."

"Like lying by omission?"

Archer nodded. "More or less."

"I probably do that a lot. Not really meaning to lie, just sort of shutting up."

He smiled a little. "I understand that inclination."

"So I don't come across as a liar, huh?"

"One of the very few people I've ever met who does not."

I shrugged and grinned. "So I've got that going for me at least."

Archer's gaze on me was direct. "Again, I ask, why have you come back? One mistake I understand, but the second time? That is deliberate."

I suddenly didn't want to admit that I'd returned on a total whim. It made me feel weak somehow. And immature. I took a deep breath. "My mother still isn't back."

Archer looked startled. "Your mother?"

"She was at Whitechapel station when I ... Clocked."

He stared at me thoughtfully for a long moment. "The woman in the green dress." I nodded. "The Ripper saw her. He heard you call out to her before you vanished."

I stared at him. "Why would he care?"

Archer looked at me carefully to gauge my reaction. "Perhaps because he knows you're a Clocker?"

"But I didn't think regular people knew about Immortal Descendants. Why would Jack the Ripper care about me or my mother?"

He'd been holding his breath. "I think he might be a Descendent too."

I stared at Archer like he had just sprouted horns. "A Clocker? Like me?"

Archer shook his head. "Not one of the born Descendants."

I stared at him. "A Vampire?"

He looked as startled as I felt. "So you know of these things?"

"Not much, but I know they're Death's Descendants."

He nodded. "It's possible the Ripper is among them. I started tracking him after they found Mary Ann Nichols in August. At first it was the wound patterns. Throats cut to mask traces of incisor wounds."

"But the woman we saw had way more than just a slashed throat."

Archer gave me a significant look. "It appeared almost as though an animal had attacked, didn't it?" I nodded and then shuddered at the memory of intestines hanging out of a slashed belly. "He's masking his murders as animal-like attacks."

"So?"

"So, who among the Families becomes animal?"

Duh. "Shifters." Archer watched my face as I worked it out. "So Vampires are framing Shifters? Again, I didn't think regular people knew about the Families."

"They're sending a message. To what purpose I can only guess, but I believe it's designed to split the Families."

"As in, pit the Clockers and Seers against the Shifters?"

191

Archer nodded. "Something like that."

"What about War? Whose side are they on?"

Archer scoffed. "War lands squarely on the side of whatever causes the most conflict. That is the nature of War."

Fricking Mongers. "Okay, why now?"

He shrugged. "I don't know. Bishop Wilder speaks as though it is a random escalation of an ongoing conflict, but I feel there is some design behind it."

"Why is Bishop Wilder so interested in the Immortal Descendants? Is he one, too?"

"Not that I'm aware of, nor is Wilder one of the family names in the genealogy."

"Then *why* do it?"

Archer sighed and paced around the room. He looked young and worried, and I felt bad for him. "Bishop Wilder enlisted my help to research the Families under the guise that they had a complex social and economic structure unto themselves. He feels this research is justified because the Families operate as though they are their own society."

He suddenly seemed very tired, like the whole thing had been weighing on him. "I was very easily drawn into this study because of my own Family ties. But as the genealogy became more complete and I was able to find Descendant Family ties to some quite surprising people, I realized the danger of such a book's very existence."

"Not something you thought about before?"

"Not really, no. The research was an intellectual exercise, no more. But once the general outlines had been done, the bishop pulled me off the project and has discouraged me from continuing. So perhaps he realized the same thing. It could be rather uncomfortable for some people if the information were ever to be made public, and frankly, I'm happy to be done with it."

"Where is the book now?"

"Bishop Wilder has it under lock and key."

That genealogy could contain pieces of my Family tree that were missing, and maybe there were other Clockers out there he'd identified. "Was my mother part of your research?"

He nodded. "She was, in theory. At least her birth was recorded."

"Was mine?"

He looked at me a long moment. "No."

I narrowed my eyes. "But you know about me."

"The bishop doesn't." Archer was protecting me? From his boss? His pacing resumed and he seemed agitated. "I really must ask you to go now. Your presence here would be very awkward to explain if anyone were to discover you."

I wasn't going to be put off easily, so I ignored him. "But what are the Families doing about the killings? About the idea that Shifters could be doing it?"

Archer shook his head. "Nothing. They've become increasingly isolated from each other, particularly in the past two decades. Whatever this Vampire is hoping to provoke among the three Families seems to already be in effect."

"So then why bother?"

"Indeed. Perhaps there's a fundamental cruelty in Vampires. This one could be just acting according to its nature."

Uh oh, dangerous territory here. "Do you believe that?"

"History and legend does. What does one man's opinion matter?"

My voice choked in my throat. "It matters."

"I believe the creature known as Jack the Ripper is evil. Do I believe all Vampires are evil? They were human once and therefore, born innocent. Whatever path their lives took ultimately ended in them being made a Vampire."

"You make it sound as if they did something to deserve it."

Archer gave me an odd look. "Why do you defend Vampires?"

"Why do you study them?"

His eyes narrowed at me. "You have to leave this place, Miss Elian."

"Not without my mother. And why are you back to 'Miss Elian'? It's Saira."

His voice got stiff and formal. "I don't presume to know you well enough to call you by your Christian name."

193

"Fine, how about this. If Silverback hears you call me Miss Elian, he will know exactly who I am."

Archer looked stricken, which was almost worse than his formal high-handedness. "Of course. I wasn't thinking."

"No, you weren't. Now are you going to help me find my mother, or do I start searching this city on my own?"

"If I help you, Bishop Wilder will know you are here."

"He doesn't scare me."

"He should."

There were things Archer wasn't telling me about his boss, but my own gut instinct said that he was right about Wilder's scariness.

Archer seemed to come to a decision and he opened a desk drawer and removed a notebook. I raised my eyebrows. "That's your safe?"

He looked startled. "You heard me speak to the bishop?"

I nodded. "I was at the window."

He went to the window and looked out in disbelief. Then he smiled. It was unexpected and it transformed his expression into one that made my breath catch in my chest. "Are you sure *you're* not part Vampire?"

No, but you are, I almost said. How the hell was I going to have *that* conversation with him?

RIVERSIDE

Archer spread the contents of the notebook around his desk and walked me through the information. There were newspaper clippings, a couple of diagrams, and some handwritten crime scene reports. Apparently the bishop had well-placed connections inside the police department, and I said as much to Archer.

"Bishop Wilder is a man with allies. Powerful ones. The kind a wise person doesn't oppose." There was a warning look in his eyes. But considering it hadn't been on my list to go up against the bishop, I thought his reaction was a little extreme.

I shrugged and rifled through a stack of papers. "I don't see how any of this helps us. You don't even have a proper suspect in here, just names of people the police have interviewed."

"The one I believe is a Vampire isn't on any list we've seen."

I stared at Archer. "And what are you, psychic?"

"Not that I'm aware of."

The dry way he spoke reminded me he had Seer blood. "Okay, so enlighten me."

He looked at me a long moment, then finally spoke. "No."

My eyes narrowed at him. No? Really? Archer met my stare with an expression that looked rebellious. Well, I wasn't going to play his game. I spun on my heel and walked out of the room before he could say a word to stop me.

"Miss ... Saira!" I didn't even pause. "Saira! Wait!"

Fortunately I have a decent memory for directions and was able to stalk out of the building without a wrong turn. A tiny rock was wedged into the doorway of the heavy exterior entrance and I silently thanked Ringo for leaving me a way out. There's nothing like fumbling an exit to ruin the effect of storming away.

Archer was still chasing after me, and when he burst out of the building I broke into a run. I could hear him swear under his breath, but to his credit, he kept after me.

I didn't have a plan, and that was my whole problem. I was back in England in the late 1800s with no money and no idea what to do next. Seeing Archer again had been a wacky little fantasy, and now I just felt like an idiot.

Hence the running. When the going gets tough, the skittish run away. It felt like whatever he was into was just one big mystery. I had way too many of those at the moment, and I didn't have it in me to solve his too.

I turned a corner and paused to catch my breath. It hit me all at once that the only thing I wanted right then was to find my mom and go home. I felt like I was about three years old and lost in a mall. But there was no mall-cop to page her on the speaker system. "Claire Elian, please come to the first floor security office. Your daughter needs you."

Unless … maybe there was a way to have her paged. Or at least this century's version of it.

Archer hadn't rounded the corner so I figured he gave up and went back to King's College. The coast seemed clear, so I took off in the direction of the bridge. If I was lucky, the loot-splitters would be gone, Ringo would be back in place by the river, and I could maybe sweet-talk him into helping me again.

I passed an older woman with a basket over one arm and two men walking together wearing workingman's clothes. I kept my head down and my hands in my pockets, trying to look as much like a young man as I could. The clothes definitely helped dispel any idea that I might possibly be female.

I found the river again by smell. I remembered reading about "The Great Stink" in London, circa 1858, where people had been dumping their sewage into the river for so long that finally even Parliament had to move because the smell was so bad. They started a big sewage works project and then the cholera epidemics stopped coming to London every year. Go figure. Get rid of the poop and the disease will follow. It still smelled bad by the river, but at least it wasn't quite so eau d'outhouse.

I made my way to the quay and searched the bank of the Thames for any signs of my guide. If Ringo was back with his hooligans, I was likely out of luck. I didn't think his reputation could stand an acknowledgment of my foreign, female self.

Just past the London Bridge there were dockworkers unloading a small barge. I hoped to spot Ringo's smallish frame among them, but he was probably still too young to take that job from the able-bodied workers watching from the quay.

Which was, of course, why Ringo worked with thieves. I figured I'd have better luck looking for him in warehouse windows than down by the river. As I turned to head back up the embankment, a guttural voice called from behind me.

"Throw us down the line, would ye, lad?"

Since I happened to be passing a heavy, coiled rope attached to the quay by a big iron chain, I figured I was the 'lad.' And because not doing it would probably bring more attention than doing it, I heaved the massive rope down the slope toward the flat boat that bumped again the wall.

"Ta, then."

I looked quickly to make sure the word didn't mean anything other than "thanks." The lone fisherman was already at work tying off his boat, so I figured it didn't.

I watched him for a quick second. He wore a thick wool sweater a lot like mine, but gray from age. The man himself was probably in his forties, small in a way that reminded me of Sanda and her people, and he had the Welsh way of talking through a mouthful of gravel. The Fisherman looked up and caught me staring. He winked through twinkling eyes.

"Looking for work, are ye? Well, if ye'll take these nets up and help me untangle them, I'll pay ye a penny."

His voice sounded smiley, even if it was only in his eyes. A whole penny? I wondered what that was worth in this time. It was a penny more than I currently had, so I figured I could help the guy out. I nodded silently and Twinkles grinned.

"Right, then." He heaved a huge, slimy net out of the boat and held it up for me to grab. I barely hid a wince as my fingers slipped through the tangled lines. The net was a disgusting mess of gunk collected from a river that had once been full of raw sewage. Ick.

I hauled the net up to the quay while Twinkles finished clearing the decks of buckets of fish. The net was like a giant Gordian knot, and within a few minutes I gave up trying to stay clean while I worked on it.

By the time Twinkles made it up to the quay with his full haul of fish, I was laying out the last corner of the net. I was absurdly proud of having untangled the mess and unconsciously wiped a piece of hair off my face with the back of a filthy hand.

The gesture caught Twinkles' attention. He looked at me a long moment. "Lass ye are, then. And most none the wiser, I'd hazard."

I froze. Just like that my disguise was seen through – by a stranger. I must have looked ready to run because Twinkles suddenly shifted his tone of voice to something deliberately calm and quiet, like he was talking to a skittish animal. "No need to bolt, lass. I've none to tell."

I took a deep breath, then nodded quickly.

Twinkles continued in the same, soft voice. I got the sense he was probably good with kids and creatures, and my shoulders relaxed a notch. "Are ye alone then?" My eyes narrowed. Not a question a smart girl answers. Twinkles read my hesitation immediately and held up his hands as if to show they were empty. "I mean you no harm, truly." He held out his hand to shake. "Name's Gosford."

I wiped my slimy hand on my jeans. Ugh, I was going to pay for that later. "Saira," I said as I shook his calloused fisherman's hand.

He raised an eyebrow. "Traveler? Are ye an Elian, then? Me missus works in the big house. Ye may know her?"

Uh oh. "Sorry, I have to go." I practically jumped away from him in my hurry to bolt.

Gosford called after me in a quiet voice meant for my ears only. "Ye ever need help, Traveler, me boat's the *Sanda* and folk here know where to find it."

I spun and stared at him, open-mouthed. "The *Sanda*?"

Gosford smiled proudly. "Named for me granddaughter, just born. She lights up me life like a beacon, that one."

"It's a pretty name." I felt like I had to say something to cover my reaction.

Gosford just beamed. "And she's a lovely bairn." He suddenly fumbled in his pocket. "Yer penny!"

I probably needed that money more than he could ever know, but the look on Gosford's face when he talked about his baby granddaughter made me wish I had a grandfather who loved me like that. "Buy Sanda something pretty with it from me."

Gosford looked a little stunned, but he touched his cap to me and his eyes twinkled. "Our luck goes with ye then, miss."

I'd take whatever luck I could get. I gave him a quick wave and a smile and headed down the quay. I thought about my options as I walked. I needed to find my mother, who might either be in hiding or in major trouble. Archer was mixed up in his own mess with Silverback and the Family war, and he had clearly made his choice about helping me. I might have an ally in young Ringo, but probably only if I paid him, and in my current state of poverty, that wasn't going to happen.

I faced the fact that my impetuous decision to 'test my skills' was completely idiotic. I had jumped headfirst into a situation that rivaled the poop-water of the Thames for stinkiness. And now it was time to get myself out.

The London Bridge was just up ahead and I picked up my pace to get there, even as waves of doubt hit me. I didn't remember having seen a spiral on this side, and now that it was probably close to quitting time, the quay was bustling with dockworkers and shoppers.

A figure stood in the distance, watching me approach. My nerves jangled in alarm until I saw the moppy blond hair falling over an eye. Ringo. I gave him a very small wave and he grinned.

"What are you doing here?"

"Came to find ye."

"Why?"

"Thought ye might need more 'elp."

More than he could ever imagine. I looked speculatively at him, and then made a really quick decision. I could do this alone, but with two people it would be much easier. But mostly, I just liked Ringo and wanted his company.

"I need to find something on the bridge. But there are too many people around and I don't want to be seen."

I needed a look out, but Ringo did one better. "So ye need a distraction. No worries, I have a great trick for the docks."

"You do? Of course you do."

He grinned. "I'll see ye in five minutes."

With any luck I'd be gone before he got back, but I couldn't explain that to the kid. And he was already scrambling across the quay.

A moment later I heard his voice yell "Pints on the 'ouse at Morton's. Get 'em while they last!" A sudden commotion went up on the quay and people started rushing toward what I could only assume was Morton's. Obviously it was an effective ploy, but I figured I only had a couple of minutes.

"Will that do for ye?" Ringo's voice popped up at my shoulder and made me jump – which made him laugh.

"What will they do when they realize there's no free beer?"

"Yell and fuss at old Morton a bit. But it serves 'im right. 'E called the coppers on me last month and I've been owin' him."

I laughed as we jumped down to the bridge footings. The area was in shadow, even in the afternoon light. It was a perfect place to put a spiral.

Without thinking I grabbed my Maglite and flipped it on to illuminate the old stone. Ringo gasped. "What's that fer magic?"

Uh oh. Was there some paradox I'd just created by revealing future technology to someone who probably would never see another flashlight in his lifetime? I spotted the spiral scratched into the inside of a piling just as I turned to face Ringo. His expression was equal parts wary and wondering. I handed him the Maglite. He hesitated for just a moment, then took it carefully in his hand.

"You turn it off and on like this." I showed him the twist top. "Inside is a battery, which powers it, but if you leave the light on too long the battery will die."

"Do ye have to feed it?"

I looked at him in confusion until I finally realized what he meant. I stifled a smile so he didn't get offended. "A battery isn't alive, it's a power-source, like coal or steam."

He held the flashlight with something like awe. "Do ye make these in America then?"

"They will." I said it before I could stop myself, and Ringo's eyes narrowed at me speculatively. He produced my fountain pen and held it out to me.

"Can I trade for the torch?"

I was probably breaking some cardinal rule of time travel, but the kid looked so eager, I couldn't resist. I took the pen from him and stuck it back in my pocket. "You can have the Maglite, but please don't show it to anyone. They won't understand." I took another step toward the spiral. "I have to go."

I reached the piling and started tracing the spiral pattern on the stone. I could feel Ringo's eyes burning into my back, but my fingers were already moving of their own accord and I couldn't stop if I tried.

"There's a fisherman on the *Sanda* who might give you work. He seems like a good man." Maybe Gosford would take Ringo on and get him away from the thieves. At least I could hope so.

"Will ye be back?"

I turned to look at Ringo even as the hum of the spiral was filling my ears. I nodded. "Thank you, Ringo."

I could see the quizzical expression on his face as he mouthed the name I'd just called him. Then his eyes widened as he watched me, but I couldn't hear anything except the buzz and hum of the portal opening under my fingers. The edges glowed and the world heaved under my feet. I was distantly aware of Ringo's shout, but it sounded like it came from miles away. I was stretching and falling and suddenly the ground rushed up and smacked me in the face.

I felt like Dorothy landing in Oz after the tornado. Except there were no Munchkins to greet me, only the ornately-framed painting of the London Bridge surrounded by the abandoned tower room of some long-ago Clocker headmaster.

I didn't puke this time, though it was close. I didn't want to have to go find water to clean it up, so maybe practicality overruled my heaving guts.

What the hell had I been thinking? Since when did I do anything without a plan, or at least without being totally prepared? As Archer had so blithely said, once was a mistake, the second time was just stupidity. Maybe he didn't exactly say that, but it was there, hanging between us.

Part of me wanted to go down to the basement and wake his Vampire ass up so I could yell at him for being such a spineless jerk. The part of me that was still slightly sane knew that was ridiculous on every count. And then my wounded pride wanted nothing to do with him ever again. Except for the fact that today's conversation with him actually happened over a century ago and I'd certainly seen him since then. My head hurt with all the twists and turns in time-travel logic.

So instead I got up, dusted both nineteenth- and twenty-first-century dirt off my butt, and closed the velvet drapes over the London Bridge. I knew I'd be going back, but not until I was armed. With what, I wasn't quite sure, but certainly with more than a Maglite and a fancy pen.

I realized I should probably bring extra batteries for Ringo the next time I went. That thought made me smile as I slipped out of the tower room and locked the door behind me.

HUNTERS

The corridors were empty so I guessed most people were already in bed. My little bedroom, with my own stuff shoved into the drawers, felt like a sanctuary.

The *Caves and Caverns* book was still open on the nightstand. I wanted my own cave or cavern in London – someplace I could outfit for my own use when I traveled, central to where I needed to be, but still hidden from sight. Like Archer had his secret room under St. Brigid's school, I wanted a cave or tunnel somewhere in central London.

I opened the book to the Blackheath Caverns, skimmed the page, and then dismissed them as unworkable. They'd been discovered in the 1700s and had been in almost continuous use since then. The next page mentioned the London Bridge Catacombs, but there weren't any pictures. Just a description of abandoned tunnels under the London Bridge, where workers had recently found seventeenth-century human remains. Very creepy, but definitely a possibility given their location. There was an entrance near Tooley St., and I wondered if I could access it in 1888.

As I rummaged through a drawer for a clean t-shirt to sleep in, I found the flat map box. I slipped the key off my neck, opened it, and carefully spread it out on my bed.

The paper was stiff but intact. I examined the marked places on the map closely. There was one in Whitechapel, one near Waterloo, and another near King's Cross station. When I found the red dot at the base of the London Bridge, I suddenly understood what I was looking at. It was a map of time travel spirals throughout London.

Fascinating.

The outlying areas around London were also mapped, and there was a portal in Epping Wood, near a little village called Chingford. St. Brigid's was on the map too, but there was no red dot to mark it.

I wondered if anyone else besides me, Doran, and Adam knew about the portal in the painting in the north tower. An idea to be pondered later, after I was clean.

The jeans I had on were crusted with Thames slime and needed to be thoroughly washed. I grabbed a towel and slipped out to the bathroom, listening carefully before I turned on the shower. Nothing. The old manor must be totally soundproof.

I basically took a shower in my jeans, scrubbing them with soap and then hanging them over the radiator in my room. I'd learned that trick from my mom through all the traveling we'd done. The regular kind, on airplanes and trains, in the life I used to have – back when I thought I knew who I was, before my identity got pulled apart at the seams.

So now it was time to put myself together.

I woke up late the next morning, but my jeans were still damp so I chose the ones that seemed the least filthy. I pulled them on, and then realized when I'd worn them last.

In my pocket was a newly minted Victoria Jubilee shilling. Archer put that coin in my hand right before he went after Jack the Ripper. And suddenly, I saw his concern for me in a totally different light. He wasn't a coward and he didn't believe I was weak. Maybe the reason he wouldn't help me find my mother was that he was afraid I'd succeed. And my success would put me in the path of dangerous people.

It was hard for me to admit I could care about or matter to anyone but my mother. My life had pretty much been all about me, and I'd never really had to do things for other people. Oh sure, I'd spent a lifetime becoming capable and independent, able to survive on my own for weeks at a time. But I'd never taken on responsibility for anyone else.

I shoved the shilling back in my pocket, pulled on a clean San Pedro Muffler t-shirt, laced up my boots, and grabbed a notebook and a pen. I had research to do, and I wasn't going back until I was prepared.

I was sorry I'd missed my tea time with Miss Simpson. Her office door was closed and there was already a study group of younger kids in the library, so I found an empty table and settled in. First, I needed a little history, geography, and wardrobe information on the year 1888. I also needed whatever else I could find on Jack the Ripper's victims.

I scanned the stacks looking for references to Victorian times and found a catalogue of paintings from the era. Lots of lace and petticoats and bustles and it looked like corsets were still very much in fashion. Totally impractical for running or climbing. I usually dressed like a guy anyway, so I decided that it would probably be my best bet in the past. I found paintings of the men and studied them. My big white sweater would probably work for the river, but anywhere else I should probably dress like a servant or a tradesman. Or maybe a student.

I thought about Archer's clothes. Black trousers, a white shirt, and either a topcoat or his fantastic cape. I wondered if he still had any of his old clothes in his basement hideaway. Elian Manor was possibly another source for the right wardrobe. I bet those closets still had clothes in them from the 1600s.

"Hey, where have you been?"

I jumped and almost knocked over a stack of books at the sound of Ava's voice. It took a minute of serious juggling to keep the whole pile from going down. Ava was grinning from ear to ear and I scowled at her. "You knew I'd do that, didn't you?"

"I couldn't have choreographed it better if I'd tried." She sat down at the table I'd covered with books. "Where were you last night?"

Uh oh. I was sure my aura flipped to green and Ava could see the lie, but I said it anyway. "Crashed early."

"And slept late, I see." She avoided my eyes and turned a book over to read the title. "Doing a little British history study?"

205

I'd never had a problem telling my mom white lies to keep her off my back, but now I felt guilty not telling Ava the truth. I took a deep breath and opened my notebook to a page where I'd written an address. "Do you know Chelsea very well?"

Ava sighed. "My mother found the perfect antique store there that she just *has* to show me."

The more time I spent with Ava, the more I liked her. I grinned in sympathy. "When are you going?"

"I've been trying to get out of it. Why?"

"I have a big favor to ask." I handed her the address and dug the Jubilee shilling from my pocket. "There's a rare coin dealer just off Kings Road, and I need as many small coins from about 1870 to 1887 as you can get for this."

Ava flipped the coin through her fingers as she studied it. "Is it real?"

"Yes."

"It's gorgeous."

"Yeah."

"And you want to trade it?"

"For as many older, small coins as you can get. Hopefully it's worth more now than it was then."

Ava looked at me carefully. "You got this then, didn't you?"

My ability to lie to her was fading fast. "When?"

She read the date on the coin. "1887?"

"A friend gave it to me."

"And you're going back there, aren't you?"

This girl didn't miss a trick, which meant her brother wouldn't either. I decided to trust them with the truth. "Can you grab Adam and meet me in the north tower?"

Ava studied me a moment, then nodded. "We have a lesson with Miss Simpson in ten minutes. We can come after that. Where's the north tower?"

"Adam knows."

Ava tucked the coin and the address into an inside pocket of her skirt. "I'll see what I can do about trading your coin in Chelsea. Maybe this weekend."

"Great, thank you."

"You're welcome, Saira." Her eyes didn't leave mine, and I had the feeling she was looking way beyond my aura. "It's going to be hard, you know that, right?" She wasn't talking about trading the coin. "You have friends that will help you, though."

"It's a new thing for me, Ava. I'll try to be worthy." I tried for self-effacing, and she got it. She waved and left the library.

I saw Mr. Shaw outside the window, striding toward the front of the school building with what looked like fierce purpose. I tucked myself behind a bookshelf and watched as Mr. Shaw threw down his mug of tea and stormed up to a sleek black Maserati that had just pulled down the driveway. Even though I couldn't hear anything, I could feel the rage pouring off him.

The front doors of the Maserati opened, and two of the scariest looking, jackbooted, leather-wearing, tattoo-sporting skinheads I've ever seen peeled themselves from the car.

I almost dove under the library table.

If I thought I'd been feeling like prey before, these two made me want to run for the hills. They had completely expressionless faces under their mirrored aviator sunglasses, and their body language was reading calm, collected, and coiled. The word 'hunters' hit me so hard it's like they were broadcasting it. I held my breath as Mr. Shaw approached them.

The driver was the one taking most of Mr. Shaw's heat. He crossed his arms and leaned insolently against the spotless luxury car. The Hunters looked like they were about twenty-one or twenty-two, and the attitude they projected was total disrespect. The muscles in Mr. Shaw's back bunched under his jacket, and I wondered if he was actually going to Shift right there.

A few other kids in the library noticed the scene unfolding outside the windows. When Ms. Rothchild stepped outside, I knew it was her the minute I saw the designer suit and stiletto heels. Everything about her was pointy and sharp and vaguely dangerous, and I thought 'Rothbitch' was a perfect name for her.

Every kid in the library stepped back a little, as if they didn't want her to catch them watching. Mr. Shaw spun to face her, and his eyes narrowed as she approached. The driver peeled off his shades and threw Ms. Rothchild the barest nod as if to say, 'I'm here. What did you want?'

Ms. Rothchild was all smiles and concern as she got between the Hunters and the Bear. The Hunters watched her placidly, and after a few more words, mostly from Ms. Rothchild, the Bear's shoulders tightened even more menacingly. Yet amazingly, he backed down. I watched in shock as Mr. Shaw stooped down to pick up his empty tea mug, throw one last hateful look at the smirking Hunters, and storm away past the library windows.

For one breathtaking moment I thought he had seen me watching through the window, but if he had, he gave no indication of it as he disappeared around the corner out of sight.

By the time I looked back at the Hunters, the Rothbitch was all smiles. Finally, the driver nodded curtly, put his shades back on, and went around to the back of the Maserati. There was a dragon painted on the back of his leather jacket and the name "Mal" tattooed on the back of his neck. What, in case he forgets his name? He opened the trunk, pulled something out, then tossed one to the other Hunter. They were both holding crossbows; the compound kind that looked totally accurate, deadly, and medieval.

Mal said something to Ms. Rothchild, got her answer, then nodded once at his partner. The Hunters flung their crossbows into the rear seat and slid into the Maserati. The powerful car roared to life, but instead of turning back down the drive, the Hunters drove the sports car past the school and out of sight.

Once they'd gone, the Rothbitch's fake smile disappeared like it was wiped off with an eraser, and her expression was cold, hard, and very pointed. I shuddered. That was not a woman I wanted to be alone with, and the Hunters she had brought to St. Bridgid's were the stuff of nightmares.

I saw the Crow come into the library with her murder, and I wanted to get out before she saw me. Mongers gave me chills, and I wasn't sure it was necessarily a personal thing. More like an animal instinct. They came, I went – it was better that way.

Adam and Ava were already inside the north tower room when I got there, and they had the curtain open in front of the London Bridge. Ava turned to me as I entered the room. "You went back through this?"

I looked at Adam. "Told anyone else about the painting?"

His spine went rigid. "Of course not."

"He showed me because we're helping you, and because we need to know our assets before we go into this."

My eyes narrowed. "I'm feeling pretty protective of this whole tower all of a sudden."

Adam shrugged. "Makes sense. It's a Clocker place and we're not Clockers." His quick agreement threw me off, and I forced myself to take a breath.

"I'm sorry. I suck at asking for help, and you guys have been really great." I caught the beginnings of Adam's smirk, and I shot him a look. "Except you, not so much."

The smirk widened into a grin, and I felt something lift off my shoulders. I stuck my tongue out at him for good measure, just so I didn't grin back, but when he waggled his eyebrows suggestively, I burst out laughing. "Pain in the ass."

"Takes one to know one."

Ava winced. "You're both shockingly adolescent."

I looked over at Adam. Yup. He was the big, charming, annoyingly good-looking version of every twelve-year-old boy I've ever known.

I forced my brain back to the task at hand. "You mentioned assets. I'm not really sure we have any."

Ava shook her head. "First we need to know what you're planning. Then we'll understand better how we can help."

Adam chimed in. "What's in Victorian London?"

I hoped they truly were my friends. Otherwise I was in very big trouble. "My mother." I could almost hear the dramatic movie music go "duh duh duhhhh." But then Adam's eyes narrowed.

"She's an Elian, right? How come she can't come back?"

"She might be a Vampire's prisoner." It's not every day a person can say that with a straight face. It kind of freaked me out that they took my announcement seriously.

"You know for sure she's there?" Adam got very business-like and it was oddly comforting.

"I saw her in the Whitechapel Underground station in 1888."

"What were you doing in Whitechapel station?"

Deep breath. "Running from a serial killer."

To his credit, Adam didn't lose the business-like tone of voice. "The Vampire?"

"Maybe." And here was the kicker. "It was Jack the Ripper."

Adam's eyebrows shot up to his hairline and I could swear I heard Ava's jaw go 'thunk' on the floor. I waited for one of them to call me a crack-smoking liar. But then Adam surprised me yet again with that dumb grin that makes him look like a kid in a candy store.

"I love having no idea what happens next!"

Ava shook her head. "Adam, we can't see the future because it's the past – it's already happened." I looked from one to the other of the Seer twins as if they'd both lost their minds. Ava's worried gaze suddenly turned to me. "We can't see into the past to help you there. The only place we can affect anything is here, in this time." She considered for a moment. "Do you think your grandmother will go back with you?"

"Millicent? Not a chance! Besides, I don't think she can travel."

"Not even to help your mother?" Ava clearly didn't believe me, though I noticed that Adam hadn't said a word.

"Millicent hates my mother for leaving her in charge of the Family. She made it very clear that it was my mother's fault she had no life."

Ava's eyes were wide. "I didn't know you were in line for Head."

I looked at Adam. "You didn't tell her? I thought you were all twisted up about your *prophecy*."

Ava's gaze landed squarely on Adam and he squirmed uncomfortably. Her expression was full of hurt. Adam took a deep breath, steeled himself with a quick glance at me, and launched into the Cliffs Notes version of my history. "It's possible that Saira is the child *fated for one, born to another* from Aislin's prophecy. If the 'one' is time. Apparently her mother is Lady Elian's great-aunt who went forward."

Hearing my story out of Adam's mouth like that made it actually sound credible. No wonder he freaked out when I told him my mom's history. Ava recited the prophecy under her breath.

"Fated for one, born to another
The child must seek to claim the Mother
The Stream will split and the branches will fight
Death will divide, and lovers unite
The child of opposites will be the one
To heal the Dream that War's undone."

Aislin's prophecy sent chills up my spine just like the first time I heard it, but I still had no idea what it meant. Apparently, neither did the twins. "You're right, if Saira was supposed to be born in another time, she could be *fated for one, born to another*. Ava suddenly turned to face me. "You're going back to 1888 to find your mum, right?"

"That's why we're here talking, isn't it?"

She turned back to Adam. "So 'the child' is seeking to 'claim the mother.' That definitely fits."

Apparently, I was invisible.

"But what's the 'stream' that splits? And 'branches' that fight?"

I refused to be spoken around. "It's the branches of the Families. You guys have been fighting forever."

Adam nodded thoughtfully. "But the in-fighting really only ramped up in the last couple hundred years."

A conversation suddenly replayed itself in my brain. "According to Mr. Shaw it happened in 1871. After Will Shaw slaughtered the council." I had their attention now.

"That was very near the time you went back to." Ava was back to her wide-eyed look.

"Seventeen years. Not that near."

211

It's weird to feel time slow down. The air sort of shimmers and gets thick, just like it did when Adam and I had the same thought at the same exact moment.

"Oh my God!"

"How old are you?"

Ava was a heartbeat behind us, but she put into words what both of us were thinking. "Saira's mum left England around the time the council was murdered and the Family branches started seriously fighting."

This time I was the one with the brilliant idea. "Not only did she leave England. She left 1871. What if she's the reason the *stream* split? What if the stream is the time stream, and it split because she left her native time and never went back?"

"But she's there now, right?"

"Hang on, I'm not through. I could be the split since I've never lived in the time I was *fated* for."

Adam spoke very quietly directly to me. "You realize you *are* the child in Aislin's prophecy. You're the one who's going to stop the war between the Families."

I couldn't tear my eyes away from his. It was like he held my gaze, and my voice, in a vise grip. All I could do was shake my head. I finally managed to croak out something that sounded completely weak, even to my own ears. "It's not my war."

"It is now, Saira. They have your mother."

THE GENE POOL

The twins had to bolt out of the tower room not to be late to their next class with Miss Rogers. I felt like there were a million things I should do to prepare for going back to find my mom, but I couldn't hold on to any one idea long enough to do it.

Finally, I locked up my tower and just started walking.

The Clocker Tower in the north corner was mine, just like the Seer Tower in the west belonged to the twins. That thought gave me an idea and I decided to take the journey at a sprint, just to stay in shape.

The third floor of the school was basically unused, and I didn't meet anyone on my way to the Seer Tower. I could picture a map of the place in my head, and it felt good to finally know my way around.

The small niche was where I'd pictured it, just outside the door to the tower. There was a statue perched on the ledge inside the niche, but I ignored it and felt up high, out of casual sight.

There it was, just where I thought. Adam's stash. It truly amazed me that confident people could be so lazy. I pulled down the envelope and opened the note.

"The apple tree at sunset."

How he was going to pull that one off I had no idea. The school was still in lockdown mode, and with the appearance of the Hunters on campus, even I wasn't feeling so confident about breaking out. But I wanted whatever information Adam could give me from his visions, and no way was I going to feed his arrogance by letting him win. I pulled a pen from my pocket and quickly wrote on the flip side of his note, then stuffed the whole thing back up in the niche.

I'd won Adam's game, so I debated what to do next. I hadn't done any classwork yet, and I wanted more time in one of Mr. Shaw's science classes, so I took off for the first floor of the school.

Class had already begun, but Mr. Shaw saw me through the window and waved me inside. The students looked a couple years younger than me and I felt like the old lady of the class, but Mr. Shaw directed me toward a seat next to the Connor kid who had flirted with Miss Rogers. The kid grinned at me and bent his head back to his notes. Shaw was talking about genetics and blood, and within a minute I knew I was in a class of Family kids.

"All right. Who can tell me the primary gene for Duncan's Descendants?"

He was talking about Mongers, and Connor's hand shot up. "Yes, Mr. Edwards?"

"A genetic variant on MAO-A, the 'warrior gene'."

"Indeed. Mr. Saracean, Mr. Rothchild, please take note." Mr. Shaw was scowling at two dark-haired boys in the back of the room. Mongers, was my guess.

"MAO-A is called the 'warrior gene' because a rare genetic variant causing its deficiency is associated with aggression and criminality." The Bear looked pointedly at the boys in the back of the room. The Rothchild kid glared back at him in a way that made me think he was the Rothbitch's spawn.

"And what is the primary gene in Aislin's Descendants?"

Connor looked around the room. No one was raising their hand, so his went up again. I saw Mr. Shaw hide a smile, and I wondered if this Connor was the nephew I'd seen in the Shifter genealogy.

"Connor?"

The kid answered in a confident voice. "DRD4."

"Which is what, exactly?"

"A dopamine receptor."

"Excellent."

Connor looked proud that he'd gotten it right. That little tweak in attitude was the difference between seeming like a know-it-all or just being smart, and it made me like him. I caught Connor's eye and smiled. He grinned back. One of his canine teeth hung a little over his lip and gave his smile a goofiness that made me laugh.

"I'm calling them 'primary' genes, not dominant genes, because they are the ones most affected by each Family's heredity. And those two are the easiest genetic primaries within the Families because they are specific genes. For the Descendants of Goran it's a bit different. A completely unique gene is present in each of the Shifter clans and provides the animal characteristics for that clan. What Goran's Descendants all have in common is an oncogene mutation which targets that specific animal gene. For example, a Shifter whose animal relies on speed as its primary physical characteristic will have an oncogene mutation around the ACTN-3 gene, which activates the muscle protein alpha-actinin 3, and that helps muscles contract powerfully at high speeds."

I spoke before I even knew I'd opened my mouth. "Is that why a lot of Shifters are athletes?"

Mr. Shaw considered for a moment. "In my estimation, a lot of the very successful professional athletes have some of the genetic markers of various Shifter clans, but I'd argue they lack the one, unifying, dominant gene that marks them as true Descendants."

Mr. Shaw looked around the classroom to make sure he had everyone's attention. "And that is the subject of today's class." Pencils came out and notebooks were opened. He spoke the magic words and suddenly everyone was paying attention.

"Genes are like a band that's just starting out." A couple of kids snickered and Mr. Shaw had his audience. "They're sort of just playing tunes here and there; maybe they even show a little promise, but nothing really happens until they get a promoter." A couple of kids laughed.

"Now, suddenly, the band gets an audience and their skills can really start to shine. The thing is, promoters are only as good as the connections they have, which means the band will only really be able to build an audience if their promoter has juice." He looked around the room.

"So here it is in genetic terms. The juice that gives the promoter its power is a protein called neuregulin 1. There's a whole lot of it in the brains of babies because, of course, the promoters are hard at work pushing the genes to do their jobs. Have a faulty supply of neuregulin 1 and problems like schizophrenia and bipolar disorder come up. But have an abundant supply, and the genes get super-promoted to be the best they can be."

I got it in a way I'd never understood genetics before, and this guy was teaching a bunch of kids. Impressive.

"That's obviously the very simplified explanation of neuregulin 1. In the average human there are five types of neuregulin 1, each one feeding various gene promoters their proteins." He paused to flip a chart on the board that outlined the various dominant genes of different branches of the five Families. I wished I had my phone with me just so I could snap a picture of it to study later. It looked like important stuff.

"Descendants of the Immortals have a sixth neuregulin 1 type of protein. Its only function is to juice the promoter of our particular primary gene. So, in Seers, as Mr. Edwards pointed out, it's the dopamine receptor on the D4 gene whose promoter gets juiced."

He looked around the room again. "Did you know that an over-abundance of any other neuregulin 1 type of protein on DRD4 can cause delusions, one of the symptoms of delusional schizophrenia?"

"So Seers are just a protein away from being delusional? Awesome." The Rothbitch's Spawn had such a sneer to his voice it completely broke the thrall of Mr. Shaw's lecture.

"I believe aggressive criminals come from any type of protein interaction on the genetic variant that causes MAO-A deficiency. That makes you rather common, don't you think, Mr. Rothchild?"

The mild tone of voice the Bear used with that brat was the perfect way to insult someone without lowering himself to the Spawn's level. I filed it away for future reference.

"In any case, it is the presence of neuregulin 1 type 6 that kicks off the aberrant primary genes in our Families."

He gave us all a very serious look. "And something to remember. Each Family has a dominant blood type to go along with their mutated genes. The introduction of blood from another

216

Descendant Family type will most often be rejected and can even cause death."

Connor nodded. "Which is why we're not allowed to give blood to common blood banks?"

"Exactly why."

The bell rang, and students immediately put away notebooks and gathered up their stuff to go. The Rothbitch's Spawn mumbled something that sounded like, "And why mixed-bloods always die."

The two Monger kids continued whispering furiously under their breath as they escaped the classroom, and I could feel the tension in my own shoulders leave with them. Weird. Mongers I didn't even know sent me into fight or flight.

I waited in my seat for the rest of the students to clear. I hoped Mr. Shaw would have time to talk, and I also wanted to study the chart on the wall. I could see the links to genes for Mongers and Seers – they were almost direct lines to MAO-A and DRD4. The line for Shifters was a little less simple, with a symbol for an oncogene mutation promoting various different gene combinations.

"I still haven't memorized all the dominant gene combinations for Shifters." Connor's voice startled me out of my trance as I studied the chart. Mr. Shaw was talking to a red-headed kid by the door, but everyone else was gone.

"You are a Shifter, right?"

Connor grinned. "And you're the Clocker. I'm Connor by the way." His grin was infectious.

I held out my hand. "Nice to meet you. I'm Saira."

"I've seen you running in the halls with the big Arman guy. You should run with me sometime. I can turn into a grey Wolf."

I laughed. "No way I could keep up with you."

He regarded me for a moment. "You're rare here, like me. Until my brother, Logan, comes next year, I'm the only Shifter kid at St. Brigid's. And my half-sister, Alexandra, was the only one when she was here too."

"Alexandra ... Rowen?"

Connor looked at me funny. "You know her?"

I shook my head. "I saw your names in a genealogy book in the library. It didn't say you guys were related."

He shrugged. "Her mum was a ballet dancer, like Alex is. She was famous when she was alive, so Alex uses the same last name."

"Can I help you, Mr. Edwards?" The Bear's voice plowed through our conversation like a bulldozer.

Connor went over to the Family genetics chart. "Yeah, I had a question. I know we don't talk about Suckers in class, but this chart doesn't show a gene for them. What's the deal?"

I looked closer. Connor was right, there were no primary genes listed for the Descendants of Aeron. Just the symbol NRG1-6, like every other Descendant had.

Mr. Shaw looked pained. "Yes, the Descendants of Aeron are part of the five Families, and thus, they carry the neuregulin 1 type 6 protein."

"But I thought it's an oxymoron for Death to be born."

Mr. Shaw smiled. "I hadn't heard it put quite like that before. That's good. It's true, Death's Descendants are made, but they are also born, just not into Death's bloodline." The Bear looked at us both significantly. Could we riddle it out? A light bulb snapped on in my head. It came from a conversation I'd had with Archer, and I tried it out on Mr. Shaw.

"What if Vampires carry the neuregulin 1 type 6 protein because they were born as Descendants of other Immortals?"

Connor stared at me, open-mouthed, while Mr. Shaw nodded with a sort of grim look on his face. "That's not possible! Suckers are … evil!" Connor's voice exploded from him.

Mr. Shaw looked at him levelly. "Some of us believe Saira is correct, though it's definitely not commonly held knowledge. Nor is it something that should be talked about outside this room. There are those among the Families who would go to great lengths to keep that information from ever being proven."

"But how does it happen?" Connor was still angry, but his desire for knowledge was winning.

"There is an ancient disorder called porphyria which produces several of the same conditions we see in Aeron's line. There are scientists among us, myself included, who believe that Vampires are infected with a deadly mutation of that disorder. When they bite Ungifted humans, the mutation infects them and they die. But when they bite those of us with neuregulin 1 type 6, the protein treats the disorder like a dominant condition, and it activates and enhances it to the point that a Vampire is created."

"But Vampires are dead." Connor said.

"You're stereotyping because they're called 'Vampires.' As far as I can tell, 'Vampire' was likely just the simplest, most universally understood way for our ancestors to categorize the state of being of Aeron's Descendants after infection. They're not dead. Their cells are in a sort of suspended animation, much like what happens to Saira's body when she's out of her native time."

Connor shifted his gaze to me. "That's kind of wrong, you know."

I shrugged. "So is turning into a Wolf."

Mr. Shaw laughed out loud. "Off to class with you, Connor. Ms. Rothchild will be all too happy to make an example of you if you're late."

Connor made a sour face. "She's even worse than her kid."

Mr. Shaw suddenly got stern. "And she's a teacher here, Mr. Edwards. I expect you to behave accordingly."

Connor mock saluted him. "Yes Sir, Uncle Bob, Sir."

Connor flung a smile at me as he raced for the door. "See you around, Saira!" And suddenly the kid was gone.

Mr. Shaw was still looking at the place where Connor had been standing. "I'm proud of him, he's a good kid. But his mouth moves faster than his brain sometimes, and I worry the wrong people will be listening." He gave himself a sort of mental shake and his eyes met mine. "I'm curious, what made you connect Family Descendants with Vampires?"

Uh oh. Not comfortable territory. But since I seemed to be stepping in things with both feet recently, I took a deep breath.

"I need to know how to defeat a Vampire."

SELF-DEFENSE

Mr. Shaw looked me in the eyes and then said with a perfectly straight face, "It's a useful skill to have. What makes you think I know how to do that?"

I shrugged. "Your prowess and strength? You're the coolest teacher I know? I'm totally desperate?"

He laughed. "I'll take 'prowess and strength' for my ego and 'totally desperate' for the truth. Can I ask why you need this information?"

I winced. "Depends."

"On what?"

"Whether you'll try to stop me?"

He regarded me for a moment. "Fair enough. How about this. Tell me the truth and I won't try to stop you. I will tell you if I think you're being an idiot, and I'll be angry if you ignore my advice, but I won't stop you."

I thought about it. "Will you get other people to stop me?"

"Do you want to be stopped?"

"No."

"Then no, I won't."

I took a deep breath and told him about traveling to 1888, and about seeing my mom and being chased by the Ripper through Whitechapel. I told him a little about Archer, but not that he was a Vampire now.

At some point during my recital, Mr. Shaw got up and locked the door to his classroom. He gestured for me to keep talking as he started pacing the room. I told him how I'd gone back to 1888 again, and what I'd overheard between Archer and Silverback – about Jack the Ripper, and about Will Shaw.

"Is there anything you want to know about him? I mean, I can ask Archer next time I go back."

Mr. Shaw's distant expression came back into laser focus on my face. "About that ..."

"If you're going to try and talk me out of it, don't bother. I have to go back there and get my mom. I'm the only one who can." I tried to keep my voice steady, but failed.

"I wasn't going to talk you out of it. Of course you have to go. As you say, there seems to be no alternative."

"Oh. Thanks."

"Don't thank me. I'm sure your mother wouldn't."

"Why not?"

"Because I am going to give you some tools that will put you squarely in the path of a serial killing Vampire."

We agreed to meet in his office before dinner, and he told me to wear comfortable shoes for walking outdoors. I shot him a raised-eyebrow look and he grinned. "You don't think you'll be safe in the woods with a Bear?" He teased.

"Actually, it's those Hunters and their crossbows I'm more worried about."

Mr. Shaw scowled. "You're right to worry about the Romanians. They're very bad news."

"So how come they're here?"

Mr. Shaw looked me straight in the eyes. "Because apparently St. Brigid's has a resident Vampire, and they've been contracted to find him."

I dragged my eyes away from Mr. Shaw's so he wouldn't see the truth on my face. Which was that I knew where that Vampire slept. Mr. Shaw let his next class in and they filed in past me with curious looks. Someone poked me in the ribs.

"Hey, stranger. First the mean roommate, and now you're hanging with the toughest teacher in school? You have a thing for punishment, huh?" Olivia grinned at me.

"Mr. Shaw's a good guy." He didn't need me to defend him, but I liked Olivia and felt she should know that.

Her voice dropped conspiratorially. "Of course he is. It's all these idiots who don't do their homework who get the rough and gruff stuff."

"See you at dinner?" she said as she went into the classroom. There was so much smile packed in that little voice it made me happy just to hear it. I nodded and waved goodbye as Mr. Shaw closed the classroom door behind Olivia.

I wasn't sure what to do next. I couldn't go to Archer to warn him about the Hunters, and I had no idea where the twins were. The library was my best bet for filling in the blanks that I couldn't learn anywhere else.

A couple of small study groups were working there, but no one I knew, so I went back to the genealogy books I'd found earlier and settled into a relatively empty corner of the room to read.

I pulled out the Shifter Family tree and realized what I'd missed the first time I saw it. Connor's mom was Mr. Shaw's sister. Connor and Logan Edwards shared their father with Alexandra Rowen, so it looked like separate branches of the tree.

Someone blocked out my light and my head jolted up to see Adam standing over me. "What are you looking at?"

"Shifters. I met this kid, Connor Edwards, today." I pointed to his name then slid my finger across the page to Alexandra's name. "You must have known his half-sister when she was here, right?"

Adam slammed the book shut and threw it onto the pile of other books. "Come on. Ava and I are leaving and we need to talk first."

"Where are you going?"

"The parentals suddenly decided we needed a family weekend. They're already on their way from London. We leave in an hour."

He walked away without a backward glance for me. I was annoyed, but I followed him anyway. He led me out a side door that put us near the conservatory, and I took off running. Adam gave a shout and came after me, but I had enough of a head start to stay in the lead.

The old apple tree was one field over, so I ran up the stone wall and across the top like I was part cat. Adam swore under his breath behind me as he tried to keep up.

I finally got to the tree, plucked an apple off a branch, and dropped down to sit on the wall. Adam skidded to a halt beside me. "I hate it when you do that." He really was mad, but that only made me defiant.

"Yeah? Well I hate being ordered around by a surly Seer."

Imagine my shock when he actually apologized. "Sorry. I don't know why my parents suddenly felt the need to yank us from school and I really don't want to go. I didn't mean to take it out on you."

"Why so agro when I asked about Alexandra Rowen?"

Adam looked me directly in the eyes and spoke very clearly, as if making sure I heard every word. "I don't want to talk about it."

Wow. Major touchiness, which of course meant I wanted to know everything about her. But I somehow managed to bite my tongue and change the subject instead.

"Your note said you wanted to meet out here?" That caught him off guard. "Your note. In your stash?"

His eyes narrowed. "Damn. You found it?"

"Of course I did, you amazingly arrogant piece of work. I told you over-confident people don't hide things well. Right outside the Seer Tower? Seriously?"

He finally cracked a smile. "And here I thought I was being really crafty. I guess that means I don't get the kiss?"

"Not a chance in hell, big guy. But it does mean you tell me whatever you've Seen about me."

"What if you don't like it."

"It's not for you to decide. We had a deal."

He grinned. "Okay fine, I've seen you naked in my bed."

I narrowed my eyes at him. "You are such a liar."

"Like or don't like?"

I bopped him on the head with my apple. "The truth. That's the deal."

He laughed. "What makes you so sure that's not the truth?"

"Because I have no intention of ever ending up in your bed, naked or otherwise."

"Ow, that hurts."

"Deal with it."

He was still chuckling, and I had to admit it made him pretty cute. But every fiber of my being knew better than to ever fall for a guy like Adam. "I'm waiting."

His expression got serious. "It's really not a good idea for us to tell what we See."

"I'm a big girl, Adam. I can take it."

He took a deep breath and studied me for a moment. It wasn't the kind of look a guy gives to a girl he likes. It was the kind someone gives when they're about to reveal bad news.

"I Saw you in London, somewhere by the London Bridge."

Interesting. "What was I doing?"

"Looking for someplace to hide."

"From who?"

He shook his head. "I never Saw who. But I Saw someone step out of the shadows and follow you."

That could be anyone. Archer maybe? Or Slick? "That's it?"

"You went underground or in a tunnel or something."

I nodded. This could be useful. "Can you describe the entrance or anything around that I could identify?"

"It was definitely under the bridge because there were pillars nearby. I think it was near some steps or something like that."

"Cool. Thanks."

"Thanks? Why?" Adam asked.

"Saves me having to look in the wrong spot."

"You want to go there?"

I shrugged. "I've been looking for my own stash spot. Someplace hidden that's been around for a couple hundred years."

"You mean for when you go back? But how can you leave something for yourself?"

"I haven't figured that out yet."

"What would you hide there?"

"I don't know, food, medicine, weapons …" I shrugged my shoulders because I truly didn't know what I might need in the past. I just hated feeling unprepared.

Adam shook his head. "You're so … not a girl."

I scoffed. "First you're talking smack about me naked in your bed, and now you say I'm not a girl? You're a very confused boy, Adam Arman."

He laughed. "I mean you're not like any girl I know. You're fearless, and smart, and much faster than me." The twelve-year-old boy was back. It was my favorite version of Adam because he lost the cool arrogance that put me on edge around him.

I shrugged. "I do what I have to do to survive. I've done it my whole life."

"I'm sorry."

I bit back the clever retort and took a deep breath. "Yeah, me too. I look at you and Ava and think you guys are so lucky you have each other, and two parents who love you."

"They're going to be here any minute, and Ava wants them to meet you. Come on." He stood up on the wall and held his hand out to help me up. I tossed my apple core down and took his hand. When Adam pulled me up, he shocked me by kissing my forehead. "You've got me and Ava, whether you want us or not." He took off across the wall at speed, and I was so surprised, I didn't catch him the whole way back to the school.

The Armans were in the main entry hall chatting with Miss Simpson when we arrived. Ava was already downstairs with an overnight bag, and she grabbed my hand. "Thanks."

I was surprised. "For what?"

"For meeting them."

She nodded at Adam who slipped quietly up the stairs before their parents could say anything. There was a pause in the adults' conversation, and Ava stepped forward. "Mum, Daddy, I'd like you to meet our friend, Saira. Saira, these are my parents."

Mr. Arman was tall and looked like the grown-up, conservative version of his son in a cashmere sweater and slacks. Mrs. Arman was

225

exquisitely elegant in that way rich women are, all the way from her simple pearl earrings down to pointy-toed boots under dark jeans. I had to work my confidence up just to shake her hand. "It's very nice to meet you, Mr. and Mrs. Arman."

When Mrs. Arman took my hand, her eyes widened and her friendly smile faltered for the barest fraction of a second. Then suddenly her smile grew warmer and she clasped my hand in hers. "It's so nice to finally meet you, Saira."

Ava and her father both had slightly odd looks on their faces as Mrs. Arman kept my hand in hers. "Will you walk with me?" Mrs. Arman's voice sounded musical with a vaguely French accent under her crisp English.

"Sure." How anyone could refuse this woman anything was beyond me. She looked back at her husband. "James, please ask Adam to bring his leather bag. The canvas one he's packing is disgusting."

Adam was clearly nowhere in sight, but she must have been able to See what he'd be bringing. It was disconcerting to hear her speak so directly about being able to See the future.

Mrs. Arman kept my hand in hers as she led me down the front steps. There was a new black Mercedes-Maybach parked in the driveway, with a driver standing beside it. It was the kind of luxury car that came with optional bullet-proof glass. These people had serious money.

"Thank you for walking with me, Saira. I don't want Ava to overhear us." She stopped and faced me, and I realized all her height was in her boot heels. I suddenly wasn't quite so intimidated by her.

"My son will get over his crush on you soon enough to make a useful ally. Unfortunately, he has learned how vulnerable he is, but the walls he has in place are good for you both." She was knocking the wind out of me with each word and I was scrambling to keep up. She barely noticed.

"Don't let him follow you into the tunnels. He'll want to protect you, but he can't. Not yet. Not until he accepts that there's someone else." The blood rushed to my face and I was about to protest, but Mrs. Arman's eyes went unfocused again, and then she gasped. "Oh!

You can trust Tom, but his mother never told— Oh dear! I'm sorry, I have to talk to my husband."

Mrs. Arman let go of my hand and started back toward the door. Right before she went inside, she turned. "I look forward to getting to know you, Saira. We'll all figure out how to be there for you in the end."

She rushed inside and left me alone on the path. Until Mrs. Arman spoke to me, I would have denied with every last breath that there could ever be something between Adam and me. And now, suddenly, I was sad that it would apparently never be anything at all.

The thing that had made Mrs. Arman go all nervous and flustery was a vision about Tom and his mother. I guessed she meant Tom Landers? And since Adam and his mom both saw me in the tunnels, I better be prepared for the London Bridge catacombs.

Ava came outside to find me. "Hey. Are you okay?"

"Yeah. I'm just processing."

She looked concerned. "Anything you want to talk about?"

Whatever I said to her would get back to Adam, so I sidestepped. "Adam once mentioned that he dated a ballerina. Was that Alexandra Rowen by any chance?"

Clearly I'd hit something raw with that question. "I can't talk about that. That's Adam's story to tell."

The front door to the school opened, and the driver exited with Ava and Adam's bags over his shoulder. I noticed Adam's was a leather bag, so his mother had won that round. Ava whispered fiercely. "Please don't mention Alex to him. It isn't fair."

I searched her eyes for some clue to what she meant, but there was only pleading in them. "I won't say anything."

She gave my hand a squeeze and palmed my coin to show me she had it. "If we go to Chelsea, I'll try to change your money." Then she raced off to join her family at the car.

Adam was watching me curiously while his parents loaded into the fancy vehicle. I tried to smile at him but none came, so I just waved instead.

"Goodbye, Saira. Bring your sweater to London this weekend; it's going to rain." Mrs. Arman's voice rang out clearly, yet with a genuine friendliness. Adam looked sharply at his mother, then back at me with a question in his eyes. I suddenly got defiant. No Seer was going to determine my fate. That job was mine, and mine alone.

I blew Adam a kiss, watched just long enough to see shocked expressions land on his family's faces, and went inside. I laughed when the door shut behind me, more from nerves than humor.

Miss Simpson stepped out of the library. "That was interesting."

I don't know what astonished me more, that she'd been spying or that she admitted it. "Which part?"

"Well, I didn't hear what Camille said to you, of course, but I imagine it had to do with her son."

"Why does everyone think there's something between me and Adam?"

She sighed. "You remember the history I told you? About Jera and Goran?" I nodded, suddenly acutely aware that I was speaking to the headmistress of the school. "Then you also remember that the Immortals declared there could never be another mix of Families."

"Mrs. Arman wasn't bothered that Adam might like me. Doesn't that seem like things might be changing?"

"Well, as I can't begin to wonder at her motives, I can only tell you that the Armans are powerful allies to have. They are also playing a game of Family politics, and therefore ultimately, have their own best interests at heart."

"So how much weight should I give to what she said then?"

Miss Simpson smiled. "If Camille offered insight or assistance, take it. If she offered advice, take it with a grain of salt."

I nodded. "Okay."

"I'm still working on a class schedule for you, dear, but I understand you've been sitting in with Mr. Shaw." I nodded. "Please continue to do that. I believe you'll find him to be most instructional."

I was relieved. "Thank you."

"You can thank Mr. Shaw. It was his request." She turned to head back into the library.

"Miss Simpson?"

"Yes?"

"What happens if Descendants from different Families *do* get together?"

She looked at me for a long moment. "It doesn't happen."

"But what if it did?"

"Their Families would shun them, they'd be cast out, and they'd be prevented from having children."

"Prevented? How?"

"It hasn't happened in decades."

"How would they be prevented from having kids?"

She looked me straight in the eyes. "It used to be death. Now there is a medical procedure."

I was horrified. "That's insane!"

Her eyes didn't leave mine. "Until a precedent has been set and the laws can be changed, the threat of barbarism seems to be enough."

"What are they so afraid of?"

Miss Simpson sighed. "The medical excuse is blood, since Family branches can't transfuse blood into other branches. The thought is that mixed-blood children would be aberrations. But in reality, everything in this world comes down to power; who has it and how it's used. The day when love is stronger than fear is the day we'll begin to discover our true power."

The bell rang and she left me with her words still ringing in my ears. The front hall was suddenly swarming with students, and I found myself being carried along with the tide toward the dining hall. Of course I was starving. My meals lately had been so erratic that I either ate like a pig when it was in front of me or I dealt with a growling stomach all the time.

I loaded up a plate with some sort of meat and vegetable pie and slid onto a bench next to Olivia. She looked around. "Where's your handsome prince?"

I scowled at her. "If you're talking about Adam, I'm leaving. There's nothing going on." She laughed at my expression and took a huge bite of her food. It was disconcerting to see so much food go into such a tiny human. "I can't believe you can actually fit all that food in your mouth."

Olivia's eyes twinkled and she swallowed. "I'm growing."

I smirked. "About time."

She stuck her tongue out at me and we both cracked up.

"Okay, I'm sorry about the handsome prince comment. I'm sure he's really a frog in disguise."

"Most good looking guys are. Didn't you get the memo?"

Olivia laughed again. "You seriously don't fancy him?"

I shook my head and it kind of felt like a betrayal. "Adam's a friend. Actually, you and the twins are my only friends here."

A voice popped up at my shoulder and I almost dropped my fork. "Not true. You just don't know me well enough yet." Connor dropped into a seat across from us and grinned. "Hi."

He reminded me of Ringo, with the mischievous look on his face. I turned to Olivia. "Do you guys know each other?"

Connor immediately stuck out his hand. "Hi, Olivia. I'm Connor."

She looked startled. "How do you know my name?"

"I was just waiting for the right time to meet you, and since you're sitting with my friend Saira, I figured now's the time."

Olivia looked from me to Connor. "You guys are friends?"

"Connor's a science super-freak with an 'in' to Shaw. I'm sure he'd be available for tutoring help if you needed it."

Connor's grin expanded. "At your service."

I could tell Olivia was charmed despite herself. She kept the skeptical look on her face though. "You're what, like, fourteen?"

"Yes, but I'm tall and smart for my age."

I laughed. "And arrogant and charming and big trouble when you get older. Get in with him now, Liv, before he gets unbearable." She finally laughed too, and we spent the rest of dinner chatting about random, entertaining stuff that had nothing to do with the Families and all their stupid intrigues.

Connor was really adept at avoiding all Family topics of conversation. I'd almost forgotten that Olivia wasn't a Family Descendent even though I was pretty sure she knew about them.

I thought about Gosford, the fisherman I'd met in 1888, and I wondered if it were possible that his Sanda and Millicent's housekeeper could actually be related?

"Hey, Liv? Where's your family from originally?"

"From Wales. A place called Gosefordsich."

"Any chance Sanda is related to a fisherman named Gosford?"

"She's my great-aunt actually, and I think her grandfather was a fisherman named Gosford."

My jaw dropped open and I snapped it shut before anyone noticed my resemblance to a fish. There was no way Sanda was born in 1888. "Liv?"

Olivia was already standing up to clear her plate. "Yeah?"

"Do the people in your family ..." How was I going to say this? "... live a long time?"

Shockingly, Olivia just shrugged. "I think it's a Pict thing."

Connor stared. "You guys are Picts?"

"Not full-blooded, of course. Our family mixed with Gaels after the Romans sacked everything. But there's apparently enough old blood for us to age in line with Saira's Family."

The casual way she mentioned something that sounded like it was out of a fairy tale left me practically gasping.

"I have to run. I have a micro-economics test tomorrow, and if I get anything less than ninety percent, the Rothbitch will have me 'removed' from her class."

Connor leapt to his feet. "Sorry, I can't help you there. She hates me, and the feeling's mutual." He bowed to both of us. "Ladies, thank you for the lively conversation." He grabbed Olivia's plate before she could clear it herself, and then said with a grin, "I look forward to our next one."

Olivia sort of included Connor in her gaze. "I'll see you guys later." She grabbed her books and left, but not before I caught her smiling.

I got up to clear my own plate and Connor waited for me. "So, do you think she's actually a 'Pixie'?" He cracked up at his own joke, and I looked at him sharply. "You want a chance with Olivia you'll never joke about her size again."

231

To his credit, he sobered instantly. "Do you think she likes me?" The bluntness of his question was surprising, but his honesty was so disarming I didn't hesitate to answer.

"I think she liked your attention. She's fifteen though."

He shrugged. "So? It doesn't matter that she's older if I'm confident enough. I learned that from watching Adam."

"Adam Arman?"

"He got Alex interested, and she's two years older than he is."

Ah hah! "They dated? I didn't think they could."

Connor suddenly veered away from a group of Ungee kids standing in the food line. He spoke under his breath as we put our dishes in the bins.

"We can't. But they did."

I stared at him, the gears clicking into place in my brain. "What happened?"

"I'm guessing they got caught."

The blood drained out of my face. "And …?"

He shrugged. "I don't know. Alex graduated early, and Adam suddenly started dating a bunch of girls from town. At least that's what I heard." Connor waved at a group of young guys across the room. "I'm not really friends with Adam, so I don't know the details. Alex moved into London where I think she's teaching ballet and waitressing in some dive in the city to support her ballet habit. She doesn't really come around anymore, so my info is all second-hand."

I thought I might know that dive where Alexandra Rowen worked. I flashed back to the coffee shop conversation I'd had with the striking waitress who moved like a dancer.

"Is her mom black?"

He looked at me like I should know. "Yeah, she was Jacqueline Rowen, a super famous ballet dancer."

Wow. I might have met Alex. She'd been generous with me in a way most people aren't with strangers and I thought I might even owe her one for her help. If that had, in fact, been Adam's ex-girlfriend, it was interesting to realize she was a Shifter.

Connor grinned before heading off toward his friends. "Thanks for the intro to Olivia. Put in a good word for me, would you?"

I checked the clock on the wall and realized I needed to run to make it outside to meet Mr. Shaw. I waved to Annie as I bolted through the kitchen and out the back door. The sun was just going down behind the kitchen garden when I got there, and I spun to find Mr. Shaw coming up behind me. "Did you hear me that time?"

"No."

"You just 'knew' I would be there?"

I shook my head. "I told you, I feel it when you approach. I don't know how else to describe it."

His tone was still serious. "What else can you do that normal people can't?" We'd had this conversation before, but there was something different about his tone. Something that said I needed to be totally straight with him.

"I can free-run. And see pretty well in the dark."

"Show me."

I looked Mr. Shaw in the eyes. "Are you going to teach me how to defeat a Vampire?"

He nodded. "I want to see what I have to work with."

Fair enough.

 ATTACK

"There's a barn in the next field over. I'll meet you there." I took off running and was almost over the wall when I finally heard Mr. Shaw coming behind me. I scrambled along the top until I could see the barn, then I dropped down and ran straight for the structure, up and over wheelbarrows, haystacks, and low hedges in my path. Mr. Shaw seemed to keep pace with me, but I could tell he was going around obstacles instead of over them. By the time I made it to the barn, he was out of breath.

But not much. Being a Bear must have advantages in speed and endurance that someone like Adam, a fit seventeen-year-old guy, didn't even have. I wondered about the genetics of that. "Do you keep the physical advantages you have as a Bear when you're in your human shape?"

My question surprised him, but he considered his answer. "Normal strength and endurance genes were super-promoted because of my particular mutation, so yes, I do."

I nodded. "That makes sense. So Connor is probably really fast then, huh?"

Mr. Shaw nodded. "He's also the alpha in his pack."

"You mean like his friends?"

Mr. Shaw was looking around the inside of the barn as we spoke. He nodded. "He'll always rise to a leadership position within any group because he's the oldest male in his family."

"What about his older sister?"

Mr. Shaw scowled. "Alexandra lived with her mother when her parents divorced, and when her father, Andrew, married my sister,

Liz, Alex rarely came around. Alexandra's mother became a Gazelle and there's a gender component to our heredity."

"So, because she's a girl, she doesn't become a Wolf?"

Mr. Shaw nodded. "Correct. However Alex also carries some of the Wolf's physical enhancements, just like I carry some of my mother's Lynx attributes."

I thought about all the possible combinations out there. It was sort of mind-boggling. "It seems like Shifter genetics would be a huge science to study all by itself. It must be pretty cool to see what different kids can do based on who their parents are."

Mr. Shaw nodded. "We're actually quite fortunate that genetic diversity is allowed with us."

"Allowed? It seems like a necessity if you don't want to end up inbred and weak."

"Genetic diversity, even between Families, is an argument that is coming up more and more among those of us who want to see the Families survive."

I climbed up a hay stack and perched myself in the rafters of the barn. I think I needed a little distance from him to ask the questions that had been burning holes in my brain. "Miss Simpson said they take 'medical steps' to keep people from different Family branches from mixing their genes." From my perch high above him, I could see the muscles in the Bear's shoulder bunch with tension. He looked up to face me, and I could see worry etched around his eyes.

"Are you in love with Arman?"

I wasn't expecting that question, at least not from him. "No. But I think he must have been in love with Alex."

Mr. Shaw closed his eyes as if to block out that thought. "I haven't seen her since she left school. You remind me of her a bit. It's probably what attracts him to you."

"Adam and I are just friends. I don't know why everyone's so freaked out about that."

Mr. Shaw sat down on a hay bale and rubbed his fingers through his shaggy hair. "This whole issue of mixing bloodlines and cross-Family mating is coming to a head right now. The leaders among the

Families come from old blood. They're jealous of their power and will do whatever it takes to keep it pure and uncomplicated."

I shuddered. "That sounds like Aryan race crap."

He gave a rueful smile. "It is. The problem is that everyone looks at the mixing up of Families as 'dilution' instead of what it really is, which is 'survival.' I mean look at your Family. No one even knows if there are any Clockers left who can travel through time aside from you and your mother. If you don't have children, that skill could very well be lost."

I grimaced. "No pressure."

"Indeed. And here's the rub. Because there are no Clocker boys your age, and possibly no Clocker men left at all, any children you have will only have half your Clocker blood."

"Can we please stop talking about my hypothetical kids? It's really weirding me out. I'm about as far from having kids right now as a person can get."

"Sadly, Miss Elian, you and I are not the only people having this conversation."

I don't know which made me more uncomfortable, the Bear calling me 'Miss Elian' or the idea that other people could be discussing anything about me.

I got up from my perch and walked the upper beams of the barn like a tightrope. It took my mind off Mr. Shaw and gave me something to concentrate on. He must have needed a change of subject too. "Regarding Vampires, they do have a couple of vulnerabilities." I dropped down out of the rafters and it startled him. Good.

"Tell me."

"As we touched on briefly after class, the mutant strain of porphyria, supercharged by a Family neuregulin 1 type 6 gene, is what halts their cell growth and creates a sort of suspended animation for all organs and tissue in their bodies. Obviously other skills are enhanced by the neuregulin 1 protein promoters."

"Like what?"

"I guess you haven't had a lot of one-on-one experience with Vampires."

I held my tongue. Explaining my very complicated relationship with Archer was not something I was prepared to do just yet, or maybe ever.

"Well, they're stronger and faster than an average human. I could go into *why*, but it doesn't really matter unless you're a scientist. They need concentrated protein to exist, and the hematocrits in human blood are the best way to stave off the painful symptoms of the porphyria. Animal blood will work too, but there are apparently conversion issues there. And whatever skills they might have inherited from their Family bloodlines are also present, so there's a wild card to dealing with a Vampire."

"In other words, if he comes from the Seers he could have Sight, or he could have animal skills if he comes from Shifters?" A fascinating and terrifying idea.

"But a Vampire would never be a true Shifter. There's an incompatibility between the porphyria and a full change. He might have latent skills though."

"What about if he's part Monger?"

Mr. Shaw looked me directly in the eye. "Then he's just a very bad guy." Somehow I thought that fit perfectly with what I was up against. I nodded.

"Okay, how are they vulnerable?"

"It's all about blood with Vampires." I rolled my eyes, but Mr. Shaw continued. "Porphyria is a blood-borne disease. Drain the blood, and the cell stasis can be reversed." He could tell I was struggling with that one and he smiled ruefully. "It's the suspended animation of the body's cells that cause a Vampire's 'immortality.' They're not truly immortal, but until their cell death cycle can be kick-started again, they might as well be. So, by draining a Vampire's blood, the cell stasis has nothing to sustain it anymore and the body's cells will start to die. Then it's just a matter of dealing what would be a 'normally' fatal wound before the body has time to generate new blood. Of course, if you've managed to get all the blood out of a Vampire, you've likely delivered that fatal blow already."

"And for those of us without homicidal inclinations?"

"In this game, it's kill or be turned, because if a Vampire gets his teeth on you, Saira, your blood will mutate and the porphyria will take hold. You will become a Vampire too."

I shuddered. "Big stakes."

"The biggest." He circled around and sized me up. "You're tall, but you have no weight to back you up in a fight."

"My physical strengths are agility and speed."

"What else?"

"I'm not sure. Night vision?"

"What else could you rely on if you were attacking or being attacked?" He was still circling me as if looking for a weakness.

I thought about that for a moment. "A very strong self-preservation instinct."

"Let's see." Mr. Shaw lunged forward and grabbed me.

I hadn't seen it coming and was instantly trapped in strong hands. I tried to spin away, but I couldn't move. Tried to kick him. Missed. I even tried to use my head to break his nose, but I only connected with his chest. I screamed in frustration! Rage and impotence boiled in me like poison as I tried to get free.

Then, a blur of movement came from the shadows.

The heavy sound of impact.

I was being pulled down. Everything felt like slow motion. I knew I would hit the ground hard and it would hurt.

Hands let go of me. Pushed me away.

The thud of a big body. A grunt of pain.

I hit a bale of hay and all the breath whooshed out of my body. I tried to open my eyes. They were open. My vision cleared. In the dim light I could see a figure huddled over another on the floor.

Archer. And Mr. Shaw.

"NOOOOOO!"

The scream was mine, and it jolted Archer out of whatever had possessed him. There was anger and fear and something else etched on his face. He turned to me. His hands were like claws and he looked feral.

Suddenly, an enormous brown Bear rose up behind Archer, towering over him with full, menacing size. The Bear growled in rage.

238

It was a sound that froze the blood in my veins. This animal meant to kill.

"Mr. Shaw!" I screamed his name hoping that sheer volume would be enough to get through to the Bear. He took a step toward Archer, who was still focused on me, not the two thousand pound Bear that was about to maul him.

I darted forward, between them. Archer screamed my name, but I barely heard him, so intent on reaching the man inside the massive Bear. My eyes were locked on the brown Bear's golden ones. I held my hand out to him and begged.

"Mr. Shaw, it's me, Saira. He won't hurt me. He's my friend. Please change back!"

I could feel Archer ready to leap at the Bear's slightest move. But I kept my eyes locked on the huge beast in front of me, and slowly, I felt the rage slip out of his glare.

With a deep "hrumph," the Bear dropped to all four legs, and after a final growl at Archer, he turned and ambled slowly from the barn.

I started to sag in relief until I remembered I wasn't alone. I spun angrily. "What the hell were you doing? You just attacked a teacher!"

The concern on his face instantly flashed to anger. "What the hell were you doing grappling with him in a dark barn? I thought I was saving your life!"

"Throw me my jeans, Vampire. They're on the floor behind you." Mr. Shaw's voice boomed menacingly from the deep shadows of the barn.

To his credit, Archer retrieved the jeans and tossed them toward the voice. After a moment Mr. Shaw emerged from the shadows, shirtless, barefoot, and scowling.

"Why are you here, Vampire?"

I'd never heard a voice so scary and fierce.

Archer held his ground. "For Saira."

Mr. Shaw's eyes narrowed. "Her blood does you no good."

That made no sense to me, but apparently it did to Archer. "I won't let them have it."

"So you'll destroy what you can't have?"

They were growling in riddles, and I didn't like being the subject of their argument.

"Not destroy. Protect."

Mr. Shaw's gaze sharpened on Archer's face. "What does the Clocker mean to you?"

Archer's voice dropped to a hoarse whisper. "I love her."

Mr. Shaw roared and lunged at Archer.

"Stop it!" I put myself between them again and almost got taken out by the force of his blow. "Enough! Archer won't hurt me, but you will if you keep attacking him." That must have gotten through to him. He stepped back, and I was able to get my feet back under me. Mr. Shaw sat warily on a hay bale while Archer retreated to the other side of the barn.

There were scars marking nearly every inch of Mr. Shaw's bare chest. I'd seen the newest ones on his back, but the crisscrossed lines on the front looked like the rake of claws across his skin. He didn't notice my horrified glance, and I was able to look away before he caught me staring.

"What is the game you're playing, Clocker?" The Bear's voice was gruff, and I didn't like how he kept calling me 'Clocker.'

"I'm not playing a game. I got thrown in the middle of one, and all I want is to find my mother." My voice broke.

"Why is the Vampire here?"

I looked back at Archer, still pacing on the other side of the barn, his shoulders tightening visibly at the Bear's tone. "I met him in 1888. He helped me escape then from the killer who may have my mother, and he found me again now. He has information I need …" My voice broke again. "And he's my friend."

It sounded lame to my ears after Archer's proclamation of love, but I honestly didn't know what I felt. And I didn't need to be announcing it to my teacher, whatever it was.

"So this isn't the Vampire you want to kill then." It was a statement, not a question, and I almost heard the hint of a joke in the Bear's gruff voice.

"No. I don't actually want to kill anyone. I just need to know how."

Mr. Shaw looked at Archer. "Got any tips for her, Vampire?"

His mouth tightened and his eyes narrowed. Archer really didn't like Mr. Shaw, and I had the sense that feeling was quite mutual.

"Go for the jugular, isn't that what you teach your Cubs?"

Okay, that was enough of that. "Archer, I need to finish my lesson with Mr. Shaw. Can we meet later?"

"You're not allowed outside at night." The Bear was back to full growl mode.

"Isn't that because of Archer though? I mean, he is the Vampire they're hunting, right?" It galled Mr. Shaw to concede that point, but he finally nodded. "If you'll leave the solarium window unlocked, I can make it back in without letting anyone know I've been gone."

"And how will you evade the Hunters?"

"She'll be with me." Archer's voice sounded posh and upper class in comparison to Mr. Shaw's, but it was equally dangerous.

Mr. Shaw considered him for a long moment, and then looked at me. "The Hunters won't be out for another hour, so you have your conversation now, and we'll finish our lesson in my office when you're back inside."

I nodded meekly. It seemed to mollify him a little.

Mr. Shaw threw one last menacing look at Archer as he stood up to go. "Your accent puts you around a hundred and fifty years old, but don't think I'm not stronger, faster, or more experienced than you, Vampire. Regardless of your age, you're still a cub to me."

Mr. Shaw grabbed his sweater off the barn floor and stalked out of the barn. I noticed the bandage on his shoulder had been ripped off again. The wound was almost healed, and I had a moment of irrational pride that my poultice had done well on him.

Archer was suddenly in front of me. "What the hell are you doing, Saira? Why do you need to know how to kill a Vampire?"

I rubbed my eyes tiredly. "I'm not planning to sneak up on you while you're asleep if that's what you're afraid of."

He scoffed. "Until the other night I wouldn't have been. Now I'm not so sure."

241

I gaped at him. "You can't be serious. I would never hurt you while you're sleeping."

"Just when I'm awake, hmm?" There was a bare hint of bitterness in his voice, but it was enough.

"I don't know how to react when you say you love me. I barely even know you."

"You know me. Better than anyone. And you forget it's been a hundred and twenty five years since we first met. That is a very long time." What could I say to that? "I'm not here to pressure you, Saira. Or make you feel anything you don't. I truly am just here to watch over you while you learn the things you need to know here." He took a deep breath. "And when you go back to my past again, you have to find me and tell me about myself."

I stared at him. "Wait ... it's already happened and you were there. You can tell me!"

He shook his head. "I can't. I've spent the last hundred years looking for memories of you, but all the ones with you in them are blurry, like I'm looking at all the possible pasts at once. Only the things that have already happened to you are clear in my head. I can't tell you what you've done because you haven't done it yet."

There was desperation in Archer's voice, and I wanted to put my arms around him and tell him everything would be okay. But I wasn't sure about anything. For all I knew, my mother had been turned into a Vampire.

I had to go back and try to find her. I needed all the help I could get, and my best shot at success was standing right in front of me. I took a deep breath. "Will you help me?"

BETRAYED

Getting into Archer's bunker was a little tricky because Annie and Mrs. Taylor were still in the kitchen. But Archer showed me a well-concealed route, and within a couple of minutes we were in the cellar. My night vision, which had been fine when we were outside, failed me completely in the cellar because there was absolutely no light coming in anywhere. So Archer kept hold of my hand until we were inside his room. When he finally let go to light an oil lamp, I felt a flash of loss, like his skin had generated warmth that wasn't actually even possible.

With the orange glow cast by the oil lamp, Archer's room felt like a cozy den where I wanted to curl up with a good book. The only thing missing was a fire in a fireplace. It said a lot for him that he had made such a comfortable place under the school.

Archer pulled open a massive, old-timber armoire. "I think there are some things in here from earlier this century, but I'm not sure about anything older." He was sorting through hangers of clothes, mostly black, but with a flash of white or gray thrown in for 'color.' I laughed, and he grinned at me. "You're just lucky I'm a clothes horse."

"Is that what you are? To me it just looks like you never threw anything away."

He scoffed. "Let me guess, everything you own is in that suitcase you brought with you."

I raised an eyebrow at him. "More or less. When you've moved as much as I have, you tend to throw stuff away instead of pack it all the time."

"I guess that's the difference then. I've had this room here for about the last eighty years, and before that I kept a room in the basement of King's College."

I stared at him. "Seriously? Didn't anyone notice the same guy hanging out year after year?"

He smirked. "Students. They've always been my camouflage. It's a little tougher here because I'm older than everyone. But this is a better hiding space, and much more comfortable. When they closed down the upper floors most of the furniture was brought here, so I've had my pick of good pieces. The bed was my favorite though. It reminds me of the one in my father's bedroom." I watched him rifle through his clothes, pulling out hangers here and there draped with dark-colored, soft-looking fabrics.

"Did you ever see your dad again ... after?" I asked tentatively.

He paused in his task. "You mean after I was turned?" I nodded. He turned back to the wardrobe and continued pulling items. "I used to go out to the estate and watch him. Ultimately, I couldn't stand to see my father get frail, and when he died I stopped going."

"So he believed you died?"

He shook his head. "He never knew. I actually inherited some land from him in Epping Place that I was able to claim after my brother died. I've kept it in my name so my tenants could stay indefinitely. Millicent's housekeeper uses the cottage as her weekend home, much like her grandmother did."

I stared at him. "Sanda? Does she know you own it?"

"She knows of me, but we haven't personally met. Her grandmother was a very good friend to me in the beginning." Archer seemed to shake himself out of his memories. He held up a pair of dark trousers and a black topcoat. "Here, these might fit the style you're looking for. Try them on and I can make any alterations you might need."

That surprised me almost as much as the change of subject. "You can sew?"

His smile was wry. "And hang a door, and re-cover a chair, and fix an engine, and patch a tire. Not too many of those services are open after dark."

"Wow."

"I'm glad there's at least something I can do to impress you." He held out the clothes. "There's a screen over there. Try them on."

Our fingers touched as I took the hangers from him, and I got that impossible jolt of heat again. I couldn't look him in the eyes as I went around the screen. What had gotten into me? Why was I suddenly acting all fluttery and lame? I had always wanted to smack the girls who acted like that around guys because it seemed so fake. Maybe it was time to let up on a few of the harsh judgments I was so good at making.

I usually wore skinny jeans because there was no excess fabric to catch on fences and door latches when I was free-running, so the trousers felt loose-fitting and almost sensuous with their silky lining. His white shirt had tiny little buttons and was huge on my shoulders, but I tucked it in and cinched the waist of the trousers with a belt.

Archer's eyes flared when I stepped out from behind the screen, and I felt a flush of self-consciousness at the intensity of his gaze. I held my arms out for inspection.

"Everything's big on me, but it's all so soft. You have nice things."

His voice was oddly husky and very controlled when he spoke. "You make them look good." I felt a little pinned by his eyes and was relieved when he finally looked away to the wardrobe. He pulled out a black sweater and tossed it to me.

"Here. A polo neck will suit the docks." The turtleneck was fine cashmere and so soft I wanted to wrap myself in it. "Try it, and then we'll see how much the trousers need to be taken in."

I slipped the black cashmere over my head and it fell perfectly around me, big like sweaters should. Archer nodded.

"If you wear the shirt under it you can quickly change looks as needed."

I smiled. "The master of disguise, huh?"

He returned my wry expression. "Often a matter of survival."

He pinched the fabric of the trousers on each side of my hips and deftly pinned it in place. It was strange to have his hands on me, but I willed myself to feel like a mannequin. After a moment he stepped back to look at his work. "The length is good, and I think taking it in a little on top will make you look less like a boy playing dress-up with his father's clothes."

"As long as I look male; that's all that matters."

He smiled wryly. "If it's night and your hair is out of sight, maybe."

"Hey, I fooled you, didn't I?"

"You couldn't now."

"Why not?"

He scoffed. "I've lived through the last half of the twentieth century. Clothes no longer define gender like they used to." He gestured to the garments I wore. "Take those off so I can fix them."

I slipped behind the screen again and quickly changed back into my jeans and t-shirt. It was cold in the cellar, so I held out the black cashmere sweater as I emerged. "Is it okay if I borrow this?"

Archer gave me a funny look. "Anything I have is yours."

"Careful, you've got some rugs down here that would go a long way toward warming up my little room upstairs."

I pulled the gorgeously soft sweater over my head as he scrutinized me. "You're no longer sharing a room with the Monger."

"How'd you know?"

"I looked for you there last night."

I couldn't believe I actually felt a sense of loss that I hadn't been there. I shook my head. "I moved myself. There's an empty wing on the north side. I'm on the second floor, down at the end by the fire escape. Did Raven see you last night?"

"Raven is the Monger? No. I saw at once she wasn't you, so I left before she woke."

"She's pretty though, huh?" I should have bitten my tongue off before admitting I cared what he thought.

He shrugged like he hadn't given it a second thought. "She wasn't you."

I moved away from that minefield of a topic. "Did you know the Monger teacher, Ms. Rothchild, brought Romanian Hunters to the school? They look like jackbooted skinheads."

"They're Weres."

I stared at him. "As in Wolves?"

He nodded grimly. "Their scent is everywhere. They've been marking the woods all around the school."

"They're here to hunt you." Now I was really scared for him.

"I've encountered Weres before. Mongers have always used them as enforcers for the dirty jobs, and though they're very good with weapons, they lack control when they change. Unlike Shifters, Weres lose themselves to blood lust, which makes them just as weak as it does dangerous."

Was he serious? I could barely wrap my brain around the idea that so many nightmares were actually true. Archer seemed to realize he'd freaked me out.

"Do you know about warded rooms?"

I shivered. "I know they're cold places I have no desire to hang out in. Why?"

"Do you know where the wards are in St. Brigid's?"

"One. It's up in the east tower."

"Could you get to it if you had to?"

I stared at Archer. "The Weres aren't here for me."

He took another deep breath and nodded. "I just need to know you're safe during the day when I can't be there."

"I can take care of myself."

Archer's gaze never wavered from mine. "Don't forget, you're also being hunted."

I suddenly shivered at the thought of Slick. "By a Monger." My voice was a whisper. "I can feel it. I get nauseous and want to bolt anytime a Monger is near me. Slick is one; I know it."

Archer accepted my words without a question. "For some reason the Mongers have painted a target on you. Until we know why, I exist in fear that they'll take you." His eyes were locked on mine.

I'd been feeling fairly secure at St. Bridgid's, but Archer's words reminded me of the predator/prey game that had played out around Whitechapel station with Slick.

"I need to go to London, Archer. Can you get me there?"

"Yes. When?"

"Can we go tonight?"

"And the Shifter?"

"I should go to his office now before he starts tearing the place apart to look for me. But if you can take me later, there's something I need to check out under the London Bridge."

Archer nodded, thoughtfully. "The dogs come out at nine p.m. and the last of the staff goes to sleep around midnight. I can come for you then, but we'll need a diversion." I thought about the different ways to distract dogs, and steak came immediately to mind. I said as much to Archer and he laughed. "I meant the Weres. Don't worry, I'll deal with them. You just be ready to leave at midnight."

The Weres. He was so casual about them, while I was practically wetting my pants at the idea of running from Werewolves. "How does one 'deal with' a Werewolf?" Archer grinned in a way I could only describe as, well, wolfish. I shuddered. "Okay, I don't want to know."

He stopped laughing. "Do you need me to bring anything?"

I smirked. "Breadcrumbs? I've never been where we're going and I don't know my way around."

He grinned. "Sounds fun."

I headed toward the hidden entrance, and Archer's voice came from right over my shoulder. "Be careful with the Shifter." I turned around, surprised at how close together our faces were. But I didn't step backwards. His eyes glinted in the dim light from his room.

"He's a good guy."

Archer grimaced. "None of us are."

And suddenly he kissed me.

His lips were soft, and their touch made my heart pound so hard in my chest I was sure he could feel it through his teeth. I couldn't breathe while his mouth was on mine.

He pulled back a fraction of an inch, just enough to break the contact between us, and my body prickled with heat all over. I backed up into the wall to hide the tremble that had hitched a ride on the air in my chest, and Archer reached over my shoulder. I thought he was going to pin me in place, but he unfastened the catch and slid the door open behind me.

"Bye." My voice didn't work properly and the word came out in a whisper. Just as I turned to leave, I thought I caught the hint of a smile on his lips, and I couldn't decide if I liked it or if it made me want to run.

I was extra careful to be quiet as I closed the cellar doors behind me and slipped around the outside of the castle to the solarium. The window was unlatched, and I was able to slither inside without any obvious breaking-and-entering noises.

I didn't meet anyone on my way to Mr. Shaw's office and wasn't sure what I'd have said if I had. My heart was still pounding from Archer's kiss, and I was afraid it was written all over my face.

I had no idea what I felt, only that I really *felt*. Everything. My skin was on fire and every nerve-ending was exposed. I felt raw and totally vulnerable, and I was about to face the Bear. But if I didn't go to him, he would come and find me.

I tapped lightly at his office door.

"Come." His voice was gruff and not terribly friendly, and my stomach butterflies turned to nerves as I opened the door.

"Close it behind you." He barely looked up from the microscope slide he was studying, and I was very aware of feeling about six years old.

I stood in front of his desk until he finally finished studying the slide. The expression on his face when he looked up was completely neutral, and I actually wished for anything else. Even anger would have been better than the wall of silence that stood between us.

Then his eyes narrowed, and I took back my wish for anger.

"You smell of him."

"I tried on some of his clothes—" Mr. Shaw's eyebrows nearly rose off his forehead and I quickly continued. "He still has things that fit the time period. I need to be able to blend in as much as I can."

"Indeed." The dryness of his voice was positively Sahara-like. He regarded me for a very long moment. "I found some of your hair on my sweater tonight after we fought."

I got defensive instantly. "So?"

"So, I finally saw what you discovered when you examined our hair side by side."

Uh oh. I winced in anticipation of the thing that hadn't been said out loud, not by me, not by anyone. The thing I'd been dreading and fearing since the last time I was in his office.

"You have Shifter blood in you."

Mr. Shaw's voice was completely dead, like he couldn't quite process the aberration that stood before him. I crossed my arms tightly and glared at him.

"My mother is the only one who knows anything about what I am, and it clearly hasn't bothered her for seventeen years."

His eyes widened in surprise and he was about to say something when his office phone rang. Saved by the effing bell. I almost turned and left, but the fierce look on his face stopped me. He held up a finger as he spoke into the phone. "Yes?" His eyes locked on mine. "Yes, Jane. She's here." His gaze was completely unwavering. "Indeed. I'll ask her." He listened a few more moments, then, "I'll let you know." He hung up the phone with a soft 'click' and took a deep breath.

Mr. Shaw's eyes narrowed. "Miss Simpson tried to find you earlier. I believe you are Miss Walters' roommate, are you not?" I didn't move a muscle to confirm or deny. "Miss Simpson said there appeared to be no trace of your presence in the dorm room that was assigned to you."

This felt like one of those moments of choice. Make up a story, or come clean? At this point it wasn't actually much of a contest, and I was trying to figure out how to explain where I'd gone when Mr. Shaw suddenly stood right in front of me in full rage.

"I take it that means you've moved in with the Sucker, in whatever den he's managed to find for himself?"

I was shocked into speechlessness. What the hell?

"Really?" I felt an unreasonable rage start to build, and I glared at him. "You're going to accuse me of what … sleeping around? Are you kidding?" I spun on my heels and marched toward the office door.

"You come back here, young lady. We're not finished yet!"

He was growling now, but I faced him and matched his tone with my fiercest voice. "I'm totally finished with you and with this whole place! I was brought here against my will, and held captive by doors, dogs, and Werewolves. It's a fricking school, but I'm not allowed to learn anything, and my roommate makes Cruella de Ville look like a fairy princess. *You* were the one person I thought was human enough to trust."

I bolted from Mr. Shaw's office before my tears of rage blinded my vision. I needed to run because I knew he would chase me. And he did. The Bear believed I was hiding somewhere in the castle with Archer, and he wouldn't rest until he found out where.

Mr. Shaw was fast, but I was faster, and way more agile than he was. Luckily for both of us, everyone was already in their rooms for the night, because we were both going full speed and would have knocked over anyone in our way.

I couldn't go to my room; that would lead him directly to my hideaway. And I certainly couldn't go to Archer's room in the cellar, even if I could think of a way to get past the Werewolves that were by now surely patrolling the outside grounds. That pretty much left the towers.

I took a staircase three steps at a time and managed to gain some distance on him as I turned down a back hallway. I could hear Mr. Shaw pounding after me, his breath coming in steady pants much like the animal he could turn into. I ducked out of sight as a bedroom door opened and Mrs. Taylor's head popped out. I was already up another staircase when I heard her exclaim, "Mr. Shaw! Whatever are you doing?"

He gasped an answer I didn't hear. I thought about going to my tower, the Clocker Tower, and bolting through the painting. He certainly couldn't follow me there. But no one except Ava and Adam knew about the painting, and I wanted to keep it that way.

So I switched direction – to their tower. If the secret doorway didn't thwart Mr. Shaw, maybe the warded room might. It was worth a shot.

I took staircases two steps at a time, hallways at a dead sprint, and slid down banisters just to gain extra precious seconds to throw him off my trail. I made it to the bookcase entrance to the Seer's tower and closed it behind me without catching sight of the Bear. Maybe he didn't know about the tower, or maybe he thought I didn't know, but I wasn't taking any chances. I bolted up the stairs to the warded room and immediately felt my body temperature drop with the cold.

There was a "bang" down below me, and the sound of something scraping on the floor. Was he forcing the door? Did he know about the hidden catch? What was he doing? How could Mr. Shaw switch gears so completely into a raging madman? Was it possible that the split personality of Shifters eventually made them insane like his ancestor Will Shaw?

I shivered. Whether fright or freeze, I couldn't tell, and not even Archer's cashmere sweater could stop the chill. The sound of pounding on the steps stopped me in my tracks, and I felt myself wrapping a mental shield around my body as if I was bracing myself for the Bear to crash through the door.

Heat suddenly poured off me and rose from my skin. I closed my eyes, feeling my mental shield go from transparent to opaque, like I was encasing myself in a solid cocoon that could protect me from Mr. Shaw's wrath.

The Bear arrived at the top of the stairs. Literally, the Bear. Sometime during his pursuit he had Shifted. He sniffed the air furiously, then began pacing the room, ignoring me completely. I was right there with him, yet he seemed not to realize it.

Then he dropped to all four feet, arched his back, and curled his head under his body as if in pain. The air shimmered around him like a heat mirage, but then the moment vanished and the air around him stilled. Suddenly it was Mr. Shaw standing there, not the massive brown Bear that he had been.

"You are in so much danger, Saira," he said into the air. His voice came out in a growl, and I didn't doubt his words one little bit. I closed my eyes expecting him to see me then. Maybe grab and shake me like a naughty kid, maybe worse. But nothing happened, and when I finally opened my eyes again the tower room was empty. I stayed completely still, not trusting my body to obey me if I tried to take a step. I heard the scrape of the bookcase downstairs, and then finally ... nothing. The only sound in the room was the pounding of my heart. The feeling of the cocoon I'd wrapped myself in fell away and the air of the warded room chilled me.

Could I possibly have warded *myself*? The wards on the room didn't keep Mr. Shaw out, and I wasn't sure how they worked anyway. But from the moment I had mentally hidden myself from him, Mr. Shaw had not been able to find me. And I had been right in front of him the whole time.

I tried to do it again. I tried to find the edges of the cocoon in my mind and wrap myself in it, but it was gone. And I was cold. So cold my teeth chattered uncontrollably and I could barely control the trembling in my hands and legs.

I tiptoed down the worn stone steps and found my way back through the old headmaster's office in the dark. The bookcase door *had* been forced open, so it took a couple of tries with the hidden catch before it finally swung freely and silently.

I was half-expecting Mr. Shaw to leap out at me from the shadows of the hall as I emerged from the Seer Tower, but the hallway was empty. My shoulders didn't relax until I was back in my north wing.

The flutter of the curtains was my first clue that someone had been in my room, but when I stepped on the soft pile rug in the middle of the floor, I knew it had been Archer.

I collapsed on the bed in a puddle. What the hell had just happened? I had spent the last quarter of an hour being chased through the school by a Bear. A Bear I had liked and respected until he turned on me and accused me of what? Being a mixed-blood?

Being of 'low moral character'? When it came down to it, I felt like someone who had disappointed her dad. A dad who didn't like who she'd become, didn't like her boyfriend, and didn't believe she was still a virgin.

That whole series of thoughts was so weird and so foreign, I almost couldn't process it. First, the idea that I could ever think of Mr. Shaw as a father figure was absurd, and yet I did. Except for tonight, he had always treated me with respect, like I was someone worth teaching. And I *wanted* to learn from him, and I had trusted him to tell me the truth.

That's what hurt the most. I had trusted Mr. Shaw. And in my chaotic, nomadic existence, trust was more rare than diamonds or gold or the same bed more than two years running. I wasn't even sure I trusted my mother anymore. She had lied to me more than any other person I'd ever let into my life. That actually made me question why the hell I was going to all this trouble to rescue her.

And to top it all, somehow I had managed to ward myself from being seen or caught by both a Bear and a human. Of everything that had happened, that was the one thing I looked forward to digging into. Archer knew about warded rooms, and the Seer Tower, so maybe he could help me.

And with thoughts of Archer flitting through my brain, I drifted off into something resembling a coma.

 ESCAPE

About two hours later I snapped awake with a gasp. My eyes went straight to my still-open window where the cold night air flowed into the room. Strangely, I was less cold here than I'd been in the tower room, even though I had run myself into a sweat to get there.

I got up to close the window, and just as I was about to reach for the sash, a hand appeared. I barely stifled a scream as Archer pulled himself into the room. His smile immediately turned to concern at the look on my face.

"Saira! Are you well?"

"You scared the crap out of me!"

Archer winced. "I've never really gotten used to the American fascination with bodily functions."

"Seriously?"

"I'm sorry. It seemed the safest way to come here."

"It probably is." The pounding of my heart slowed to something less like a jackhammer. "Thank you for the rug."

He grinned. "Getting up here with that on my shoulder was a bit of a trick. I have a new respect for firemen." He looked around the room quickly. "Are you ready to go?"

I shrugged. "I guess so. I had a couple hours of sleep."

Archer reached up and pulled a piece of hair off my face where drool had stuck it to my cheek. Nice. He grinned. "I see that."

I scrubbed at my face with my hands. "Give me a minute to wash my face, and I'll be ready." I ran out the door to the bathroom down my hall, suddenly mortified. Since when did I care what any guy thought about how I looked?

Cold water on the face, a rough towel, brushed teeth, and re-braided hair and I was back in my room feeling much more human, if not properly awake. Archer was looking at something on my dresser when I walked in. "Now I'm ready."

He smiled and indicated a leather jacket on the bed.

"I wasn't sure if you had a warm coat, and despite how good you look in my sweater, it's not enough. The English cold is finally setting in."

I picked up the soft leather and slipped it on. It was a road bike jacket, sporty and simple and totally my style. I couldn't help it; I had to check myself out in the mirror.

"You look good in my clothes."

I turned to him with a grin. "This jacket would make anyone look good. Thanks."

As an afterthought I grabbed the portal map and a Maglite and shoved them in my back pocket. The pen and ink portrait I'd done of Archer was staring back at me from my dresser. I didn't have time to wonder what he thought of it though. The minute we left the room it was game on.

It was quite an experience to scale the walls of the school with Archer at night. He was good, that was for sure. He had a solid instinct for foot placement, and he seemed to know exactly which drain pipes would support our weight before grabbing them. It was a challenging climb down, and one I could have done alone if I'd had to, but with Archer it was actually fun. Until we hit the ground. Suddenly the sound of baying dogs from around the front of the school assaulted us, and Archer shoved me forward with powerful arms.

"Run!" His voice was a low growl in my ear, and it held all the urgency of life and death in it. So I ran. Faster than I've ever run in my life. The baying of the dogs suddenly changed to a yip and fell off. And was replaced by a deep, low growl.

Crap. Those weren't dogs chasing us anymore. These bad guys had four legs and the hunting instincts of both man and beast.

Archer was really fast. Vampire strength had given him speed that pushed me beyond limits I thought I had. And still the Weres were gaining on us.

We were sprinting through dense woods behind the school in a direction I hadn't explored before. The groundskeepers were shouting at their dogs, their voices getting farther away as we outpaced them.

But the Wolves were getting closer.

I had my doubts about Archer taking on one, much less two badass Romanian skinhead Weres. I was basically Were-bait, so I found more speed and kicked it in. Archer's path seemed very deliberate, and I knew he could hear me right behind him. The Wolves had stopped growling now, which I took as a bad sign, since the sounds of crashing through the underbrush were getting closer.

"We'll gain some time at the wall, but you'll have to be fast." He didn't even sound out of breath. I saw what he meant a moment later. A six foot high stone wall loomed up in front of us, and Archer practically vaulted to the top. I could already see handholds I wanted to use, and my feet were off the ground a second later.

I felt a Wolf leap for my lower leg just as Archer hauled me out of the way. Then he dropped down to the other side and waited for me to jump. I didn't hesitate, and he caught me neatly.

"This way." His voice was low in my ear, and I could barely make it out over the din the Wolves were making on the other side of the wall.

He led me to a clearing where his silver Aston Martin was hidden. Moments later we'd left the clearing behind. I looked for any sign of either men or Wolves. Nothing. I almost dared to breathe until Archer spoke. "If they're smart, they'll try to head us off at the main road."

"Let's hope they're not smart then."

He smiled wryly. "You run well."

"So do you."

"One of the few advantages."

I winced. The few advantages to being a Vampire, he meant.

"How did it happen?" A question I'd dreaded asking.

He shrugged noncommittally. "I'm not entirely sure, which in my experience means it has something to do with you." His voice was more casual than it seemed possible to be. "But since it hasn't happened in your life yet, I can't remember it."

"Oh, God."

"I doubt He had anything to do with it, actually." The wry smile was back and took away a little of the nausea that hit my gut with its fist. I had something to do with him being turned into a Vampire? I couldn't imagine anything worse. Guilt gnawed at me like a big, mangy rat, and I turned away from Archer's face.

He shifted gears, and then touched my knee lightly. "Whatever happened, it's not your fault."

"How can you say that? You can't even remember it." My voice cracked, and I worked to get myself under control.

He took his hand off my knee and looked away. His voice was low when he spoke. "If I hadn't been bitten, I wouldn't be here with you now."

I groaned and shut my eyes. I couldn't deal with this. I really couldn't. I put my feet up on the dashboard and gripped my knees tightly.

My life had suddenly gotten very messy, and I realized with a jolt that I really didn't have a safe place to call my own anymore. Just like that, I was homeless and running again, with even less of my stuff than I'd had before. It was not a comforting feeling, and combined with guilt about what I'd done to Archer, my stomach was in knots.

When we entered London proper, I sat up and pulled Archer's leather jacket close around me.

"London Bridge, you said?"

I nodded. "The catacombs. I think the entrance is on Tooley Street."

Archer's eyebrows rose. "They're still there?"

"You know them?" It was my turn to be surprised.

"I used to drink with the dockworkers when I was out of sorts, just to feel human again." The wry grin was back.

"Get enough ale into men of the docks and they'd scare each other with ghost stories of buried plague victims and hidden rooms under London Bridge."

"Have you ever been there?"

"Once. I ducked into a tunnel to get away from a bobby who didn't like the looks of me."

"Lurking in the shadows? You're such a cliché."

He smirked. "What? You don't think I have it in me to be scary?" That was a startling thought. Did Archer the Vampire scare me? "I don't know? What do you eat?" It was a matter-of-fact question that was like throwing a bucket of ice-water on the conversation. All playfulness left Archer's tone.

"Right, we're here." He suddenly swerved down a narrow alley and parked the Aston Martin behind an old warehouse. Archer leapt out of the car in one smooth movement. He was changing the subject, and I could have pushed him to answer my question, but honestly, I didn't really want to know. Not when I was alone in nighttime London with a Vampire.

We emerged from the alley, and the dark, looming presence of the bridge felt ominous over my head. I was disoriented for a moment as I tried to find the quay I remembered from my last visit to the bridge. But everything had changed since 1888.

My thoughts must have echoed in Archer's brain, or it was just an occupational hazard of long life. His voice was deadpan. "The buildings used to be a lot shorter."

I sniffed with a grin. "River smells the same though."

Archer agreed drily, "Even the Nile smells better than the Thames."

I stared at him. "You've been to Egypt?"

"Finding nighttime transportation has become easier in the last thirty years."

The realities of his life suddenly hit me. "You can't be out in the daytime."

"Can't and shouldn't are two different things. Sunlight won't kill me. But it kick-starts the cell death that my ... condition has arrested. And it's very painful."

"So you do burn in the sun?"

"Something akin to what I imagine radiation sickness would feel like."

"Wow. That's not good."

"Very little about being a Vampire is."

There was no discernible bitterness in his voice, but his words sent the knife of guilt through me. We passed a homeless guy lying in a doorway, and I thought I saw a glint of open eyes. Fear suddenly curled itself around my guts and every instinct in my body screamed 'run!'

Archer must have sensed something because he grabbed my hand and held me next to him as we continued down the street. "Easy, Saira. Don't let him know you know."

"What? What do I know?" I whispered furiously under my breath.

"The vagrant is a Monger."

Thunk. Of course. Mongers triggered my fight or flight. The question was what had he heard, and who would he tell? Archer steered me around a corner onto Tooley Street and suddenly we were heading down a concrete staircase. "Nancy's Steps. Named after the Dickens character in Oliver Twist."

I stared at him. Either the man was totally unconcerned that a Monger had just seen us, or he was the greatest subject-changer in history. So I played along. "Never read it."

"Great story, full of Mongers."

I stared at him. "Seriously?"

He shrugged. "Criminals, pickpockets, workhouses where orphans are abused. If the shoe fits ..."

I shuddered. "So, who's Nancy?"

"A pickpocket in love with an abuser who betrays Oliver on these steps. Her lover beats her to death later."

"Charming."

"No, Dickens."

I smothered a laugh and we started down the steps.

There was a heavy iron gate wrapped in a thick-link chain at the bottom of the steps. I half expected Archer to muscle it open, but he surprised me. He pulled a slim leather case from an inside pocket of his jacket, and opened it to reveal a set of delicate tools that looked like something from a dentist's office. A Vampire with lock picks was somehow scarier than one who could open a chain with brute strength. He nodded at me. "Your torch?"

I shone it on the padlock while Archer went to work with the picks. In less than a minute the heavy lock was open and Archer was unwinding the chain from the door. When we were inside, he wrapped it up again and snapped the padlock shut.

"You locked us in." I was trying not to freak out.

He shook his head. "I'm buying us time."

I suddenly had a very strong compulsion to keep Archer alive and functioning so he could get us back out of the catacombs when we were done. I aimed my light down the dank tunnel and started forward. Archer pulled me back as my light flashed on a pair of eyes glinting from the wall.

"It's just a statue." I kept my voice low in case anyone was still around, but I knew the London Bridge and Tombs Experience exhibit had closed a couple of hours ago. Funny that the animatronic Halloween monster had freaked Archer out.

He stared around the room at the dark corners. "They're everywhere."

"It's a special exhibit to scare the tourists. Nothing down here is real." The sound of skittering feet made me a liar.

"Real is entirely relative." His voice held that droll tone that I was beginning to understand represented a very dry sense of humor.

I turned down the farthest tunnel, and Archer fell in right behind me. Despite knowing the creepy corpses and robotic zombies were animatronic fakes, I was glad to finally come to an empty tunnel. It was pitch-black down there, and therefore a little unnerving to sweep the Maglite past plague-dead bodies and silently screaming faces.

We explored the caverns methodically and I was careful to memorize landmarks along the way. Most of the rooms off the main tunnels were empty. Presumably they'd been storage rooms for dry goods when the caverns were first dug. But one room was an archeological dig in progress, and I took an involuntary step back when my light illuminated a skull.

"A plague pit?"

"Apparently so." Archer seemed as intrigued as I was. I aimed my Maglite so his face was visible.

"You like this stuff?"

He nodded. "Since I was a kid. I once found a Pictish stone carving in the woods behind my father's manor. I turned it into kind of an altar, and anytime I found something interesting I brought it there as an offering." Archer smiled at the memory. "I haven't thought about that in a very long time."

"My friend Olivia said her family comes from the Picts. She said it's why Sanda is so old."

Archer looked thoughtful. "It wouldn't surprise me. Sanda's grandmother, the Missus, also lived a very long time, and she had skills modern healers have long forgotten. I believe she kept Elian Manor well into her nineties."

I hadn't made that connection before. "Sanda's grandmother worked at Elian when you knew her?"

"She told me she inherited the job from *her* grandmother."

I gasped. "She must have known my mother and Emily when they were little."

We suddenly heard the clank of metal at the gate far down the corridor, and Archer and I froze in place. I instantly shoved my flashlight against my thigh to hide the light. I could hear voices, but I couldn't make out more than a couple of words. But it was enough to hear "... in there" and "Clocker."

"They're in."

My light swung onto Archer's face. "How do you know?"

"They've stopped working the chain."

"They could have left." I was grasping at straws. "So what do we do, hide?"

He looked at me for long enough that I started to get nervous. Then he finally spoke. "We can try. But this is a closed tunnel system, and if I were them, I'd post someone at the entrance while the others search."

"So we're trapped like rats?"

"Essentially."

"Well, I'm not waiting for Mongers to find me. Let's go deeper." Archer followed me further into the tunnels, past long forgotten storage rooms, and into a section that seemed much older than the brick-clad walls of the main caverns.

Finally, Archer stopped me. "They won't stop looking, Saira. I'm going to have to fight them to get you out."

The yellow light of my Maglite made his eyes seem golden. "You say 'fight' but you really mean 'kill,' don't you?"

"I can't risk turning any of them."

"Because they're Mongers."

"Yes. I can try to disable them, but if I pull punches, we'll both be at risk."

Cool. I was standing next to a Vampire discussing the costs and benefits of maiming versus killing. It's one thing to have to defend yourself from an attack, but something entirely else to decide to murder. I didn't like it, not one little bit.

"I don't even know what they want from me, Archer. I can't let you plan to kill them."

"Would you rather we sat down and bartered for you like eighteenth-century slave traders?" His voice was tight, and I had the distinct sense he was digging in on this.

"What if there's another way?"

A shout down a tunnel sounded much closer, and the answering voice wasn't too far away. Archer whispered furiously. "I'm open to suggestion."

"I could try to make a portal and get us out of here that way." I had no idea if it was even possible.

"Can you do that?"

"I don't know." I spotted a pile of chalky stone that had broken off one of the walls. I picked up a piece and tested it on the brick. It made a mark. "I can try though."

We continued moving down the corridor. "Fine. But if it doesn't work, I'm not going to let them take you." I wasn't sure I was okay with that ultimatum, but I didn't think I had much choice.

Archer's voice didn't invite negotiation. After a moment, he spoke again. "I've never heard of a Clocker being able to take anyone with them."

"Me either. But until last week, I'd never heard of Clockers."

"Point taken." The tunnel wall ended abruptly on the far side and I followed it down to see where it went. "If I can't go, at least you'll be safe. And I can take care of myself if I don't have to worry about you."

We probably didn't have time for one of my arguments about my own self-preservation, so I didn't bother. "I've never done this before."

"That doesn't mean you can't." His tone changed to completely pragmatic and there was nothing I could say to that. There was a sharp corner in the wall leading to what must have once been a small storage room. The room was shaped like a square, so there was another sharp corner just inside the door with a piece of wall that I thought looked big enough for a Clocker spiral.

"Why here?" Archer's voice whispered in my ear. He was really close and my heart pounded a little faster.

"Every spiral I've seen has been hidden from casual view. I think so people don't freak out when a Clocker just suddenly appears."

"So you're a Clocker now?" There was a grin in his whisper.

"What's your point, Sucker?"

"Ouch."

"Exactly."

I shone my light up the section of wall I'd chosen. I didn't know why, but it felt like the right spot.

The wall was relatively smooth, and looked like it would hold the chalk pretty well. The rock worked almost as well as sidewalk chalk, and I concentrated on the main center spiral while Archer held his own flashlight pointed at the wall. My Maglite was clenched between my teeth and aimed at the back of my hand as I drew the design.

Archer tensed behind me, and then I heard the sounds of raised voices. There was a yell from the main Hall of Horrors, and I

264

imagined a Monger leaping away in terror from one of the plague-dead statues.

"Can you work faster?" Archer's voice was a whisper directly into my ear, and I shivered with the heat of it. I didn't say anything, just took a breath and continued drawing. I had just moved to the fourth outer spiral when the sound of pounding feet down the tunnel made Archer growl in his throat. He flipped off his light and turned his back to me, shielding me from whatever was coming for us.

"Now, Saira!" His voice was just a breath, but it could have been a scream. I finished the spiral, but nothing was happening. No buzzing, no light, nothing. The Maglite was still between my teeth, the nearly finished chalk rock was in my left hand, so I started tracing the spiral with my right index finger.

"They're down here!" A male voice yelled from the nearest tunnel.

"Do you see 'em?" That voice was gruff.

"It's where I saw her." That one sounded young and scared.

"Doing what?"

"Drawing something ... on the wall."

"She's trying to escape!" The blood froze in my veins. Slick.

I traced faster, and Archer pressed his back against mine. He went rigid as the beams of their flashlights illuminated the edges of our small room. The spirals were starting to hum; the edges glowed faintly as my finger moved even faster around the pattern. The throbbing of sound began in my brain, and I could feel something inside my body stretch and pull toward the spirals.

Pounding feet halted and a voice yelled, "They're here!"

Archer snarled and tensed, ready to pounce. The last spiral was almost complete.

"It is a spiral!"

"Stop her!" Slick was almost there.

Archer pushed himself back against me, pinning me to the wall ... sending me through the wall ... falling, stretching, pulling, with the deep throbbing hum of time being crossed.

.

CATACOMBS - 1861

I think I puked even before I landed.

I was still heaving when I felt a heavy weight crush my back. I shoved with all my might to get air.

There was a moan in the pitch blackness. And the sound of someone retching in the corner.

"Saira?" Archer's whisper in my ear sounded pathetic and weak, and it nearly sent me through the roof. He came with me? A choked sob came from the dry-heaver in the corner, but I had no idea who it was. Archer seemed to pull himself together. "C'mon. We have to go." His voice was louder now.

But then the dry-heaver moaned from the corner. His voice sounded kind of pathetic and ... young? "Don't leave me!"

"Who is that?" My whisper was furious as I got to my feet. This was the fifth time I'd traveled and it was by far the worst. I was annoyed at how shaky and sick I still felt.

"I think he came with us."

"What?" No longer whispering, I squeaked now.

Archer grabbed me by the arm and pulled me out of the room, away from the moaning guy. I could only assume we were in the same catacomb storeroom where I'd opened the portal, though *when* we were was a complete mystery.

Archer moved precisely while I fumbled for my Maglite. I flicked it on to see the catacomb tunnel, now stacked with boxes and bags of goods against the walls. "Off!" Archer hissed at me, and I jumped at his command. "There are people down here."

Now I could hear the scuffle of feet and the sounds of heavy sacks being dropped into piles. They were toward the entrance, but the sound carried fairly well in the underground cavern.

"Workers." I tried to fathom the significance of that. From what I read, the tunnels hadn't been properly used as storage for the river merchants since the early 1900s.

But if time was truly spiral-shaped, what were the chances that we had landed back in 1888? Archer flicked his flashlight on quickly and aimed it at one of the stacks of boxes against the wall. There was a shipper's stamp on the seal of each box, and Archer moved in for a closer look.

"1861"

Archer seemed stunned. "I haven't been born yet."

"Doran said I couldn't be in any time I already was. It must work for you too. We skipped past your lifetime."

"Who's Doran?"

I didn't have a chance to answer. A heavy, cockney-accented voice called from just down the tunnel. "Down t'end, against t'wall. Stack 'em 'igh." Archer clipped off his light just as a lantern swung into view at the far end. My first instinct was to freeze in place for invisibility. But common sense and Archer finally kicked me into motion. We slid back down the tunnel, and fled into a smaller corridor. It was stacked, floor to ceiling, with precariously balanced boxes. There was just enough room to slip past them into another storage space.

The sounds of the workers had faded behind us, but I was beginning to wonder if we'd ever find our way out of the catacombs.

Archer flicked his light back on and shone it around the small storage room. There was a thick layer of dust on the few boxes left in the small space, and a spider skittered out of view of the light, leaving an intricate web behind as evidence of her industry.

I wiped dust off one of the box labels, but it only gave me the name of the shipper. Archer stood next to me. "That's a cloth manufacturer." I pried open the lid and found stacks of folded linen. I took two large pieces out of the box.

"What are you doing?"

"Gathering supplies."

"For what?"

"I don't know. For later."

Archer looked at me like I was a little mental, and to be honest, I wasn't exactly sure what I was doing. But I wanted supplies that I could stash for 1888. Who knew if they'd even last, but it was worth a shot.

The next box held what looked like linen bandages, and I took a couple of rolls of that out too. There was also rope and some wire, both of which I added to my growing pile.

Archer watched me with fascination as I scavenged through the forgotten boxes and crates in the small storeroom. Finally, deep in a corner, I hit something good.

A shallow wooden crate lay on its side, behind other boxes. I hauled it up and pried the lid off. Inside were rows of small, brown glass bottles with white, handwritten labels. A couple had broken and released a sweet-smelling vapor.

Archer suddenly grabbed my hand and pulled me back from the box. "That's chloroform!" he hissed.

Cool. I've always associated the knock-out drug with horses or a cloth to the face by the Victorian murderer. Which is why it sounded perfect for my purposes.

"Does it have any effect on you?" The curiosity in my voice made Archer look sharply at me.

"I presume so, why?"

"Let's test it."

His eyes narrowed. There must have been some excitement in my tone because he looked very skeptical.

"To see if it'll work on the Ripper."

"The Ripper?"

"Yes, the bad guy." I was trying to keep amusement out of my voice. I'd made Archer nervous.

He considered me a long moment, then let go of my arm and took a hesitant step toward the chloroform box.

"Don't inhale too much. You're too heavy for me to carry anywhere."

That seemed to give him confidence enough to bend closer to the broken bottles. He took a shallow breath, waited a moment, and then took another. It was taking too long and I'd just made up my mind that it wouldn't work when he suddenly staggered backwards away from the box. I grabbed his arms. "Are you okay?"

His eyes were unfocused and he swayed on his feet. His voice came out broken. "It works."

"What do you feel?"

"Dizzy. Unsteady. Like I've just fed from a drunk."

"Seriously?"

He nodded. "I learned not to take them fresh from the pub."

"Okay, someday we're going to have that conversation about your eating habits. How are you feeling now?"

"A little better."

"Do you think a full dose would knock you unconscious?"

His lips curled up in a wry smile. "Why? Are you considering taking advantage of me?"

"Would I have to knock you out?"

"Touché." He was properly smiling now, and I was proud of myself for a quick comeback. I was still holding his arms, which put his face very close to mine.

Archer's hands came up to my cheeks. His skin was cool and soft and it made my breath catch in my throat. "Would I?" His voice came out as a whisper that packed more power than a punch.

Despite seventeen years of hard-wired self-preservation instinct, I shook my head 'no.' And then he kissed me. Again.

And my knees went weak. Again.

Suddenly, we heard shouts from several tunnels away. Archer went to the doorway of our little storage room to listen, while I quickly wrapped several small bottles of chloroform among the folds of linen in my little bag. He was back almost immediately. "Something's happening on the street. They're all leaving."

"Should we go too?"

"Now might be our only chance." I slung the small supply pack over my shoulder as Archer grabbed my hand. We slipped down tunnels quickly, aware of the growing sound of some kind of danger coming from above us. Men shouting, and then a klaxon. "Fire." Archer pulled me along faster, and we navigated stacks of boxes and sacks of cargo. In the last tunnel before the Tooley street entrance he slowed his pace abruptly. His hand went up in a warning, and I barely had time to stifle a very unladylike word.

The sounds of alarm on the street were nearly deafening in the quiet of the catacomb. And then my body went rigid with the desire to run. I saw the glint of metal, and then the outline of the guy holding it.

"What did you do to me?" It was the Monger who fell through the portal with us. Fight or flight kicked in hard.

"Put the gun away, Monger." Archer's voice was low, tight and controlled. He sounded very dangerous.

"I'm not a Monger!"

"Yes, you are!" I gasped before I could stop myself.

Archer's voice was low and controlled. "If not a Monger, then what are you?"

"It doesn't matter. You're a Sucker, so you have to die." There was an edge of desperation to the young guy's voice that made him sound a little nuts. Not good in someone holding a gun.

"So this is about me? You'll let the girl go?" Archer's voice sounded like velvet-covered steel.

The Monger's voice shook a little. People with guns shouldn't shake. It's not good for the people they're pointing the gun at. "No, I have to take her with me."

Archer gave my hand a warning squeeze. "Why?" The casualness of the Vampire's tone was impressive.

"I don't know. They just want her."

"So, what do they have on you?"

"What makes you think that?"

I could hear the smile in Archer's voice. I would be very nervous if I were the guy with the gun. "I know lots of things. I know you have no idea how to use that gun. And I know you're scared. But I'm not the scary one. The people you're doing this for, they're doing things you can't even imagine. And they're going to let you take the fall."

As he'd been talking, Archer had let go of my hand and was easing himself in front of me. And while I appreciated the gentlemanly gesture, he was blocking my view. So I moved almost directly in line with the Monger. I gasped. Everything clicked into place. The 'Sight,' his youth, and his face. "You're Tom Landers."

There was a sliver of light coming from above, and his resemblance to his cousins, the twins, was remarkable. He was like a more angular version of Adam, but with dark hair instead of surfer-blond. I also recognized him as Slick's young companion outside Whitechapel station.

The expression on his face was instantly terrified. "How—? You can't know that!"

Archer kept very wary eyes locked on Tom, who seemed unaware of anyone but me at the moment.

"He's a half-Sight. And the other half is Monger." I said this for Archer's benefit, but the reaction from Tom was instantaneous. He lunged for me, and I stumbled backwards into a stack of boxes.

Archer moved fast. He put himself between Tom and me, and was like a brick wall for Tom to smack into. Then, with barely a second glance, Tom bolted up Nancy's Steps and out of the caverns to Tooley Street.

"What the hell was that all about?" I rubbed my shoulder gingerly. Archer had halfway followed Tom up the stairs, but returned to me when he lost sight of him. "How do you know him?"

"I don't. He's Adam and Ava's cousin who disappeared a couple of months ago. I just took a guess."

"Apparently an accurate one. Why do you think he's half-Monger?"

"Well, he's their cousin, so he's at least half-Seer. And the physical reaction I've been having to him is like I need to get as far away from him as I can. All Mongers inspire it."

"Do you have any proof of it?"

"No … wait, yes. Maybe. Why?"

"Because if it can be proven, that young man is as good as dead."

COTTON WHARF - 1861

Of course. The Family moratorium on mixing bloodlines. No wonder the kid freaked out. I would too if I thought someone might kill me because of my DNA. It was weird to think I was on the same list, even if only my mother, Mr. Shaw, and I knew it.

I had a little compassion for Tom Landers. Maybe the moratorium why he was running with the Mongers now. Maybe they knew about his family history and were holding it over his head like a guillotine. It would explain a lot of things that had made no sense to Adam and Ava.

A woman's scream echoed down from the street above. "We should go after him."

On Tooley Street the scene was chaos. People ran like herd animals being chased by something with sharp teeth, and in a second it became clear what that predator was. Fire.

The night sky was glowing with orange and yellow flickering light, and when we turned the corner we could see a massive warehouse burning like a bonfire down the quay. The street was crowded with people either running away, running to help, or standing around gawking. I'm not sure why we ran toward the fire to find Tom; maybe it was because I felt some kind of connection to this half Seer, half Monger kid.

There was a massive crashing sound ahead of us, and we both darted to the shelter of a building. A piece of wall shattered on the street in front of the burning warehouse, and men with water buckets scattered, shouting warnings to their comrades. I scanned the street for any sign of Tom, but it was hard to make out individual features in the smoky light from the flames.

Another series of klaxons rang out, and a team of draft horses clattered past, pulling a heavy carriage behind them. They halted, and helmeted men poured off the carriage, dragging a heavy hose under their arms.

"What's inside?!" One of the firemen shouted to the crowd.

"It's the cotton mill!"

The fireman nodded grimly and called to his men. "Wash down the walls on either side. It's going to spread!"

"Unbelievable!" I didn't realize it was Archer who spoke until he continued. "The technology is fantastic for its time, isn't it?" I stared at him in amazement. I was fascinated by how primitive firefighting was in 1861, and he was practically glowing with pride at the efficiency of it.

A movement in the corner of my vision made me turn. Tom, wearing a denim jacket and combat boots, of all things, darted out from between two of the buildings the firemen were about to spray.

"Tom!" He turned like a deer caught in the headlights, and I watched in shock as a fragment of wall broke off the building above him. "Move!" I could feel my throat burning with the force of my voice. Tom leapt forward, just as the fragment shattered to the ground behind him.

"You there! Get out of the way!" The fireman at the end of the hose shouted at Tom as he strode forward, dragging the hose behind him. Tom bolted past the firemen, toward the buildings where Archer and I stood.

The fireman yelled to the man on the carriage. "On!" The hose was aiming at the spot above the wall where Tom had just been standing, and before I could open my mouth to scream "NO!" the stream of water dislodged a huge section of the wall. It came crashing down to the street, sending huge chunks of burning wood and stone debris flying.

The rubble sent up a cloud of dust that made visibility impossible, but I knew the fireman had been buried underneath the fallen wall.

"Oh God!" My words came out as a choked sob, and Archer grabbed me as my knees sagged. Suddenly, Tom was in front of us, his face blackened with smudges of soot, and his eyes wide open in horror and fear.

"Get me out of here!" His voice came out as a croak, and his eyes stared right through me.

Archer grabbed my hand and gestured to the young Seer. "Come on. Back to the catacombs."

The fire was like a war zone behind us as we raced down Tooley Street toward the bridge. The klaxon rang again and more people joined the rescue operation. We should have stayed to help, even though I knew in my gut the fireman was dead before he hit the ground.

We scrambled down Nancy's Steps, and Archer led us unerringly down the pitch black route through the tunnels, back to the tiny storeroom where we'd come through.

I pulled the Maglite out of my pocket and flicked it on for those two of us without Vampire vision. The catacombs were silent except for the pounding of our feet as we ran. Tom's breath came hard and fast, probably the aftermath of panic. He could have been killed by that wall, and I didn't envy him the flashbacks.

"It's in there." I waved my flashlight toward the small storage room off to the right. Archer was already inside, but Tom halted outside the door.

"You're with the Vampire." Tom's voice was filled with disgust.

"So, you're with Mongers."

"Vampires are worse." The certainty in his voice was absolute.

"Not in my world."

Archer stepped into view. "Why do they want Saira?"

His directness startled Tom, who stepped backwards as if he was about to bolt. "If you run again, I'm leaving you here." I loaded my voice up with as much edge as I could find. The young Seer responded kind of like he had when I'd yelled at him up on the street, like he needed a mom or something.

"They say she's on their list." Tom's words were tentative.

"What list?" Archer growled.

Tom looked frightened. "I've never seen it. I don't know."

Archer's patience was thinning. "What will they do with her if they get her?"

"I... I don't know."

Now I was mad. "You were willing to take on a Vampire just to get me, and you have no idea why? Are you out of your mind?" I was ranting and I didn't care. It felt good to let go of all the stress and fear, and frankly, Tom Landers deserved it. "What if those Monger jerks wanted to kidnap me?" From the shock on Tom's face he clearly hadn't thought about it. So I pressed harder. "Everyone in your family thinks that's what happened to you, by the way. Adam thinks it's his fault you're gone, and your dad keeps threatening Miss Simpson and the whole school with shutdown until you're found."

Tom finally found a little courage in his voice. "My dad's a jerk."

"Clearly. And so are you."

He took a deep breath. "I don't know why they want you."

"And you also didn't think about what it feels like to be hunted, did you?" Again, the shocked look in his eyes. "Well, let me tell you, it sucks! People you don't know following you everywhere, chasing you down dark tunnels, threatening to kill your friends. It's not fun, Tom."

"I'm sorry." His voice was small, and to his credit, he cleared his throat and said it again in a stronger tone. "I'm sorry."

I looked at Tom Landers, a guy my age, a little shorter than me, who had spent the last few months running with a bad crowd, making bad choices. With those two words he actually took some responsibility, and I was impressed. I made my expression hard. "Don't do it again."

"I won't."

Tom Landers was a decent guy, and I decided I could like him. Archer spoke from the darkened doorway. "They may be waiting for us when we go back."

"Crap. You're right. We can't go back to the same place we left."

275

Tom was looking back and forth between Archer and me like he was watching a tennis match in Japanese. But Archer was a step ahead of me. "Can you make another portal?"

Of course. Think like my mythical friend, Doran. "I don't have to. Let's go up to the base of the bridge."

Archer nodded. "There are places to hide, and we wouldn't be trapped if the Mongers remain."

"Wait. My stash-bag." I ran for the little room with forgotten boxes and grabbed the bag I'd filled with random supplies. When I got back to the portal room, Archer was working at something on the wall while Tom watched him warily. "What are you doing?"

"Finding you a hiding place." Archer gave a great heave and a flat stone pulled out of the wall. Behind it was a smallish void.

"Nice." I pushed the small bag into the void, mindful of the chloroform bottles wrapped in linen inside, and Archer replaced the stone. I pulled out the last of the chalk rock and marked a corner of the stone. Probably wouldn't last, but worth a shot.

"Try it. Make sure you can pull the stone out by yourself."

"You won't come with me?"

I started working the stone, and found that with a little leverage I could wiggle it out.

Archer shook his head. "I don't think I can because I already exist in 1888, remember? And I don't think I want to explain this to me." He meant his Vampire-ness, and I grimaced. I didn't want to explain it to him either.

I took a deep breath. "Okay guys, we have to go." Tom and Archer both nodded and we took off running. On Tooley Street the mayhem seemed to have died down a little. People were still standing around watching the Cotton Wharf Fire, but the klaxons had stopped, and the frantic running and gone silent too.

I tucked my Maglite up into the sleeve of my coat to hide it from casual view, and all three of us slowed to a walk at the top of Nancy's Steps.

Archer took a protective position by my right side, and Tom took a place slightly behind me on the left. It could have been a total accident, but it gave me the feeling of being flanked by bodyguards.

The fire was a great distraction, and we made it to the base of the bridge without incident. I went to the pillar where the spiral had been, and very cautiously flipped on my flashlight. The pillar was blank.

"There was a spiral here before." My voice was a whisper, but both Tom and Archer stopped in their tracks.

"What do you mean? Before when?"

"Crap. 1888." We were in 1861. I'd traveled through that spiral to 1888. I shone the Maglite at the other pillars just to be certain, but there was no doubt in my mind. This was the place.

Archer looked at me a long moment. "What did the spiral look like?"

"When?"

"In 1888. What did it look like?"

"I don't know, I didn't really think about it. It was painted or drawn with some dark color." Archer looked around at the ground. Behind the pillar were the remains of an old campfire and he picked up a charred stick.

"Would this do?"

"It won't last 27 years."

"It doesn't have to. It just has to be the foundation for the one to come." That sounded as reasonable as anything I could come up with, so I took the stick from Archer and started drawing.

Tom watched me, fascinated. "So, you draw that spiral thingy and it turns into a door?"

"A portal, and yeah, I guess that's what happens."

Archer shifted impatiently. "It's almost morning and the fire's dying down."

Tom grimaced. "I puked when we came through before."

I shuddered. "Me too."

Archer stared out into the pre-dawn darkness like a statue. I knew he was impatient to leave, and we were at risk every moment we stood out in the open, no matter how dark and quiet it was. I was almost done drawing the last spiral.

Archer suddenly stiffened, though it was a little like a statue going even more rigid. "Someone's coming."

Tom and I froze in place. I could hear the faint shuffle of someone coming toward us, but I couldn't see anything yet. I gestured to Tom, and he and Archer were beside me in a second. "Hold on to me," I whispered to them.

I felt a hand grab my coat, and another snake around my waist. "Tom! Hold me, not my clothes." The hand on the jacket moved to my arm, which he grabbed like he was hanging on for dear life. The edges of the spiral had begun to glow when I heard the off-key hum of whoever was approaching.

I traced faster, and the humming grew louder and louder until I realized it was in my ears and my body, and I could feel myself being stretched and pulled and drawn into the spiral itself. The last thing I saw before the darkness was the shocked, soot-blackened face of a drunk staring in horror as three people vanished in front of his eyes.

I clutched at the pillar for support. The darkness was clearing from my eyes, and I barely managed to keep my heaving guts from emptying all over the ground. Archer's arm was still around my waist, but he was sagged against me as if he was unconscious. Tom! Where was Tom! His hand wasn't on my arm anymore, and I looked around wildly. He was there, on the ground behind us, just starting to open his eyes.

"Are you okay?" Archer's voice was soft in my ear. I leaned back into his arms for a moment and nodded.

"It wasn't as bad this time."

"Maybe not for you. But I feel like I just got hit by a truck." Tom's voice croaked from the ground as he struggled to sit up. Archer helped him to his feet and Tom reluctantly thanked him.

I was already on the alert for Mongers. Being around Tom for the past couple of hours hadn't dulled my fight or flight instinct at all. And now I sensed three more Mongers moving around in the darkness. My courage instantly liquefied, and I wanted to run more than anything in the whole world.

"They're out here." My whisper was sharp, and both Tom and Archer immediately stiffened. The night was not as black here as it had been in 1861, and I looked around to see if I could tell exactly *when* here was. The streetlamps were electric, and the sound of a car engine gave me confidence we were back in the twenty-first century.

One of the Mongers spoke. "If the kid is with them, he's as good as dead. If they don't kill him, Walters will, just for contamination."

Walters? Like, someone related to my ex-roommate, Raven Walters? A different Monger scoffed. "Come on, contamination?"

"A Sucker bites you, and that's it. You're better off dead."

The voices were getting closer.

"I don't get how they got out of the catacombs."

"Walters told you, the girl's a Clocker. She got them out. It's one of the reasons he wants her so bad."

Suddenly, Tom stepped out from behind the pillar where we huddled. "Bering? Is that you?" Tom's voice was strong and confident as he called out. And my heart sank. Archer's hand tightened on my waist and we both prepared ourselves to run.

"Kid? Is that you?" The older one's voice got a little shaky. He was nervous.

"Who else? Is Seth still down in the catacombs?"

"He's looking for you. Where you been?"

"The girl and the Sucker disappeared. I thought they went down the tunnel, so I went after them and found myself halfway down the river. Did you catch them?"

Tom was buying us time. Archer signaled me it was time to move, and we started backing away.

"Nah, Walters thought they went through a door or something. He thought you went with them."

Tom's voice was confident and cocky. "A door? There was no door in that room besides the one we came in."

"Not that kind of door, you idiot!"

The voices were fading as Archer and I moved farther away. I was worried for Tom. I didn't trust that Slick would believe him, and I hoped Tom would be able to get away from them soon. Archer whispered to me as we got back to the road. "He might actually turn out to be a good kid."

"Should we help him?"

"We have to help ourselves right now. He'll be okay."

I wished I had as much confidence as Archer did. Everything about Slick felt wrong to me, and it was impossible for me to trust that anything would ever be okay where he was concerned.

We wound our way back toward the alley where Archer had parked the Aston Martin. He spoke in low tones. "They were talking about Seth Walters back there. That's not good."

I looked at him in surprise. "Do you know him?"

"His brother is being groomed by Markham Rothchild to be the next Head of the Monger Families."

"Which means what?"

"Which means Seth is probably the Mongers' enforcer."

"You think he's the one who's been hunting me all this time?"

"Like I said, it isn't good."

As we approached the alley, it became immediately clear that our luck had run out. I was able to sense the Mongers before I saw them, and my hand on Archer's arm stopped him in his tracks. "There's more than one." Archer nodded once and then looked up at the sky. The sun was just beginning to color the eastern edge pink, and I was standing next to a Vampire who equated the sun with nuclear radiation. We had to go.

Archer grabbed my hand and pulled me after him. He dodged down a side street and we started running. "Where are we going?"

"To King's College."

Of course. It's about to be dawn, the streets are full of Mongers, and we're headed to one of the most populated places in all of London. Made perfect sense to me.

We made our way to the outer wall, but this time we went through the gate instead of scrambling over the top, like I'd done with Ringo, my street urchin friend.

"Over there is the chapel." He wasn't out of breath at all.

"I remember. I've been here before."

Archer had to dig way back in his memory for that one, but he smiled. "Of course."

"You don't still have an office here do you?"

280

He laughed. "I left the college soon after I was turned. Bishop Wilder had disappeared, so my reason for staying at King's College disappeared too."

I stared at Archer. "Bishop Wilder? You mean Silverback? Where did he go?"

It was Archer's turn to look startled. "I don't know."

I was getting a bad feeling about this. "Because …?"

His eyes met mine. "Because it might have had something to do with you?"

I sighed. I hated that. The sky was almost light enough now to see details of the landscaping around the old university campus. There were a few lights on in some of the upper floor rooms, and I suddenly got very nervous. "Why are we here again?"

"I have a resting place in the chapel."

"Of course you do."

Archer led me in through an unlocked side door. The King's College chapel was beautiful in the early dawn, and the only sound in the cavernous space was our feet on the old stone floor.

"I take it you've slept here before?"

"There's a comfortable spot under the altar. Most churches have them, though priest holes in Catholic churches are more comfortable than those built by the Church of England." Archer grinned like there was a lot more he could say about that subject.

We approached the altar, a big stone edifice that looked like it was an extension of the floor. Archer felt around the side and sprang a hidden latch. He had to put some muscle into it, but the front slab of stone moved and revealed a fairly deep hole underneath. A spider scurried out of the way as Archer broke through its tiny web.

"I've found some interesting things hidden in altars around the city."

"Like what?"

His grin turned mischievous. "Like bottles of wine, street clothes and cash, some bones, a dagger." He was ticking things off on his fingers like a laundry list. I laughed.

"Sounds like my kind of archeology."

"There are fascinating things hidden around this city if you know where to look."

"Will you show me sometime?" I was conscious of how close together we were standing, and also very aware of the brightening sky outside the big stained glass windows.

Archer's voice was gentle, and his eyes held mine in a gaze that made the butterflies jump in my stomach. "I'd love to." He spoke like a caress, and my skin shivered. His kiss felt like slow motion, with every molecule in my body anticipating the touch of his lips. My heart was pounding when he stepped back. "I'm not powerful enough to stay awake."

"Some of you can?" I was shocked.

Archer nodded. "I've heard it told."

"That's comforting." I dripped sarcasm and Archer smiled.

"I have to go under."

"I know."

"You can stay with me if you like."

Part of me wanted nothing more than to be wrapped in Archer's arms and sleep the day away. But the thought of lying in a cold stone hole under a church altar seemed a little too much like a crypt for my comfort. I shook my head. Disappointment flitted across his face, but his voice was carefully neutral when he spoke. "What will you do?"

I shrugged. "Stay out of sight. Maybe do a little exploring."

"The Mongers will be looking for you."

"I can feel when they're near. I know when to hide."

Archer searched my eyes and then kissed me on the forehead before crawling down into the hole under the stone altar. "I'll be up at sundown. Will you come back?"

I nodded with a smile. "Sleep tight."

He pulled the heavy stone slab across the opening and it clicked into place. Anyone who didn't know about the catch would never be able to find him. A beam of sunlight shone in through the top of the eastern window and lit up the raised dais. It was so beautiful, and yet so deadly to someone I cared about.

And I realized I did care. Archer had kissed me three times, and each one made my heart slam like a jackhammer in my chest, butterflies the size of sparrows flop around in my stomach, and my knees turn to jelly in an instant. It was pathetic, and it made me want to do backflips down the aisle.

Archer had told me he loved me, but I hadn't been doing too much introspection lately to figure out my own feelings. Much easier to 'do' than to 'feel' when faced with the tough stuff.

Maybe because the 'feeling' part *was* the tough stuff.

I needed my mom. We used to talk about everything when I was younger. We'd have as straight a conversation about politics, religion, and sex as we would about food, books, and friends. Usually it was when we were working in a garden. I think maybe side-by-side made for more honesty than face-to-face. Politics and religion made me tired, food and books were always fascinating, discussions about friends I tried to avoid whenever possible, and sex had never inspired more than a passing interest in the mechanics of it.

I wondered if my mother had ever worried about my lack of interest in boys – or girls for that matter. I think she would have been fine with anything that smacked of an interpersonal relationship for me, and yet I had never had anything to model one after. She didn't date and barely made any friends of her own in each of the places we lived.

I didn't really dig too deeply into her feelings for my dad after the first hundred times she shut me down, but now, as I learned more about her 'real' life, I wondered if she'd still been in love with him all those years.

The idea of being 'in love' was definitely a foreign concept to me and had never been a topic of discussion between us. When I looked at it that way, I totally got why I'd been avoiding the whole 'love' thing with Archer.

I had no idea what love felt like, looked like, sounded like, or was. Books had given me an idea of what other people's love was, but it had never been a personal thing for me.

How depressing.

SILVERBACK

I took stock of my situation. I'd slept about two hours last night before we left St. Brigid's, and I was starting to feel it. Which meant I needed coffee.

Of course I had no money of my own, and I felt about as unprepared as I'd ever been. I checked the pockets of Archer's leather coat, which I was still wearing. The outside pocket held my Maglite, but I discovered two inside pockets I hadn't noticed before, and there was an envelope in one.

I pulled it out, curious. My name was written on it, and inside was five hundred pounds in cash, with a note from Archer.

'Just in case we get separated. You can stay in my rooms at St. Brigid's if you need to and anything that's mine is yours. –Archer.'

A warm flush spread through me. He was taking care of me. I tucked all but twenty pounds back in the envelope along with the note, and put it back in the pocket.

There was a coffee cart parked right around the corner from the chapel, and the lady manning it actually looked happy to see me. Her eyes narrowed slightly as she took in my appearance. "Black coffee and a croissant?"

"Sounds like heaven."

"My version would have French bread and red wine, but I can see the allure of yours." The man's voice at my shoulder nearly sent me up the stone wall, but the coffee lady laughed.

"I'll have your tea and scone in a minute, Bishop Cleary."

The lady handed me my change, and I opened the lid to blow on the coffee. A bishop. From the chapel? I smiled at him as he paid for his tea.

I wanted to know what happened to Bishop Wilder. What Archer had said about Silverback disappearing put that question at the top of my list. Something about that long-ago bishop's desire for a Family genealogy felt wrong, or maybe I just didn't like him. In any case, here was my opportunity.

Bishop Cleary was wearing a pair of jeans and a sweater. His gray hair made him look about fifty years old, but his face was a lot younger than that. And the jeans made him seem like a student. He caught my eye and grinned. I held out my hand. "Hi. My name is Saira."

He took my hand easily with a smile. "I'm Bishop Cleary. Please forgive the jeans. I was working on a sermon in my office when I smelled Mrs. Lasky's scones, and a powerful thirst came over me." Mrs. Lasky chuckled as we stepped away from her cart.

"I think it's cool to see a bishop in jeans. Makes you look approachable." I had no idea where all the confidence was coming from, but I was on a roll. He was walking back toward the chapel, and I kept pace with him.

"I wish I could convince the Silver Sneakers lot of that. Though the robe does have its uses in the winter in this drafty place."

I liked this guy. "The Silver Sneakers lot?"

Bishop Cleary looked abashed. "I suppose I must count as one of them to you with this head of hair."

I laughed. "I like your name for bossy old ladies better than what we call them in the States."

He smiled. "Which is?"

"Blue-hairs."

He burst out laughing. "I love it." I could see he definitely wasn't as old as his hair made him look. His eyes sparkled with amusement, and the trace of five o'clock shadow didn't have any gray in it. "Are you coming in to light a candle, or can I help you with something?" He held the door open for me and I stepped into the chapel with him.

"Actually, I was wondering if you keep records here of the bishops from the late 1800s. A friend of mine is related to one and I wanted to surprise him with a genealogy." I felt bad lying to him, but I didn't think I'd get anywhere with the real story.

Bishop Cleary looked thoughtful. "The relation was a bishop here at Guy's Chapel then?"

"We think so. His name was Bishop Wilder."

The sparkly amusement disappeared from Bishop Cleary's eyes in an instant. It was replaced with wariness and anger. "If your friend was related to Bishop Wilder, I'd advise that you find new friends."

The coffee soured in my stomach. "Wow. Okay. Let me start over." The coldness in Bishop Cleary's eyes remained as he waited to see how I'd come back from that. "I lied. I'm here to investigate Bishop Wilder because he disappeared in 1888 and I want to know why."

His eyes were still fixed on mine. "You have my attention."

Something about this jeans-wearing, white-haired bishop made me trust him. "And … I didn't like him."

His eyes widened a fraction. "You didn't …" Finally, he nodded. "Alright."

"Really?" My surprise at being believed was clearly written on my face, because the bishop cracked a very slight smile.

"I keep the chapel archives in my office if you'll follow me." Bishop Cleary headed toward the door in the wall behind the altar. I practically tripped over my feet to catch up with him, impressed that he wasn't calling the cops on me.

The bishop's office was surprisingly casual for being part of such an elaborate church. There were a couple of low-slung chairs from the 1950s in front of a big dining table used as a desk. Besides shelves and shelves of books, the art on the walls were the only fancy things in the room.

Bishop Cleary sat behind the desk and I sank into a chair. He looked at me across folded hands supporting his chin.

"Saira is your real name?"

I nodded. "Saira Elian."

An eyebrow arched up. "I've read your name in Bishop Wilder's genealogies."

"You have? *My* actual name?" Talk about creepy.

Bishop Cleary's gaze on me was unwavering. "Written more than a hundred years ago in his own hand."

Ho boy. This was going to get interesting.

"I trust you have an explanation?"

I nodded, and he seemed to accept that I'd tell him the truth. "Unfortunately, the books were stolen last month. After a request very much like your own."

My heart sank to my stomach, and I knew the answer even before I asked the question. "A well-dressed Russian-mob-looking guy, slim, blond, in his late thirties with a soft voice?"

Bishop Cleary looked startled. "That's him."

I winced. "His name is Seth Walters, and he's been after me for about the last two weeks. I don't know him; I just know he's not someone I want to meet in a dark alley ... again."

The bishop's eyes narrowed. "Have you gone to the police?"

Why hadn't I gone to the police and sent them after Slick? Allowing people like the twins and Archer to help me was hard enough. Handing the whole mess over to the police was way outside my experience. I shook my head. "I don't have anything *real* to tell them. I have no proof Seth Walters is after me, and to be honest, I have no idea why. But that's part of what I'm trying to find out."

"And that's why you want Bishop Wilder's records?"

"Actually, I didn't know they had anything to do with each other until just now. I heard the bishop had left King's College in 1888 and I wondered why?"

Bishop Cleary sat silently for a long moment, and then finally nodded. "As I said before, I've seen your name in Bishop Wilder's genealogy, which was a book he'd apparently been compiling for much of his time here at King's College. His research seemed to focus on five families in particular, though 'Elian' and 'Shaw' are the only two that stand out in my memory."

Of course Silverback had been tracking the Shaws in 1888, but it still made my spine tingle. He had talked about Will Shaw with Archer that day in his office.

"When Mr. Walters liberated the genealogy from my office, I did some searching through the chapel's library for any other references to Bishop Wilder. Nothing was written of his departure except that Bishop Malcom had arrived on December 14th, 1888 to fill his vacant post."

"There was nothing about why he left or where he went?" I expected that all churches were like libraries, with every record meticulously kept.

"Not in the chapel books. However, I did find mention of Bishop Wilder in an unexpected place: the psychiatric notes from Bethlem Hospital."

"Bedlam."

Bishop Cleary smiled. "I have to admit a morbid fascination for the place myself, which is why I was poking around the special exhibit of Bedlam's records we had here at the New Hunt's House Library."

"Is it still here?"

The bishop shook his head. "It went back to their archives last week. But I do have this." He pulled out his cell phone, scrolled through the menu and handed it to me. There was a picture of some handwritten text, and I had to zoom in pretty close to read it.

1 November, 1888. Bishop Wilder here to see SHAW. Patient agitated and unresponsive upon bishop's departure. It was signed in some illegible scrawl that looked distinctly doctorish. I looked up at Bishop Cleary. "He went to see Will Shaw."

"Is that significant?"

"I don't know, but I think so."

Bishop Cleary sat back in his chair and thought for a moment. "Why was your name in Bishop Wilder's genealogy?"

I'd told Bishop Cleary I didn't like Silverback, and I had said it in present tense. "I honestly don't know, because as of now, I haven't actually met him."

Bishop Cleary's eyes narrowed. "But you could still?" I nodded. "And that could explain your name in his book?" I nodded again. He took a deep breath. Either he knew something about the Families, or he was used to hearing things that defied rational explanation. "Who was Will Shaw?"

Good question. And one that deserved the truth. "Apparently, he was the inspiration behind 'Jekyll and Hyde.' He went crazy in 1871 and they put him in Bedlam."

"I have a feeling that is one small part of a much bigger story."

"It's probably in the public record."

Bishop Cleary had a very disconcerting way of looking into my head. I might have thought he had some Seer in him.

"I don't know why you're not telling me the whole truth, but I do believe what I've heard is true."

"Bishop Cleary, I don't even know what's real, and I'm way over my head in a game I don't know the rules to. I'm sorry I'm not telling you everything, but I'm pretty sure knowing more would put you in danger. And you seem really cool, so I don't want to do that."

He gave me the ghost of a smile and stood up. "Well, Saira, shall we go to Bedlam then?"

I stared at him. "Really?"

"Well, not the current hospital, that moved outside London in the 1930s. But the Imperial War Museum in St. George's Fields still maintains a very small collection from the old hospital chapel, and I just happen to know the way into the archives."

"It wouldn't happen to involve a secret passageway, would it?"

"How did you guess?"

I laughed. "Because you looked like an excited kid when you said it."

Bishop Cleary pulled an old set of keys out of his desk and indicated I should lead the way out of his office. "You're not afraid of the dark, are you?"

I pulled the mini Maglite Archer had given me from my back pocket, and grinned. "Nope."

He grabbed a huge Maglite from behind the office door as he shut it behind us. "Me neither."

Passages

The tunnel entrance was under a spiral stone staircase in the chapel. There were even brackets along the walls to hold torches, which Bishop Cleary pointed out with enthusiasm. I'd found my match in secret place exploration; the bishop had combed every inch of the network of tunnels under King's College and delighted in explaining the purpose of each one as we passed it.

"The tunnel between Guy's Hospital Chapel and the old Bethlem Chapel was built so that Bethlem didn't have to keep a full-time chaplain on staff. Sometime in the early 1800s the doctors realized that holding weekly services at Bedlam actually helped them keep the 'Unfortunates' peaceful. Before then the Bedlam docs had believed the word of God inflamed their patients to violence."

"Considering some of the vicious things people have done in the name of God, I can see how they might think that." I was taking a chance on my companion's open-mindedness, and I wasn't disappointed.

"I didn't go to church for a year when I was a kid. I'd studied the Spanish Inquisition and was horrified by the torture done by the Catholic priests. As I got older though, I realized that the horrors are all committed by men, twisting the word of God to suit their own desires for power." Bishop Cleary reminded me a little of Archer, and I thought they might get along if they ever met. Given that Archer was sleeping under the bishop's altar, that was a distinct possibility.

"But what about the people who would argue that if God were real and good, He wouldn't let so much violence be done in His name?"

Bishop Cleary was leading the way down the dark tunnel since his flashlight was so much bigger than mine. He stopped and faced me with a smile. "Personally, I think the perfection of God can be seen in all of his creations, and even the flaws of humanity, terrible though they sometimes are, are part of His design."

I could see myself debating with this guy for hours over cups of tea in his cool, mid-century modern chairs. I raised an eyebrow. "So a murderer is all just part of the plan?"

"Not the act of murder itself, but free will which gives the person the choice to do right or wrong, yes."

"What if it's not a choice. What if it's a predator that has to kill to survive?" I wasn't sure where I was going with the conversation, but I was thinking about Archer, and about Will Shaw.

"There are those who would say true predators are animals that don't have free will. I say everything's a choice. All creatures can choose to live or die, eat or starve, love or hate according to their will."

"What about the scorpion who stings the frog midstream because it's his nature?"

Bishop Cleary laughed. "Even Aesop believed in free will, otherwise the frog wouldn't have agreed to take the scheming scorpion on his back in the first place."

The tunnel was fairly long, and conversation between us went from theology to history to geography. We finally arrived at a heavy wooden door.

"Until Lord Rothermere bought Bedlam in the 1930s, this door was always locked." I shone my Maglite at the old iron lock. It was the kind that took a big skeleton key and could be locked on both sides. I looked up at the heavy stone lintel above the door.

"Do you have the key now, or is it still kept up there?"

Bishop Cleary looked at me in surprise. "How did you know that's where it was?" I reached up and felt for the key. It was almost exactly where my hand went. "Because the chaplains on this side were very confident the inmates wouldn't be trying to get in."

I stuck the heavy iron key in the lock and turned it. The door opened and I re-shelved the key as the bishop laughed. "Well done, young lady, well done." We entered a stone basement with a high, arched brick ceiling crisscrossed with big old water pipes.

"I haven't done a lot of poking around in here because it technically belongs to the War Museum now." He shined his light around the cavernous room, illuminating smaller offshoots and passageways. "The old Bethlem items have been kept in an antechamber off this passage." The bishop led the way past a couple of sealed off walls.

"How come those are closed?"

"There was a cave-in under the men's wing in the late 1800s. They filled the basements and sealed them off after they demolished that wing."

We reached a small room with dusty metal file cabinets, probably from sometime around the '30s, and Bishop Cleary went in. "I've found a couple of logbooks from Bethlem here, as well as the mostly indecipherable doctors' notes that the modern museum didn't have use for."

"I'm looking for anything from 1888 that mentions either Will Shaw or Bishop Wilder." Bishop Cleary scowled, and I read his expression clearly. "Yeah, you wouldn't have liked him in person much either. I call him 'Silverback.'"

"Why?"

"Because he had wiry gray hair, and carried himself like he was a big silverback gorilla that everyone should be afraid of."

Bishop Cleary opened one of the file cabinets and started leafing through the folders. "So, tell me Saira. How is it you know how Bishop Wilder carried himself?"

"You'll think I'm nuts."

"Maybe. But I won't think you're lying."

"I'm serious about the fact that you could get hurt if anyone thought you knew."

"Then no one will know. At least not from me." His voice was calm and matter-of-fact, and I figured it couldn't hurt to have a regular human know in case things got crazy among the Families.

I opened a filing cabinet to search for files so I didn't have to look at him, and then started talking. I'm not sure how long I spoke, but between us we managed to search through every cabinet in the room. I had about five files pulled from 1888, and Bishop Cleary's stack was about ten files deep, but nothing interrupted my story. I brought him up to the present moment, and then paused to breathe.

There was complete silence in the room for a long moment, and then the bishop finally spoke. "So you're saying there's a Vampire asleep in King's College?" I nodded and winced, expecting anger or disbelief to come pouring out of him. "Cool." I stared at Bishop Cleary. "Do you think he knows any forgotten hiding places?"

"Considering he's probably the one who made sure the places stayed hidden, I think he might be willing to show you some." What else could I say? The bishop was blowing me away with how calmly he took everything.

"And time travel. Do you think someone like me could travel with you? I mean both Tom and Archer have Family blood in them. Is that required for traveling?"

I rubbed my eyes with the backs of my filthy hands. "Do you realize that right now I think you're the one that's nuts? You should be calling the cops on me or something, not asking about Vampires and time travel like it's normal. It's not normal!"

Bishop Cleary smiled happily. "But it's part of the perfection of the plan. Remember, I come from a school of thought that believes in angels, demons and a zombie Jesus who rose from the dead."

I grinned at that. The Silver Sneakers lot would be shocked by the bishop's irreverence. He continued merrily. "And the existence of your Families explains things that were missing from my education about God and the world and human history."

Something that sounded like a "thunk" of stone and metal came from somewhere overhead and Bishop Cleary suddenly gathered up the files we'd pulled. "I think perhaps we better go." We hurried to the main room and the bishop locked the heavy tunnel door behind us.

"They don't know you come here, do they?"

He smiled at me as he replaced the key above the door lintel. "Sometimes I find it's easier to ask forgiveness than permission."

It wasn't until we were back in Bishop Cleary's comfortable office that either of us spoke. "Why are you helping me, Bishop Cleary?"

He put the stack of old files in the middle of his desk, then gave one to me and one to himself. "Because I'm fascinated by everything you've told me. And the little boy in me wants to go digging for secrets and uncovering mysteries."

I grinned at him. "It's too bad you're not a free-running tagger. You'd be a good wing-man."

The bishop stared for a second. Then he laughed. "It's too bad I'm not twenty years younger. You'd be a good teacher."

We settled into a companionable silence as we each tackled the stack of files between us, skimming for "Wilder" or "Shaw" among the notes.

Doctors must take classes in how to write badly, because I'd never seen worse handwriting. Only when the nurses had done the paperwork could I read a word on the page. I was almost to the bottom of my stack when Bishop Cleary suddenly stopped moving. I looked up.

"I think I found something." He pushed his open file across the desk to me and I looked at a sign-in log. There, the third of five entries, was Bishop Wilder's name and signature. I looked at the date: 9 November, 1888, and his name was signed at 05:45.

"Is that five forty-five in the afternoon?"

"I don't think so. This page here is written in military time, so five forty-five pm would have been written 17:45."

"What the he— heck was he doing at the hospital at 5:45am?"

The bishop smiled at my midstream shift of language. "A very good question indeed. But here's an even better one. Why is your name on this page too?"

I stared at the name he was pointing at: 'S. Elian.' It was the last name on the sign-in sheet, and it was completely ridiculous that it was there. "Maybe that's not my name."

Bishop Cleary shrugged. "Sure, there could be other S. Elians in the world. It's just interesting that it happens to be the same day Bishop Wilder signed in, don't you think?"

I didn't want to consider the implications of any of it, so instead I focused on the date on top of the page. "The ninth of November, 1888. That date sounds familiar somehow."

Bishop Cleary spun around in his chair and booted up his computer. "I can Google it and see what comes up." I flipped backwards through the log book, absently scanning pages for other mentions of the bishop's name. I inhaled sharply.

"What is it?" I had Bishop Cleary's full attention.

I turned the book around to face him and pointed to a name halfway down the page. He read the name. "C. Elian. A lot of Elians seemed to hang out at Bedlam then, huh? A relation?"

"My mom."

His eyes widened. "Oh." He found the date. "September 29th?"

I suddenly felt sick. "The day before I went back the first time." I rubbed my exhausted eyes in a pointless attempt to see things clearly. But I needed Seer vision to understand what it all meant.

The sun was going down and Archer would be rising soon. I felt like I hadn't eaten or slept properly in days. I sat back and closed my eyes for just a moment. If only I could clear my head I would be able to make sense of all the puzzle pieces.

I had been on a plane to England the day my mom went to Bedlam. I had a sudden thought and sat up, startled.

"Did we get any logs from earlier than 1888?"

Bishop Cleary looked up from his computer and shook his head. "Nothing further back than September of that year. Why?"

"I need to check something from the last time my mom disappeared. Two years ago."

"So, you mean 1886?"

I nodded and got up. "Think I could go back through the tunnel and poke around a little?"

The bishop stood and leaned over his desk to log off. "By the way, the first five Google hits for November 9, 1888 are all about Jack the Ripper."

I gasped. "Of course! It's the day Mary Kelly died."

"Think it's related?"

"At this point, I just figure everything's related, and I'll sort it all out later." We walked through the sanctuary toward the cupboard under the stairs. Late afternoon sunlight was still shining through the stained glass, which is what made the shadows that crossed the window so obvious.

My guts suddenly clenched in fear. "Mongers," I whispered.

Bishop Cleary spun to glance at me. "Saira, what's wrong?"

My gut was telling me there was a whole lot of wrong outside the chapel. "We're surrounded by Mongers. How did they …?" I finally put it together, the thing that had been staring me in the face. "They have a Seer. Tom is still with them, and they made him find me. It's how he's always done it. It's how Slick found me all those times."

"Then I can't hide you here."

"Give me the Bedlam logs. I'll take them back through the tunnel so Slick doesn't get anything else with Bishop Wilder's name on it."

He nodded and was gone and back in a flash, wearing his black bishop's robe and carrying a bag full of notebooks. "They're heavy." I slung the bag over my shoulder. The bishop opened the secret staircase door in the cupboard and stepped back. "I'll keep them occupied here for as long as I can. The War Museum should be closed by now, so maybe it'll work as a hiding place if nothing else."

"I'll find a way out if I have to." Impulsively I leaned forward and kissed Bishop Cleary on the cheek. "Thank you."

I could just see two guys coming up the stairs to join one knocking at the door. The Hunters.

My voice dropped back to a whisper. "There are two Weres outside; they're the skinhead-looking guys. Archer needs to know about them."

Bishop Cleary looked stunned, and for the first time I noticed a hint of nervousness. "Weres?" I nodded and pulled a pen off the offering stand. I took Bishop Cleary's hand and drew my spiral question mark on his forearm under his robe. "Show Archer this and tell him where I am. He'll help you."

"He won't eat me?"

"He actually studied theology and ethics when he was here. I don't think killing a bishop fits his moral code."

"Well, that's good to know." I stepped down out of sight just as the knocking on the door turned into a pounding. "Be safe, Saira."

"You too, Bishop Cleary." I turned and slipped out of sight.

LONDON - 1888

The door closed behind me and the tunnel went pitch black again. I didn't really have a great plan, but I felt like I had a new ally in Bishop Cleary.

I stumbled, and my head swam a little. I was going to pass out from weakness one of these days because I kept forgetting to eat. Not good for someone who needed to stay strong to stay free.

I jogged through the tunnel to put that War Room basement door between myself and the Mongers as soon as possible. Then a smashing sound, deep in the tunnel behind me, turned the jog to a sprint. The clenching in my gut said Mongers.

I made it to the Bedlam door before I passed out, and I was only hyperventilating a little bit as I grabbed the key and shoved it in the lock.

When the door opened, the key went back in my pocket. Lock myself in the basement, or leave the key for Mongers to find? It was no contest.

I headed straight for the small storage room where we'd found the file folders. There was a dank, musty smell in the basement that I thought was probably from wet paper somewhere.

I dumped the files and made my way back to the main chamber of the cellar to find the stairs. They were old stone, with grooves worn into them from all the feet that had passed here for hundreds of years. There was a gate at the top with a door beyond it. The gate was chained shut.

"Crap." I headed back down the stairs, thinking furiously. I'd have to wait it out until the Mongers were gone and then go back through the tunnel to the chapel. Except then I heard a slam into the heavy wooden tunnel door. I froze in horror. The Mongers were coming to get me and I was trapped like a rat. I swung my little Maglite around wildly, hoping a way out would suddenly jump up and bite me.

And then one did.

I was looking down the passage where the cave-in had happened, and I gasped when I saw what my Maglite illuminated. Part of a time spiral was etched into the wall. I ran to it and pulled at the crumbling wall covering the rest of the design.

The pounding on the cellar door intensified. It took several minutes of heaving and throwing before I had finally cleared enough debris away to see five spirals, perfectly visible, etched into the plaster that still covered the wall. The fifth spiral had been damaged by the plaster wall and parts were scraped bare.

I picked up a sharp rock and started filling in the design.

The pounding outside the wooden door had paused while I'd been clearing rock, but then resumed. It seemed like the Mongers were trying to pick the lock.

I closed the last spiral with my rock, and I felt a jolt of electricity in my fingers when I started tracing. I could hear voices outside the door, yelling, hammering, and the chink of something sharp biting into the metal lock.

I knew it had to be full dark now, and Archer would have risen. I hoped he had trusted Bishop Cleary, but I was scared for him. He would come after me and run into an ambush of Mongers, plus two very nasty Weres.

The spiral glowed under my fingers, and I could feel the pulling and stretching begin. The yelling got louder, but the humming in my body was drowning it out as I traced.

The door splintered. There were shouts of triumph.

Falling. Tumbling.

Retching.

I was on my hands and knees and would have been puking if there had been anything in my stomach.

When my nausea was back under control, I stood up and took stock. I was alone, as far as I could tell. There wasn't a sound to be heard once I'd stopped retching.

And the smell was the same – the dank odor of something molding in the walls, which meant I must still be in the same cellar. Question was, was it Bethlem Hospital or the Imperial War Museum?

It seemed like I might be in the same passageway, except it wasn't full of rubble from a cave-in. Which meant the men's wing must still be above me.

"Fabulous. I'm officially in the nuthouse."

"Join the club."

I practically left my skin in a puddle on the floor. Seriously?! A man's voice echoed in the cavern, and I had no idea where he was. I fought the urge to run screaming around the cellar like a beheaded chicken with vocal cords, then took a deep breath and winced.

"Hello?" My voice broke, and I'm sure whoever was there could tell I was scared out of my wits.

"Hello." The man's tone was actually kind of pleasant in a low, growly kind of way. At least it sounded entirely reasonable.

Right. Now what.

"Um. Where are you?" At least I wasn't squeaking in fear anymore. I scanned the cellar but just saw stacks of boxes and discarded broken furniture.

"If you're in the cellar, I'm above you."

"You are?"

I looked up. Nothing but stone and bricks.

"There's a vent in my cell that has wonderful acoustics to the passages below, as I discovered when they used a storeroom to hold a particularly violent inmate."

I must have gasped, because the man above me chuckled softly.

"I don't believe there's anyone else but you there now. You did arrive rather suddenly though. Which means you either came through the tunnel from King's College or by another means entirely."

Ho boy. Time to change the subject. "Can you see me too, or just hear me?" Too creepy to think I was being spied on.

"Oh no, it's only sound that travels up through the vents. It's become somewhat of a game though, guessing what the noises are in the cellars. One does what one can to pass the time in Bedlam."

"So you're a ... patient?"

"I prefer inmate. 'Patient' implies that my health is being cared for." He chuckled again. I sort of enjoyed the repartee with the Bedlam nutjob. He had a nice voice.

"Let me guess, shock therapy and prayer groups aren't your idea of healthcare?"

He laughed again, properly. "Shock therapy sounds quite unpleasant, so I'd have to agree that they are not."

I got my bearing in the cellar and was very happy to find my mini Maglite still in my pocket. I clicked it on to look around me.

"What was that sound?"

This place had seriously good acoustics. I could lie about the flashlight to protect the guy upstairs from knowing things that couldn't be explained. But frankly, I was sick of all the lies. Everyone around me had either lied by omission or lied right to my face. And I was done lying.

"I just turned on a flashlight."

There was silence, then, "An electric torch, do you mean?"

"I guess you'd call it that." Goosebumps raised on my skin. How could he know?

"You're not English." It was a statement, not a question.

"No. American."

Another silence. "What is your name?"

"Saira."

His intake of breath was sharp enough I could hear it.

"It's very nice to meet you, Saira. I'm Will."

My turn to gasp. "Will Shaw?"

His voice was very quiet suddenly. "Yes."

Wow. The sound of clanging metal came through the grate.

"You have to leave now, Saira. It's not safe for you down there."

"Will? What's happening?"

His voice dropped to a whisper. "Don't say another word. They've come for me." The clanging sound grew louder, and I could hear a deep voice talking to someone else as they approached Will's room.

"It was very nice to talk to you, Saira." His voice was barely audible, and I made mine as quiet as I could.

"You too, Will."

The voices grew louder, and suddenly they were in Will's room.

"It's a little late for you, isn't it, Bishop?"

"I could say the same thing to you, Mr. Shaw."

I recognized that voice. "Bishop Wilder, you want I should cuff him, sir?" That must have been a guard talking.

"Yes, I believe Mr. Shaw is looking a little fierce tonight. Restraints are definitely in order." I could hear sounds of a small scuffle, and then the thud of something hard hitting something not so hard – like flesh. Then a moan. Not good.

"Take him downstairs to the cellar. I'll deal with him there."

Oh crap. My flashlight shone directly on my spiral portal, but this one hadn't been carved that long ago and was complete. I had no idea what was going on in the War Museum basement with the Mongers, but I didn't think there was any chance they were already gone, especially not if Archer followed us through the tunnels. I quickly shone my Maglite around. This version of the Bedlam cellars looked like it was in full use, so I was taking my chances to hide anywhere. But maybe I'd be able to see what Will Shaw looked like and find out what the hell Bishop Wilder was up to.

I looked around and finally settled on the bottom shelf of an empty cabinet. I felt like I should have a 'do not fold, spindle or mutilate' sticker stamped to my forehead as I origamied myself inside.

Despite the cool damp of the cellar, it was stuffy inside the cabinet and very hard to breathe. I took a risk and cracked the door just enough to get some air. It gave me the sliver of a view into a dark room across the way.

Grunts and shuffled footsteps. Someone was dragging something heavy down the stairs. Then an oil lamp came into view, painting a circle of yellow light around the man who led the way. Bishop Wilder. My fight or flight instinct kicked in so hard I almost bolted right in front of him, and gripped knees were the only thing that kept me hidden in the stifling cabinet.

Right behind the bishop was a big, goonish guy dressed in a uniform. Goon was walking backwards down the corridor dragging an even bigger man.

Bishop Wilder was going to pass my cabinet, and I instinctively pulled all the heat from the tiny space into myself and wrapped my body in a warding cocoon. It was such an automatic response to the bishop that I suddenly realized he had to be a Monger. He passed by me without seeming aware of my presence at all. And when I let out a breath, I released the ward in the same moment.

"Strange temperatures down 'ere, ain't they?" Goon was hauling the big man past my cabinet. The man was wearing something vaguely like modern-day scrubs, but in a homespun variety, and he was possibly the hairiest person I'd ever seen. Longish, light brown hair shot with gray and a beard that hadn't seen a razor in a long time. Was this Will Shaw, famous scientist and the disgrace of his family?

Suddenly, the man's eyes flashed open and locked on mine. He absolutely, positively knew I was there. I couldn't blink or look away, and I felt like he was consuming me with his eyes. In that moment I knew for certain this was Will, the inspiration for Jekyll and Hyde and the Shifter who had murdered the council. And then he closed his eyes and his limp body was dragged out of sight.

"Strap him to the table in here." The bishop's voice commanded Goon imperiously. There were more sounds of grunting and heaving, and then the heavy slap of flesh on a hard surface. Will was clearly conscious. Why wasn't he trying to stop them?

"Lock the straps you imbecile! He will try to kill us both if he returns to consciousness. I can't have any questions about his physical condition before they take his mind." The clicks of locks snapping into place brought bile up into my throat, and I was starting to flush in that way that predicts imminent puke.

I had to get out of there or risk gagging on my own vomit. I didn't know if I could make it to the tunnel door without being seen, but I needed air like I'd never needed anything before in my life. I pushed the cabinet door open as slowly as I could with a badly shaking hand. The men in the room down the hall seemed to be too focused on their tasks to pay attention to the darkness outside their door.

My body slithered to the floor, and I felt literally spineless as I tried to get to my feet. The light caught my eye as I half-stumbled away from my prison-cabinet, and burned into my brain was a glimpse of Will Shaw, strapped to a metal table. I ran.

"Find out what made that noise!" The bishop's command sent chills up my spine. "You locked the gate upstairs behind us, didn't you?"

Light illuminated the corridor I'd just left, and the Goon answered gruffly. "'Course I did. I'm not an idiot." There was just enough to show me the way to the tunnel door.

"That's a matter for debate. Go find the rat. You should be familiar enough with its kind."

I truly, truly hated that man. The bishop's smug imperiousness was the worst kind of arrogance, and it wasn't just Monger-ness that made me want to get as far away from him as I could. I made it to the tunnel door and tried the handle. Locked.

A shock, but definitely not a surprise. Silently praying that the lock hadn't been changed in the last hundred plus years, I pulled the key from my pocket, fitted it into the lock, and turned. The door opened.

I slipped through and closed the door quickly, then locked it behind me and pocketed the key again. I gulped the cool air from the tunnel and stumbled toward King's College. I had to hold myself up against the wall about every ten steps to suck air into my lungs. What was wrong with me? This wasn't just a lack of food and sleep. I was so weak and hot. When I'd warded myself before, it hadn't set my skin on fire like this.

I didn't have a plan, just some half-baked idea of making it out of the chapel and back to the river so I could find my way home by way of the London Bridge. I don't know how long I stumbled down the tunnel between King's College and Bethlem insane asylum, but crawling up the stone steps to the cupboard under the chapel stairs took everything I had left.

And it was the last thing I remembered.

RECOVERY

My arms felt like they were strapped to my sides, and I couldn't see through the blinding light. I moaned and a glass of cool water was held to my lips. I took a couple of small sips, then finally forced my eyes open.

I was in a white room with a big window. A face swam into focus, and I recognized the worried eyes of Ringo. I tried to smile, but it might have looked more like a grimace.

"Hi." I croaked. The wave of relief on Ringo's face was like watching a waterfall wash away worry lines.

"Hi yerself."

I struggled to sit up, and Ringo darted to help me. I was in a single bed, wearing my camisole and underwear, and covered by the softest white linen bedding I'd ever felt.

I spotted Archer's sweater and my jeans draped over the back of a chair by the window. Ringo wasn't looking at me, and I realized my camisole didn't cover all that much. Not that I had all that much to cover, but I pulled the linen up to my shoulders anyway. Ringo practically sighed in relief.

His eyes searched my face. "Ye're here again."

"I guess so." My voice still sounded like an old rusty hinge.

"I was worried."

"How did I get in this bed?"

"Archer found ye. In the chapel. Ye told him to come and get me."

"I did? I don't remember."

"He had trouble carryin' ye upstairs."

"Upstairs? Where am I?"

"You nearly died." Archer's voice cracked. I turned to find him standing in the open doorway, watching me carefully.

"Hi."

He smiled very slightly. "Hello." I suddenly saw the tired lines etched in both their faces.

"What happened? I don't remember." With use, my voice was coming back to normal. Archer entered the room, and Ringo gave him the seat next to my bed. I threw my young friend a quick smile as he retreated to the window.

Archer was dressed the most casually I'd ever seen him. His white shirt was open at the collar and the sleeves were rolled up to his elbows. His hair was a mess, and I saw why as he ran his fingers through it distractedly. He noticed my scrutiny. "Sorry. I haven't slept much the past few days."

I was shocked. "Days? How long have I been here?"

"Since Saturday night. Today is Tuesday, Miss Elian."

"Call me Saira already. I mean, you've clearly seen me in my underwear." That underwear situation was going to have to be remedied very quickly. When I thought about wearing the same pair for three days I wanted to strip them off and burn them on the spot.

Archer smiled tiredly. "Of course, Saira. As you wish."

"Tell me what happened."

"As your friend, Ringo—" Archer paused, and I looked over at Ringo in surprise. He grinned back. I liked that he had adopted the nickname I'd given him, even if he had no idea what it meant.

"—mentioned, I found you in the chapel, just outside a cupboard beneath the main staircase. When I was unable to carry you up the stairs, you ordered me to find this young man at the river. His employer was able to direct me to him."

I interrupted and looked back at Ringo. "Employer?"

He nodded proudly. "I work for Gosford on the river."

I grinned at him. "Good for you!"

Archer watched the exchange between me and Ringo with tired amusement. I think he'd come to appreciate the kid.

Ringo continued the story. "I helped his lordship carry you up here—"

"I'm not a lord." Archer's voice cut in dryly and Ringo grinned even wider. It was clearly a game they'd played before.

"Oh right, his not-a-lordship then."

Archer grimaced and I laughed, which felt strange, as though it had been a very long time. "Where is 'here' exactly?" I looked around the room. It was nearly bare of furniture, and totally nondescript in the way hospital rooms can be.

Archer answered. "You're above the chapel at Guy's College." Oh wow. Equal parts relief and trepidation flashed through my gut. Where was Bishop Wilder? "I know it's a men's college, but given the clothes you were wearing, we were confident we could sneak you in without anyone the wiser."

"Who undressed me?"

Now Archer seemed positively mortified. "I did."

Ringo piped up quickly. "I didn't want no part in that. Whatever else yer clothes say, you're a lady." I almost laughed out loud at the expression of pure shame on Archer's face.

I changed the subject quickly. "Does anyone else know I'm here?"

Ringo shook his head. "No one."

I looked closely at Archer. "Does the bishop know I'm here?"

"He does not. Though I'm afraid he's starting to get suspicious about my behavior. I believe he thinks it's tied to a case at Bethlem though."

I'd been there three days. Three days since I'd seen the bishop in the cellar at Bedlam. I gasped. "Will Shaw."

Archer stared at me in shock. "How do you know about Shaw?"

"Is he still ..." I couldn't say the world.

"Intact? Yes. Though not for lack of trying on the part of Bishop Wilder. Apparently there was an incident a few nights ago, and Shaw has been placed in restricted quarters. The bishop hasn't been able to see him alone since then, and it's been very frustrating for him. He's been taking it out on all his students."

Ringo nodded. "Oh, that's who ye're talking about. The old codger what's been 'asslin' ye all in the 'alls. I've seen murderous looks on yer faces when 'e leaves a room."

Glad to hear I wasn't the only one who hated the bishop.

"Are you still working for him?" I was tentative in my choice of words because I didn't know how else to describe the bishop's control over Archer.

Archer hesitated for a moment. "He is still officially my tutor."

"How's your hunt for the Whitechapel killer going?" I looked pointedly at Archer, and he met my eyes.

"There's been no progress."

"Ye're after that rotter what's been killin' the ladies across the bridge?" Ringo looked at Archer in wonder.

"In a manner of speaking, yes."

"Well, for what it's worth, I think 'e's gentry, or church or somethin' 'igh up. Someone with means."

This startled Archer. "Why is that?"

Ringo shrugged. "The knife. It's 'ard work to keep a knife sharp enough to cut meat, and not many 'ave such a blade. No, a workin' man is more likely to bludgeon someone to death than cut them up. It's less work and less mess. And when a man gets blood on 'is only suit of clothes, people tend to notice."

Ringo had a point, and while Archer pondered it, I had a chance to look at him more closely. He looked so much like the Vampire Archer, with the same tousled, longish dark hair, the same smooth skin and deep blue eyes. But the expression in these eyes was much more innocent than the one Archer wore in my time. As if my Archer had seen more of the world than he ever wanted to see, and this Archer hadn't yet experienced all those worries. Even weirder to me was that I thought of Archer as *mine* in any sense of the word.

"'E's not killed again, though." Ringo's voice pulled me away from that disturbing train of thought.

I responded. "He will." I could feel Ringo's eyes on me, but I only had eyes for Archer. "Remember I told you there was another victim? Her name was Mary Kelly, and the Ripper killed her on November 9th, 1888."

Archer stared at me a long time, and Ringo was practically bursting at the seams wanting to know what I was talking about, but he held his tongue.

"I have to find Mary Kelly. I don't know if I can change anything, but I have to try. I have to warn her." I tried to sit up, but my head swam and my stomach heaved. Archer practically pushed me back to the pillow.

"Miss Elian, three days ago you were dying. Your fever was ridiculously high, you were delirious, and you were rapidly dehydrating. You must recover before you do anything at all. Please."

"I'm sure it was just the flu; I'll be fine. Just let me get up."

Archer glared at me. He actually looked fierce, and I flashed forward to his Vampire self. "People die from influenza every day, and I will be damned before I allow you to die, do you understand?"

I looked at him in surprise. The intensity of his gaze reminded me of the way his Vampire self had looked at me the first time he declared his love. He didn't know how right he was about being 'damned.' Guilt churned in my guts, and I slid down in my bed and pulled the covers up to my chin.

Archer's voice was suddenly contrite. "You're tired. Of course. Forgive me for keeping you up so long." I rolled over to face the wall. I couldn't stand to see him feeling bad about anything, not when I knew what he would become. The hurt in his voice was palpable. "It's just … I was so afraid."

His fingers must have just grazed my hair, because I first thought I'd imagined his touch. And then I wished he'd do it again. I had closed my eyes in a feeble attempt to shut out the guilt, but I guess I really was exhausted, because the next thing I knew I woke up to a dark and silent room.

I had been dreaming. Of spirals and tunnels and running. And of the bishop and Will Shaw. I rolled over and let my eyes adjust to the dim light. I heard whispered voices in the hall outside my door.

"Hey guys. What's up?"

Archer came in and immediately relit the lamp by my bed. He searched my blinking eyes. "You are well? We didn't wake you?"

"I'm fine. Just curious what you're talking about?"

310

Archer and Ringo looked at each other quickly. Quite the little conspirators they'd become in their short acquaintance. Ringo spoke up. "We was discussin' yer ma."

Oh. I wasn't expecting that. "I presume that's why you've come back?" Archer asked.

Ringo stepped into the ring of light. "I already knew ye was special from the things ye could do. His lordship just filled in some blanks."

Archer winced at the title, but said nothing. "So, have you decided if you're going to help me yet?" I directed my question at Archer.

"'Course he's goin' to help. We both are." I loved Ringo for that. And especially for the look he gave Archer that said, 'Are ye daft?'

"Good. Because I have an idea how to find her."

A Night Abroad

My plan had to wait until the next day, after Ringo's work on the river was done, so I slept until my body ached with inactivity, and restlessness drove me out of bed. I was up and already dressed in some of Archer's era-appropriate clothes by the time Ringo had returned with fish pies and news.

"They said your notices will be in tomorrow's papers," Ringo said between bites. The one for Mary Kelly was straightforward enough, but the one describing my mother and her green dress I had less hopes for. Still, it was as close to paging Mom on the shopping mall PA system as I could get.

After his classes, Archer joined us in the alley behind King's college for our shopping excursion. It had taken a bit of convincing to get them to let me go out with them, but I played the 'you're not the boss of me' card, and then threatened to follow them in my underwear if they tried to leave me behind. That did it. Archer paled, Ringo shuddered, and I got to leave my sickbed.

Things felt different in London since the last time I'd been here – more familiar. Maybe it was because I actually felt a little bit educated about what I had gotten into. I adjusted my stride to match Archer's and Ringo's – a slight swagger for Ringo, unapologetic confidence for Archer.

When we got to the commercial district, Archer had tried to give Ringo his shopping list. Ringo took it, but shoved it deep into a pocket without looking at it. Because he couldn't read, of course. Archer seemed completely unaware.

So I asked to see the list, and after glancing through it quickly, tucked it into my own pocket. I was sure Ringo had memorized the list while Archer made it, but I had his back just in case.

Ringo wouldn't let either of us go into shops with him because he said our clothes were too fine and he'd never get deals like he could alone. So Archer and I loitered outside, talking in low tones.

I learned that Archer had been shut out of the bishop's confidence since I was last there, and it seemed as though Bishop Wilder had holed himself up in the chapel for more and more time each day.

"Does he keep an office there?"

"His office is upstairs, but he keeps a small study in the room behind the altar. He's never there though, even when he's left word he will be, so I don't know where he goes."

"What about your investigation into the Ripper? How's that going?"

"The bishop seems to have lost interest in the case. I've continued my own work though, unbeknownst to him."

"And your theory that it's a Vampire doing the killing?"

"Well, since the police received the 'From Hell' letter last week, the investigation has been madness. I haven't been able to see Inspector Lusk at all, and I'm not entirely comfortable showing my face at the station in case the bobby who saw us at Dutfield's Yard is there."

"I guess that could get a little awkward."

"Indeed." The wry smile on his face was cute, and I struggled with myself over the fact that I noticed.

"Our history books say the police never caught him; the murders just ... stopped after the one on November 9th. There's a photo of Mary Kelly's slashed-up body in her room that's pretty disgusting."

Archer considered. "I do hope your notice is able to find Miss Mary Kelly before that happens."

"I don't know if I can change anything, but I can't know it and not say something. If she answers the ad, at a minimum we'll know where the Ripper will be on the 9th, and maybe he'll lead us to my mom."

"Saira ..." Archer hesitated.

"Yeah?"

Archer exhaled. "There's one bit of information I have that perhaps no one else would know to link the victims. Not even the bishop knows the extent of my research on this."

"What is it?"

Archer hesitated so long this time I thought he wasn't going to speak. "The victims all had links to Clocker bloodlines."

I stared at Archer in horror. "How is that even possible?"

"It seems weak even to my ears, and none of them was more than a Quarter-Time."

"But all those women had Clocker blood in them? Even the two ...?" I couldn't finish the question, but Archer was already nodding. "After their names were released I did the research. The genealogy work I'd done for the bishop helped me make the connections."

I stared at Archer in the orange light from the gaslamp, and I could tell he was very uncomfortable with my scrutiny.

Just then, Ringo emerged from the shop with a bag under his arm and a proud grin on his face. He held out some coins.

"I told you I'd get change."

"You keep it, for a job well done. As you yourself pointed out, if I'd gone in I likely would have been charged double."

"Well, in that case, the pint's on me."

We found a pub that wasn't too crowded and took a table at the back near the fire. Ringo ordered a hard cider for me when I told him I didn't like beer. It came in a mug and tasted like apple juice gone off, but I sipped a little to be polite.

The only women in the place were behind the bar or serving the customers, who seemed to be a mix of working men and students. The three of us blended with the clientele as well as a fifteen-year-old ex-thief, a girl from the future, and a second-son-of-a-lord could.

I stumbled as we left the pub, and both guys were instantly at my elbows practically propelling me along the street toward King's College. As much as I wanted to rebel, I actually did need their support. I'd gotten really weak from the fever that might have just been a bad flu, and I seriously hoped I hadn't given it to Archer or Ringo. It's the kind of thing that could run through 1888 like the black plague.

"You guys took care not to get too close to me when I was sick, didn't you?"

They looked surprised. "We had to nurse ye, didn't we?" Ringo said.

"But if you got too close I could have given you the germs. You could be getting sick right now."

"Saira, you were in your undergarments. How close could either of us have possibly gotten?" Obviously someone had kept me hydrated and changed the bed sheets when I sweated through them. I just hoped that by some miracle whatever virus had taken me out would miss them both.

We slipped inside King's College and made it upstairs without running into anyone. "Wait. Your office."

Archer was fumbling with a key attached to a long chain as we waited to enter the tower. "We'll get you upstairs first."

"Unlock the door and I can make it upstairs myself. You guys need to get in there while no one's around."

Ringo looked at Archer. "She's right. The guards do their rounds every hour. We'll 'ave fifteen minutes if we go now."

Archer sighed as his key finally fit into the lock. "Alright, but if you can't make it up the stairs, just wait here for us. We'll be back shortly.' I nodded and entered the stairwell. The guys closed the door and I started climbing, but I was weak and exhausted, even holding onto the hand rail. I made it to the first landing and sank to the ground. My heart was pounding so hard from exertion I felt like I'd just run a marathon. And maybe in my condition, I had.

I needed to get my strength back, but it was hard to do when I was trapped in a tower all day like Rapunzel. The sound of a key in a door startled me out of my reverie. I almost called out to Archer to come and help me up when I realized the door being unlocked was above me, not below.

315

Crap! The landing I was sitting on was fairly large, and part of it was entirely in shadow. As long as whoever was coming didn't have a light, I might not be seen. I quietly scooted to the back of the landing, made myself as small and dark as I could, and held my breath.

I felt a sudden warmth come off my body through the pores in my skin, and I worried that maybe I'd gotten the fever back. But then I realized I was warding myself. I hoped it would work again.

Two men came down the stairs. They were speaking in whispers so I couldn't hear what they said. They had to be men because women weren't allowed in this wing, not even servants.

As they descended I could make out the odd word of their whispers. "… tower room …" and "someone sleeping there …"

Crap. Crap.

Okay, if I survived the next five minutes, I had to find a new place to stay while I recovered my strength.

The whispers were silent for a moment, and the only sound was their footsteps on the stone stairs. The heat of my ward hovered over my skin, but it left me cold, huddled in my little dark corner. I willed myself not to shiver.

The men got to my landing and fortunately, they didn't carry a light. A wave of revulsion and fear hit me so suddenly I nearly gasped out loud. I felt it in my gut and instantly recognized the reaction. At least one of the men was a Monger.

One of the men stopped suddenly and sniffed the air.

"Whatsit?" The other man's whisper sounded thick and accented.

The other whisper sent a chill down my spine. "I just caught a scent I thought I recognized." Who has that kind of smell-sense? I mean I washed, but not thoroughly. The only thing I could smell was fear rolling off me in waves.

The men seemed to listen to the darkness for a long moment, then the same guy spoke in a normal voice. I almost lost my cider then and there. "Perhaps some student has a girl in his rooms. I'll have the housemen do a search in the morning to find the tart and send her packing."

"I'll take her, Your Grace." The Ruffian's voice was still a whisper, but I shivered at his words.

"You'll do nothing of the sort. Things have finally quieted down again in London, and I'll not have that rabble roused until I'm ready."

The men continued down the stairs, but not until they opened the door at the bottom did I dare to breathe again. I knew that voice. The man the Ruffian had called 'Your Grace' was Bishop Wilder.

I don't know how much time passed before Archer and Ringo came up the stairs, but I think Ringo nearly wet himself when I grabbed him on the landing. "We can't go back to the room. Bishop Wilder knows we're there." My voice came out in a terrified whisper. Why that man scared me so much was a mystery to me, but he did, much more than my normal reaction to a Monger.

Archer went stock-still as Ringo helped me to my feet. "We got the notebooks with none the wiser." Ringo's voice in my ear was proud, and I smiled at him.

"Then let's go. We can leave here and find a room to rent somewhere in town, couldn't we?"

Archer shook his head. "I have to stay. If I go missing, my career here will be finished, and then I'll have nothing." My eyes found his face in the darkness. This was not easy for him. Of course it wasn't. Here I was relating to him like the Vampire I knew in the future. But this was the still-human Archer. The second son whose only prospects were tied up in his education. I'm sure my mom would have applauded him for sticking to his guns about staying in school.

I did too. "I'm sorry, of course you have to stay."

He still sounded stricken though. "I occasionally use rooms that belong to my father. You can stay there for a time. He never comes to London anymore."

"Thank you. I'll take you up on it. My money's still at home, hopefully being changed into something I can spend." I smiled faintly. "Actually, it's your money. From the coin you gave me when we first met."

Archer's tone softened. "So it was worth something after all?"

"More than you could know." I sounded sappy, but it was true. It was the act of a friend to give me that coin, maybe the first friend I'd ever had.

Ringo cleared his throat. "Is there aught to clear from the room before we go?"

"I wore my jeans under Archer's trousers, so I'm good." The men stared at me. "What? It's cold outside."

"Right then, back out into the night we go. I'll meet you two by the gate. I just need to stop at my rooms for Father's keys."

Ringo and I didn't speak until we were safely out of earshot of anyone at King's College. "You don't need to do this, you know. You have a job and a life to live. Helping me could be hazardous to your health, Ringo."

Ringo gave me a dazzling smile, one a fifteen-year-old kid shouldn't be allowed to have in his repertoire. "Ye make things interestin', Saira. And I like you. Yer not like other girls. Ye know 'ow to do things, and yer not scared of much."

That was high praise from a kid who had basically raised himself. I grinned and pushed him in the shoulder. "Careful. You're starting to sound a little sappy."

He grimaced. "I'll leave that to Archer. But if 'e doesn't marry ye, give me a few years to make my fortune, and I will." My mouth dropped open, and thankfully Ringo didn't see it because Archer arrived just then.

Weirdly, the back-handed marriage proposal made me respect Ringo even more. He was thinking about his future and what he wanted from it. That was way more than I'd ever done.

Archer looked at us both expectantly. "Ready to go?"

"Lead the way."

Lord Devereux's apartment wasn't far from King's College, but it might as well have been a whole other world. I looked up at the grand Georgian building and shook my head. "I can't stay here."

Archer stared at me. "Why not?"

"I'd stick out like a sore thumb in this neighborhood." I remembered the slang. "I don't fit in. I'm not money enough to be a guest and not outfitted to be a servant. And there's no way Ringo could get in and out without being questioned by everyone he met."

Ringo looked startled. "I wouldn't be stayin' 'ere, I 'ave my own digs down by the river."

I turned to him. "Can I stay there with you?"

Both guys looked positively pale at the thought, and it seemed like it was misplaced Victorian modesty that was making this so hard. "Okay, look. You can't think of me as a girl, because to outside eyes, I'm not. And we're friends, so I don't think you're going to suddenly try to ravage me in the middle of the night."

I tried not to laugh, but really, the twin expressions of horror on their faces were way too funny.

"And besides, I'd probably win the fight if you did." I did burst out laughing then, because Ringo went bright red, and Archer's shock finally shifted to amusement.

"She's right about that, you know." Archer said.

I felt a little sorry for Ringo since I'd just insulted him, but really, they were being ridiculous. I decided to hit him in his pride to get my way.

"That is, of course, unless where you sleep is just too gross."

Ringo looked at me with suspicion. "Gross?"

"Disgusting. Flea-ridden. Filthy with bedbugs. Gross."

Ringo puffed up like a stuffy Brit. "I certainly do not live in filth, nor are there any fleas or bedbugs allowed in my flat. In fact, it's cleaner than the room ye've been livin' in, and bigger, too."

"Good. Then it'll be perfect."

"It's not proper for ye to stay with me. It's just not done."

I started walking away from the big Georgian house, back toward the river and the neighborhoods I was becoming familiar with. I was definitely much more comfortable blending in as a guy in those parts of the city, and despite the dark alleys and criminal element that lurked in the shadows, I somehow felt less exposed in the places where people were too busy worrying about their own survival to pay much attention to me.

Archer and Ringo caught up with me a few moments later. They'd obviously taken the time to have a private chat. "I'll give ye my flat, Saira, and I'll find another place to sleep."

I turned to Ringo. "Not a chance. I won't stay there if you go. It's your home."

Ringo and Archer exchanged a look, so I pulled them both into my gaze. "Look, guys. I know I'm an inconvenience, and like I was telling Ringo before, hanging out with me is potentially hazardous to your health." In more ways than you could know, I thought to myself as I interrupted Archer's protest. "No, listen. I know I'm already asking the world, but I can also admit that I need your help, and I'm learning how to put my pride away to ask for it."

I looked them both in the eyes. "And here I go, asking for more help. I need a place to stay, for just as long as it takes to find my mother. I'll stay out of your business and try not to bother you—"

Ringo interrupted. "It's not that ye'd be a bother. But 'ow could ye ever look yer mother in the eye again after stayin' in my flat?"

That surprised me. I thought it was all about what was proper for them. He was actually thinking about my reputation, and again, I was impressed. I smiled at him. "My mother trusts me." I actually wasn't sure how true that was, given that she had lied to me my whole life, but I plowed on. "In my time, guys and girls live together as roommates all the time. They go to school together, they work together, they even play sports together. So the only weird thing to me about staying with a fifteen-year-old guy is the fact that that fifteen-year-old has his own place."

Playing on his pride worked, and I could see Ringo's arguments fall. But when I looked at Archer there was a different expression playing on his face. Maybe envy? I wasn't sure, but I thought it was ridiculous for him to be jealous of a kid. Even if that kid had basically proposed half an hour before.

"So if you'll give me a piece of your floor to sleep on, I'd be very grateful, Ringo."

"I 'ave a chair that I'll be very comfortable in while ye take the bed, of course."

I grinned. I'd won. "It would be my honor. Thank you."

Archer said nothing, but he seemed to walk a little closer to me than my masquerade required, and he brushed my arm or bumped me slightly with nearly every step we took. For having spent my first seventeen years with total blinders on, I was starting to learn a lot about people.

Ringo led us back down to the Thames. He lived very close to where I'd first encountered him, by the London Bridge. We turned down an alley, and he opened a door into a dark hallway. It was the back entrance into some sort of office or business. As soon as the door closed, Ringo opened a closet and stepped inside. There were a few coats hanging on the rack, but he slipped between them.

"Close the door behind ye when ye come in, would ye?" His voice was just above a whisper when he spoke, and I had the impression that his apartment was not exactly sanctioned.

There was a ladder at the back of the coat closet and he climbed it with ease. The space at the top of the ladder was huge, like an attic with one room the size of the entire floor below it. Ringo was right, it was much bigger than the tower room at King's College. The space reminded me a little of the great room in our Venice loft. Dormer windows lit a seating arrangement of chairs and a table at one end. A twin bed, tightly made, was positioned under another window, and a bathtub was oddly, fantastically placed in the middle of the room.

Ringo noticed my eyes on it. "I get water from the cistern on the roof and 'eat it over there."

He indicated a small hearth in a tall chimney at one end of the room. Wood was stacked neatly next to it, with a kettle and a cast-iron pot placed carefully on either side. The entire space was very neat and tidy, with everything carefully in place.

"This is cool!"

Ringo suddenly looked a little stricken. "If ye're cold, I 'ave extra blankets. I don't usually light a fire at night because the light is too obvious through the windows."

"I didn't mean I'm cold, I meant I really like your flat."

Archer arrived at the top of the ladder and looked around in surprise. Ringo lit a small lantern in a windowless corner of the room, and I could tell he was proud of his home.

"Ringo, I am stunned. I had no idea you lived this well." It was kind of a pompous thing to say, but Archer spoke with such frank admiration that Ringo was disarmed. He shrugged.

"I found this place a coupla years ago, when the blokes sent me in through the upper window. The accountants downstairs 'ave no idea about the attic, which suits me just fine. And as ye can see, Saira, not a beastie in sight. I learned a long time ago that if I left food out, the beasties would come. And since I'm not an official resident of the buildin', I didn't like to think of anyone pokin' about lookin' for the source of an infestation."

Archer smiled. "Wise beyond your years, Ringo." He turned to me. "Saira, are you sure you'll be okay here?" I kind of liked that he seemed so worried.

"I'm fine. And I really appreciate everything you guys are doing for me. Thank you." His gaze never left mine, and my stomach threatened to backflip with the intensity of it. Finally he nodded and included Ringo in his question.

"Where shall we meet tomorrow?"

"I'm workin' with Gosford in the mornin', and was goin' down to the newspaper office after lunch to see about any responses to the notices." Ringo said.

"And Saira, what will you do in the morning?"

"I want to go to Bedlam." Both guys stared at me. I seemed to be fairly good at horrifying them.

"Whatever for?" Archer was the first to speak, and his voice broke on the words.

"I found my mother's name on the sign-in sheet for September 29th, and I want to know why. I also want to make sure Will Shaw is still alive."

Archer looked like he'd just seen a ghost. "You can't."

"Why not?"

"He's … he's …"

"A murderer? I know. But I want to talk to him."

"No."

I narrowed my eyes. "Archer Devereux, I will be going to Bethlem Hospital tomorrow with or without your approval." His

322

eyes were locked on mine, and Ringo looked from one to the other of us like he was taking bets on who would swing first.

I didn't even blink, and Archer, to his credit, knew he was beaten. He sighed and rubbed his temples. "Good Lord," he said under his breath, then finally looked at me again. "I'll meet you outside at Nancy's Steps at ten. Borrow a cap if you can."

He turned to go with barely a nod at Ringo and not a single other glance for me. I'd pissed him off, and I told myself I didn't care. But I wished he had looked at me to say goodbye.

Ringo gave me some cold water and a towel to wash with, while he rigged a sheet around the bed to give me privacy. I tried to protest that he'd seen me in my underwear when I was sick, but he set his jaw and ignored me.

When he had partitioned the room to his satisfaction, he grabbed an extra blanket from a trunk and curled up in a soft-looking armchair to sleep.

I watched Ringo from a break in the curtain for a while. He actually looked a little angelic in the dim moonlight. I could see the promise of handsomeness his face held, with broad cheekbones and a strong jaw. I hoped with all my heart that his association with me wouldn't end badly for Ringo.

I didn't go to Bedlam the next day or the day after that. I could barely crack my eyelids open when Ringo shook me awake. "What time is it?" I croaked. Ringo looked worried.

"It's after noon. I've been to work and the newspaper office already. Didn't ye meet Archer at ten?"

I tried to sit up and failed miserably. Ringo eased me back down to the pillow, looking more and more worried. "I think maybe I overdid it last night."

"I think perhaps ye did." He poured me a mug of water, and had to hold it for me to drink.

Archer's voice called quietly into the room. "Ringo? Saira?"

"We're here." The sheets Ringo had rigged for privacy were still draped around the bed, and Archer stopped outside them. "What's happening?"

Ringo pushed the sheet aside and looked up at Archer. "I found 'er like this." Archer rushed forward and put his warm hand on my head. His touch felt good. I sank back down to my pillow, and looked at Ringo. "Were there any responses to our notices?"

He shook his head. "Not yet. But they've only been out since this mornin'. If anyone's seen either woman, we should 'ear about it by the time the office closes."

Archer checked his pocket watch. It was the gesture I'd hated the most when I first met him because it reminded me so forcefully that I was not in my own time. If I ever had a chance to come back here again, I'd bring the man a wristwatch. "I have to get back to the college. I'm teaching one of the bishop's classes this afternoon," he said.

"Have you seen him?" I could barely keep the fear out of my voice even talking about him.

Archer shook his head. "There was a note with the Head of House that I should take his Biblical Literature class today. Usually one of his other graduate students takes it, but apparently he's ill."

"Biblical Literature? Like, the Bible as a work of fiction?"

Archer grinned. "The bishop would have you drawn and quartered for saying that. But essentially, yes. It's one of my favorites, though I'm not often asked to teach it. The students apparently get too inquisitive about fact vs. fiction after one of my seminars."

"My mother read the Bible to me when I was small." Ringo said.

Archer and I turned to stare at him. "The whole thing?"

Ringo shrugged. "I don't know. I never learned to read for myself because she died before she could teach me."

"I can teach you, if you want." I said it without thinking, but the way Ringo's eyes lit up at the idea told me I'd figure out how, no matter what.

"Ye would? Really?"

"I could teach you, as well. Perhaps in the evenings when Saira is tired?" Another point for Archer. He was learning.

Ringo jumped up and ran to the trunk where he kept his blankets. He pulled out a book and brought it to the bed. "We could start with this."

"Where did you get that book?" Archer's imperious tone startled me.

But Ringo didn't back down. "I took it from the study next to the bishop's office. What's it to ye?"

Archer grinned suddenly. "No wonder Theo thought he'd gone insane. He tore his office apart looking for that book."

I flipped open the first page and started reading out loud, following along with my finger and reading slowly enough that Ringo could see each word. Archer quietly got off the bed and waved to me before slipping out of the room. Ringo didn't even seem to notice.

GATHERING STRENGTH

We settled into a routine of sorts. Ringo checked the newspaper office twice every day, but so far there hadn't been any response to the notices. I was still recovering my strength, which took a whole lot longer than I thought it should. Even though the fever never came back, it was another day before I had enough strength to walk again. Archer had set strict rules about how long I was allowed to be up every day, and I actually followed them. The wide-open floor space of Ringo's loft was perfect for yoga stretches and strengthening exercises, so I worked at that to keep my free-running skills intact, despite my limited endurance. Ringo laughed at me every time I stretched, until I challenged him to hold a plank pose and he face-planted on the wood floor.

After that he did the stretches with me.

Otherwise, when Ringo wasn't working, he was learning to read. I taught him during the day, and usually by the time he was ready to throttle me in frustration, Archer would arrive with dinner.

When it was just Ringo and me, discussions were about what was happening outside in the neighborhood, who he'd seen that day, what Gosford had been hauling, and how often he'd had to dodge any of his old comrades in crime.

But when Archer was there, discussions touched on theology, history, sociology, and literature. It was a little like being in college, because he used us as guinea pigs to test his theories. When Archer arrived, Ringo usually left his seat next to me and retreated with his food to the shadows just outside the open curtains. I could see him listening intently as Archer and I discussed everything under the sun.

It wasn't one-sided though. I talked about growing up in America, and the things I'd learned in school there. But so much history had happened between 1888 and my native time that I felt like my stay at St. Brigid's was more easily relatable to them.

So even though I'd barely spent any time at the school for Immortal Descendants, I told them everything that had happened there. Ringo was fascinated by our skills, and he thought the Shifters were about the coolest thing he'd ever heard of. I thought young Connor, the Wolf, and Ringo would have been great friends.

Archer was able to contribute to discussions about the Families. And even though we both knew we were breaking all sorts of rules by telling Ringo what we knew, we trusted him with the knowledge. I just kept hoping we weren't putting him in danger.

When we were done with dinner, and I was tired and talked-out, Archer and Ringo would retreat to the chair where they would read whatever books Archer had brought with him.

I often drifted off to sleep to the words of Voltaire or Charles Darwin or Lord Byron. One night I heard Mary Shelley's Frankenstein being read aloud, and the next morning Ringo was curled up on the floor next to my bed.

At my urging, Archer had gone to Bedlam to check on Will Shaw. He found out Will was alive, but still in solitary confinement, so no visitors were allowed. Not us, and not Bishop Wilder. Shaw was due to go back to his regular room any day though, and I was determined to be well enough to visit him when he did.

So I threw myself into my recovery. I told myself this was necessary to regain my strength as quickly as possible, but deep down I knew that I was really just avoiding having to think about what was waiting for me in my own time. When I'd left, I'd been running from Mongers and two very vicious Werewolves, and for all I knew, Archer had been ambushed in the Bedlam cellar. Instead of rushing right home, I'd convinced myself that my mother needed me more than Archer did.

So, rather than dwell on the very uncomfortable thoughts of what waited for me in the future, I focused my brain on the one thing I could control – my recovery.

Archer was watching me climb ropes I'd had Ringo rig in the rafters of his attic flat. My upper body had actually gotten stronger since my fever, but I wondered if maybe I just weighed less. I was wearing my jeans, which were a little loose on me, but still much more suitable for rope-climbing than Archer's trousers were.

"You are amazing."

I pulled myself up to the rafter beam and stood for a moment, catching my breath. Archer was looking up at me in awe. I grinned.

"It's fun. You should try it."

"I don't even know if I could."

"Come on, I dare you." I was in a playful mood because I was so happy to have some strength back.

Archer considered the rope, then unbuttoned the cuffs on his shirt, rolled up the sleeves, and started climbing. He was strong and graceful, and I admired the way he pulled his body upward with sheer arm strength. He could be a really good free-runner with some training, and I found myself imagining what it would be like to play around a nighttime city with him by my side.

He reached the rafter and pulled himself up to sit next to me. I was happy to see he was a little out of breath too. "Nice view."

"Yeah, I like Ringo's flat."

"I wasn't talking about that."

I looked at Archer and found his eyes locked on mine. My heart began to hammer.

Falling for Archer the Vampire had been like getting hit by a truck. I didn't see it coming, so all I could do was get swept away with the impact.

And now, here I was, knowingly falling for Archer. Just Archer. A nineteenth-century college student who talked to me like a friend and intellectual equal, had nursed me through a fever, saved me from a murderer, and who treated me like a lady without acting like I was helpless. He hadn't driven a truck that swept me away this time. Instead, he had walked up to me at the corner café and held out his hand to introduce himself. I'd only just realized I was still holding that hand.

He shifted closer and his eyes hadn't left mine. There was a tiny smile at the corners of his mouth, like he knew something I didn't yet. Like maybe he was going to kiss me.

I found myself anticipating that promise of a kiss with every cell in my body. He leaned so close that I could hear his heart pounding. I couldn't tear my gaze away. I was captivated by the flecks of green in his deep blue eyes and wanted, more than anything—

"Saira? Are you here?" Ringo's voice cut through the room like a knife, and I closed my eyes in disappointment. I expected Archer to be halfway down the rope by the time I opened them again, but he wasn't. He was still staring at me, still close enough to kiss me, still smiling.

"Soon I'll know the taste of your lips." His voice was a whisper, and it was the most provocative thing I'd ever heard in my life.

Archer stood on the rafter and called down to Ringo.

"We're here. Do you want to try your hand?"

Ringo grinned at us and shrugged out of his coat. He grabbed ahold of the rope and shimmied up it faster than I've ever seen a human climb.

"Fancy meetin' ye up here." He was so proud of himself, I laughed out loud. "I 'ave good news. A young woman answered the notice about Mary Kelly. She's available to meet tomorrow."

"What time? Because I'm teaching another class for the bishop during the day, and then Saira and I are going to Bedlam."

"Mary wakes at six."

"In the morning?"

"No. I gathered she's a workin' girl."

"Working girl, as in …?" I already knew the answer, but I'd forgotten the reality of it. The Ripper's victims were all prostitutes. Intellectually, I didn't have a problem with it, but I would be lying to say the prospect of hanging out with a person who trades sex for money was one I looked forward to.

The guys looked embarrassed. "Let's discuss this over dinner. I brought some beef stew and fresh bread if anyone's hungry." Archer said.

We all slid down the rope and gathered three chairs around the small square table Ringo had found on the street and repaired with the help of some of Gosford's tools.

Archer spooned the stew into bowls. "Maybe Ringo should meet the girl on his own. He knows enough about the Ripper that he can decide what to tell her."

"I know enough about people to know when they're lyin'. That's what I know." Ringo spoke matter-of-factly.

"Then I can take you to Bethlem Hospital, and we can see about visiting Will Shaw."

"Before Bishop Wilder gets to him."

Archer nodded solemnly. "I confess, I haven't felt easy about Mr. Shaw's prospects since his hearing several weeks ago. Frankly, I'm a bit surprised he's still alive."

"I heard you and the bishop talking about that hearing when I saw you in your office. What was that about?"

Archer put down his spoon. "Every two years Will Shaw's condition comes up for review with the hospital board. Because he's considered a violent patient, the normal course of events is to consider permanent action."

"Permanent?"

Archer hesitated. "They've been discussing doing a new type of Swiss psychosurgery on him because of the danger he poses to guards when he Shifts."

I stared at him. "You mean a lobotomy?" I was horrified, but it fit something I'd heard the bishop say in the Bedlam cellar about Will Shaw losing his mind. "But why now? He's been in there forever."

"This year, like each one before it, the hearing occurred on September 30th. However, this was the first year that someone hadn't stood before the board to plead Will's case."

I stared at Archer in growing horror. Someone *had* come on September 30th. And that someone was me. "What if it was my mother who had been coming to speak for Will Shaw? What if she couldn't come on September 30th because Jack the Ripper heard a Clocker call out for *her mother!*" I took a deep breath and dared them to stop me. "I have to get Will Shaw out of Bedlam."

BETRAYER

It was decided. Ringo would meet the 'lady of the evening' at six pm the next day, while Archer and I went to Bedlam after his classes to try to see Will Shaw.

Ringo went up to the roof to wash the dishes, and I was standing at a dormer window, looking out at the night when Archer came up behind me. "I brought you something to wear when we go out tomorrow. I hope you don't think it too forward of me."

I turned in surprise to see Archer holding a dress. I took it from his outstretched hand. "Wow, it's heavy." What an idiotic thing to say. "I mean, thank you."

"You should try it. I'm not much of a tailor, but I can make some adjustments if need be."

You will be, I thought. I took the dress behind my bed curtain and quickly stripped out of my clothes. I pulled the white under-dress on — the chemise, I think it was called. I'd seen the barmaid at the pub leave it open to the top of her cleavage. I didn't have anything like cleavage to be showing off, so I didn't untie it.

Next came the corset. My mom told me about corsets once. Of course, I didn't realize at the time she'd had first-hand experience with them. I pulled the corset over my head and struggled with the laces. Not a chance. This was why women had dressers. I figured that with the long chemise on I was more covered than when I wore my jeans, so I opened the curtain and found Archer waiting at the table.

He almost knocked over his chair as he stood.

"I can't get the laces."

"Oh." A flush crept up his neck as he came toward me. I turned away and moved my hair so he could help me. His fingers were tentative and fumbling at first, but the corset lacing was no joke, and to get the thing closed took some effort.

Archer yanked hard to pull the corset closed, and I gasped. "Sorry." He sounded sheepish.

"No worries." I didn't know how nineteenth-century women could ever get enough air in their lungs. No wonder they kept passing out all the time. "It's hard to believe my mom wore these every day. But then again, I feel like I barely knew her."

Archer pulled another lace tighter. "Perhaps your friendship with your mother is just shifting to something more … adult."

Ringo returned with clean dishes and almost dropped them as he stared at me. I suddenly realized I was in the Victorian equivalent of my underwear, and I hurriedly stepped behind the bed curtain again. "Sorry, I'll just be a minute."

I picked up the heavy brocade dress. It was made from beautiful midnight blue fabric that looked black until the light hit it. I pulled it on over the chemise and corset and buttoned it up the front. The dress was actually long enough and fit perfectly, which surprised me because I'd never seen another girl my size in this time. Of course I was corseted to within an inch of my life and could barely catch my breath, but I suddenly felt almost beautiful.

I opened the curtain. The guys had pulled out the chess set Ringo had assembled from various games and were starting to play. But at the sight of me, both of them stood and stared. I twirled for them with a smile. "I don't know how you found it, but it's actually long enough. I'm impressed."

Ringo looked like he was about to applaud. "Ye look fantastic, Saira! Like a Lady. Except ye can't ever leave this place wearin' that dress. Ye'd be well and proper ruined to be seen with a bloke like me."

I laughed and went to him to give him a kiss on the cheek. He blushed furiously, which made me laugh even harder. I turned to Archer. "Well? What do you think?"

He looked in my eyes. "I think Ringo's right. You can't wear that."

I stepped backward, deflating like a popped balloon. "Why not?"

He was silent, but the longing on his face was naked and raw and I took another, involuntary step backward. In seconds the fashion show had gone from playful and fun to something so intense and honest it made my breath catch against the rigid boning of the too-tight corset. My face flamed as I turned and stumbled behind the curtain again, and my fingers fumbled with the buttons while I struggled to unfasten them.

When I'd finally gotten the brocade gown off I called out. "Ringo, will you help me with the laces?" I turned my back and stood at the edge of the bed curtain with my head down so I didn't have to make eye contact with either of them.

I felt fingers tugging at the ties and an instant sensation of freedom as the corset finally opened. Then a soft caress on the back of my neck made me spin in surprise. Archer stood there, so close I could feel the heat of his skin. "I'm sorry," he whispered.

He closed the bed curtain behind him and went back to the chess game. I dropped to the bed, trembling, then finally pulled myself together again to get dressed in my own clothes.

I brought the gown out with me and draped it over a chair. "It's lovely. Maybe you could sell it back to the shop where you found it?"

Archer's eyes found mine and he shook his head. "It's yours. It was made for you."

I must have looked as shocked as I felt because Ringo explained. "No one else looks like ye, Saira. Ye'd always need custom clothes in this time."

I touched Archer's hand to get his attention away from the chessboard. "Thank you. It's a beautiful dress."

He finally met my eyes again. "You're welcome."

The guys bent their heads back to their chess game and I knew that whatever had just happened between us wasn't going to be mentioned again. Ringo was studiously avoiding my gaze and Archer was unreadable. So I surrendered to the fact that I might never fully understand, and settled in to watch.

I was starting to get nervous about visiting Will Shaw. While he was in solitary it hadn't been possible, so I didn't really have to think about it. But now that we were actually going to do it, I suddenly wondered what I would say. The whole 'Jekyll and Hyde' thing was weighing on me too. What if the nice, reasonable guy I'd spoken to through the vents was the costume, and the horrible monster was the real deal?

I hadn't told Archer that I'd already met Will. We'd talked about nearly everything else, so I wasn't sure why I was being cagey about that. But that wasn't the only thing I'd been keeping from Archer, and that other secret was so big, I didn't even know where to begin.

Archer beat me in a game of chess, but this time I got both of his knights and a bishop before he did, which made me think of the other bishop I wished was out of the game. "Have you seen Bishop Wilder?"

"He accosted me when I returned last night." Archer's tone was grim. "He's suspicious."

"Of what?"

"Of my absences every evening."

Ringo suddenly jumped up and climbed out the window to the roof. Startled, I looked back at Archer. "What was that?"

He sighed. "He's probably gone to see if I was followed here. I don't believe he sent someone after me tonight, but he will tomorrow. He didn't believe my excuse, and I honestly believed he would forbid me to leave."

Ringo reappeared and closed the drapes tightly over the window when he came in.

"I took care to pay attention behind me, if it's any consolation." Archer told him.

Ringo looked equally grim. "Ye weren't followed so I could tell, but I wish ye'd told me when ye first got 'ere. They might 'ave gone back to report."

"I'm sorry, Ringo. I'm putting you both in jeopardy by coming here."

Oh God, the pity party wasn't just limited to me. "Then you shouldn't go out after your classes tomorrow. Don't give him any reason to doubt you."

"You're not going to Bethlem Hospital alone, Saira, and that's final."

"So meet me there." Archer had just opened his mouth to protest when I continued. "There's a tunnel under Guy's Chapel that goes to the Bedlam cellars."

"How do you know this?"

"It's how I got to the chapel when you found me."

He looked me steadily in the eye. "Where's the entrance?"

"Under the stairs to the loft. But if it gets you in trouble, I don't have to go …"

He grimaced. "We both know that you'll go with or without me. Your curiosity is too great not to."

"But it's not like I haven't already talked to him—" I flushed at my own stupidity. If I'd just told them about it, I wouldn't feel like such an idiot.

Archer stood up suddenly. "I'd better be going. Good luck to you tomorrow, Ringo." The way he avoided looking at me made my skin crawl with guilt.

I got in his way as he turned to leave. "I'm sorry I didn't tell you the truth before. I don't know why I hid that from you."

He finally looked me in the eye again, but his voice was cold. "You forget, Saira, I can see your lies. Green has glowed around you since you returned."

Oh God, I *had* forgotten about Archer's Seer gift. He'd known I was keeping secrets from him every day and must have been waiting for me to come clean without having to bust me on it. I felt sick.

"I've been afraid to tell you the truth." I practically whispered in my desperation.

His voice was mocking. "About Shaw?"

"No, not about that. That was just stupid." I included Ringo in my gaze and gave them both the Cliffs Notes version of the night I got there. Ringo seemed a little impressed with my adventure, Archer just looked disappointed.

"And you couldn't see fit to tell me about either the bishop or the tunnel? It certainly clears up the mystery of what Bishop Wilder has been doing these weeks that he has holed himself up in the chapel. He's been using the tunnel to go to Bethlem."

I winced. I hadn't been thinking of that, and if I had been straight with him from the beginning, he would have figured it out right away.

"But there's more, you said." The chill from Archer's voice was practically arctic, and I deserved every degree of it. I nodded.

"There's more."

A pin dropping would have sounded like an anvil in that room. I took a deep breath, and looked Archer in the eyes. His arms were crossed in front of him and disappointment was coming off him in waves.

"If you stay with me, you'll die."

HOME

"I'll … die?" The look on Archer's face was one part incredulity and one part disgust. This was the conversation I'd dreaded since I found Archer's hideaway under St. Bridgid's, and every day I hadn't told him made it ten times harder now.

"Well, not exactly, but you'll think it's worse."

"What could be worse than death, Saira?"

"Becoming a Vampire."

He looked at me for an instant like I'd gone insane, then wouldn't meet my eyes. "I become a Vampire." He seemed to be talking to himself, testing the word out on his tongue. Ringo looked a little pale and sat down hard on a chair behind him.

Archer finally looked at me, his voice curiously flat. "How?"

"I don't know. You don't remember." I whispered, "I'm sorry," as if by taking my words back I could take away the outcome.

Archer's detachment ended suddenly as he turned cold anger on me. "How dare you, Saira!"

I was shocked into speechlessness.

"How dare you insist we track down Mary Kelly to warn her of her impending demise, and yet you hid mine from me! Do I mean so very little to you that you'd leave me to that fate with no warning?"

He paced the room with a wildness I'd seen in trapped animals. I think Ringo might have stood up for me then, but my spine went rigid and I bit back like I was the cornered one.

"You were testing me! You knew I was hiding something and you waited to see if I'd come clean. Do you have any idea how much I've been dreading this conversation? Every time you talk about

338

Vampires you sound disgusted, and I've practically bitten my tongue off not to say, 'Oh, by the way, you're one too.' I have to defend you to everyone! My teacher practically attacked me to get to you, and I don't even know if you're alive or dead now. When I left you were about to be ambushed by Mongers and Werewolves, you hadn't eaten in I don't know how long because you won't tell me, and I had to leave you behind because you were still sleeping when the Mongers came after me. And to top all that, I'm somehow at fault for all of it!"

I felt like poisonous toads had just fallen from my mouth, and I wanted to rinse out the words I'd just spewed. It had not made me feel better to unload all that garbage, and the deadness in Archer's eyes dug a hole right into my soul.

He spoke more stiffly than an English king. "I apologize for any inconvenience I may have caused you, Miss Elian."

I couldn't even find breath to protest as he left the loft. Guilt and shame crawled up and down me like spiders. I sank onto my bed, still staring at the place where Archer had stood, shocked beyond recognition by the vacuum he'd left behind him.

Ringo didn't speak, presumably disgusted with me too, and I could hear him shutting the flat down for the night. I closed the drape around my bed so I didn't have to see his disappointment, and I lay back to try to stop the spinning in my head. Finally, I found something that resembled my breath again.

"I have to go home, Ringo."

He paused outside the bed curtain. "For good?"

"No. I'll be back."

"When do ye need to go?"

"Now."

He flipped open the curtain and looked at me. "Ye should 'ave told 'im. Ye should 'ave told us both."

"I know." My voice was as small as I felt.

His gaze held mine for a long moment, and finally he sighed. "'Is lordship won't like it."

"His lordship has taken himself out of the game." Not that I blamed him.

339

Ringo's eyes narrowed. "Why are ye going back?"

Because I was running away. Because that's what I did when things got tough. But I couldn't admit it out loud. I couldn't say it to Ringo and lose whatever respect for me he might have left. "There are things I need to get. Things my mother left me."

He nodded curtly, and I wondered if he could see through my excuses. "Come. I'll walk ye to a spiral if ye'll bring me back some torch food." I stared at him in surprise, then finally cracked a very small smile.

"You mean batteries?"

He nodded. "Yeah. Those."

"You got it." I got up from the bed, took a deep breath, and grabbed Archer's leather sport bike jacket. "Let's go."

There were probably safer places to go through, but Ringo wanted to see the Bedlam cellars, and I wanted to travel back to the last place I'd seen Archer. My Vampire. The one who loved me even though I sucked.

Ringo didn't have any trouble breaking into the King's College chapel, and he loved the hidden staircase and the connecting tunnel. We slipped inside and down the stairs without anyone the wiser.

The Bedlam cellar was empty except for the moaning echoes of patients above us. If I thought of it like the wind blowing through old castle ruins, it didn't make my skin crawl. I tried to whisper for Will Shaw through the vent, but Archer had said he was in solitary confinement until tomorrow, so I presumed his usual room was empty.

Ringo was a silent companion through it all until we found the spiral. I hugged him, and in that moment, I knew my run would be temporary. I wasn't sure exactly what I needed from home, but I still had a job to do here. "I'll be back tomorrow, through the spiral at the bridge. I'd like to go see Mary Kelly with you."

"It's not fit company for a proper girl to keep."

Stuffy Brit. I didn't even have it in me to scoff, so I just sighed. "We both know I'm not a proper girl. Just let me come with you, please. I failed miserably in my warning to Archer about his future, maybe I can do some good for Mary."

Another pause. "Right, then. I'll set the meetin' for seven. That way, if 'is lordship does come for dinner, we can all go together."

We both knew that was about as likely as us growing wings, but we tactfully didn't say it. I walked him back to the tunnel door so I could lock it behind him.

"I'm sorry, Ringo. I screwed up and I apologize. It won't happen again."

Ringo gave me a solemn look for a long moment, then grinned. "Oh, ye'll screw up again, just not like that."

I closed the door on his jaunty wave, and I went back to face my spiral. My fingers traveled with practiced swirls, and I almost welcomed the nausea and humming before they happened. It was kind of like a train rounding a corner: I could hear it coming before I felt it, and I surrendered to it.

The sound of a chain being unwound from a metal door was the last thing I heard when the humming in my body sent me through the portal.

I was still hearing it when I landed, on my knees, barely able to keep my heaving stomach under control. I was in the same dank, moldy cellar. But the air felt different. Deader, somehow. I reached out my hand and felt along the wall until I found the cave-in rubble. So I was back in my time, maybe.

And maybe it was Archer unwinding the chain from the metal door. Or maybe I was really an inmate at Bethlem Hospital, and none of the last hour or week or month had really happened.

The creak of metal as the gate upstairs opened finally galvanized me to move.

I inched my way along the wall and out to the main chamber with the stealth of a ghost. I didn't want to use my Maglite in case someone with nefarious intentions was down there with me. Although at this point I was pretty sure all my pursuers had long gone.

Until I kicked one.

Ick.

The second time in my life I'd ever kicked a dead body was two too many for me. And it was as unmistakable as it was disgusting.

Every hair on my skin shot straight up, and I practically wet myself trying not to run and scream like the blonde in a horror flick.

Instead, I very calmly flipped on my Maglite and aimed well above the floor. I didn't want to look directly at it, but I had to make sure it wasn't Archer.

It wasn't. I saw the chain and leather jacket of one of the Weres. Mal, I think, based on the tattoo on his neck. He was facedown, thank God, so I deliberately stepped over the body, which was lying against the wall at the edge of the room, flipped off my Maglite, and continued my mostly silent progress toward the stairs. I say 'mostly' because hyperventilation doesn't lend itself to silence.

Fortunately, by the time I got to the stairs I had finished gasping and stepping on dead people, so I was pretty prepared for the next thing to startle me out of my skin.

Hands grabbed me in the dark, and at that point I was no longer capable of screaming so I just gave in to them as my knees let go. Stunningly, it was Archer, and he pulled me into his arms and held me close to his chest until my heart stopped hammering and my throat reopened.

"You came back to me." His own voice was pretty tight, and I didn't realize until that moment that his heart was hammering too.

"You're still here." My voice came out somewhere between a squeak and a whisper, and without meaning to, my arms wrapped around his body.

"I waited for you."

Seriously? For more than a week? With a corpse? Ugh. That was hardcore. But I couldn't say it freaked me out. I was way too glad to see him. Archer held my hand as we stepped through the metal gate. He had opened the wooden door beyond, and I watched as he rewound the chain around the gate and pushed a broken link back together to make it seem whole.

"How did you—?"

"I fed."

"From the Were?" I squeaked. I couldn't help it.

"No. Him I killed. There was another."

"Oh." The morality of this might have kept me up at night before, but at this point, I wasn't feeling so spotless myself.

We made it out of the Imperial War Museum without difficulty, and we spent the next ten minutes walking in silence. After a quick recon at Archer's car to determine no one was watching it, we got in and he finally turned and looked at me.

His eyes seemed to scan every inch of my face. There were about a million emotions zooming around my brain as I watched him, but I waited for him to speak first. And he did. "I'm sorry."

That wasn't what I expected him to say. If anything, those words belonged to me, but I didn't even know how to begin. So I didn't. "Why?"

"I don't usually feed from humans anymore. And I'm sorry you know about it."

I seriously was not in any shape to deal with the philosophical ramifications of sustaining a Vampire. I had much bigger conversations to avoid with him. I closed my eyes and sighed. "I need to sleep."

"Where should I take you?"

"Elian Manor."

Archer watched me for a moment longer, then he started the car. I must have passed out, because I had very vague impressions of trees, and being carried, someplace very cold and dark, and then warmth.

My surroundings gradually came into view, and I sat up in confusion. I was in a bedroom; that much was clear. Heavy drapes were mostly pulled around the four-poster bed, and I was alone. The light outside looked like either evening or very early morning, which meant Archer was resting somewhere else. My chest tightened with thoughts of everything that was unsaid between us, and I willed myself to get out of bed just to avoid thinking.

Every muscle in my body was achy and stiff. I had no idea how long I'd slept, but I clearly hadn't moved much. Someone had undressed me, and I was very grateful to find my clothes, clean and folded, on the wing chair next to the bed.

There was a very light tap on the door and I froze, then quickly scurried back under the covers. The door creaked as it opened, but the heavy drapes blocked my view.

Sanda didn't seem surprised to see me awake, and she placed a tray full of food on the table next to the bed. "Old 'un said ye'd be tired."

I smiled at her. "Hi, Sanda."

She gave me one of those looks mothers give kids they don't know whether to hug or spank, then the deep lines around her eyes softened and twenty years fell off her face. "Gone a week, eh? Good yer back."

"Does my … Millicent know I'm here?"

Her look said 'are you insane?' "Himself said as ye'd be hungry when ye woke." She indicated the food she'd brought. "Ye're skin and bones, lass."

I grabbed an orange from the tray and started peeling it. Sanda took it from me, and in about three seconds had completely removed the skin with a little knife she whipped out from somewhere in her skirt. She handed me slices like I was a little kid, and I honestly didn't mind being fed like that by her.

I watched Sanda while she worked. I could see she had been pretty once, and she still had bright blue eyes, and long, thick hair she wore in a braided bun at the back of her neck.

"I met your grandfather."

She looked up from the orange and regarded me steadily.

"At least I think he was. His name was Gosford, and he had a boat called the *Sanda*."

After a long moment, she finally spoke. "He said he'd met a traveler. Said she gave him aught fer the bairn I was."

I shook my head. "He paid me for work I did on his nets, and I told him to keep the money to buy you something with." Sanda's eyes were shining very brightly as she looked at me, and I smiled. "He was very proud of his baby granddaughter."

She looked down at her hands, still holding the last slice of the orange. She gave me the piece, then carefully wiped her little knife on her skirts and folded it closed.

For the first time I could see the handle was inlaid with little bits of shell. It was quite beautiful for something so useful. When she looked up at me there were tears in the rims of her eyes. "My grandda bought me this knife wi' yer penny. Said a lass as pretty as I'd be had need of something wicked to keep the lads mannerly."

She smiled at the memories as she turned the pretty knife over and over in her hands. "I've much more wicked tools to work wi' now. She'll be useful to ye, and me grandda'll smile to know she's wi' ye." Sanda handed me the lovely little knife and clasped my hand with it between us. "Thank ye fer that memory. And fer the penny she cost him."

I opened my mouth to protest that I couldn't accept such a precious gift, but closed it again. I realized that the gift of the knife meant more to her than the knife itself, and I'd be dishonoring her not to accept it. I studied the knife in my hand. "It's beautiful."

Sanda's dreaminess was gone, replaced by the no-nonsense voice I'd come to expect. "'Tis deadly sharp and opens like this." She showed me a hidden catch which sent the blade springing open. It was the size of a paring knife, and flat, so it would fit easily in my pocket. I closed the blade carefully.

"I'll take good care of it."

"And she'll take care of ye." She bustled around the bedroom. "Now, herself is in London 'til past dark. Ye have a wee bit o' time fer wandering. The old 'un said he'd wait for ye in the garden when ye're ready to go."

"You mean Archer when you say the 'old one' right?"

She looked at me strangely. "None else here is older than me."

Wow. Okay. "And you know he's a ..." All of a sudden I couldn't say it out loud.

Sanda shrugged. "Makes as much difference as any of ye lot. Good and bad is all that matters. Good and bad."

An excellent point, and one to remember the next time I got squeamish about what he needed to eat to survive. She turned just before she left the room.

"It's a deep love he bears for ye. Mind you're careful wi' it."

She left me alone with that cryptic thought, and a bowl full of lamb and potato shepherd's pie. I tucked in with relish while I thought about Sanda's parting shot. 'Be careful' because it's dangerous how much he loved me, or 'be careful' not to take Archer and his love for granted? Probably both.

I swung my legs out of bed again to get dressed. I'd forgotten to ask Sanda whose room I was in, so I did a little snooping. The bookshelves were a good place to start, and from the titles on the shelves (dusted, of course) I got the feeling no one had added to the collection in about a hundred years. Everything was classic, from Shakespeare to Jane Austen. I'd read some of the books on those shelves, but most of them had intimidated me with difficult language and hidden meanings about politics, sex, and religion.

So whoever's room this was had been well read.

I opened a big wooden wardrobe. There were no clothes hanging in it at all, just empty hangers. The dresser was empty too. When I tried to close the bottom drawer it got hung up on something, so I took it out to reset it on the track. There was a packet of papers attached to the underside of the drawer. Someone's secret stash.

They were letters. Addressed to *My Love*, and signed *Your Love*. Nothing so easy as an actual name, of course. The paper looked old and yellowed, and the ink had the kind of perfect indigo blue that only came from fountain pens. The handwriting was sort of masculine, in that practiced way Europeans have of writing, and based on the words, I guessed the letters were from a man to a woman.

There was a lot of talk about her eyes, her lips, and the way she looked when she laughed. People in my world barely seemed to speak anymore, much less actually take time to write something longer than a twitter post.

I had the sense he was being deliberately vague about where they met and how often they saw each other, as if he expected someone would find the letters and not approve. And then this paragraph jumped off the page at me:

We don't have to run away to be together. We can stand side by side and convince the Families there is only right in our union. They will have to listen to us because we are their heirs, and they've been grooming us to lead after them. You will be mine, Claire, as I am yours. For all time.

It was signed like all the others, *Your Love*, but I knew it was written by my father to my mother, Claire. I stared around the room in wonder. My mother's room. Cleared out of any personal possessions after she left, yet the packet of letters remained hidden for me to find almost a hundred and fifty years later.

Sanda had said I had until dark to snoop around the house, and I made my way down the hall in the direction I thought would take me back to the main staircase. When I passed the Epping Wood cottage painting outside Emily's bedroom, I knew I was on the right track.

The house was silent. Whatever Sanda was doing was far enough away that she could claim plausible deniability if I got caught. Smart. I'd have done the same. I headed straight for the keep, where I hoped there was a spare key hidden. It was worth a shot.

The hallway leading to the keep was noticeably colder than the rest of the house, and I pulled Archer's leather jacket around me. He'd been so silent last night, and yet he must remember everything now - the week that I'd spent in the past with Ringo and ... him, and how I'd betrayed him with lies. Guilt was quickly becoming my very least favorite emotion, and the avoidance of it kept me very busy.

As I expected, the door to the keep was locked. I felt up around the lintel but didn't really believe a key would be there. Millicent was not the over-confident type.

But then I looked low, for no particular reason except that Sanda was tiny, and if she had been inclined to help me out it wouldn't be with a high hiding spot. And there it was, shoved under the threshold in a crevice just the right size for an old-fashioned iron key.

I turned the key in the lock, and the heavy wooden door opened smoothly. The darkness inside the room was absolute, and only the dim glow from the hallway let me find my way to the table with the gas lamp and lighter. When the lamp was lit, I inhaled the room and its contents as if it was a place I could take into myself.

It was strange that this room was warded, since the Clocker tower at St. Brigid's hadn't been, but maybe because it was a stronghold for my Family's records, the wards gave it vault-like protection.

I found myself drawn directly to the painting of the Immortals. Jera still looked like she was gazing straight at me, and now, knowing what I knew about their history, I could see so much more on their faces.

Goran was looking at Jera with pure love in his eyes, while Aeron looked at Goran with something closer to hatred. And still, there was that sense of wrongness about the painting that I couldn't shake. The missing person between Goran and Aeron who had deliberately *not* been painted.

I suddenly wondered who had made the magnificent art. I searched the corners for a signature and found nothing. I lifted the heavy artwork off the wall and searched the back of the canvas. Still nothing.

There's one last place an artist is likely to hide a signature, and I couldn't imagine a piece like this one going unsigned. So I carefully pushed the canvas out of the elaborate gilt frame and searched the edges. There, in the bottom left corner was a signature.

Doran. My long-lost cousin, the spiral-maker. Either he had an amazing imagination, or he had been around for a very long time. From the canvas and the style of framing, I thought that the painting was probably as old as Elian Manor. I carefully replaced it on the wall and sat back to think.

There were big things at play among the Families; things I hadn't really given too much thought to because they didn't seem to be my problem. But maybe I was wrong.

Why were Bishop Wilder's Family genealogies important enough to make in the first place, and then steal from Bishop Cleary's care? Why was Slick after me, and did he know Tom Landers was a mixed-blood? And since I was on the subject of mixed-bloods, who was my father?

Then there was Doran, this sort of mysterious, omnipresent, peripheral member of my family who casually dropped by for lessons and left clues for me to find. Where the heck was he in all of this?

I had no idea what time it was, but figured dark wasn't too far away. I didn't want to be caught in the keep by Millicent, so I blew out the lantern, relocked the big door, and then headed down the hall toward the main entrance to the manor. I wanted to retrieve my mother's drawings before I slipped out to the garden to meet Archer, so I stopped by Emily's room on my way.

I retrieved the key to the locked cabinet from Emily's headboard, then carefully pulled the drawings out from under the stack of her journals.

"What the bloody hell do you think you're doing in my grandmother's room!?"

Millicent's voice was laced with poison, and it had made me jump. But I didn't turn around until the drawing I'd wanted was folded and tucked into my coat pocket.

"Hello, Millicent." I was proud of my neutral tone when I faced her, since part of me wanted to rage at her, and the other part wanted to run.

"How dare you come into my house and behave as if you've done nothing wrong. Between acting like a vagrant and God-knows-what kind of relationship you're having with a Vampire, I'm frankly shocked to see you. I thought you'd have crawled back to the hole in which your mother saw fit to raise you.

Calm passivity was not going to win this one.

"You know, Millicent, I'm sorry my mother left you with the shitty job of running this Family. It has clearly made you a bitter, hateful old woman who would rather drive away the little family she has left than admit she could be wrong. And lady, you've been wrong about me from the moment you laid eyes on me!"

Her glare narrowed to pinpoint sharpness, like she was trying to burn me with laser-eyes. "I knew you for the abomination your parents created and you haven't disappointed me yet."

I stared at her in shock. "How am I an abomination?!" I was furious, and my bearing must have made that very clear because she took a step backward. So I went in for the kill. "How is it not you that's the abomination? The Clocker who can't Clock? Or is it that you won't? You're too cowardly to try something you were born to do. You're the Elian who might as well be Ungifted for all the skill – or the will – you have. I can travel through time, Millicent. What can you do?"

I pushed past her and strode out of the room. The look of shock on her face was about the most satisfying thing I'd ever seen, but I wanted to get out of there. Just as I stepped out the kitchen door, Sanda appeared at my right elbow.

"Where are ye going then, lass?"

"Back to find my mother." Until I said it out loud, I hadn't been entirely sure.

She touched my arm to stop me, and then gave me a fierce hug. "Keep yer friends close, lass. Ye've made good ones."

I hadn't thought of myself as the friend-making type, but I realized that was an old story. And a boring one. "Thank you for everything."

"Ye'll be back. Ye can thank me when it's all done."

I guess after my fight with Millicent I didn't think I'd ever be welcome back at Elian Manor, so to hear Sanda say I'd return was oddly comforting. I gave her a quick smile and slipped out into the darkness to the garden, where I hoped Archer was well hidden and waiting for me.

Unlike the kitchen garden at St. Brigid's, which was strictly tended by Mrs. Taylor, this garden was wild and overgrown in a way I knew my mother would have loved. Paths meandered around aimlessly, brambles twisted together combining roses and raspberries in a riotous pile, and herbs, edibles and weeds seemed to thrive in each other's company. I couldn't believe Millicent allowed such disorderliness on the manor grounds, and the garden instantly became my favorite place at Elian.

"You still look tired." Archer's voice was low and gentle, and I felt all the tension seep out of me with the sound. He was seated on a low garden wall in front of a large tree. I sat next to him, and he pulled me against his shoulder comfortably. "I saw Millicent come home."

"Did she see you?"

Archer shook his head. He wrapped his arm around me and I snuggled into him for warmth. I was in a weird state of complete denial, as if I could pretend my life wasn't fractured in about a million different ways. Dealing only with what was right in front of me was protecting me from the insanity.

"She thinks I'm an abomination."

He held my chin in his hand and looked into my eyes. "You are not an abomination. You are extraordinary and remarkable and you completely captivate me." The seriousness of his tone made the breath catch in my throat.

Impulsively, I kissed him on the nose. "Thanks."

He looked surprised. "For what?"

"For being here with me."

"You're welcome. But we should really consider getting out of here before Lady Elian realizes I'm here and sets the dogs on me."

"She has dogs?"

"Her gardeners do."

He got to his feet and held out a hand to me. I looked around us at the overgrown garden as we left. "Why do you think she let this garden grow wild?"

"I know why."

I stared at him. "You do?"

He nodded. "I've been watching your family for a hundred and twenty-five years. This garden was her grandmother Emily's favorite. She used to come out here and sit for hours, maybe clipping back a rose or dividing some herbs, but mostly just sitting. When Millicent was a child and Emily an old woman, they spent many evenings out here. Emily would tell her granddaughter stories about her sister, Claire, and how much they loved this garden when they were little girls. She told her how the wildness inspired their games, and the stories her sister made up of fairies and wood nymphs and creatures of the forest. Emily wove such wonderful tales of sister magic that Millicent kept the garden exactly as her grandmother had."

I stared at Archer. "This was my mom's garden." I felt a wave of sadness for the lonely little girl Millicent had been, even as I hated the bitter old woman she'd become.

Archer nodded. "I gathered that from the way Emily spoke."

I squeezed Archer's hand. "Thank you for that."

"I didn't remember it until just now."

"Makes me hate her a little less."

"I've always understood her loneliness."

My voice didn't work properly, and I whispered, "I'm sorry."

He gave me a tiny smile. "Where to, milady?"

"I have to go back, Archer. From the London Bridge. I can't hide here anymore."

I could just see the look of concern in his eyes by the light of the moon. He nodded and wrapped his arm around me protectively. "Then we'll go."

LONDON CALLING

Archer had hidden his car in the woods behind Elian Manor, and we made it there without incident. I scanned the drawing I'd taken from Emily's room, which I now recognized as a scene from Bethlem Hospital. The building matched the façade I'd seen in old photographs from the files I'd gone through with Bishop Cleary.

The drawing in my hand was the one with the man in the Bedlam window, who I now thought might be Will Shaw. Retrieving it had been my vague excuse to Ringo for coming back here, although he and I both knew better. Now, armed with a bit more knowledge, some restored courage, and Sanda's little knife, it was time to finish what I'd started. Too bad I hadn't been able to grab a change of clothes, too, before I stormed out of Elian manor in a huff. I sighed. "I thought I'd be able to get more things together to take with me."

Archer indicated the back seat. "I finished the tailoring on my clothes and packed them for you. You can take the whole bag or change before you go."

I stared at him in wonder. "You're amazing. Thank you."

He smiled, but after a minute his face darkened. "You have to leave from the London Bridge? The Mongers know about your spiral there, and probably have someone watching for you."

Frustration bubbled up in me. "Because finding my mom in Victorian London isn't hard enough? Why are they after me? What did I *do?*"

His voice was quiet as he navigated. "I don't know, Saira. You haven't told me yet."

"I haven't … Oh right. You don't remember because it hasn't happened. Like everything else I've somehow caused." My voice was bitter, mostly directed at myself. Archer's eyes stayed glued to the road. I didn't blame him though. It was my fault he'd become a Vampire, and here I was whining about everything that didn't make sense about this world I'd dropped into. I looked away at the city lights that became brighter as we got closer to London. Suddenly, Archer pulled the Aston Martin over to the side of the road and parked. Before I could speak, he took my face in his hands.

"I love you, Saira. I've spent several lifetimes waiting to see you again, watching over your family, imagining what it would be like to be with you every night, to run with you, laugh with you, hold you in my arms. I wouldn't know you now if I hadn't become what I am. And to me, it's worth it."

Archer leaned in and kissed me, very slowly and very softly on the lips. It took my breath away. To be honest, I wasn't sure exactly when I'd stopped breathing.

I still hadn't said anything by the time he started the car and pulled out onto the road again. Guilt about the human Archer who despised me and the Vampire who loved me was tangled up inside my head, and I couldn't unknot even one thread of it. So I sat there, totally silent, feeling like an idiot for everything I didn't know how to say. And then, just when I'd worked up the courage to breathe again, we were in London. Not actually at the bridge, but the neighborhood looked familiar.

"Stop, Archer! I need to check something."

He pulled over to the side of the street and I jumped out of the car. "I'll be right back." I ran across the road, dodging traffic, before he could say anything. The Whitechapel Underground station was halfway down the block, but I was headed to the little café where I hoped Alexandra Rowan worked.

Adam and his mother had both envisioned me at the London Bridge, and whether or not I believed in fate, I knew I had to go there. If I was going to step into Slick's playground at the bridge, I wanted to go armed with any information I could get.

The bell above the door rang when I entered, and except for a family sitting at one of the tables, the place seemed deserted. A red-haired waitress in her fifties came out of the back carrying four plates in her arms. "Just take a seat anywhere, love." My shoulders sagged. It was evening and the dancer had been working the morning shift then.

I was about to walk back out the door when she came down the hall from the bathroom. She was wearing a turquoise leotard and black sweats, and against her mahogany-colored skin it was the most striking thing I'd ever seen. She had a big bag slung over one shoulder and was tucking a stray piece of dark hair into the bun at the back of her neck. Everything about her screamed 'ballet dancer.'

"Alex?" My question was tentative, but she looked up at me in shock.

"Yeah?" Her expression said, 'do I know you?' and 'you look familiar' all in one.

"You're Alexandra Rowen?"

Her eyes narrowed suspiciously just as Archer flung open the door. She took one look at him and backed up a step, her eyes widening in fear. It was exactly the way an animal might react to a predator.

"What do you want?" Her voice had a challenging tone, but it came out in a whisper.

"You okay, love?" The red-head called from across the café.

"I'm a friend of Adam and Ava Arman. I'm a Clocker." I held my hands out as if I was showing I was unarmed. Alex's glance flicked to me, but she barely took her eyes off of Archer. She was terrified of him.

I turned to face him. "Can you wait in the car? I'll be right out." Archer's eyes moved between Alex and me, and finally he nodded and left. The coil in Alex's spine seemed to let go, and though she was still tense, she didn't look quite so ready to bolt.

"Do you have a minute to talk?"

She checked the clock on the wall. It was almost six. "I have a class." She seemed really nervous, but she indicated a booth and I sank into the bench across from her.

355

"I'm Saira." I held out my hand to shake.

"I remember you. A couple of weeks ago. You're American."

I nodded. "Seth Walters tracked me down to the Whitechapel station. He was after me that morning when I came in here."

She stared at me, the fear back in her eyes. "Why?"

"I don't know. I was hoping you might have some idea. I saw you notice him through the window."

"He's a predator. Like your Sucker friend."

"Archer's a Seer."

"I sense predator in him. Seth Walters is different, but maybe even more dangerous." She hesitated a long moment, but I could see she was trying to find words. "Seth threatened me. He found me at a dance recital. Adam wasn't there. He said if Adam and I ... he said we'd be hunted." Her voice finished in a terrified whisper. I looked at the graceful girl across from me and wondered how anyone could let themselves be scared that badly. But then I remembered Mr. Shaw said she shifted into a Gazelle and it made sense. She was prey, with absolutely no defenses except her ability to run.

And then it all clicked into place. "Seth is hunting anyone who threatens Family 'purity.'" Nothing like one of those ah-ha moments to open up a whole other bag of questions. "But why does he keep Tom with him?"

"Adam's cousin. I don't know. I saw him too."

Something in her voice when she said Adam's name made my instinct ping. "Do you still care about Adam?"

She didn't look away. "I can't put him in danger. That's why I left St. Brigid's."

"Adam thinks you left because of him. Because he wasn't worth the fight."

Alex looked stricken. "No." There was anguish in her voice.

Alex and Adam deserved a chance to be together. A chance to see if they fit each other. A chance their Families were too scared to let them have.

Impulsively, I reached out to touch Alex's hand. "Adam still loves you. He's hurt and he's mad, but he never stopped."

She closed her eyes. "I miss him."

"I'll tell him." We stood up to go. "If his vision was right, I'm going to see him tonight."

Alex gave me a tentative smile. "Thanks."

She looked past me, out the window, and across the street to where Archer waited, leaning against his Aston Martin. "Be safe."

I followed her gaze to my Vampire. "With him, I am."

We left the café together, but Alex jogged down the back alley toward her class, and I crossed the road to meet Archer.

"Everything okay?" He sounded so solid and sure of himself. And safe. He nodded at the Whitechapel station entrance. "Do you want to go back through there?"

Despite the Armans' vision, I could skip the bridge and travel through the Whitechapel spiral to get to 1888 faster. But I thought I could find Ringo better from the bridge, and I needed his wits to help me with my half-formed plan to find my mom. I shook my head. "The bridge is better."

He started the car and pulled away from the curb. I took a deep breath. It was time to actually spell out something I hadn't said to anyone. Not out loud, and barely even to myself. "Did I tell you I'm a mixed-blood?"

Archer glanced over at me quickly, and then looked back at the road. I suddenly wondered if he had the same prejudice everyone else seemed to have ingrained in them. Everyone except maybe Adam and one or two other liberal-minded Family Descendants. But Archer's voice was even and completely reasonable. "That explains why they're after you."

"Does it? How do they even know about me? *I* don't even know about me."

"Your friend, Bishop Cleary, told me they have the genealogy."

"But you said you kept my name out of it."

Archer's voice went quiet. "But you were all over my notebooks, Saira."

I stared at him. "Your Ripper investigation?"

He shook his head. "My private journals. I destroyed them later. But they were locked in my safe."

I finished the sentence for him with a feeling of dread. "In your desk drawer."

Archer nodded miserably. He stared straight ahead as he drove toward London Bridge. My own brain was curiously blank. I didn't even know who my father was, so who else, beside my mother, could possibly have that information? Which meant everything was just pure conjecture at this point, and the only thing I had to go on was literally splitting hairs.

Archer tucked the sports car into a little alley just around the corner from the London Bridge, and I reached behind my seat for his leather messenger bag. "I should probably change here before I go."

He nodded and helped me out of the car. He pulled a blanket from the back, held it open and turned around to face away from me. In a couple of minutes I had changed all but my boots.

Archer's trousers fit beautifully. The lined wool fabric hung really well from my hips, and with the black cashmere turtleneck, I felt like I was dressed for Park Avenue. I threw my jeans back into the duffle bag and slung it over my shoulder.

"Thank you for these. They're gorgeous." I smoothed my hands down the wool slacks.

Archer's gaze was direct, and he wasn't smiling.

"What's wrong?"

"If I didn't know how important this is to you, I'd ask you not to go." That was about as loaded a statement as he could have made, and I stared at him.

"But I do go; otherwise you would already remember what happens to you."

"I know. That's the part I can't stand. Here I am, sending you within reach of one of history's most notorious serial killers, and it's making me insane that I can't help you or protect you."

And I suddenly realized how tightly he'd been holding himself since I came back. I'd been so wrapped up in my own miserable guilt, I hadn't seen his pain right in front of me. My voice had conveniently stopped working and I could barely meet his eyes, but I took his hand in mine and we left the shelter of the alley.

I spotted a little all-night market and pulled Archer inside. It was a magazine, packaged food, and cigarette kiosk, but they had batteries for Ringo's Maglite. I added some Chapstick, paid the guy behind the counter, and stuffed them into Archer's bag. I slung it across my body like a bicycle messenger would, and we were out the door.

There was nobody visible out on the streets, but as we got closer to the bridge I began to get a very itchy feeling at the back of my neck. Archer must have had the same instinct because we moved toward the shadows of the buildings and slowed our pace. And then he stopped.

"There's someone up ahead." His voice was the barest whisper in my ear. I shivered. The feeling of prowling Mongers made my stomach clench in fear. Only Archer's hand in mine kept me rooted to the spot.

"They're everywhere." My whisper sounded squeaky to my own ears. "They knew we'd come." Suddenly there was a commotion on the next block and we could hear a man's voice shouting.

Archer pulled me away from the noise. "Let's go."

SHOWDOWN

We turned a corner and slipped between buildings, finally emerging near a bus stop and the entrance to Nancy's Steps. We stayed tucked just inside the alley, deep in the shadows, but still able to see the scene in front of us.

And all of a sudden I got it. "They're not here for me." My whisper was incredulous as I spotted the twins' uncle, Mr. Landers, standing near their parents, Mr. and Mrs. Arman. Facing him was a man I'd never seen before, wearing really expensive, all-black clothes like a ninja. I loathed him on sight.

"Send Tom out here!" Mr. Landers yelled at the Ninja.

"I don't know what you're talking about, Landers. My understanding is that your son ran away from you, and it's no surprise to me that he did." The Ninja's voice was pure Monger, and it slithered up my spine.

Mr. Arman spoke in a calm, placating tone. "Rothchild, my wife Saw Seth Walters here, holding Tom against his will. We all know Walters works for you."

The Ninja must be Markham Rothchild, the current Head of the Monger Family, and Seth's boss. "There is no truth to whatever little 'vision' your wife had, and it's slanderous for you to even suggest—"

Mrs. Arman's voice was so very bored-sounding I almost felt sorry for Rothchild. "Don't be ridiculous, Markham. Let Tom go and your exposure at the Descendants' Council will be mitigated by your willingness to help. If you insist on continuing this charade, we will see that you're removed from the council."

Suddenly, a very fancy car screeched up and parked, and Ms. Rothchild emerged from the passenger seat. There was a Hunter driving. The one who wasn't a corpse in Bedlam's cellar.

It was everything I could do not to run.

Ms. Rothchild strode to her father and whispered something in his ear. The expression on Markham Rothchild's face darkened instantly. He raised an eyebrow at his daughter in question, and she nodded grimly. His eyes narrowed, and his voice took on a tone of hatred as he turned back to the assembled adults. "Apparently there may be an issue of mixed blood with Tom."

Mr. Landers exploded in rage. "That's outrageous!" But Mrs. Arman touched her brother's arm and stepped forward, glaring at the Rothchilds as if she wanted to tear out their hearts.

"The issue may be one of force, Markham. Something you would do well to ask your … enforcer about."

Oh. My. God. *I* knew Tom was a mixed-blood, of course, because I could feel the Monger in him. But somehow Mrs. Arman knew too. I flashed back to the shock on her face during our conversation about Tom's mother, and it fit. But was it really possible that Seth Walters, the Monger enforcer, was actually Tom's dad? The thought made me feel so sorry for Tom I could barely stand it.

Next to me, Archer hissed. "They'll have to kill him now."

But wasn't this calculated? I mean, they were talking about Rothchild's man having committed a horrific crime, and I couldn't imagine Mr. Landers or the Armans calling for Tom's blood if the Mongers didn't.

But Mongers could be trusted, and I whispered back. "Then we have to save him."

Ms. Rothchild had begun screeching at Mrs. Arman, and Mr. Landers was yelling at Markham Rothchild so fiercely I thought he would burst something. Archer touched my arm to direct me away from the scene.

"Is there another entrance to the tunnels?"

I shook my head. "I haven't heard of one. Nancy's Steps is the only thing that's been written about."

He seemed thoughtful. "Why do you think Tom is here?"

"Because *I* am here." A voice growled from the shadows, and my guts liquefied. Seth Walters stepped from the shadows, pushing Tom in front of him with a gun. The gun was one of those little sleek, modern, totally deadly-looking ones and was loosely aimed at both Tom and me.

I felt Archer spring-load beside me, like he was using every ounce of self-control not to leap at the guy and take him down. Seth must have sensed that too, because his loose aim at me suddenly tightened.

"What do you want?" I was proud that my voice was steady, but the leer in Seth's voice made me want to smack him.

"Same thing I've wanted all along, dear girl. You."

Which was about the scariest thing I'd ever heard. "Why?"

"Oh come now, haven't you figured out what you are? Suffice it to say that unless your blood-sucking friend lets you go peacefully, I will kill you."

Right. I'll kill you unless you come with me so I can kill you? I looked over at Tom, who was positively white-faced with fear. This whole gathering here tonight was about him. Finding me was just opportunity. And now I had to figure out how to get us both out of here.

Archer must have been having similar thoughts because he suddenly stepped right in front of me. "No." His voice was matter-of-fact, but he might as well have been yelling for the jarring effect it had on Seth.

Suddenly, there was a Vampire between Seth's gun and me. A Vampire who wouldn't die if he got shot. Which is handy if you're me. Not so much if you're Seth.

So, outmaneuvered on that one, he suddenly changed tactics. He grabbed Tom's arm and yanked him forward. For some reason, Tom closed his eyes. And then Seth shot him.

Just like that.

Shot him.

The sound was so deafening I felt like I might never hear anything again. Except Tom's screaming. And suddenly it was the only thing I could hear. Seth kind of went crazy because Tom was screaming so loudly right in his face. He pushed him away, toward Archer, who grabbed Tom and pulled him behind his body.

Archer locked his eyes on mine. "Run!"

Archer stepped forward, straight at Seth, who backed up and forgot to look at me. I grabbed Tom's good arm, dragged him behind me, and we ran.

Tom's gunshot wound must have been a flesh wound, because he could run just fine. As soon as we were moving he stopped screaming. I could see shadows on the walls as the adults came running from Nancy's Steps, and I flashed back to what Ava told me about seeing me and Tom running away from shadows.

Score one for the Seers.

I headed straight for Nancy's Steps. I knew Archer was buying me time to get there, and I wasn't going to waste the opportunity for anything. But my Vampire was back there, face to face with Seth and his gun. It wouldn't kill him, but I had no idea how badly Archer could be hurt.

And then there were the powerful Immortal Descendants headed right for them who probably hated Suckers as much as their kids did. I wanted to vomit. But I had to trust that Archer would be okay, even with the Seer and Monger Heads about to descend on him. Fear for him threatened to overwhelm me, but I kept running.

Just before the entrance to Nancy's Steps, I pulled up to catch my breath. Blood was seeping down Tom's sleeve, and he clutched the wound in his arm with blood-stained fingers.

"Are you okay?"

Tom winced. "Even though I knew it would happen, it bloody hurts to be shot."

"You knew and you didn't try to stop it?"

"It doesn't work like that. You can't change your fate."

"I don't believe that!" I was suddenly, irrationally furious at him. "I think it's just one possibility. Not the *only* one!"

"Tom?"

An urgent whisper called out from behind one of the bridge columns. I tensed and very nearly bolted, but then Adam emerged into the light from the streetlamp and I fought back the crazy urge to run into his arms.

His eyes locked on mine for a second, and then he spotted the blood on Tom's hand. His face went rigid. "What happened?"

"Seth Walters shot me."

I wondered if Tom had heard the conversation among the adults about his alleged parentage. I hoped he hadn't. I couldn't imagine anything worse than finding out the Monger enforcer could be your dad. A dad who shot his own son!

Adam grabbed Tom in a rough hug in that way guys have of being affectionate and still cool. Tom winced in pain and Adam let go quickly. Then he turned back to me. His eyes quickly searched me for any signs of injury before he wrapped me in his arms. It felt good to be there. Really good. But like a brother, good, not like a boyfriend.

I thought maybe I already had one of those.

"I have to go, Adam."

"I'm coming with you."

Ava stepped out of the shadows. Mr. Shaw was right behind her. My eyes caught the Bear's. I couldn't even describe the relief I felt at seeing him there. Like maybe the grownups would take over and make everything okay.

I spoke directly to Mr. Shaw. "The Mongers will kill Archer if they can."

Adam looked confused. "Who's Archer?"

I ignored him and focused on Mr. Shaw. Tom backed me up. "Seth Walters shot me. If he can, he'll kill the Sucker to get to Saira."

Adam sounded appalled. "Sucker? You're here with a Sucker?" Now everyone ignored him.

Mr. Shaw looked at me for a long moment. "Do they know?"

They, who? I was guessing he meant do the Mongers know I'm a mixed blood? "There's a book. A genealogy that might name me. But I don't know."

Adam was about to speak again but Ava shushed him fiercely. He shut up.

Mr. Shaw's gaze never left mine, but I could swear his eyes softened slightly in sympathy and pain. "I'll do what I can."

I'd been holding my breath. "Thank you." Mr. Shaw started to stride away, then stopped and turned back to me. He handed me a package wrapped up in cloth and tied with twine. "What is it?" The package was fairly light, an about the size of my hand.

"A neuraminidase inhibitor." I waited for him to translate and he smiled faintly, the first smile I'd seen from him. "It stops the spread of viruses through the body."

I narrowed my eyes, understanding slowly dawning. "Like maybe porphyria?"

He smiled then, properly, and I could tell he was proud of me for getting it. "We don't know exactly, but we suspect it can. It was designed to stop the spread of H1N1 and avian flu."

Valuable stuff. I put it in my bag. "Thank you, Mr. Shaw."

He hesitated, and then finally said. "I'm sorry … about before. I was scared for you when I saw … in the microscope." He glanced at the others and said simply. "Forgive me, Saira." He turned and headed back down the alley. I suddenly didn't want him to go. "I met Will." I called after him.

The science teacher stopped in his tracks, but didn't turn back to face me. His shoulders tensed and he growled. "Tell him I have his microscope."

"I think he'd probably like that."

Mr. Shaw hesitated a moment, like there was something else he wanted to say, but he must have changed his mind, because he strode away from me, toward Archer and the Mongers. I couldn't tell if the news made him sad or angry, but I suddenly wished I could bring Mr. Shaw back with me to meet his great, great, great uncle.

Ava was tending Tom's arm, and Adam watched me carefully. I spoke to Tom. "Tell Ava and Adam everything, including the half part."

Tom looked scared and shook his head 'no.' I wouldn't let go of his gaze. "Tell them, Tom. It's why they took you, and why they want me too."

He stared at me in surprise. "But you're not half!"

"Ask Mr. Shaw about that."

Adam had been watching us like a tennis match, but then he fixed his gaze on me. "I don't know what's been going on, and I'm pretty bummed you didn't trust me enough to tell me. But you're my friend and I'm coming with you." His jaw was set in a way lesser mortals would have been swayed by, but today I was not feeling lesser. If anything, I was more confident and sure of what was right than I'd ever been before.

"We *are* friends, Adam. But you have to stay here. I need your help."

"With what?" He sounded skeptical.

"Archer is a Vampire, but he's been protecting me. *Please* help Mr. Shaw save him from the rest of the Families. They'll hate him because of what he is, but they don't know *who* he is."

Adam's skepticism hardened on his face. He really didn't like what I'd asked him to do. But then Tom spoke, and I could have kissed him. "The Sucker's not that bad. For a Sucker."

Ava suddenly piped up. "Of course we'll help him, Saira."

I included them all in my relief. "Thank you guys. For everything." Then I focused my gaze back on Adam. "I saw Alex. She said to tell you she misses you." Adam stared at me in shock. For all his Sight, he hadn't Seen that one coming. "She didn't leave because of you. She left *for* you. Seth Walters threatened her and she ran, because she knew you wouldn't."

"Where is she?" His voice practically shook with emotion.

"There's a café near Whitechapel Station. She works there. Archer can show you." If he lives. The thought weighed so heavily on me, it was everything I could do to keep moving forward toward Nancy's Steps.

I included Ava and Tom in my gaze. "I have to go back. I have to get my mom."

Ava suddenly leapt forward and pressed a small linen sack into my hand. "Your coin. I got a lot for it. The guy wants more if you can get them." I gave a half smile. "I'll see what I can do. Thank you, Ava." Impulsively I hugged her, and then I looked at Adam. "Try to find the genealogy book. I think everything's in it. Ask Archer about it because he was there."

Tom sounded surprised. "I've seen that book. Seth showed it to the Rothbitch."

I shot Tom a quick look. "Will you tell Adam what you know?"

Tom nodded and Adam hugged me, hard. "Come back to us. I still have a lot to learn from you, Clocker."

"And a lot to teach me, Seer."

Ava suddenly jumped up and took my hands. "I can't see the past, you know that, right?" I nodded. "But you bring your mom back here. I've Seen it."

"What else did you See?" Ava looked at Adam as if to ask permission. My eyes narrow. "Adam, we had a deal about the visions."

Adam nods at Ava. "You're sad when you come back. Profoundly sad. I don't know why."

And how do you like them apples? That's what I get for asking. "Well, at least I'm coming back, huh?"

Another gunshot rang out, and shouting echoed down the alley. I started to bolt toward the sounds, but Adam grabbed me. His voice was low in my ear. "They want you, but they can't follow you back there. Go now. We'll help Shaw with your Sucker." I almost cried with relief. I didn't know if Archer and Adam would ever be friends, but at least Adam was willing to help.

I nodded, my eyes filling with tears. "Tom, you can come with me if you want to. Adam's right. They can't find us then."

Tom paled a little. "I'd rather take my chances here, but thanks."

"We'll keep you safe. And you too, Saira, if you want to stay," Adam said.

I shook my head. "Jack the Ripper disappears from history after his last murder, and if I don't go now, I may never be able to track down my mom." My voice broke as I looked at Adam. "I have to go."

"And you'll be back." His whisper sent a shiver through me.

With a last, lingering look at friends I never thought I'd have, and now couldn't imagine living without, I turned and ran down Nancy's Steps into the London Bridge catacombs.

INTO THE DARKNESS

I barely even noticed the animatronic ghouls and ghosts as I sprinted for my spiral room at the back of the tunnels. I found it easily enough, and after checking that I wasn't being followed, started tracing the design. Between the slamming of my heart and the clock ticking on an appointment I wasn't sure I'd be able to make, I was barely even concerned about the impending nausea of traveling through the time portal.

The edges of the spiral glowed, and the humming filled my ears and whole body with the sensation of being pulled. I felt my stomach drop somewhere around my knees, and when everything finally stopped, I was barely conscious.

Fortunately I'd landed with my back to the old brick wall, because it took a long time for the dizziness to pass. The room looked different than either of the two times I'd been there before. It was empty and dusty and very, very dark. I fumbled in my bag for my Maglite. I'd put fresh batteries in and it clicked on with a satisfying white glow. Okay, now to find my other supplies.

My old knapsack was still where Archer had hidden it behind a loose brick in the wall. If I had traveled back to 1888 again, the bag had been hidden in the wall for over twenty-five years, which meant the chloroform inside was older than I was. That couldn't be good. I wondered if chloroform was an unstable compound. Hopefully not.

I emptied the contents of the knapsack into Archer's leather bag, but barely took stock of my supplies. For the first time in my life I wished I could wear a watch. It had to be very close to seven pm, the time Ringo had set to meet Mary Kelly, and if I didn't get back to the loft to go with him, I'd have no idea how to find them.

The corridors of the tunnel were lined with boxes, much like they had been when Archer and I had hidden the bag, but there was a new gate at the bottom of Nancy's Steps and the chain wrapped around the iron bars was fastened with a heavy lock. I shook the gate and rattled the chain. It was fastened tight. And bolt cutters hadn't been part of my survival kit.

"Help!" I shook the gate again for emphasis. I honestly had no idea how I was going to get out of this locked catacomb. I yelled again, but only the scurrying rats answered. I supposed I could go back to my time, get out of the tunnels, go past the Mongers with their guns and who knew what else was still lurking, and go through the spiral under the bridge. Or maybe …

I ran back to my spiral room and found the design on the wall. What had Doran said? It was possible to travel *between locations* as well as times, but I needed a clear picture in my mind of where I wanted to go. I held my Maglite between my teeth and started tracing the spiral. My fingers found their own way, so I closed my eyes and imagined myself tracing the same spiral outside on the bridge column. I felt the hum and stretch come on, and for the first time since I'd discovered I could travel through spirals, I surrendered to it, trying to keep my focus on the image in my mind. It was taking too long. It wasn't working.

And then suddenly it did. I was outside in the dark and chill of a November night under the London Bridge. I peered around, almost afraid to look too closely in case I had jumped time. But everything looked almost comfortingly familiar, and despite the horrors that might await me, I was glad to be back.

The quay was still populated with drinkers, shoppers, and a few laborers wrapping up their day's work. I climbed up to street level and took off running. Ringo's loft was only a couple of blocks away, but I was afraid he was already gone.

I couldn't dwell on what might have been happening in my own time. Archer the Vampire had survived a very long time without help from anyone else, and I hoped that maybe Mr. Shaw and Adam would get past their prejudices against Suckers long enough to see him as a person worth helping.

I slowed to a casual stroll as I turned the corner to the back alley. My run from the river had caused enough raised eyebrows; I didn't want to draw attention to Ringo's hideaway.

"Ye came back."

I nearly left my skin in a puddle on the street at the sound of Ringo's whisper. "What the hell?!" I got a scampy grin in return.

"Come on, I figured ye'd be late, so I pushed off our meeting to later. Let's eat."

I followed Ringo inside the back door and up the ladder to his loft. A ridiculously big part of me hoped Archer would be waiting inside, and it was hard to control my disappointment. Ringo noticed. I had the feeling there wasn't much he didn't.

"I 'aven't seen 'im."

It took a huge effort to shrug like it didn't matter. "I didn't think you would." My blue dress was lying on the bed, and I shut the curtain on it, trying to close off my heart with it.

Ringo had brought two fish and a loaf of bread home with him. I set about starting a fire on the hearth of the chimney while he filleted and boned them.

We did all of this without really talking, a fairly comfortable silence between people used to working together. I knew that if Archer had been there, he would have been filling the silence with talk about his philosophy lecture or my favorite of his classes, the Bible as literature. I loved to listen to him get fired up about biblical history: what archaeologists had proven to be true versus what was likely filled in by someone's imagination or political agenda.

I missed the sound of Archer's voice as Ringo and I prepared the simple meal. Ringo absently set three plates on the little rescued table. When the fish was finally cooked and we sat down to eat, he finally realized his mistake and took one away again.

"Thank you. It was staring me in the face."

Ringo looked at me speculatively. "Ye love 'im?"

I hesitated, and then nodded.

"Then choose 'im."

Those simple words startled me completely, and I stared at Ringo. I waited for a translation.

He shrugged as if it was obvious. "Ye're 'ere to find yer mother, yeah? Well, whether or not ye find 'er, ye're just assuming ye'll go back."

I nodded again. To my native time was what he meant.

"Why not just stay 'ere? Marry 'is lordship, live a decent life on 'is salary, maybe even take work as a governess or a shop clerk since ye can read and figure. Choose 'im."

Now that was something I'd truly never considered. Not once.

Ringo shrugged again. "Anyway, I'm just sayin' it's what normal people would do."

And there you had it. I wasn't normal. I hadn't even been normal before I knew I was a time traveler, when life was midnight tagging excursions, free-running through the city, and avoiding everyone because the potential for pain was too high every time we left. Actually, to be perfectly honest, the most normal I'd been was since I discovered what a freak I really was.

No, I didn't see a normal life in the cards for me and Archer. And if that wasn't enough, Ava had seen me come back with my mother, but profoundly sad. A prospect I most certainly did not want to think about.

"Thank you for being such a good friend, Ringo. I'm really lucky I met you."

"Yeah, well, I did 'elp save yer life, didn't I?"

I grinned. "You did."

"And ye taught me 'ow to read. That makes us about even."

"Good."

"Ye're not goin' to stay, are ye?" All the smile had gone from his voice.

"I don't think so."

Ringo nodded solemnly. "Will ye come back and visit me sometime, then?"

"I'll try, but I'm not gone yet." I stood up to clear the dishes. "And we still have a job to do, and a woman to see, right?"

He took the dishes from me to clean them at the cistern. "Right."

The wind had come in off the river, and the night was cold when we stepped out for our meeting. I was wrapped in every layer I had with me, and Ringo had loaned me his cap to hide my hair, which was braided and tucked down the back of my sweater.

We were headed toward Spitalfields to our meeting on Dorset Street. I could tell Ringo had an eye behind us the whole way; I just wasn't sure who he thought would be there.

Spitalfields was definitely on the lower-income end of London, and we passed a couple of women in doorways who seemed to be of the 'working' variety. Most of them were missing teeth and looked like they were in their 40s or even 50s. It was hard to tell a person's age when poverty had probably robbed them of good health a long time ago. I thought the same was pretty much true for the homeless people I'd stepped around in Venice.

There was a boy waiting for us when we arrived at the meeting place. Ringo stopped short and looked the boy up and down suspiciously.

"I thought ye was comin' alone." The kid accused Ringo.

"'Ow'd ye know it would be me?"

"Saw ye at the paper office. Who's this?" The kid threw his head in my direction but barely spared me a glance.

"Question is, who are ye?"

"Name's Charlie. I'm to take ye to Mary if I think ye're safe enough."

Ringo stood still, regarding Charlie steadily. "Well? Are ye done lookin'?" His voice took on the same street quality he'd had when I first met him. He'd been matching Archer's and my speech patterns for so long I'd forgotten how tough he could sound.

Charlie's arms were crossed in front of him as he made a show of looking us both up and down. Then he turned without another word and started off down the street. As one, Ringo and I followed behind.

"Charlie ain't a bloke." Ringo's voice was a whisper in my ear. I was startled. It hadn't occurred to me that it was anything but a boy leading us toward Mary.

"How do you know?"

Ringo arched an eyebrow as if to say 'seriously?' "'Ow'd I know ye wasn't?" He had a point.

"Look at the 'ands. They're lass's 'ands. The eyelashes are too long, and the collarbones too fine." Charlie stopped at the entrance to an alley, looked back at us just long enough to make sure we'd seen, and then turned down it.

Ringo hesitated. "Maybe ye'd better wait 'ere for me?"

"And let you go down a dark alley by yourself? No way, Jose. I've got your back that that's final."

"I don't know Jose, but I thought ye should have an out if ye wanted it."

"Well, I don't. But thanks anyway." Ringo looked halfway between kid and man in that moment. The man wanted to protect me and do the chivalrous thing; the kid didn't mind having me at his back. We turned down the dark alley together.

Charlie wasn't in sight, but a light was on at number thirteen, and the door was slightly ajar. Ringo knocked once, and a woman's voice called "Come."

We stepped into a dimly lit room, smoky from the fire in the wood stove and smelling of ash and boiled cabbage. It was a smell I'd become familiar with as it wafted in through the open window in Ringo's flat.

Someone was sitting on the bed in the shadows, smoking a cigarette. Charlie stepped in from the other room, and I could instantly see what Ringo had already noticed. She was definitely female. Probably about Ringo's age, with high cheekbones and delicate collarbones just visible above her sweater.

"This is my sister, Mary. Mary Kelly."

Mary leaned forward into the light and stubbed her cigarette out in a dish on the bedside table. She was actually kind of pretty, with thick, reddish hair and the same high cheekbones Charlie had. But where Charlie had a more delicate look in her bones, Mary seemed coarser and tougher, as if she would have had a lot more success pretending to be male than Charlie did.

"Wot's t' reward for findin' me?" Mary's voice was rough and sounded like the whisky voice of a country singer.

"A quid." Ringo spoke with confidence, and I could see him sizing everything up in the room.

"Give it 'ere."

"Not 'til we know ye're who ye say. T'was in the advert."

Mary sighed as if we were testing her last nerve. She couldn't have been more than about twenty-five, but she already had the mannerisms of an old lady.

"Show us, then."

I pulled a gold sovereign out of my pocket. It was much more battered than its age would suggest since it was one of the coins Archer's new shilling had bought. I held it up for Mary to see and she squinted at it in the dim light.

"Check it's real, Charlotte."

Charlie scowled at her sister and looked quickly at Ringo and me, but we were expressionless. Charlie came closer to me and examined the coin.

"Looks real enough. Can't tell for sure without feeling it, though." Without a hesitation I dropped the coin in her hand. I could see Ringo about to pounce if she made one move to pocket it, but she weighed it carefully and handed it back.

"Real." Charlie moved back into the shadows and sat behind the wood stove. Mary coughed a great big, loud, juicy hack that reinforced every anti-smoking ad I'd ever seen, then she settled back into the shadows again. I didn't like not being able to see her eyes, so I moved forward and sat on the chair next to the bed.

I hoped I wasn't close enough for bedbugs to make the leap to my clothes, but at least I could see her eyes properly.

It seemed like Mary could have been a beauty, but life had been a bit too harsh for it to stick. I'd always assumed I'd grow old like my mom, who had a few laugh lines around her eyes and a couple of gray hairs peeking through whenever she went too long between highlights. Mary had broken capillaries on her cheeks, from too much drinking I supposed, and deep bags under her eyes from not enough sleep. Both were hazards of her occupation.

I was startled to realize Mary was studying me with the same intensity. "Ye've the look of someone I know."

That surprised me. "Who?"

She suddenly shrugged and looked away, and as she did I caught sight of her necklace. Or rather, my mother's necklace. Around Mary Kelly's throat.

The room swam before my eyes, and I gripped my chair to keep from lunging at her and ripping the clock pendant from her neck. It was the one my father had given my mother; the one that I thought had been stolen from our loft in Venice. Ringo looked at me with concern, and even Charlie had noticed my reaction. Only Mary seemed oblivious.

"Yer a fancy brother or a cousin or something," she muttered under her breath. Only then did I realize she hadn't seen through my disguise. Considering how easily Ringo had spotted Charlie through hers, I just assumed I was equally transparent.

I clenched my teeth. "That's a pretty necklace, Mary. Where'd you get it?"

She looked at me with a sudden narrowing of her eyes. "It was a gift."

Liar. My mother must have brought it to 1888 with her, but she would have never given it away. I quickly weighed my options and decided to go with capitalism. "I'll buy it from you if you tell me the story."

"'Ow much?" I could see the wheels turning in her head, or maybe it was the jackpot dials and they'd suddenly come up cherries.

"The quid, plus this." I held out the entire bag of coins Ava had given me and emptied it in my hands. Mary's eyes widened fractionally. Ringo grimaced as she nodded. "A customer ..."

"The truth or no deal." Whatever sympathy I'd walked into the hovel with was gone. And maybe Mary heard it in my voice, because she flinched. "The bastard who lives next door pays me to clean for 'im sometimes. 'E's a pig, so I wait until 'e's out to do it. The necklace was on the floor by the bed."

It took every ounce of my self-control not to leap up and run next door, and Ringo knew it too. He'd moved closer to the exit and was basically waiting for me to give the word. Charlie's eyes were locked on him, but he didn't notice. He was watching me.

I casually bagged all the coins and handed them to Mary. "He there now?" I was trying for conversational instead of desperate. Mary shook her head. "They left last night and I ain't seen 'em since."

"They?"

Mary's eyes narrowed. "There's the ratty-faced, pockmarked one. 'E's the one who pays me. 'E's mean and sneaky and I don't trust 'im as far as I can spit. 'E's had the place next door since summertime, and 'e's been a nasty piece of work since day one."

"And?" I was holding my breath for a description of a woman in a green dress.

Mary shuddered. "I never see's 'im. Pitch black it always is, and 'e's careful, that one. Big man, but not tall. There's power there. 'E moves with it. But I ain't never seen 'is face."

A deep dread was beginning to grow in the pit of my stomach. The pockmarked face could be the Ripper. But working with another man? A powerful one that made someone like Mary shudder? Could that possibly be Bishop Wilder? Were they both somehow connected to my mother's disappearance? Mary had stopped speaking, but I knew there was more. There had to be.

"What about the woman?"

Mary looked at me, clearly startled. "I ain't said naught about a woman." Her eyes shifted from Charlie to me, and there was guilt written in them. Something I was beginning to recognize all too well.

I didn't let up. "She's wearing a green dress. And she's posh-looking. What did you call it? Fancy. The necklace belongs to her."

Mary's eyes narrowed as she gazed at me. And then she made a choice. I watched her decide to lie. "If your fancy lady was lyin' with that ratty-faced bastard, I don't know nothin' about it. I told you, I found the necklace on the floor by the bed."

My fists clenched unconsciously, but I kept it together as Mary unclasped the necklace. She looked at it a long moment, her expression shifting into something unreadable. "Our ma 'ad a thing for clocks. Charlotte's too young to remember, but she 'ad 'em everywhere in our house in Dublin." Mary hesitated, and then finally handed over the necklace. The minute my hand closed around the woven brass choker I felt instantly better. And totally worse. Even though she was holding something back about my mom, if Archer's theory was right, Mary and Charlotte Kelly had Clocker blood in them. Which made us related. Sort of.

I stood to go. "Mary?" She was counting out the money from the little cloth bag I'd handed her. She looked up, distracted, as if she was surprised I was still there. "Is there someplace you could go? Someplace outside of London. Just for a few days?"

She stared at me for a moment. "Oh sure. I keep a country 'ouse in Surrey. I'll just pop out there for the weekend." And then she cracked up like I was the headliner in a comedy show. It was an ugly laugh designed to make me feel stupid. But, better me stupid than her dead.

"Or maybe you could work the other side of town for a few days?"

Her laughter dried up and she glared at me. "Listen, Fancy. No one tells me what to do, or lords over me like I was some *girl* to do their biddin'. I've earned my freedom, such as it is, and none can say otherwise. I work 'ere when I choose, and while it may not be work ye respect, it's what keeps us alive and together." She cast a look at Charlie who seemed just as proud of her sister as she was mortified.

Mary's glare dismissed me. She took the gold shilling out of the pouch and weighed it in her hand just as Charlie had done. Then she tossed it to Charlie, who caught it in mid-air like she had magnets for hands.

"Get me some rye and a loaf of day-old bread. Mind ye bring the rest back 'ere. The landlord's waiting 'is due and won't take 'is payment any other way no more."

Charlie scowled and slipped out of the room without a backward glance.

I joined Ringo at the door and he led me outside. Just as I was about to close the door behind me Mary called out from the bed, "Who's the fancy lady to you?"

I turned to face her, my expression carefully schooled to hide how mad I was at her for lying to me. "She's my mother." I pulled the door closed so I didn't have to see her face, and then turned to rest my head against the cool bricks.

"She okay?"

Charlie's voice was tough, but quiet as she spoke to Ringo. I looked at him quickly. He was glaring at Charlie in a way that recommended no argument.

"'E's fine, *Charlie*." I loved Ringo. In three words he told Charlie, 'mind your own business and we'll mind ours."

She hesitated a moment, then nodded curtly. She was about to run off down the street when I called to her.

"Charlie?"

She came back to face me. "Charlotte Kelly, sir, but Charlie's fine."

I guessed she'd accepted the rules of the game. "Which place does Mary clean?"

She squinted at me and pointed at the row house door next to theirs. She was about to run off again but then turned to face me. "I seen that fancy lady. She's been there a few times, but always sick or somethin'."

My breath caught in my throat. "Sick?"

"Them two always come in holding 'er between 'em. Supportin' 'er."

"Is she there now?"

Charlie shook her head. "I ain't seen 'er in a couple days. But I ain't seen 'im neither, and 'e's usually in and out."

I itched to get into his row house, and I could tell Ringo felt the same. But I felt somehow responsible for Mary and Charlie because of what I knew. "Would Mary listen to you about going away from here?"

Charlie's eyes narrowed. "Why should she?"

I sighed, and then took a page from Ava. "I *know* things sometimes." I looked Charlie straight in the eyes to make my point. To her credit, she met my gaze. "And Mary's in danger here. She will die in her bed tomorrow night if you stay."

Charlie looked from Ringo to me and back to Ringo.

"We've no place to go."

I could have kissed Ringo when he said to Charlie, "Come to my place. If ye don't steal nothing, ye can stay the night." My jaw dropped open, and after a quick glance at me, Ringo told her how to find his loft. "And mind ye come tell us if the fancy lady comes back." One raised eyebrow and a nod later, the deal was done and Charlie had scampered off.

I stared at Ringo for a long moment. "That was awesome."

He snapped at me. "I'm not 'appy about it."

"Then why'd you do it?"

He shook his head at me. "Some thin's ye just 'ave to do, right?"

I studied his face for a moment, and then nodded. "Right." I looked at the windowless room. "Think we could get in?"

Ringo smiled suddenly and it transformed his face. He held up his fingers and waggled them. "Give me thirty seconds."

I gaped at him and he laughed. First he tried the door. Locked, of course. Then he used the doorknob to lift himself up to the transom window above it. He pushed the top and it creaked backward, opening a gap that barely looked big enough to fit an arm through, much less a teenaged thief. But somehow, impossibly, Ringo slithered through the transom and in less than a minute had opened the front door for me to slip inside.

"Spectacular." I whispered. Ringo flashed me a grin, and then we got busy prowling the room.

If I thought Mary Kelly's room was gross, this one was like a science experiment gone horribly wrong. There were plates of half-moldy food stacked on the table and a layer of scum covering the bottoms of three glasses. The bare mattress was in one corner with a blanket wadded up at the foot of it. I shuddered to think of the petri dish that mattress probably was.

"Animals don't live like this," I said.

"So apparently the Ripper isn't a Shifter?" Ringo tried for humor, which was the only antidote to the revulsion the room inspired.

"Guess I'm not hiring Mary as my housekeeper." We dissolved into fits of laughter, but there was an edge to it, and when it faded away the silence in the room was deafening.

"I want anything that could tell us where my mom is."

"Right."

I found a small stick at the wood stove and used it to poke around in piles of filthy rags. I pushed aside a ratty curtain and got a sudden chill. My backpack, grabbed by the Ripper so long ago in the Whitechapel station, sat on the floor in a tired heap. I quickly slung it over my shoulders and turned to tell Ringo. But he beat me to the words.

"Saira. I think I found something."

I went over to the shelf that sat above a rusted enamel sink. On it were old-fashioned glass bottles with handwritten labels. Ringo held one out to me to read. The cursive was tight and proper and I could just make out the word 'hyoscine.' I looked at Ringo. "What's hyoscine?"

He shrugged his shoulders. "Don't know." He suddenly noticed the pack on my back. "Where'd you get the kit?"

"Long story."

Ringo pointed to the bottle. "Look closer at the label." The decorative border of the label had some initials incorporated into the pattern. "B R H? Is that someone's name?"

"Not someone, someplace. Bethlem Royal 'Ospital."

"Oh my God! Are they keeping her there?"

Ringo grabbed my shoulders and turned me to face him. "We 'ave to go get Archer."

I could feel my expression tighten. "He doesn't want—" But Ringo cut me off. "'E does. And 'e will."

The dread that had settled into my stomach was like a hard knot that made any other feeling impossible. "Okay," I whispered.

"Good. Let's get out of 'ere!" Ringo pulled me out of the horrible room and closed the door behind us. I gulped the night air trying to clear the stench out of my lungs, and we took off running.

We practically flew from Spitalfields back down to Southwark and King's College. I could only imagine that Ringo felt the same way I did – lucky to be free of the conditions that had trapped people like the Kellys into the limited options of their lives.

We crept our way up and over the walls and across the grounds at King's College. We had a shorthand now and didn't need to speak as Ringo scaled the wall, slipped through a window, and a few moments later, opened a door for me to scoot inside. Archer's room was on the second floor near the chapel, but I'd never actually been to it, so Ringo led the way.

We didn't run into anyone, which I thought was weird until I heard the sounds of singing coming from the chapel. So, if that's where Archer was, we'd just have to break into his room and wait for him. I had become very casual in my relationship to locked doors with Ringo around.

He slipped a thin piece of metal into Archer's lock and had the handle turning in under a minute. The room was dark and oddly closed, like there wasn't enough fresh air to breathe. I crossed to the window and flung open the drapes to crank the window up while Ringo lit a lamp. We gasped at the same moment as we saw Archer on the bed, as pale and motionless as a corpse.

And I was horrified to realize that the first emotion that flashed through me was relief.

FEVER

The second emotion was terror. But both were caused by the same thought. Had Archer already been turned into a Vampire?

Ringo reacted faster than I did. He checked Archer's pulse and listened to his chest, then looked at me with a combination of relief and fear. "'E breathes. But 'is lungs sound full of liquid and 'e burns with a fever."

I knelt by Archer's bed and touched his skin. He was on fire, and he'd probably spent the day bathed in sweat that had dried and made his hair stick up at odd angles. I brushed it back from his forehead and Archer turned his head away. I flinched back as if I'd been slapped, but Ringo brought me back to my senses.

"'E's unconscious."

Was that better? Was his loathing of me so deep that his unconscious mind pulled back from me too? Wow. I had sunk to some pretty impressive depths of self-pity to even have that thought. I was punishing myself for being relieved that maybe I hadn't been directly responsible for Archer becoming a Vampire.

Ringo moved Archer's head from side to side, looking around his neck for bite marks I supposed. I shook my head. "I don't think I get off that easy. I think I'll probably be there when he gets turned."

"So what is it then? What's wrong with 'im?"

I felt his skin again. It was burning with fever. I don't know how to check for a pulse at the neck, so I put my head on his chest and listened to Archer's heart. It was beating, but it didn't sound strong. I looked up at Ringo.

"Is this what I looked like when I was sick?"

Ringo looked from Archer back to me, his eyes wide and scared. He nodded.

I cringed. Swine flu maybe? Definitely something he had no immunity to. Archer took a shuddering breath and then didn't breathe for a long moment. I panicked and pushed down hard on his chest with both hands. "Archer!" He gasped and started breathing again, but that shook me badly.

"Can you find some water for him to drink?"

Ringo went to a pitcher on the dresser, but it was empty. He grabbed it and took off. "Be right back."

I fished in my messenger bag for the little cloth-wrapped parcel Mr. Shaw had given me. The anti-viral drug I'd been hoping to save for Archer after … I couldn't even say it to myself … after he was infected by a Vampire.

But the way he looked right now, he wouldn't make it long enough to be bitten. Ringo returned with a full pitcher and poured a glass full. He brought it to me just as I opened the parcel. Inside were three pills.

"What are they?"

"Medicine from my time that I hope will cure him."

Ringo looked impressed, but I was terrified the pills wouldn't work. If I had given Archer my flu, one from the future that he had zero antibodies to, he was in real danger. As he had pointed out, people died from influenza every day in 1888.

"Help me sit him up, but then you should probably stay away from him. And wash your hands." Ringo nodded and lifted Archer's upper body enough so he wouldn't choke on the water. I opened his mouth and put one of the pills as far back on his tongue as I could reach. He gagged involuntarily, but I quickly put the glass to his lips and tipped it back. Thank God he was still aware enough to swallow, and after he'd taken a few sips I checked his mouth again to make sure the pill was gone.

I'd never actually done any of this care-taking before, and it felt very strange to be someone's nurse. I remembered my mom giving me all her home remedies when I was a kid, and fevers always got lukewarm baths until my temperature came down, or a spot sleeping next to my mom so I could use her body heat when the chills set in. Archer's skin was still hot, so I pulled the bedclothes away from his body and opened his nightshirt.

His chest was smooth, and I could see the flutter of his pulse under his collarbone. My own heart thumped in a sympathetic response. Then again, it might have been the sight of lean, coiled muscle under the broad expanse of his skin.

"He has to cool down." Or maybe I did. I blushed at the heat that suddenly spread its way through my body. Ringo nodded, a little embarrassed for me, and turned to open wide the window I'd cracked. "I'll stay with him if you want to go."

"We'll both stay." Ringo pulled a chair over for me and I sat by Archer's bedside. Ringo stayed closer to the door, guarding it, or maybe just giving me time alone with my patient.

I fell asleep with my hand on Archer's arm, and woke up when he started shivering. His skin was freezing cold and clammy, but he was still unconscious.

Ringo had blown out the lamp and was asleep in his own chair by the door. The only light coming in was from the still-open window, which I got up and closed. Archer's blankets were damp from the fever sweat, and I could only find one that was dry enough to cover him with. It wasn't enough.

The best way to warm another person up is with body heat. And at that point I didn't really care how it would look to the very Victorian guys when they woke up. Archer was shivering too much for just one blanket, so I kicked off my boots and climbed into the single bed with him. I rolled him to his side, facing away from me, so I could fit my body to his back and wrap my arms around his chest. I pulled the blanket up to cover us both and then just listened to the chattering of his teeth as it quieted and then finally stopped. Archer sighed and seemed to settle back into the curve of my body, and I heard his breathing return to something regular and deep.

I lay in Archer's bed wrapped around him like a cocoon. He fit against me felt like we were built for each other, and despite his chill, my own skin burned where his body touched it. Instead of torturing myself with physical thoughts of Archer, I tortured myself with mental ones, wondering how I'd allowed myself to get in this deep after a lifetime of keeping people away from me.

The irony was that I was trying to save a guy's life so he could lose it later to a Vampire. I buried my face in the back of Archer's neck to escape my own awful thoughts, and thankfully, I fell back to sleep.

I dreamt I was wandering around the halls of Bedlam trying to find my mom. Then the dream switched locations to a long, dark corridor. I opened a door to find her strapped to an operating table and attached to a blood bag hanging from an IV pole.

I jerked awake with a gasp. The soft light of early morning was enough to see Archer's eyes, about a foot away, staring into my own. He was conscious, and my heart caught in my throat to see him looking at me.

"Did you see that?" I'm not sure why I said that, except maybe what I had seen in the dream felt so true I had to make sure it wasn't. His eyes clouded for a moment.

"What?" It was enough to wake me up and remind me what was real.

"Hi."

The barest of smiles tugged at the corners of his mouth. "Hello."

I rolled over to look at the chair by the door for Ringo, but the room was empty. "Where's Ringo?"

Something shifted in his eyes. "You're really here, then?"

I frowned. "Yeah." Were we both losing our grip on reality? My tone questioned his sanity, and for some reason it made him smile.

"I thought I was dreaming. Or maybe ..."

"Maybe what?" I prompted.

"Dead?"

"You almost were. You're lucky Ringo and I broke in last night." I started to sit up, suddenly aware that my head was on Archer's chest.

But he clutched me to him. "Don't go."

His reaction surprised me, but I was grateful that he didn't actually seem to hate me. I settled back into the crook in his shoulder and was instantly self-conscious about morning breath and bed-head and anything else that he could see so close. "You were freezing last night. You started shivering, and the blanket wasn't enough."

"Thank you." The expression in Archer's eyes was naked and raw, and made every background conversation in my head fade to silence. Until he spoke again. "I owe you my life."

Bam! The guilt hit me like a freight train, and this time I sat up before he could stop me. "At least until I deliver you to a Vampire." I couldn't look at Archer as I got out of his bed and busied myself putting on my boots. I could feel his eyes on me.

"Saira—" Just then Ringo slipped back into the room carrying a loaf of bread under one arm, and a hunk of paper-wrapped cheese in the other. He instantly caught the weird vibe in the room and stopped in his tracks.

"Should I give ye a minute?"

"No."

"Yes." Archer's look said I wasn't going to get out of talking to him, so I glared back.

"It can wait. We need to talk about my mom."

Ringo seemed to decide I would win this one and stepped tentatively into the room. He opened up the cheese and carved a big slice off to add to a torn chunk of bread, then handed us both our breakfast. I took a bite to avoid having to speak for another minute. It didn't suck having a friend who knew his way around the markets.

But Archer hadn't taken his eyes off me, and I knew I had to surrender. I swallowed the last bites of my food and finally met his gaze.

"Ringo and I went to see Mary Kelly last night." I cringed in anticipation of his disappointment, but his expression didn't change. "I tried to warn her about the Ripper without making her think I was crazy, but I don't think it'll make a difference. She laughed at me." Still no comment, so I took a deep breath and pulled down the turtleneck of my sweater to reveal my mom's clock choker.

"She had this. It's my mom's necklace. It was the last thing my dad gave her before she left." I let that sink in and based on his raised eyebrows, it clearly had. "Mary said she found it when she was cleaning next door. She didn't admit to having seen my mom, but her sister did. The sister said two men had to support my mom, men who sounded like the Ripper and your bishop."

Archer struggled to a sitting position. I moved to help him up, but he waved me away and managed on his own. I was back to feeling like a leper where he was concerned, and after waking up in the man's arms, it was a little disconcerting. I shook it off and continued.

"We found a prescription bottle there from Bethlem Hospital, and my backpack from Whitechapel." Another raised eyebrow.

Archer opened his mouth to speak, but then closed it again and looked from one to the other of us. Ringo finally obliged.

"The sister, Charlie, said she'd come for us if she saw Saira's mum again." Ringo looked at me directly. "Which means I should probably stay close to home. And ye never know, they might actually take your advice and leave Spitalfields tonight."

Archer looked at me in surprise. "Tonight?"

"It's November ninth."

He winced. "Right. So I suppose the question is, do we try to save Mary Kelly from the Ripper despite the inevitability of his attack?"

I glared at Archer. "*We* are not doing anything. *You* can barely sit up straight, much less fend off a serial killing Vampire. And just because my history books say it happened doesn't mean it's *inevitable*." I wasn't sure why I was so angry with Archer, except that maybe I needed to believe things could be different.

Ringo watched us like he was waiting to jump into the ring and separate the fighters. But Archer wasn't up to fighting with me. He sighed and closed his eyes. The effects of the flu were all over him, from the paleness of his skin to the flutter in the hollow below his throat. I suddenly felt very protective of him, and guilty that I'd pushed so hard.

"Saira, I See things sometimes, so I have a Seer's respect for fate. I don't want to argue with you, and I do believe it's possible to change your future with the choices you make, but not your past." Archer's voice was tired, and I knew he needed much more sleep.

I got up and busied myself pouring a glass of water. I unwrapped the little cloth package from Mr. Shaw and took out both remaining pills. I held one up for Archer. "I gave you one last night. It's an anti-viral-something. You should take this one now and the last one when you wake up again."

"I'm not going back to sleep. We haven't finished talking yet."

I scoffed. I couldn't help it. "You're practically in a coma, and you pretty much were last night."

Archer tried to hide a smile. "Not totally."

I stared at him. "What do you mean, not totally? You were out cold." On second thought, he had settled back into the curve of my body rather snugly.

He tried to look innocent. "If you say so."

Ringo stifled a laugh, and I shot him a look that said 'shut up or I'll beat you.' I thrust the pill at him. "Take it, or I'll have to force it down your throat again."

He looked a little embarrassed. "You did that?"

"I did that." I must have looked fierce because he meekly took the pill and the water and swallowed them both down. "I'm counting on this having a big effect on you because I only had three, and I was hoping ..." There was no way I could finish that sentence, and Archer zeroed in on it.

"What were you hoping?"

I sighed. "It's an anti-viral, and the modern theory about Vampires is that it's a virus that gets super-promoted and mutates because of Family genetics." Both Ringo and Archer looked at me like I'd just sprouted a trunk. I shook my head. "It doesn't matter anyway. You needed them now."

Some glimmer of understanding must have dawned for Archer. "Maybe it'll stay in my system long enough ...?"

"I thought of that, but probably not. It's too busy attacking the flu that took you out. Oh well, it was worth a shot. I hope you thank Mr. Shaw someday. He tried to help."

I could tell that mystified them as much as the genetics talk had, so I leaned over Archer's bed and messed with his blankets. He watched me silently for a moment, and then he caught my hand in his. "What are you going to do today?"

I shrugged. "Go back to Ringo's and hope Charlie and Mary come. Maybe try to figure out where someone could hide my mom in Bedlam."

He looked concerned. "Don't go there without me."

"You're not fit to go anywhere."

"I will be later, I promise. Let me sleep now and bring me some bread and I'll go with you. Please don't go alone." I thought he was probably delirious, but there was no point in arguing with crazy people so I just nodded.

"Okay, fine. But you have to rest now."

He looked me straight in the eyes. "You lied to me before, Saira. Don't do it again."

That cut me right to the core. He was right – I was dismissing his request because he was sick, and because I thought I would probably do what I wanted anyway. I sat back down next to him and took his hand. I stumbled for the words that I needed to say. "I'm here because I have to find my mom. And I can't wait anymore. The Ripper has her, Archer, and he's a killer. But you're right. I won't lie to you again …" I saw relief in his eyes that I shattered with my final words. "… so I can't promise that I won't go to Bedlam without you."

Archer looked at me a long moment, then he sank back into his pillow and closed his eyes. "I'll just sleep for a few minutes."

"Archer, I …" He turned his back to me and there was nothing else to say. I felt like he'd been on the verge of forgiving me for a moment, but I'd just slammed the door on that, maybe forever. The pit in my stomach grew to Grand Canyon size, so I caught Ringo's eye, and we silently slipped out of the room, closing and locking the door behind us.

We didn't say much on the way back to Ringo's loft. My conscience was a mess, and I don't know what Ringo was thinking about, but he suddenly went on alert as we rounded the corner to his alley. Every muscle in his body tensed, and then I finally saw it. A bundle against the wall that I had taken for a pile of trash was actually a small person wrapped tightly in a blanket. The eyes opened and watched our wary approach. Ringo opened the back door to his building and gave the bundle a nod. Charlie stood and dropped the blanket down around her shoulders as she followed us inside the hall.

I was about to speak to her, but Ringo shushed me until all three of us were up the closet ladder to his loft. He checked the windows, lit the fire, and put the tea kettle on to boil. I gestured for Charlie to sit while I gathered cups and saucers for all of us.

I picked up my old backpack and started poking through it to see what the Ripper had left me, so Ringo spoke first. "Ye spent the night in my alley?"

Charlie nodded; her expression hadn't changed since she got here. She opened her mouth to speak, couldn't find her voice, then cleared her throat and tried again. "'E came last night. Alone. Mary lied to ye about not seeing the fancy lady, and I think she felt bad. She faced 'im down. Said 'e best turn 'er loose or she'd put the coppers on 'im."

I gasped. The thing I hadn't told Mary Kelly was that the pockmarked man was a serial killer who had already murdered four women. The guilt which had been lurking since my conversation with Archer suddenly gnawed its way through my guts like vermin. Charlie turned her vacant gaze to me as if she had just read my mind.

"*I* knew 'e was bad. Anyone with 'alf a brain could see the rot in 'im. Mary didn't care … and 'e killed 'er."

I knew what that murder scene looked like from the grisly police photos in the Ripper archives, and dread filled me. "Where were you?"

Her eyes were still frighteningly empty. "'Idin'." Anguish suddenly flooded her face. "There was nothin' … I couldn't …" She closed her eyes, took a deep breath, and then faced us both again with a spooky calm. "I just shut my eyes and 'eld my ears until it was done."

Ringo's voice was kinder than I'd ever heard him speak. Kinder than I thought it was possible for a teenaged boy to be. "And ye lived. There's no shame in 'iding, Charlie. Mary wanted ye to live, and it's what she would 'ave chosen."

The kettle whistled, and I got up to pour the tea. "I don't understand how she could be dead? He didn't kill her until November ninth."

Ringo whispered. "But it's been November ninth since midnight, 'asn't it, Charlie?"

She nodded mutely. I wanted to kick myself for not making them come with us. Mary certainly wouldn't have confronted the Ripper if I hadn't made her feel bad about it, which meant I had caused the death of Mary Kelly.

Just like I'd caused my mother's abduction by calling out to her in Whitechapel Station, so she couldn't speak on Will Shaw's behalf. And Archer would somehow be made a Vampire *because of me*.

I opened a window and took gasping breaths, trying to clear my head of the terrible things I'd done as I stumbled around in time.

The morning was crisp and the marshy scent of the river carried on the breeze. I leaned my head against the window frame and looked out at the gray sky. I had to fix this. I had to fix all of it.

I faced Charlie. "I'm so sorry about your sister."

"And me, lass." Ringo's quiet voice filled the silence.

"Mary was my only family." Charlie looked at both of us through tears. I could guess at the wall she must have built around herself to be able to survive her sister's murder. And now how much it cost her to let it down.

"Well, if ye'll have us, we'll be yer family." Ringo looked to me for confirmation.

I nodded. "I've never had a sister before."

Charlie looked me straight in the eyes. "Mine meant well, but she wasn't good at it. Maybe ye'll be better?" I nodded and pulled her into a hug. I think she was as startled by it as I was, but it felt good to let go of a little of the misery.

BEDLAM

I transferred the contents of my old backpack into the leather messenger bag. Most everything was still there except the stabbed can of red paint. The leather bag was getting kind of full, and I briefly considered leaving behind the bandages and chloroform from my catacomb stash, but in the end decided it was better to be prepared. I did allow myself one last lingering look at my dress though, before I left it behind on the foot of the bed Charlie was asleep on.

Will Shaw might know where my mom was being held inside Bedlam. And hopefully, he still had an intact brain. My mother's drawing of Bethlem Hospital showed the window where Will Shaw had stood. I needed to find that room.

Ringo led the way to Bedlam. He was silent for much of our walk, and when he finally spoke he surprised me with his anguish.

"'Ow am I goin' to take care of 'er?"

"Huh? Who?"

"Charlie. She can't stay with me, it'd be improper. Where can she go?"

"In case you've forgotten, I've been staying with you for the past week and that worked out just fine."

"But ye said it doesn't matter in yer time. 'Er reputation would be ruined if anyone ever found out."

I stopped on the street and stared at Ringo with my hands on my hips. "First, no one knows where you live anyway, so keeping her presence a secret will be easy. Second, in case you hadn't noticed how she disguises herself, and who Charlie's sister is ... was ..." Instant stomach-ache. "I don't think Charlie's too worried about her

393

reputation. As long as she stays in boy's clothes, you have no issue. And why is it *your* problem anyway? We're in this together."

Ringo considered my arguments for a moment, then finally grinned in a way I could only describe as cheeky. "Because I'm the responsible one in the bunch, or hadn't *ye* noticed?"

Just for that I punched him in the arm. Not full strength, but enough to show what I could do. He looked surprised for about a millisecond, and then scoffed. "Ye 'it like a girl."

"Wanker." British insults made me laugh, but the surprised look on Ringo's face almost sent me into hysterics.

"Muck snipe."

"What's a muck snipe?"

Ringo's mischievous look was back. "If ye were on fire ye'd be put out with a shovel."

"Nice." The light banter continued until we got to the wall around Bethlem Hospital. I recognized the rotunda at the entrance and pulled out the drawing my mother had made.

"I think this is looking at the back side of the building." Ringo agreed and we found a climbable section of wall, overhung by a stand of trees, to get around to the other side. There were several wings that extended off the main rotunda, so our first challenge was figuring out which one was the right wing.

My old cal-louses from free-running had softened, and the new ones I'd gotten while climbing the ropes were still sore. So it hurt to climb that wall, but it was the right kind of pain. The kind that could be fixed with a Band-Aid.

Ringo's eyes were glued to Bedlam. "There are outdoor courtyards behind those walls." Of course the only way to get to one was to bolt across open park-land. He looked at me. "Ready?"

We left at the same moment and sprinted across the wide-open grass. Less than a minute later we were at the perimeter wall. This one was smoother, with no obvious handholds. I guess that if you're keeping crazy people in, you don't give them easy ways out.

Ringo boosted me, and then I reached down and pulled him to the top. It only worked because we're both strong and fairly light.

Archer might have been able to do it, but I'm not sure Adam could have.

I said a silent prayer that this was the right wing, otherwise we were going to have to do this all over again. We tucked into the corner of the wall, and I pulled the drawing out of my messenger bag, then scanned the edifice in front of us.

"It looks like the right one." Ringo's voice was a whisper at my shoulder. I thought so too. The angles and perspective seemed correct, and I counted windows at the far end of the building until I found the one I thought was Will Shaw's.

"There." Ringo followed my gaze and nodded.

"Let me see if I can find a way in." He took off toward the end of the wing, and I stayed in my hiding spot watching for observers. I began to worry after about ten minutes. Finally, just as I was about to charge in after him, Ringo appeared at my shoulder. He looked disappointed. "No way in. Place is locked up tighter than a prison."

"Will called himself an inmate."

"Right, well yer inmate is definitely behind bars. I don't see any other way in than yer tunnel from King's College."

I'd been thinking about the name that Bishop Cleary found in the Bethlem Hospital logs, and realized that, like it or not, there may be things I was fated to do after all. "Or the front door."

Ringo stared at me. "Ye're not thinking of waltzing up to the entrance like ye 'ave legitimate business, are ye? Why would they 'ave any reason at all to let ye in?"

"They already have."

I told him about my signature as we ran back to the outer wall. He understood why I had tried every other option first – the place was an insane asylum, and there was no logical business either of us could think of for me to walk in the front door. But necessity – and desperation – are the parents of invention, and we formulated a plan on the way to the rotunda. After he helped me get into Bedlam, Ringo would check on Archer, who may have been waking up and ready for his next med by then. We both knew it couldn't be me who went back, because there was a very good chance Archer would never speak to me again.

Ringo would then go through the tunnel to the Bedlam cellar so he could help me get my mother out, assuming she was there, and Will could tell me where to find her. It was sort of a feeble plan, but it was the best we could do with the information we had.

Ringo grabbed my hand before I headed toward the massive front doors. "Do ye want me to tell him anything from ye?"

I searched his face. Ringo looked worried, and it made my heart hurt for him. He was a kid who had been taking care of himself for so long it made him more adult than most men. "I think I pretty much said it all, don't you? I mean, I chose my mother, right?"

He shook his head. "I think 'e understands."

The too-familiar ache started working its way into my chest. "It's better if he doesn't come. Because the way things are going, it'll be just my luck to run into a Vampire."

Ringo scoffed with a mischievous grin. "That'll get 'im 'ere for sure." Then he took my hand and kissed the back of it in a very gentlemanly move. "Let's do this."

On a whim I pulled the leather cord out from under my sweater and tugged it over my head. I handed the necklace to Ringo. Two keys dangled from it. "The big key opens the door to the Bedlam cellar. If I get caught I don't want to have it on me." The other key was to the Clocker map case, back at St. Brigid's, which felt a million miles away. Ringo nodded and slipped the cord around his neck.

I gave him a small wave before I headed up the stone steps. I had Ringo's cap on and had tucked my hair down the back of Archer's black cashmere turtleneck. I was hoping that I'd be treated differently as a guy than if I'd come in wearing a dress, but other than that, I had a fairly simple plan.

The guard behind the desk looked at his watch as I entered the lobby. "It's ten minutes until end of visiting hours."

"No worries. I'm just here to pick up a hyoscine prescription. If they have it ready, I'll be back out in less than five."

The guard barely heard my explanation as he pushed the sign-in sheet toward me. I signed, 'S. Elian,' just as Bishop Cleary had found in the Bedlam papers. "You know where to go? Straight ahead and to your left." I nodded and headed in the direction the guard pointed.

The moment I was out of sight, I stepped behind a column and waited, counting silently to myself. I heard a door slam down a hall and quickly bent to tie my boot laces, but no one came. Then, a minute later, I turned back toward the lobby. The guard looked up in surprise. "That was fast."

I shrugged, trying my best to look nonchalant. "Not ready yet. I'll be back tomorrow."

Just then a rock went crashing through the glass window on the far side of the rotunda. The guard bolted toward it, calling out 'stop!' I instantly changed direction and slipped behind a column so I was hidden from the guard's sight. I knew Ringo would get away before anyone spotted him as the rock-thrower, but my plan relied on the guard believing I'd left the building. Hopefully the broken glass was diversion enough.

I scanned the hall around me for other staff, but none came, so I opened the left wing door and slipped inside.

The long gallery hall was empty, and I tried to walk as casually as I could down the carpeted length. The room we'd spotted from outside was at the end of this wing, and I was hoping my luck would hold long enough for me to get there.

I heard a moan from behind one of the doors and stopped in my tracks. I listened carefully, heart pounding and muscles trembling with the effort it took to stay perfectly still.

There was no other sound. I wasn't really thinking about the fact that this was a patient wing, but I couldn't very well crawl down the rest of the hallway. So I stood up very slowly and looked in at the window of the door.

A face stared back at me. Wide-eyed, female, and very definitely crazy. I ducked down instantly, but it didn't matter. She's seen me, and she started to scream.

Oh. Crap!

My feet grew wings, and I was down that gallery corridor so fast it was like I wasn't even there. A door slammed upstairs, and running feet echoed above me.

I turned a corner and found myself in a separate waiting area, with another closed door. The door had been wedged open the tiniest bit by the floor mat in front of it. The handle was locked, but it hadn't latched properly so I was able to pull it open and slip inside. I made sure the mat was still in place so it didn't close behind me. I could hear Ringo's voice in my head warning me to 'have a plan to get out or it could cost your life.'

Well, there was my plan. A rug in the door.

The general alarm was sounding, and inmates were starting to show their faces at the windows of this smaller wing. They were men, which meant I was in the right place, but some of them were downright creepy.

"Will! Will Shaw!" I yelled in a voice just above a whisper. No need to bring the guards down before they thought of coming themselves.

A man's face popped up in the window close to where I stood. He was scabby-looking and revolting, and for a moment I wondered if I hadn't made a massive mistake.

But Scabby pointed next door and mouthed the words "Will Shaw" to me. I smiled at him, and he tipped an imaginary hat to me like a gentleman.

I looked in at the window to Will Shaw's room. A large man was sitting on the edge of the single bed, rubbing his eyes tiredly. His fingers ran through scruffy, badly-cut hair, and I was forcibly reminded of his descendent, Mr. Shaw, by that gesture.

He must have sensed my presence because he looked directly at me, then moved like predator might: all liquid grace and deadly strength. He pulled a sweater over his head and came to the door.

"Saira."

Will Shaw said my name plainly, with no question in it at all. It was the strangest feeling I've ever had, being known to this man I'd barely seen once, from a cupboard, as he was being dragged down the hall. A man who had no reason at all to know my face.

My hand instinctively found its way to the handle of his door. And strangely, the door opened. Just like that I was face-to-face with Will Shaw.

"I need to find my mom." If I thought it was strange he knew me, it was madness that he would understand what I was saying.

398

"They have her in the cellars. Where they bled me. I've heard them down there." Right, the floor vent with great acoustics. Will's voice sounded like he was strangling on the words.

"We need to get her." I said it like I had a plan. Like I'd been rehearsing those words in my head and knew what to do next.

A door slammed above us and running feet headed toward the rotunda. I took off toward my rug-in-the-door, not even waiting to see if Will was behind me. He kept pace with me easily and probably had a good five or six inches on me in height, which made him massive for this time. I guess massive must run in the Shaw family.

The rotunda had big, round columns that kept us out of sight from the guard's desk. I indicated the heavy wood door to the cellars where Archer and I would escape in my time, and we were able to make it there unseen by the guard. No gate was in place and the door was locked, but the lucky Gods were still on my side because a heavy iron key was perched in the lock. I turned it and the door opened.

Footsteps were now running down stairs from above, and I knew we'd be seen in a second. I locked the door behind us, and in the darkness we each held a wall to guide ourselves down to the cellars beneath Bedlam. I hit the bottom and pulled my leather bag around to the front of my body. Stashed in the pocket for easy access was my mini Maglite, which I clicked on to survey the room.

Will looked around to get his bearings. I remembered that the hall he'd been carried down was beyond us, and I started toward it at the same moment he did. His hand touched my shoulder. "Wait," he whispered hoarsely. "Let me go first." I stepped back and held out my flashlight to him. He shook his head. "It's better if we don't use it. You can hold my shirt if you need to."

I flipped off the Maglite and waited a moment for my eyes to adjust. Will was right, it actually was better, because without the light, there were no shadows for things to lurk in. My night vision was good enough to see shapes in the passage using just the light seepage from above, and I thought, judging by his confidence as he moved, Will's was even better.

We reached the door to the room where he'd been held, and I suddenly felt a massive sense of déjà vu as Will silently inched the door open. There was my mother, lying strapped to the table, with a blood-bag attached to her arm.

It was exactly what I'd seen in my dream.

I flicked the Maglite on involuntarily, and it lit up my mother's face. That was a mistake. She looked dead, or at least as dead as someone can be and still have a pulse, which was what Will was checking.

"Turn it off!" His voice came out in a growl, and for the first time I wondered if he was actually the beast everyone said he was. I shut off the light and shoved it in my pocket.

My voice caught the edge of tears that suddenly threatened to spill over. "Sorry."

Will's voice was as gentle as a growl can possibly be. "She lives. But not much longer without help. Can you shine your torch away from me, in the corner, so I can find something to bind her wound?

The room was completely devoid of supplies, but I had 25-year-old linen bandages and chloroform in my bag from my catacombs stash. Will dismissed the chloroform, but within a couple of minutes he had the needle out and a bandage around her arm. I caught sight of the inside of her elbow and was shocked at how bruised and battered it looked. My mom looked like a junkie from the streets with her torn and dirty shift, matted hair, and bare feet.

Will scooped her up into his arms and nodded at me. "You lead this time. You can keep the light on." I did, careful to shine it away from our eyes. We were moving toward the tunnel, and I thought we both wanted to see what trouble we might be heading into.

The main cellar was still empty, but from the echoes above us, it was clear there was a major commotion going on upstairs.

Will came in behind me, carrying my mom like she was a sleeping baby in his arms. Except her head lolled around on her neck like she was made of stuffing instead of flesh and bones, and her arms and legs were completely limp. I'd never seen a living person look so pale, and I could only hope, with every fiber of my being, that she hadn't been turned into a Vampire. "Help me." Will indicated stacks of folded blankets in a corner. I pulled some out and made a sort of nest for him to lay my mom down on, then I covered her with two more until only her face and head were visible. There were deep purple rings under her eyes, and her thick, auburn-colored hair was a dull brown tangle. The only proof that she was more than a corpse was the weak flutter of her pulse at the base of her throat, but I couldn't shake the feeling that she was like a clock winding down to a stop.

"We have to find a way out." Will had tried the tunnel door and found it locked, but I nodded toward it.

"My friends will come that way. They have a key."

Will's expression darkened. "Wilder and his thug came that way."

I sat down on a crate that was stacked against the wall and looked up at Will, who was quietly pacing around the cellar, presumably looking for another way out. "Why does he want her blood?" I was near enough to touch my mother, but I didn't. I was afraid to.

Will shook his head. "I don't know. They've had her here off and on for days at a time." He knelt down and checked her pulse again. It must have still been there because he stood up and resumed his pacing.

"Are you certain your friends will come?"

"They should be here any minute." Ringo would come. I only hoped Archer would be well enough to be with him.

My impression of Will Shaw as a large, predatory cat was reinforced as I watched him move around the cellar. On his next pass I handed him my Maglite, which he took with a raised eyebrow, but not a word, before slipping down darkened passages off the main chamber.

My braid was itchy down the back of my sweater, so I pulled it out and unbound it to scratch my head. I absently hoped the itchiness was just from being dirty and not from something crawling in it. I had just finished combing through the mass of hair and started re-braiding it when Will returned.

He looked at me for a long moment, and I tried not to feel self-conscious. "You look just like your mother."

I glanced over at her and involuntarily winced.

"As she looked at your age."

That surprised me. "You knew her then?"

He smiled the kind of smile that heats up the space around it, the kind that comes from a secret place inside a person where the best things get hidden away. "I fell in love with her when we were fifteen."

My fingers fumbled with the braid, but finishing the task gave me something to concentrate on while my brain spun in my head.

I finally looked back up at Will, and the look of tenderness in his eyes was the answer to the question I hadn't asked.

"Who are you, Will Shaw?" My voice was the smallest whisper because the answer I expected was the biggest one of my life.

"I'm your father, Saira Elian."

BLOOD

I've always said I have big feet so I don't blow over in a stiff wind. Well, they didn't help. My butt was planted on a box, both feet were on the ground, and I still hit the floor.

Will was next to me in an instant, pulling me back up to something resembling a seated position. His hands were strong, but his grip was gentle, like he was afraid I could break. I suppose with that kind of reaction, I probably was a little more fragile than usual.

"You and my mom …?"

I couldn't even finish the thought. Everything was off balance, like someone put the wrong prescription in a pair of glasses, and I was getting woozy just looking out through my own eyeballs.

"I love your mother like I've never loved another soul on earth, and I have given up everything I've ever known for her … and for you."

Wow. And said with so much conviction there wasn't a doubt in my mind it was completely true. I sat still for a moment, silently catching my breath, watching him with the same intensity with which he watched me.

"Why did you kill the council?"

He shook his head. "I needed them alive. They were going to rule in our favor until Rothchild let the Weres in." He knelt in front of me, his arms supporting me on the box so I didn't go keeling over again. "The Weres slaughtered Lisette, Melinda, and my father. I had to Shift to defend myself, and their own blood lust finished off the ones I wounded." He took a deep breath. "Rothchild had a knife to Claire's throat. He would have killed you both. It's what he intended from the beginning with the whole council, but I couldn't let him take everything from me. They found me standing over him and assumed I had slaughtered them all. But before they could bind me, I gave Claire Melinda's necklace so she could escape."

Will's gaze was steady and unblinking, and I suddenly got that he *knew* me. He knew me, and he loved me. In that instant I realized I had a dad. And then, more than anything in the world, I wanted to put my arms around his neck and hug him.

But I've never hugged a dad before, and it was completely new territory. So I hesitated. And it was the worst mistake I've ever made. Because a key turned in the lock to the tunnel door. We both stood up to face whatever was coming, and the moment was lost.

Ringo stumbled through the door, his face bloody, holding his arm in pain. I almost ran to him but he caught my eye and shook his head quickly before he tripped and went down.

And then Jack the Ripper sauntered in half-dragging, half-carrying a very pale and bloody Archer. Whatever color was left in my face drained on the spot, and despite the fact that my flight instinct was in full gear, I was completely rooted to the floor.

Was it true, then, that the Ripper was a Vampire? He looked red-faced and sweaty and pissed off at having to drag Archer's heavy body down the long tunnel, presumably from the chapel.

I dropped to the ground to shield my mother's body from view. And then my dad launched himself at the tunnel door, and something moved past him with inhuman speed. I couldn't get a clear view to see who else had come in, but when I heard the voice, and felt the roiling nausea of Monger-gut, I knew.

"Will Shaw. What a surprise." Bishop Wilder did not at all sound pleased to see him. I shrank back involuntarily, and my motion attracted his gaze.

"Now *this* is a pleasant surprise. The offspring of my two favorite donors, and a proper mongrel herself."

Will growled fiercely. "Hold your bloody tongue, Sucker!" Will's voice had gone from tender dad to growling beast in an instant. I suddenly understood Jekyll and Hyde a whole lot better.

"Actually, I've finished with the pure-bloods. It's time to uncover the properties of your little mix." He swooped down to grab me so fast I was off my feet before I even realized he was in motion.

And then I got who the Vampire was.

Oh. Crap.

Bishop Wilder held me with a strength that could break the bones in both my arms. And when I looked into his face, I saw the same ultra-smooth, alabaster skin that Archer would have. Oh God, I hoped it hadn't happened yet. He seemed to hang limp from the Ripper's slack grasp and I desperately hoped the bishop hadn't infected him. All of this flashed through my mind in an instant, and then everything went into slow motion.

Will lunged for the bishop and slammed into him with a force that almost took me out. The suddenness of the attack startled Wilder, and he let go of me to defend himself.

Archer suddenly sprang into motion, pulling me away from the bishop. "Give me your knife." Archer's voice was barely a breath in my ear, but I understood immediately. Sanda's little knife was in his hands in an instant.

My father and the bishop were circling each other warily, like wrestlers in a ring. Archer had backed me up against a wall and was shielding me with his body as he watched the two men. Everyone was waiting for their chance to strike, and the air shimmered with deadliness.

The bishop taunted Will as they circled each other. "I have tasted her blood, Shifter. I have her skills now."

I could see startled shock in my dad's eyes, and then they narrowed. "It's not possible. You can't become the thing you ingest."

"Ah, but I follow different rules. In fact, there are no rules for me. I drank your woman's blood and I feel her power. And soon I'll have the girl's as well."

Archer was practically spring-loaded, he was so tense, and his gaze never wavered from the bishop as he circled my father. Ringo was still down, but I could see him inching toward me and Archer. His gaze darted around the room warily, but I was the only one who noticed.

Jack the Ripper was a few yards away from my mother, who was still tucked in her blanket nest against the opposite wall from me. His eyes found her and a slow, nasty smile spread across his face. The look he gave her was feral and hungry, like he'd been anticipating this for a very long time. He actually licked his lips. Ringo and I saw him draw a wicked-looking knife at the same moment, but Ringo got there first. The surprise attack sent the knife into the air and Ringo to his knees. Enraged, the Ripper swung his powerful fists at Ringo and knocked him about five feet backwards. The back of Ringo's head hit the floor with a sickening thud, and he didn't move. Jack the Ripper had killed my friend. I was sure of it.

Bishop Wilder grabbed a piece of iron pipe and swung it at Will before he could leap out of range. The pipe knocked Will off balance and he went down. I shrieked reflexively as the bishop stepped forward, raising the pipe over his head to brain my dad.

But Archer saw his chance and lunged at the bishop. He stabbed with my little knife and must have caught him in the side, because the pipe fell from Wilder's hands with a clatter. Wilder spun on Archer, his fist connected with the side of Archer's head and sent him reeling back. The bishop roared with anger as he grabbed his student and pulled Archer into his arms. "You dare attack me? I should have killed you long ago."

Archer was trapped in the bishop's grip, and for the first time I saw the glint of teeth. Blood was leaking down Archer's face, and the bishop practically tasted the air for the scent. He drew Archer to him. I grabbed the fallen pipe and rushed forward just as the Vampire's mouth descended to Archer's neck.

The air blurred.

And was full of fur. And claws. And teeth.

A huge cat, like a Mountain Lion or a Puma slammed into the bishop and Archer. I was knocked backwards from the force of the impact as the Lion tore into the bishop's arm. And suddenly Archer was free. He crumbled to a heap on the floor, and I ran to him. His eyes were open and staring. Blood poured from a fresh wound in his neck. I crawled to Archer and shielded him with my body from the fierce attack of Lion and man above us.

But the bishop was not a man. He was a Vampire.

And the Lion was not an animal. He was my father.

I heard a new sound above the snarls and shrieks. The groans of brick and mortar columns being slammed into with superhuman force as my dad and Wilder fought.

My arms were wrapped so tightly around Archer's neck, I think they stopped the hemorrhaging. He wasn't moving though. And I couldn't see a pulse.

A flash of movement caught the corner of my eye. The depth of evil in Jack the Ripper's eyes as he sighted me was truly terrifying, and my Monger flight instinct was only quelled by the dying man in my arms.

And then suddenly the Ripper's eyes opened wide in surprise. He stopped moving, and blood bubbled from his lips before he fell, his own wicked-looking knife stuck in his back. And the look on Ringo's face, standing behind him, was pure shock. He had just killed Jack the Ripper.

Ringo turned his eyes to the battle raging at the other end of the room. The Lion had drawn the bishop away from us and they were like a deadly tornado. The last of Ringo's strength deserted him entirely and he stumbled to me, dread in his eyes as he looked at Archer dying in my arms.

"What can I do?"

I didn't want to let go of Archer, but a surge of … something … had begun to build in me. Something that pushed me into motion – to do something, anything to save the people I'd endangered with so much carelessness.

"Hold him for me. Keep him alive." My voice was barely a voice anymore, and the words came out half-formed. Ringo understood what I needed, and he sank to his knees beside us. He pulled Archer off my lap and pressed down on the wound in his neck to free me. I picked up the piece of pipe Wilder had dropped and surveyed the room.

Vampire and beast were destroying everything around them. They'd rammed each other into the columns behind them so fiercely that brick dust was falling from the ceiling.

I ran toward them, oblivious to the sound of Ringo yelling my name, or the blur of battle that raged in front of me. I knew where I was going, and it was up. I rebounded off the cellar wall, to the top of a dresser, and up to the huge metal water pipes that spanned overhead. I crawled along the biggest pipe until I was just over the fighters. The Lion sprang for the bishop again, but slammed into the column next to me as the bishop spun away. More brick dust fell, and I saw the fissures in the column widen.

And then the room was quiet except for the groans of the battered room. Bishop Wilder stood below me, panting and bloody, barely recognizable as a man, over the human form of Will Shaw who lay immobile on the ground at his feet. Brick dust rained all around us, and the last thing I saw of my father were his eyes, looking straight at me, with more emotion in them than I thought was possible. "Do it," he whispered up to me. And I knew what I had to do.

I screamed then, a primal sound that drew every bit of strength in my body to my arms as I swung the pipe at the crack in the column. The bishop finally saw me above him as I swung again.

And then the walls came crashing down.

The water pipe I straddled was wrenched from its moorings and swung away from the collapsing ceiling, taking me with it. I was flung clear and landed in a tangle of limbs. The sound I heard was horrific, like the earth itself was groaning in pain, as the cellar under the men's wing collapsed on my father and the monster that had killed him.

The room was instantly filled with a blindingly thick coat of white dust. We had to get outside. We had to get fresh air to breathe, and help for my mother and Archer.

I found my mother's unconscious body first and I dragged her to Archer and Ringo. The dust was so thick, the ground was completely covered in a layer like baker's flour. I pulled my mother into my lap and grabbed for Archer. That left one free arm.

So I started to draw. First one spiral, then the others bloomed in the stilling dust on the floor. "Ringo, hold on to me!" I could barely croak the words out, but he must have heard me because I felt him clutch at my waist. I hoped our grips on Archer and my mother were strong enough, because my arm was starting to tingle and the humming had begun in the air around us. The only thought in my head was to get to a place where there were trees and air and shelter from things that go bump in the night. And my mind flashed to the map of portals that Jeeves had hidden in my bag, so long ago. There was a portal in Epping Wood, and didn't that sound nice and peaceful and far away from the horror of tonight?

And then we were traveling. Pulling. Stretching. The sounds of thrumming making the bile rise in my throat. And just as suddenly, it all stopped.

I looked up to see the barest light shining through the window of a tiny house. A house I recognized from a painting I'd seen on a wall at Elian Manor. And then the light came toward us and a gravel voice spoke.

"And there ye finally are. The People have been waiting."

EPPING PLACE

It's possible I passed out then, because I experienced what followed in flashes. I wouldn't let go of my mother or Archer, and they had to pry my arms from them. My mother was carried away from me, and I thought her eyes focused on mine for just a moment. Ringo went with her.

The woman with the gravel voice was small, like Sanda, and she bustled in a way that no one could oppose. She directed two young men with her to carry Archer into the cottage, and I stumbled along behind them.

Inside the cottage, I snapped back to myself as the Sanda-like woman had Archer put into a room at the back of the tiny house that was dominated by a small iron bed. When the wound at his throat was uncovered, it still pumped bright red blood. The woman spoke to one of the young men in a low tone.

"Get me fresh marsh woundwort, some shepherd's purse if ye can still find it, and I've some puffball fungus in me wee box that I'll be needing. And any spider webs ye find on the way would be good too."

"Yes, Missus." The guy was gone in an instant.

Then the Missus looked me up and down in the most efficient glance I've ever been on the receiving end of. Her eyes narrowed for the barest moment.

"Can ye make a poultice, lass?" I nodded, barely registering the fact that she saw me for a girl. "Good. Put the kettle on the fire and get the water good and hot. When my lad comes back with the woundwort, mix in a little of the puffball fungus and make a paste. I'll need it for yer lad here."

My lad. Those two words resonated with me like I'd never imagined they could. Archer was *my* lad, and I'd been careless with him. I'd taken him for granted, and now I might have lost him.

Like I'd lost my dad.

The image of Will's eyes seeking mine was burned into my head. He had saved me and Archer, and had lost his life in the process. My heart felt like it had been torn to shreds, with pieces I'd only just discovered gone missing forever. I took a last lingering glance at Archer, but was bustled out of the room by the Missus.

"The faster the water boils, the faster we can draw out that what ails him."

"But ..." I tried to protest that there wasn't a cure, but she looked me straight in the eye.

"Old one was it that bit him? We'll do what we can." And if there was anything at all that could draw the porphyria out of Archer's blood, I suddenly knew the Missus was the woman to find it.

I left the room and went back into the front living space of the cottage. A young kid was just coming in with two cast iron pots, full of water, hanging from a branch slung across his shoulders. He heaved them down and I grabbed one. "Tongs are there, rack's in the fire." The kid who brought the water was already busy washing something at the sink.

"Thanks."

He made a noncommittal grunt and kept working. I found the tongs and hung the ridiculously heavy iron pot on the rack, as deep in the fire as I could reach. Then I went looking for my mother.

I found her in a corner of the cottage off the main room that must have been the Missus' bedroom. Ringo was by her side, and he looked up at me with hollow eyes.

"Archer?"

"I don't know." My voice was flat. I truly didn't know if he lived or died in that little back room, and the only thing I could do was trust his care to the Missus.

411

I went to my mother's side and studied her face. The soft English face I was so used to had become hard lines and crevices. I picked up her hand, and it was ice cold and limp.

"They've drained her." Ringo's voice sounded as flat as mine did. He was battered and exhausted, and yet here he was, still helping me, still standing.

The Missus had just entered the room when he spoke. She looked at me through narrowed eyes again. I felt like she was sizing me up to see what I was made of.

"She needs blood and it'll not come from ye. Descendants don't trade blood." As shocking as it was that the Missus knew that, I couldn't keep the indignation from my voice.

"I'm her *daughter!*"

"And yer da was Shifter. Yer blood'll kill her."

I stared at the Missus in horror. How could she possibly know … everything?

The Missus crossed her arms in front of her. "I can give her teas and such to help her keep the blood she's got, but I can't make it for her."

"Aren't there doctors who can do transfusions or something?"

Again with the narrowed eyes. "I wouldn't trust a doctor with something as precious as a life. No. Ye'll have to take her back."

"Back … to my time?"

If she knew this much, I was betting I wasn't going to shock her with that statement. I was right. "She's told me what it's like then, in yer time. They can save what I can't."

I started to feel frantic. I couldn't leave, not with Archer on the precipice, barely hanging onto whatever life he had left. The Missus must have seen my widening eyes for what they meant. "I can take care of yer lad for ye. It'll be hard for a bit, and he'll not be whole – none can change that – but he'll live."

Her boy came back into the cottage with the herbs and plants the Missus had requested, and he stood in the doorway of the bedroom. "I've got what ye need, Missus."

"Thank ye lad, leave 'em for the lass. She knows aught what to do." The boy gave me a quick, shy glance, then bobbed his head and ducked out of the room. The Missus went right behind him, leaving me and Ringo alone with my mother.

He had heard everything, and he looked worried. "You'll have to go back then?"

My eyes were trapped by my mother's motionless body. She looked so frail and small, and I felt what it must be like to take care of a parent when they get old. The tables were turned and I was the one to make the decision for her welfare. "I have no choice, do I? If she dies now, everything will have been for nothing."

The words threatened to release the searing pain I felt when I looked at my father's dying eyes, and I pressed the tainted blood back inside Archer's body. I shoved the pain back and began to bustle like the Missus.

"Will you stay with her for a while longer? I need to make a poultice for the Missus and see what else I can do for Archer before I take my mother back." I almost choked on the words, but got myself under control. Ringo seemed to be wrestling with his own demons though.

"We were in the tunnel when they jumped us, Saira. We never even saw 'em comin'."

Abruptly, I sat down. My legs gave way and wouldn't support me anymore. "Tell me."

Ringo hesitated a moment, as if the memory pained him. "I'd gone to get Archer. 'E 'ad already taken the last pill 'imself, and was up and pacin' 'is room. When I told 'im where ye were, 'e came right away. 'E was so worried about ye."

Those five words were like an icepick in my heart. Ringo looked me in the eyes to drive the point home. "The whole way down to the tunnel 'e cursed 'imself for not being *enough* for you. Not strong enough or skilled enough. 'E was almost relieved when they jumped us."

That shocked me. "Why?"

"Because maybe you wouldn't 'ave to be there when 'e was turned."

The hollowness in my heart was unbearable.

"First it was just a beatin'. The bishop made a big show of bein' so disappointed in Archer, but 'e was like a kid with coins in a sweet shop every time the Ripper landed a punch on either of us."

Ringo's gaze was faraway, like he was seeing the memory play out in front of him. "We fought. Both of us did. But there was somethin' about the Ripper that was meaner and tougher and didn't back down with any amount of pain. And worse, 'e was boastin' about 'ow much fun 'e'd have carvin' us all up like 'e'd done to the Nosy Parker next door. And after us, what 'e'd do yer ma, since the bishop 'ad taken all 'er Clocker blood."

"Did he ever say why he'd killed the other women?" I forced the words past the knot in my throat.

Ringo shuddered. "'E said somethin' about blood. I think 'e asked the bishop if there was any value to our blood or could 'e butcher at will like 'e'd done to Mary."

"What did the bishop say?" I whispered.

"'E said there was a little Seer blood in Archer, but not enough to keep 'im alive. Useless, just like the part-Clocker girls 'e'd tried first. It was the strong bloods 'e wanted."

I couldn't trust myself to speak, so I nodded.

Ringo suddenly remembered something and reached into his pocket. He pulled out the little cloth bag of coins I'd paid Mary for my mother's necklace. "I got this off the Ripper. 'E must've taken it from Mary's place." Ringo held it out for me, but I shook my head.

"You keep it. Buy Charlie a meal."

He nodded and dropped it back in his pocket. "So that was your father? The Lion?" There was awe in his voice, and, I thought, respect.

"His name was Will Shaw. He was a Shifter."

"So you're a Clocker and Shifter mix?"

"I am."

He looked at me with exhausted admiration. "Brilliant." Even though Ringo might be the only one in my world to think so, I'd take it.

"I have to go make the poultice. Can you stay?"

"As long as you like."

I gave him a kiss on the cheek and a tired smile. "Thank you, Ringo. You're a true gentleman." I headed for the door, but turned back for just a moment. "What's your real name?"

He smiled wryly. "Jonathan Starkey."

"I like Ringo better."

"Agreed."

The poultice was simple to make, and I was happy to have busywork to do while the Missus bustled and her lads rushed off to do her bidding.

When it had cooled enough to be used, I brought the poultice to the small room in back where the Missus was cleaning and dressing Archer's other wounds. The one at his throat had a clean bandage for pressure, but seemed to otherwise have been left alone.

"May I?" I indicated the bandage and the Missus nodded curtly. Archer was still unconscious, and I wasn't entirely sure he hadn't slipped into a coma. His skin was pale, and in the candlelight it seemed to be adopting the smooth, waxy look I'd seen on the bishop's face.

I lifted the bandage, and my stomach lurched at the sight of the jagged bite mark in the soft flesh where Archer's neck and collarbone met.

"Pack it with the poultice, and don't be shy with it. As much as can be drawn out will make the transition easier."

I didn't ask what she meant because I was too busy pushing the green mess I'd made into the wound. His hand twitched, and he grimaced once, so I guessed it probably hurt. But he didn't wake up. Not once.

When I'd finished, I replaced the bandage and wound a soft white strip of gauze loosely around his neck to keep it in place.

I gazed down at Archer's sleeping face.

I loved him. And I'd never told him.

And now I had to go.

Archer would wake up and think I'd abandoned him, that I got what I came for and went home without another thought.

415

I turned to find the Missus watching me. "Claire used to watch yer da like that when 'e slept."

"You knew them then?"

She seemed to permit herself the smallest of smiles. "I helped raise yer ma and 'er sister Emily. I'd bring 'er 'ere with me on my day off sometimes. It's where she met 'im ye know. Out in the woods."

"He died tonight."

The Missus nodded grimly. "I 'eard it told." She looked me straight in the eye. "'E loved ye both with all the fierceness a man can love. And now, ye do right by them and take 'er 'ome to get well. The Other one 'urt 'er something bad." The way she said 'the Other,' I knew somehow she was talking about the bishop. "And I don't trust 'e won't be back someday."

The bishop was a Vampire who technically hadn't been drained of all his blood before the ceiling came down on him, so I supposed it was possible he hadn't died. And if Bishop Wilder was alive, I had to make this a safe place for Archer to heal.

My body began to generate heat, like something was lit from inside. And then I felt it leave the surface of my skin almost like the heat of a sunburn.

"Well aren't ye fancy."

The Missus was looking at me with approval, and it was like she'd given me a gift. I smiled quickly. "Maybe it'll help keep the bad ones out."

"As long as my family can come in, I'll give ye thanks."

The Missus saw me look back toward Archer, and she busied herself with tasks at the other side of the small room. I went to the bed and held Archer's hand. It was cold, ice cold. I tried to generate some warding heat to give him but none came, so I could only give him the warmth of my skin.

"I'm so sorry," I whispered to him. "I didn't mean to hurt you."

I realized I'd seen Archer sleeping like this before – in my time, when I found his secret room under St. Brigid's School. That man felt like a worldly, sophisticated stranger to me now that I knew this one so well.

And just as I'd done then, I leaned forward and kissed him softly on the lips. But this time, his lips were warm and I could feel the slightest breath coming from them. And then the barest hint of a smile, just turning up at the corners. I could have totally imagined it, but the smile gave me hope, and melted a little of the ice that had formed around my soul.

"There's a spiral in the woods not far from here. Claire used it to come from the manor. The lads can help ye with 'er and guard ye while ye go."

I nodded silently, my eyes locked on Archer's face. Finally, I tore them away and followed the Missus to the door. "You'll care for him?"

She nodded. "The change'll take three days. The longer 'e stays down, the easier it'll be for us all."

I had a sudden thought and flung my leather satchel around to rummage through it. "I have chloroform in here. Could that help?"

The Missus looked thoughtful. She took the cloth-wrapped package from my hand carefully and nodded. "It could get him through the worst of the pain."

I dumped some things out of my bag on the small table next to the bed. There were linen bandages, a flashlight and batteries, and Archer's shirt. I pocketed the batteries for Ringo. "Use whatever's useful and hide or destroy the rest."

The Missus nodded. "Thank ye, lass. Yer ma's brought me bits and bobs from yer time as well. It's always welcome." I sighed. There was so much I needed to ask my mom, but she had to live first if that was ever going to happen.

I stood to go, and the Missus brushed a lock of hair off Archer's forehead with tenderness I hadn't seen coming.

"When yer lad comes out of it, I've enough learning of the Old Ones to guide 'im some. We'll see 'e's looked after."

"Will you tell him why I left?"

"If 'e loves ye like ye love 'im, 'e'll understand."

Again the tears threatened, and again I choked them back. They hardened in my throat and made my voice crack. "Thank you." I was suddenly shy with her until she pulled me to her in a fierce hug.

"Ye're the one to end it, lass. Ye have the strength to make them understand it's wrong what they're doing."

I had no voice left, even for desperation. "I don't understand."

"Ye do. Ye know from what's right, and ye stand up for what ye believe. It's enough."

She hugged me again, quickly, and then pushed me out of the room. The Missus bustled us all out of the cottage with maximum efficiency and minimum discussion. The lads wrapped my mother in a rough wool blanket and carried her to a sheer face of granite not far from the cottage. Ringo held me up as I followed them. When we rejoined the lads at the granite wall, I gave him the extra batteries for his Maglite. "Torch food." His smile was gone as quickly as it came, and he kissed me on both cheeks. "Be safe, my friend. Ye always know when to find me."

I smiled at him. He'd become my brother. "Explain it all to Archer, would you? About my dad? He might be able to forgive me easier if he knows."

"But will 'e forgive 'imself?"

I stared at Ringo. "It's not his fault! He has to know that!"

"I don't know if it's the same in yer time, but a man needs to be able to protect 'is woman. And 'e's going to feel like 'e failed."

"Oh God. Please try to make him understand, Ringo. Please."

He hugged me to his chest, and his arms felt strong wrapped around me. "I'll stand by 'im, Saira. 'E'll get through it."

The tears I'd been choking back for hours finally started. They ran down my face unchecked, complete with snotty nose and great, wracking sobs I couldn't control. I couldn't look at Ringo again as I caught sight of my mother's helpless body lying in front of the granite wall.

Behind her, etched deeply into the stone, was a spiral portal. Without another word, and despite the huge sobs that shook my body, I knelt down, picked up as much of my mother's body as I could hold, and started tracing.

 AFTERMATH

I had no conscious thought in my head as I traced the spirals, but somehow I was operating on a default homing instinct.

I recognized my mother's walled garden the minute I opened my eyes. The sun was just starting to color the morning sky and the pre-dawn cold was bone-chilling. Her body, wrapped in its rough blanket, sucked heat away from me rather than providing it, and I was absurdly grateful when strong hands lifted her off me and others carried her away.

My eyes were open, but I registered nothing as I was helped out of the walled garden and into the manor house. There were voices around me, but my mind refused to recognize the words they said.

Once I thought I heard Archer's voice, but it wasn't *my* Archer, so I closed my mind to it.

It was different than when I had the fever, because my body felt normal, exhausted but essentially the same. It was my brain that had taken a powder. I'd retreated from anything that resembled emotion, and I was a walking, moving husk. And I looked the part, with pale, dry skin, lank and stringy hair, and clothes that bagged off me. Thankfully, no one had too much time to fuss. They were too busy keeping my mother alive.

I hid from all of it. My mother, my father, Archer, and everything I'd experienced that night under Bedlam. They put me into my mother's old room in the Family wing, and I must have slept for a time, because when I woke up the light was different, and I had a screaming headache. I heard a deep male voice outside my door. It

419

sounded vaguely familiar, but I ignored it, shut the heavy velvet drapes, and crawled back into bed.

The next time I woke, the headache had faded to something dull and nagging, and thirst was my primary motivation for getting up. It was full dark outside, and I had to consciously use my night vision to find my way down the hall. A bedroom door near the stairs was open, and a dim light was on inside.

I peered in, almost by accident, and realized it was where they'd put my mother. The inertia that had carried me from my bed dropped away, and I nearly stumbled with the weight of ... everything.

Mr. Shaw was napping in a chair at the foot of her bed, and he woke when I came into the room. His smile was something between warm and grim.

In one fluid motion he stood and pulled me into his arms in the perfect definition of a bear hug. It was the hug of a parent when their child returns home safely.

When he finally released me his voice was low and near my ear. "Millicent has given her blood. She gave it willingly, and perhaps even happily."

I smiled wryly at that. I couldn't even imagine how that conversation had gone. "You did the transfusion?" He nodded. "Thank you."

"You brought her home."

"She was dying."

"Not now."

I looked over at my mother, lying asleep on a lace-draped four-poster bed. There was some color in her cheeks, even by the dim light of the lamp by Mr. Shaw's chair. She looked better, almost as if she was really only asleep. I looked up at her savior.

"What's your proper name, Mr. Shaw?"

He grimaced. "William Robert Shaw."

"Oh." Somehow I remained standing, but it was only by force of will. Will. Dad.

"They call me Bob though. Less ... controversial."

"He died, you know."

"Will Shaw?"

I nodded. "He was my dad."

The Bear looked at me for a long moment, and then nodded again. "Well, that explains some things." I nodded silently, fingering the ratty braid that hung over one shoulder. "We probably shouldn't talk too much about that beyond closed doors." He sounded concerned. And tired.

"It's all to do with blood, I think. That's what the bishop was after. Her blood. My blood. He said it gave him power." My voice broke.

Mr. Shaw's expression darkened. I realized I needed to talk about it with someone who understood. And remarkably, that person was right in front of me. So I told him everything.

The night passed quietly. The sound of our murmured voices the only thing breaking up the deep silence of the house.

Toward dawn my mother began to stir. Mr. Shaw moved quickly to one side, and I slid next to her on the other. She saw him first when she opened her eyes, and there was a flicker of surprise, but no recognition. Her voice was barely audible as she whispered a word. "Saira?"

I took her hand and squeezed it gently. With effort she turned her head toward me, and her eyes lit up, but dimly. Her lips were parched and cracked, and her skin was still pasty, but she looked beautiful to me. She looked like my mother.

"Hi, Mom." Her eyes searched mine, like she was looking for something that I knew, or maybe didn't know. I decided we'd talk about it later. "Have you met Bob? He saved your life last night."

She turned her head toward Mr. Shaw again and gave him a quiet smile. "Thank you, Bob."

He grinned down at her. "My pleasure, Ms. Elian."

"Claire. It's Claire to one who's saved my life."

He brought her a glass of water and helped her sit up to drink it. She was so weak and so fragile; it hurt me to see her. I met Mr. Shaw's eyes over her head, then gestured toward the door with my head and raised my eyebrows. He nodded.

"Mom, I need to take care of something. I'll be back in a bit."

She reached for my hand and held it with surprising strength, considering how frail she was. "I love you, Saira. I wanted to say that to you every day I was away from you. I love you with all my heart."

I took a deep breath. It felt like the first one in days. "Me too, Mom."

The sun hadn't risen yet, but the sky was starting to purple as I slipped out of the kitchen door. I found my way to my mom's garden and closed the door behind me.

"Hello, Saira." His voice was behind me. I turned to face him, just able to make out the planes in his face.

"Archer."

He finally spoke. "I remember it all now." His voice was rich and deep, but it had a tone I didn't recognize as his. I couldn't move and could barely breathe. He only had a few more minutes before the sun came up.

"I remember falling in love with you, first in the room at King's College, then completely during our evenings at the flat. I felt I knew you better than I knew myself."

"I knew you too." My voice was a whisper, but his acute hearing had no trouble picking it out above the sounds of insects buzzing to life.

He smiled at me then. A smile full of understanding, and the wisdom of the very old looking down on the very young. "But not anymore."

"It's not that ..." I tried to protest, but it sounded feeble even to my ears.

Archer's smile grew sad at the edges, and he stepped closer to me. "Forgive me, my love." He pulled me to him then, and kissed me in a way he'd never done before. It was a kiss full of passion and longing and the promise of more. And then it was done.

When I opened my eyes, Archer had gone.

The sunlight drew a golden breath over the horizon, and suddenly the sky was more light than dark. I knew he was waiting for me. Just as he'd spent more than a century waiting for me. But the next move was mine.

I took over my mom's old room. She didn't want it anymore. She preferred the room she'd spent her time convalescing in. The light's better, she said.

The manor was decorated for Christmas in a way I could tell it hadn't been in years, maybe even decades. Some of the decorations were probably from Victorian times, and I thought bringing them out from the attic rooms was a way for Sanda to keep my mom and Millicent from sniping at each other.

It was Millicent's blood that saved Mom though, so their disagreements were basically just personalities clashing. Underneath all that, there seemed to be something real. Maybe the fact that they shared their own memories of Emily, or maybe it did all just come down to blood.

And while the new blood was settling into my mom, and after Mr. Shaw left each night, we talked. Really talked. For maybe the first time ever.

She told me about her childhood. About distant, emotionless parents, about her fragile sister, Emily, and about the Missus. Emily was scared of the Missus, but my mother loved her, and her cottage in Epping Wood was a haven.

It's where she met my dad. And where they fell in love.

She was glad I'd found his letters, and we spent a long night reading them. She explained references, secrets, and hidden codes so I could understand what they meant to each other.

They were married by a parish priest in secret, with only the Missus and her husband there to witness. They didn't ask permission because it wouldn't have been given, but when my mother got pregnant with me, they hoped forgiveness might.

They were wrong.

At the council meeting, in front of her aunt and Will's father, they declared their love. They didn't expect approval, and they had been prepared to take banishment if it meant they could be together.

What happened next was a blur for her. There were Weres … and screams … and when Rothchild grabbed her arms and began to drag her away, her swollen belly hit a table and she cried out in pain. Her husband somehow heard her through the haze of battle, and the

423

next thing she knew, Rothchild was dead and Will was covered in blood.

Then sounds of people shouting and running. Will pressed something into my mother's hand and told her to take me someplace they could never find us. "Go forward," he said. And though she'd never gone forward before, the clock necklace had given her the focus to travel.

My mother wanted to go back instantly, but the travel had sent her into labor and I was born in London in 1995. One day, soon after that, she ran into a Rothchild, and she knew we had to go.

And so began our vagabond existence, first San Francisco, then Oregon, and finally Venice. And she timed her trips home to be able to testify at Will Shaw's insanity hearings. The morning she saw me in Whitechapel, she'd been on her way to Bethlem Hospital for one of them, but when the Ripper saw I was a Clocker, he figured my mom would be a prize for the bishop.

He was right.

She didn't know why the bishop wanted her blood; she thought he was drinking it. But he always took her to Bedlam so a doctor could drain it and then patch her back up before she died. Bishop Wilder was very careful not to infect or kill her ... too soon.

The Ripper took her necklace, so she was never able to escape. She was horrified to realize there was a spiral in the Bedlam cellars, so close to where she'd been kept, and stunned to learn I could draw my own spirals to travel. It was something she couldn't do.

My mother was glad the Ripper was dead and afraid the bishop wasn't. And the giant pink elephant in the room, which neither of us could talk about, was the death of her husband – my father, Will Shaw.

After those first few nights, when the stories were pouring out of us, we didn't talk again. It was hard to find our balance with each other, so we retreated to our separate corners to figure out what our relationship would become.

I'd wanted to go back to St. Brigid's after the Christmas holiday. At first Millicent put her foot down and forbade me to return to school. She said it was clearly too dangerous now that there were rumors circulating among the Mongers about me being a mixed-blood. But we were going to stay in England for a while if Mom and Millicent didn't kill each other first, and I needed to learn everything I could about the Families. And for the first time in my life, I had friends. So Mom overruled Millicent, and I'd be going back to St. Brigid's.

Ava came to see me and told me I was going to spill it all anyway, so I might as well get it over with. I recounted everything. Even that I'd fallen in love with Archer from the past and how hard it was now to see him without the guilt of knowing how deeply I'd betrayed him. And worse, it almost felt like I'd be cheating on my innocent Archer by taking up with the worldly Vampire he had become.

She listened with compassion and then said something to me that began to rattle the lock on my heart.

"The thing that has gotten Archer through all these years of having to hide from people he used to know, and being reviled and hunted by those of us in the Families, was the knowledge that he'd see you again. It probably saved his life a dozen times since he met you. He had to stay alive, you see, so he could be there when you needed him."

Mr. Shaw told me Archer had been shot once in that showdown under the bridge, and cut up with some sort of switchblade, but that he'd already been healing by the time they'd gotten back to the school. He said Archer disappeared soon after, and I didn't mention the hiding place in the cellar of St. Brigid's. Mr. Shaw still mistrusted Archer on principle, but I thought he had begun to accept that Archer was still human.

I found Doran in the library at Elian Manor one day. He was pacing the room, looking at books on the shelves, and saying nothing. I finally asked him why he was there. He sighed and scowled as if I should have read his mind. He said a piece of me was missing and I had to find it again before I could continue the game we were playing.

"What game?" I'd asked him, but of course he didn't answer. He just left the words hanging in the air behind him, "The piece is behind the locked door. Open it and we'll be back in the prophecy business." Typical, enigmatic, infuriating Doran.

I didn't want to be in the prophecy business the night before Christmas. My heart was hammering in my chest as I tied a red and gold bow around a present I'd just wrapped, and nerves were making me fumble with the knot.

Finally I finished with something that looked passably festive, and then checked my appearance in the mirror. I'd found a long, hooded cape in one of the closed-off bedrooms. It was black wool and lined with silk velvet. I wore the velvet on the inside, with my long hair unbraided under the hood. I'd finally recovered my eyeliner from my missing backpack, and with a little lip balm, I felt dressed up. The bones in my face weren't quite as severe as they'd been before, and the bruise-colored circles under my eyes had finally given way to my normal complexion. At the last minute, I put on my mother's pearls, and the perfect pale balls glowed at the open collar of my white shirt.

I passed Mr. Shaw in the hallway downstairs. He'd come to see my mother, as he'd been doing every week since she'd been able to leave her bed. His eyes were admiring, even as his eyebrows questioned my appearance. Then he saw the wrapped gift in my hand.

"I'm going out." I tried to sound casual, but my voice betrayed my nerves.

"Not far I hope." He tried for casualness too.

"Just to my mother's garden."

He nodded slowly. "Don't stay out too late."

He sounded like a dad. I wasn't sure how I felt about that. "Okay." He went toward the drawing room, and I stepped out the kitchen door and made my way down the path to the walled garden.

I sat on the bench among overgrown rosemary and twisted brambles. It was a huge leap of faith to imagine he would come to this garden on this night, just because I was finally ready to face him.

"Hello, Archer." I'd been sitting so still, and my eyes had grown so used to the dark, that I saw him slip in like a ghost.

"You look lovely, Saira. Those pearls suit you."

"Thank you. They were my mom's."

"She's well?"

"If you call daily catfights with Millicent well, then yes, she's spectacular." He was close enough now that I could see the smile on his face, and it made my heart jump in my chest.

"And you?"

There it was. The loaded question. Did I pay lip service or be honest? Honest then. "I miss you."

He stood stock-still, and I swore I could hear the frost forming on the rock walls. "I suppose it's too much to ask which me you miss?"

That hurt, but I deserved it. I guess a century of life brings a fair degree of understanding with it. And in all honesty, I couldn't answer that question. So I didn't. And he didn't press the issue. "I brought you a Christmas present." I held out the wrapped box, and it hung there in the air for a long moment before he finally took it from my hand.

His voice was a whisper. "Thank you." He opened the wrapping slowly. "It's been a very long time since anyone has given me a gift."

I could feel the key turning in the locked door to my heart, and tears welled in my eyes for the man he'd been, alone for so very long. But he couldn't see them. He was intent on opening the box.

Inside was a wristwatch. A simple gold face with Roman numerals and a leather band. His expression betrayed his surprise and delight. "Beautiful," he said as he looked into my eyes. And I wasn't sure he only meant the watch.

"I always hated your pocket watch."

Archer laughed. "I got rid of that long ago. At a certain point in time, only old men wore those things."

"Exactly."

He took the watch out of the box and held it to his wrist. "I love this."

"There's something engraved on the back."

He turned it over, and by the light of the moon read the words the jeweler had inscribed there for me. *Yours for all time.*

He stared at the back of the watch for a long time, and his fingers shook a little when he finally strapped the band to his wrist. When he looked at me there were tears in his eyes. "As I am yours."

I touched his face softly, wiping away a tear that had fallen. He smiled and rubbed the backs of his hands across his cheeks. Such a guy thing to do.

I kissed him then, before he could say anything. And I spoke the words that had been locked up inside me.

"I love you."

Fated for one, born to another
The child must seek to claim the Mother
The Stream will split and branches will fight
Death will divide, and lovers unite
The child of opposites will be the one
To heal the Dream that War's undone.

The End

A WORD ABOUT THE HISTORY

Time travel is my very favorite vehicle for absorbing historical facts. Take a character who thinks they have everything figured out, then drop them into a time where nothing makes sense, and go on the journey with them as they learn it all. Add a historical mystery to it, and I'm hooked.

One such mystery that always captivated me was the identity of Jack the Ripper, which is at the heart of the history in *Marking Time*. His "canonical five" victims were all prostitutes working in and around Whitechapel, London, and my retelling of the night of Jack the Ripper's double murders – at Dutfield Yard and Mitre Square – contains true details from police and eyewitness accounts. The location of the Ripper's victims, the descriptions of various persons of interest, and life in Victorian London were derived from hours and hours of down-the-rabbit-hole research.

The Cotton Wharf fire of 1861 actually happened, and was remarkable for the death of the fire chief. The rumrunner tunnels in Venice Beach, and the London Bridge catacombs exist. St. Brigid's School is loosely based on Ingatestone Hall in Essex, and Bethlem Hospital is drawn in words as precisely as I could make it from blueprints and old photographs.

In fact, all the history and settings in *Marking Time* are as accurate as I could make them without having actually been to the nineteenth century ... until, of course, they're not.

AN EXCERPT FROM *TEMPTING FATE*
Book Two of the Immortal Descendants Series

I almost laughed when I recognized the pungent scent of the river in Victorian times. The lapping of the water against the pillars of the London Bridge felt like home, and the only people I saw on the street were the ones stumbling out of pubs. As long as I kept my head down and walked fast, I thought I could disappear into the background of the wharf.

But then again, I used to think there was no such thing as time travel, and look where that got me.

I was just about to turn into an alley when someone bumped into me, hard. I'd been so focused on listening for the sound of footsteps behind me that I forgot to look up, and whoever it was came at me from above.

"Oy! Watch where yer goin'!"

"Sorry," I mumbled, trying not to let the guy know I was female. Instantly, three more toughs materialized out of the shadows, and the certainty that life in the next five minutes was going to get very interesting walloped me upside the head.

The ringleader seemed vaguely familiar. His cap was slung low over his eyes, and he had the wide stance of a guy who didn't often have to run for his survival. When he spoke again I knew. He was one of the thieves I'd first encountered with Ringo. The guys he'd been proud of having ditched when he went to work for Gosford at the river.

"You'll not be needin' yer hock-dockeys then."

This was not going to go well for me; that much was clear by the shoulder-to-shoulder stance of the ones closest to me. Not that I had a clue what hock-dockeys were, but I didn't think they were planning to leave me conscious while they took them.

Two options instantly flashed through my brain. Well, three, but succumbing to their fists wasn't so much an option as a price for failure. I could stand up to them and reveal I was female, in hopes that at least one of them was raised not to hit a girl, or I could run and take my chances. I didn't know if Victorian sensibilities included rape, but I thought it would be a stretch to imagine any of them was gentleman enough to back off just because of a difference in plumbing.

Right. Run then.

The toughs, including a Nervous Nelly who couldn't stand still on his pegs, pretty much had forward and backward covered. So my options were limited to up and down. My eyes flicked above me and I flinched. Someone was there, calmly crouched on a window ledge as if waiting for an escape-to-the-roof attempt.

Which left down.

"Yer not movin' fast enough, nib-cove. I'll be 'avin' yer upper-ben too fer me trouble."

Yeah, right. What he said. Marble-mouth would have made me laugh if I wasn't so sure I'd die before the sound made it past my lips. With another quick glance up to see the Roof-Tough hadn't moved, I dropped to the street, and in one fluid motion of my leg, swept the feet out from under Nervous Nelly. He went down like a bowling pin, taking out Rough and Tumble next to him. Marble Mouth lunged for me, but I was already up and dancing to the side away from his grasping hands.

Even with two down, the alley was too small to stay out of their reach for long, and when Roof-Tough dropped down behind me I knew I was screwed.

Except Marble Mouth's eyes narrowed as he looked past me at Roof-Tough. His voice was an angry growl. "Yer dead, Keys."

Keys? Ringo!

I felt him take a step closer and mumble in my ear. "There's a bottle on the step behind me. Break it and arm yerself." My heart slammed in my chest at the sound of his voice. If I was going to die a bloody death tonight at least I'd have the company of one of my best friends.

"I've done with ye, Lizzer. We've no more at stake wi' t'other. The lad's a mate, and ye've no call to harm 'im."

"Mate o' yers is enemy o' mine, Keys." Lizzer spat the words as his toughs regained their feet and arrayed themselves around him. I felt the step behind me and never took my eyes off Lizzer as I reached for the bottle. It felt heavy, like a wine bottle, and Ringo's voice mumbled at me again. "Smash it on the wall when 'e moves." I gripped the neck of the bottle tightly and felt every muscle in my body coil.

"Ye'll let us by or ye'll get cut." There was an authoritative tone to Ringo's voice I'd never heard before, and I had to remind myself he was only sixteen.

Lizzer barked out a laugh as he lunged. I swung the bottle at the corner of the brick wall, and the bottom shattered off, leaving a jagged weapon in my hand. Ringo had been standing just behind me, so I hadn't seen him until he blocked Lizzer's lunge with a swing of a knife. Lizzer dodged the blade in my direction while the toughs jumped in, and I swiped the bottle up in front of me.

Lizzer's eyes went wide and then he howled.

"Bastard cut me!"

Crap! I was the bastard who cut him with my makeshift weapon. The toughs froze at the sound of their leader's outrage, and Ringo and I saw the opening at the same moment. We didn't even have to say the word, we just ran.

Tempting Fate is currently available in paperback, ebook, and audiobook formats.

And finally …

Thank you so much for reading *Marking Time*. If you enjoyed this book, your review on Amazon or Goodreads would be very appreciated. You can find more information about *Marking Time* and the Immortal Descendants series on Facebook at April White Books, and on my website www.aprilwhitebooks.blogspot.com.

I sincerely appreciate hearing from readers, and thank you, again, for joining Saira, Archer, and Ringo on their adventures in time.

~April White

CPSIA information can be obtained
at www.ICGtesting.com
Printed in the USA
BVHW042219110720
583515BV00015B/768